THROUGH
THE ARCHWAY

To

My siblings, cousins, and all my childhood friends

ACKNOWLEDGMENTS

I am very grateful to Anita Barry, Brian Armitage and Ans Dodd
for reading the manuscript and for their positive and constructive
comments on it, and I would like to thank Jim, and others, for
supplying some useful data.
I would like to thank Michael March of March Design for his
book design and layout, and his general assistance in the
production of the book.
Special thanks go to my son Mark for his very helpful editorial
advice and for his proofreading.

Published by ARO Books UK
Book design by March Graphic Design Studio, Liverpool

ISBN 0 9546139 1 0

THROUGH THE ARCHWAY

Memoirs of Mouse,
Day Boy at Penly Grange School

Andrew Rice-Oxley

A R O BOOKS

We'll go no more to the woods,
The laurel-trees are cut.

Banville (from an old French nursery rhyme)

The mind of man is framed even like the breath
And harmony in music; there is a dark
Invisible workmanship that reconciles
Discordant elements, and makes them move
In one society.

Wordsworth (The Prelude)

Evening harmonises all today
Looking back.

Christina Rossetti

CONTENTS

Strange Meeting

Burton

I have always tended to believe in luck and coincidence rather than in providence and design, but something happened to me a year ago which has led me to change my view. An odd reunion, it was, and completely unforeseen.

It was last autumn. I was in hospital, in the south of England, recovering from a long overdue hernia operation which had not been entirely straightforward. Nothing serious, I was told, but my recovery was probably going to take a little longer than usual. For some reason, which may have been connected to my slow progress, I was moved from a main ward into a side room on the third day of my hospital stay. There were just two beds in this side room and I was only dimly aware of the occupant in the other bed for much of the daylight hours. I might have been oblivious of his existence altogether that night too if he had not started talking in his sleep. I was not happy about this, to say the least, because I had already had two sleepless nights. I had dozed a lot during the day but there's no substitute for a good *night's* sleep.

The first night after the operation, despite pain-killers, I had been very uncomfortable and quite unable to sleep, and I had eventually called the night nurse and asked for a sleeping pill. She had told me I was not 'down' for one so this wasn't possible. An injection was a possibility if I was in acute pain but not a sleeping pill. I was in some pain, unquestionably, but I couldn't honestly say it was *acute* so I just said, 'O never mind, I'll survive', and the nurse went away saying something about looking into it. The following night I fell asleep as the night wore on, only to be woken by another nurse. She wanted to give me a sleeping pill! When I protested that I had actually been perfectly happily asleep she brushed aside my objection and said I had to have the sleeping pill because I was 'down' for one. The sleeping pill didn't work; I was awake for the rest of the night.

During the third day I was just about capable of seeing the funny side of all this, but it was less easy to appreciate when my third night's sleep was also broken. The man in the other bed in my room was mumbling, then speaking quite noisily in short, indignant phrases. He was saying things like, "You can't say it was me! ... I didn't start it ... I didn't! I didn't! ... He asked for it ... he did!" Then he would mutter some names, or what I assumed were names, of people or places. None made any impression on me until he uttered words which sounded like 'Penby Range'. When he repeated the phrase a couple more times it sounded more like 'Penly Grange' and I realised why it was ringing a bell with me. Penly Grange was the name of the prep school in the north of England which I had attended way back in the 1950s. Could he have been at the same school as me or was he thinking of another Penly Grange? Or was I, maybe, imagining he had said Penly Grange because I was trying to relate his words to my own experience as we tend to do when faced with the strange and unintelligible? I was intrigued but not excessively so because I had other things running through my mind and I was more interested in sleeping than interpreting the mind of another patient whom I didn't know from Adam (or so I thought).

Eventually I did get to sleep and didn't hear any of the morning noises I had heard the previous two mornings – the sound of voices in the corridors, doors opening, footfalls, comings and goings, the blare of a distant radio or television, the squeak and rattle of a trolley going down the corridor, the clatter of breakfast being wheeled into the wards. I didn't wake until I heard a bright cheery voice right up close to me.

"Morning, Mr Moss! Here's your breakfast! Let's have you sitting up, shall we?" I was aware of warm steam and the smell of toast but found it impossible to respond to the invitation to sit up. I found myself saying, "Do I have to? I'm really not hungry." Of course I wasn't, I was barely awake. The voice persisted, "Come on, make an effort, we can't have you fussy about your food as well as Mr Burton." At which moment, another voice, from the area of the other bed, spoke out and I woke up a little more,

"I'm only fussy about my food because you don't bring me what I've bloody well ordered!"

"We bring you what's on the card, Mr Burton, what you're down for," said the first voice firmly.

"Well, what's on the card is wrong then, isn't it? And don't call me Mr Burton, call me Max. The others do." I was now sufficiently awake to register the fact that my companion in the room was called Mr Burton but it didn't mean anything to me until he began talking to me a few moments later, after the auxiliary had left us.

Mr Burton's bed was not adjacent to mine; mine was at one side of the room and his was along the end of the room so that I did not have to turn my head much to talk to him. That was an advantage in one respect, if I wanted to talk, but his bed was further away than the next adjacent bed in the room would have been so that it was necessary to speak up in order to be clearly heard. This was no drawback for him for he spoke in a loud, barking voice, but I have a quiet voice and usually have to make an effort to speak up when not close to someone. When fit and well I can do so without much difficulty, but in my sleep-deprived state it did not come easily to me and this was perhaps another factor in my later decision to say as little as possible. Fortunately, he seemed to hear me perfectly well whenever I did speak and I only had to repeat myself once, when trying to make a clever remark.

My eyes were fully open now and I was almost fully awake. I saw that my breakfast had been taken away except for a glass of orange which I drank gratefully. I looked over at the other bed and laid eyes on its occupant for the first time. He was quite an old man with a few wisps of grey hair across a bald head and he had a plump, pink and purple face. More striking than his face however (I had after all seen other old men looking very similar) was the fact that he was lying on his back with raised, thoroughly bandaged legs, and one of his arms was also bandaged, though not strung up like his legs. He saw me looking at him and threw a question at me,

"Did I disturb you last night? Talking in my sleep?" It was delivered in a 'come on tell me frankly' tone of voice so I felt obliged to respond truthfully, if tactfully.

"Well, I did hear you murmuring a bit. Now and again."

"Sorry about that, mate," he said, and sounded genuinely sorry. "I do sleep-talk sometimes. I'm usually on my own so it doesn't matter. Are you BUPA too or some other health scheme?"

"No," I replied, in an unintended apologetic tone, "I'm here on the National Health. I don't know why they moved me in here last night", and I added light-heartedly, "Ours not to reason why."

"What?"

"Ours not to reason why!" I repeated a little louder, trying to give my quip a little more edge, but wondering whether I should have bothered to make the remark at all. Anyway, it set him off all right.

"You can bloody well say that again! I never know what the hell is going on in here. They wheel me in, they wheel me out; they wheel me up and down the corridors into the theatre and back; they stick needles into me; they patch me up, they bandage me ... doctors and nurses come and go ... there's no end to it." In the pause that followed I wondered whether to ask him what had happened to him or whether to let him tell me himself. He certainly wasn't afraid to talk, indeed he soon broke the silence with another blunt question:

"What was I talking about? In my sleep? Can you remember?" I could indeed, some of it, and since there was no good reason not to tell him the little I'd heard, I did.

"You said things like 'No I didn't!' and 'He asked for it!' and mentioned a lot of names."

"Such as?"

"Penly Grange ... several times." I was very interested to hear his response to this. Had he really uttered those words? And even if he had, would they mean anything to him? Could he have been thinking of the school I'd been to, or was he perhaps thinking of another Penly Grange?

"Did I mention Denham, Conninghurst and Broad Oak Hall too?" he enquired.

"I don't know, you may have done."

"They're all schools I went to. I've slept-talked about my past 'education' before, I'm told. I don't know why. Waste of time and money, if you ask me. Those private schools. They were all bloody useless, worse than useless!"

I felt a little surge of excitement. This seemed to be one of those 'It's-a-small-world' experiences. So he *was* at Penly Grange School. I recognised the names of two of the other schools he mentioned, they were in the same county as Penly Grange. In over forty years I had actually met very few Old Boys, only the ones who had gone on to Marby College, Penly Grange's senior school, and I'd kept in contact, intermittent contact, with only one or two of those. So, quite a coincidence to meet an Old Boy, in hospital, after all those years, and in a completely different part of the country. How unusual!

He didn't like the school? So what? I wasn't starry-eyed about it either, though my memories weren't all bad by any means. And I was about to ask him what years he was at Penly Grange and what his name was when I was hit by a hammer blow of a realization. I knew his name – it was Mr Burton. Take the 'Mr' away and you had just 'Burton'. Mention the name Burton in the context of Penly Grange and you had a name resonant with notoriety. For Burton was no ordinary pupil, someone hazy or non-descript in the memory: Burton was the obnoxious, unforgettable school bully! Could this man in the hospital bed just a few feet away from me be the hated Burton, the last person I'd ever want to see again? Except to wreak some terrible revenge on him! But then, I thought, surely he's too old to be a contemporary of mine? Or perhaps he's prematurely old? Or, unwelcome thought, could I be deceiving myself about how old *I* look now?

Part of me didn't want me to know if this was *the* Burton or not, it was such an unpleasant thought. And how would I respond to the knowledge if it *were* him? Tell him plainly how he'd made our lives at Penly Grange a misery? Laugh off all his bullying as just a little bit of rough, boyish behaviour from long ago, just a bit of youthful mischief, of no significance now? Or not mention the bullying at all? All of these options seemed injudicious or evasive, wrong. So it was better not to know. But the other half of me wanted to know, and it proved the stronger impulse of the two. I would find out for sure, first, whether or not he was the notorious Burton and, if he were, decide what to do about it afterwards. If I questioned him too pointedly, though, he might guess I was from Penly Grange myself and start questioning *me*. I would have to get him to talk of his own accord.

I was about to frame a suitable question or make a remark which would prompt him to say more about Penly Grange when a nurse entered the room and asked me a question which I was able to steer in the right direction. She routinely took my temperature and pulse, asked me about my 'waterworks' and my appetite etc., and then remarked,

"And you've been talking to Max, have you? Cheering him up?"

"O sure," said Max sarcastically, "we've been having some great conversations. Lovely place to have them too. I've really been cheered up." I seized my opportunity and hit the ball back into Max's court.

"We've been talking about Max's school days," I chipped in. "He's been telling me about a school he went to called Penly Grange."

"Oh, well, don't let me interrupt you then, if you're enjoying yourselves", said the nurse, using this comment as her exit line. As soon as the nurse had left, Max, as I'd hoped, took up my reference to Penly Grange.

"Penly Grange was a dump!" said Max, "it was a rubbish school, best forgotten."

"In what way?" I innocently enquired.

"It was old-fashioned, antiquated, Victorian, and the teachers were all bloody sadists and bullies!" Yes, I thought, much of the teaching was old-fashioned and one or two of the teachers were sadists and bullies, one at least, but you, *you*, if you were *the* Burton, you were the worst bully, you terrorised us more than any teacher. At least they were meting out punishments, you were just being cruel. My instinct now told me this was indeed *the* Burton of Penly Grange and my instinct was soon confirmed when he continued to talk about the teachers there and what he'd been like at school. He was not a bad boy at all, it seemed. He was misunderstood and mishandled, that's all.

"That headmaster, Teddy Elgan" (actually it was Eldin), "thought he could tame me, with his big stick! Didn't work with me. And those stupid conduct marks! Blue stars and red stars! They were no good for a natural rebel like me. Not at ten years old or whatever I was." 'Rebel', I thought. So sticking a compass into someone's back while they were trying to work was an act of rebellion was it? Why hadn't I realised that?

"I was a bit of a teaser, I admit, egged on by that Jackman boy (he meant Jakeman); maybe I went a bit far at times but it was only a bit of fun." 'Teaser'? Oh yes, Burton, you were a teaser all right. But not a *bit* of a teaser. You never let up. I will always remember your face close to mine. Your incongruous baby face, small nose with freckles; your wishy-washy grey-blue eyes lit up with hostility and aggression. Threatening, taunting, tormenting. The only respite I got was when you turned your attention to someone else; an even softer target like Bookworm Beddoes or Critchley, the 'worm-that-turned'.

Burton droned on. He was a 'rough diamond', and sometimes wild and 'given to pranks', he admitted. He would occasionally 'throw his weight around' and 'get into fights'. I didn't hear everything he said because I began to doze off despite my keen interest in all his recollections: my lack of sleep was catching up on me. But his phrases echoed round my head as I fell into a sort of semi-conscious reverie and recollected Burton and the Penly Grange of nearly fifty years ago. Thoughts and memories mingled together in no particular order ...

Burton was 'throwing his weight around' at the billiard table. He was grabbing the wooden cue off Nevan who was in the middle of a game and pushing him away. Jakeman was standing by, laughing as usual. What was particularly annoying was the fact that Burton was useless at snooker and billiards; he couldn't hold the cue properly and was always in danger of damaging the cloth. We had to walk away and give up our chance of playing at all or watch Burton and Jakeman play out a tedious game of snooker or billiards (usually the latter) and hope they would soon get bored. It was never a proper contest anyway because Jakeman could play well and spent the whole game humouring Burton and trying to make him feel better about his appalling standard of play.

' ... wild and given to pranks' ... Burton loved grabbing people's things and throwing them around. School caps were a favourite of his since he never had his own and seemed to resent any boy who looked after his, especially if it looked smart. Caps would be thrown out of the window, into puddles or stuffed in the wrong desk or string bag. He would seize your book when you were doing your homework or 'prep' and throw it face down on the floor so that it got smeared and you would then get into trouble for untidy work ...

... 'Get into fights'? He provoked them with his continual baiting and insults. In lessons he would flick your ears from behind, and make it very painful, it was one of his 'skills'. In the playground he would pick on someone and harry them: punch, run off, then come back and punch again. If you stood up to him, which rarely happened, you always came off worse for he was a hard puncher and merciless fighter who observed no fighting codes. Even Rigby Smith, my friend from the first, who was quite tough and independent and usually stood up to Burton's bullying ways, eventually suffered at his hands. I remembered the fight between them outside the classroom which hadn't lasted long. After a brief skirmish, Burton, with his bare fist, landed a ferocious blow on Rigby Smith's face, close to his eyes, which reduced Rigby Smith to tears and ended the fight.

Maybe we were just a load of middle class softies but we never fought like that. We always punched the shoulders or the top of the arm. You could hurt someone quite sufficiently punching in that less fragile area. The fact that the shoulder was normally covered by a shirt and a jumper or blazer not only provided some protection from bare fists but also ensured blows sustained there were not visible so no one got into trouble. If you really wanted to hurt your adversary a lot you tried to land as many punches as possible on the same area of his arm. But you didn't punch anyone in the face, not in a normal playground fight. I had never seen Rigby Smith cry before and the sight deeply disturbed me and made me resent, and fear, Burton even more, if that were possible. An older, bigger boy, Hatchman, had told Burton off for his unethical way of fighting but it had no effect on him; he just glowered defiantly and slunk off to bully someone else.

"If only we could do what the villagers did to Bad Sir Brian Botany," said Rigby Smith to me one day.

"What do you mean?"

"In that poem in *When We Were Very Young* by A.A. Milne."

Rigby Smith had probably got the poem from his mother who was always quoting poems and sayings, and he usually remembered them. He'd probably had the poem read to him when he was younger.

"Sir Brian is the village bully who picks on people every day of the week, kicking, bashing and thumping them all the time. And he goes on doing it until all the villagers get together and deal with him. That's what we should do. Band together and sort Burton out." A great idea but who was going to do it? No one had sufficient courage to organise it. So Burton's bullying went on unchecked ...

There was one glorious moment however, which we all treasured, when Burton got his comeuppance. He had been tormenting Critchley, a shy, feeble, dark-haired boy who didn't say much and worked conscientiously in the corner of the classroom. Critchley had a new white plastic ruler, broader than the standard narrow wooden one that most of us had, and he was obviously pleased with it. Burton had got hold of it in break time and was taunting him to come and get it off him. Critchley, aroused just as Burton intended, began chasing Burton round the teacher's table at the front of the classroom. Burton was holding out the ruler tantalisingly, mockingly, just out of Critchley's reach. Round and round the table they went. Critchley getting more and more angry, Burton more and more provocative with that insolent, cocksure grin of his. He was loving every minute of his little game and clearly felt in control, changing direction as he circled the table, making Critchley change direction too, getting him more and more flustered, making him look more and more of a fool. But Critchley wasn't, in fact, such a fool.

12

He suddenly stopped chasing Burton, and, when Burton stopped too, Critchley feinted to move round the table in one direction and Burton fell for it. He ran round the table the other way and to his surprise met Critchley coming towards him. Any fear Critchley might have had of Burton had by this time been completely overtaken by his blazing indignation at the theft of his precious ruler, heightened by the baiting he was getting from the perpetrator of the crime, and he just lashed out at Burton's nose, that maddening freckly nose. Blood poured out of it. Burton dropped the ruler, put his hand up to his face to staunch the blood and swore at Critchley but did nothing. Then he ran off. We clustered round Critchley, patting him on the back, each of us wishing we'd done that and hoping this would mark the end of Burton's bullying, that he'd learnt his lesson. Sadly, it didn't and he hadn't. After a couple of days Burton was back to his old, familiar bullying self. There was one good outcome for Critchley, however. Burton never touched his ruler again. In fact, he never went near him again.

Yet all bad things, like all good things, must come to an end eventually and the Burton era did finally end. And I remember when it happened. It was the beginning of the summer term. Rigby Smith had said he'd had enough and was going to do something about Burton once and for all. He'd been thinking about it all the Easter Holidays and was determined to 'have it out with him' now. I'd no idea what he intended to do and I'm not sure he had. But he did seem determined. We were expecting the first confrontation to come at the lunch table. Burton had been on our table the previous term and we saw no reason why he shouldn't continue to be on it. But he wasn't. We looked round the dining room and he was nowhere to be seen. We didn't think anything of this; other pupils did sometimes miss the first day of term. He might of course have been off sick, though that would have been something of a surprise since, regrettably, Burton was never sick (except when he had a bleeding nose!). No one said anything and we didn't ask anyone, 'Where is Burton?' Burton wasn't in lessons the next day and was again absent from the lunch table. What had happened to him? On the third day we got the answer.

Teddy Eldin, the Headmaster, often gave a little talk after lunch which consisted of exhortations and admonitions, a little second-hand educational philosophy and important announcements. Sometimes his idea of an important announcement did not coincide with ours but on this particular day it most certainly did. Eldin announced with much gravity that Burton was not returning to school this term because he'd been asked to leave. 'Asked to leave'? Did that mean he'd been expelled? If so, why on earth didn't Teddy Eldin say so? Thereafter, no boy was ever 'expelled' from Penly Grange. The few who disappeared from the school community before their normal time in the school was completed had been 'asked to leave'. Occasionally we were told their parents had moved and once it was suggested that the boy who had left would 'probably be happier in another school'. The euphemisms amused but didn't bother us, except in Burton's case. We were indignant that Burton's reckoning was described in such a mild fashion. We wanted to hear that he'd been thrown out, on his ear; better still, on his freckly nose! Not 'asked to leave' which sounded far too nice and polite.

Nevertheless, Burton had gone and the final confrontation had been averted. We all breathed a massive sigh of relief, none more so than Rigby Smith whose resolution had not been put to the test. There were other bullies after Burton but they were nothing compared to him. I had my bad days at school, days when I wished I was somewhere else, but undoubtedly a dark cloud had rolled away from Penly Grange for good and all my contemporaries – my peers and those the year below us – felt the lightening of the atmosphere and now feared or hated the teachers again more than any other boy. The teachers generated a different fear, but it was the fear of authority, a little easier to accept, and it wasn't unrelenting. Burton had always been around: there was no escaping him, in the classroom or playground. The teachers went to the Common Room or out somewhere, the Headmaster to his study or his home in the grounds. You didn't always see them or hear them. But Burton was always with you or nearby, and for the poor boarders (happily, I was a day boy) he was around in the evening too, so his permanent absence made a huge and wonderful difference.

Sometime later I awoke to another voice, a female voice, saying something about bandages and almost immediately drifted back into semi-consciousness again. Ten minutes or so later, or whatever it was, I awoke to a face leaning over me. The face spoke,

"Been having a nice sleep, have you? We're going to have to move you out of here soon, Timothy, so you'd better wake up now. Max tells me you've been having an interesting chat." It was a different nurse, I didn't recognise her voice. Max chipped in,

"He hasn't done much chatting. *I've* done the talking, and he must have been bloody bored with it because he fell asleep, or was just ignoring me."

"Sorry," I said, "I fell asleep, I haven't slept much at night – it wasn't boredom." I was astonished to hear myself speaking so apologetically to this man I now knew to be Burton. All right, what he had done was a long time ago and he might be a reformed character by now – though I'd seen no evidence of it from the way he talked – but he still showed no remorse for what he'd done at school. That was what was bothering me. He'd re-cast his Penly Grange school days in his mind as a time in his life when he was a little wild and out of control, that's all, something quite understandable for a ten or eleven year old. But should he be allowed to go on thinking it was nothing more than that? Totally unaware of the harm he'd done? He was, as they say, 'in denial'.

Yet, was he, in fact, in denial, deep down? Why did he mention Penly Grange and the other schools in his sleep if he no longer cared about them? Why did he say Penly Grange was best forgotten and then talk about it so readily? Perhaps he needed to deal with those past experiences?

I didn't like the train of thought I was now following. It was getting too complicated, too involved, and I was starting to feel some concern for Burton, some responsibility even, which was the last thing I wanted to feel. It was much easier just to condemn him and despise him for his past behaviour, keep him in the past as an unchanging, hated object. It was at this point that the nurse only made matters worse for me by saying, "Max is a very brave man, you know."

"Oh, come off it," interposed Max Burton, "that's rubbish!"

"He's just being modest," the nurse persisted. "He's had so many operations and he hardly complains."

"Like hell I don't! I'm always complaining about something."

"Oh yes, but that's just your manner, you don't really complain. Not about the pain. All the skin grafts."

"That would be daft, wouldn't it? Whose fault was it? I'd had one too many, I admit that now. There were no blood tests, though, I don't know why." Max saw me looking quizzically at the nurse and said,

"Oh go on, tell him! He might as well know what we're talking about." The nurse obliged:

"Max was in a car accident. He swerved off the road one night to avoid a pedestrian and crashed into a tree. The car burst into flames. Max was lucky to come out of it alive."

"I was bloody lucky!" added Max. "And thank Christ, no one else was involved! Just me."

"But he had severe burns on his legs, broken ribs, pelvis and collar bone, and his arms didn't escape completely either," the nurse resumed, "so he's had to have lots of operations and there's more to come. He'll be in hospital for quite a while. Not like you. You'll be out in a day or two. So if he swears at us occasionally we don't mind, we know what he's going through. He's really very brave."

Wonders never cease! Burton, irredeemable thug and immortalised villain, seemed to be breaking out of the mould I had forever cast him in. The nurse thought he was brave. I hadn't seen much evidence of that but then I hadn't

15

seen him over a period of weeks, maybe months. I had to admit, though, that he'd never said anything to me about being in pain nor made any self-pitying noises that suggested he might be in pain, physical pain. He was relieved no one else had been hurt in the accident, so he was aware of the harm he could do to other people – not the Burton I remembered. What struck me most of all, however, was the fact that he accepted the accident was his fault: there was no blaming the pedestrian, he was not in denial about *that*. Perhaps his acceptance that he was entirely to blame himself was making it easier, at least psychologically, to put up with the painful, drawn-out treatment he was having to undergo.

The nurse was right. I was back in one of the main wards for a couple of days and then they hoofed me out, although I was still feeling poorly, to convalesce at home. I had plenty of time to reflect on my encounter with Max Burton and the more I thought about him the more positive my thoughts became. If he was prepared to admit he was to blame for his car accident, could he not come, perhaps, to recognise the error of his ways when he was at school, all the harm he had done? That was a very different matter, of course, and a very long time ago – and just how morally culpable are you when you're only ten or eleven years old, what about your home background and upbringing etc.? – but if he was talking in his sleep about Penly Grange and those other schools, then thoughts about his time in them must still be playing some part in his subconscious. Maybe he needed to talk about it with someone?

Could that someone be me? I knew he would be in hospital for many more weeks, months even, waiting for the skin to heal. Even if he went home for awhile he would still have to come back to hospital from time to time, I was told. There was plenty of time to visit him. We could talk – at closer quarters and for longer. And I would be less likely to fall asleep! But what if I was wrong and he didn't want to talk? What if he backed off, mystified, or clammed up? Might I do more harm than good?

Actually, although I now clearly felt some sympathy for Burton, which I would never have thought possible before entering the hospital, I had another motive for wanting to talk things over with him. If he had residual feelings to deal with from Penly Grange days then so had I. If he was guilty of lack of remorse and repentance, then I was guilty of harbouring a grudge and not allowing things to rest. Maybe we needed to talk for both our sakes.

A week after leaving hospital I still wasn't sure about doing any soul-searching with him; maybe it was all too late and the notion somewhat ridiculous after all that time, but I had vowed I would, at least, visit him in hospital. And then something might come of it, I thought. Who knows?

I was sure about one thing, though, whatever happened. He'd done me a favour. For years I'd carried memories of Penly Grange around in my head, using a few occasionally to spice *talk* of distant school days, but had done nothing to preserve them. Meeting Max Burton was the spur I needed. He'd lost his grip on his past, on his time at Penly Grange anyway, and had no reliable record of it in the top of his head, whatever he retained of it deeper in his mind. I must set down *my* memories before they became too blurred and their reality too faded, too glossed over or airbrushed. Not just the memories of Burton but all I could remember of those harsh, oppressive and frightening times, those arbitrary, absurd and funny, and, sometimes, happy and exhilarating days at school, in the 1950s; some years after the Second World War, closer to the revolutionary 60s in time, yet a whole era away from that liberated, permissive decade.

As soon as I felt well enough to sit at the computer again, I did so with fixed resolve. I had time available because my boss in the Civil Service had given me another week off without any homework. (I was still working then, I was a Planning Officer). I opened a new document on the computer, a window on the past, as it were, and gave it the working title 'Prep School in the 1950s'. I began to marshal my memories and sketch out a framework for my many recollections of Penly Grange School. I recalled its situation, its ethos and manner of education. I recalled its teaching staff and the boys – my fellow pupils and friends – and one of them, in particular. Some people and things in my memory were dim and hazy, some dead and beyond recall, but many were vivid and very much alive, just waiting to be given expression in some shape or form.

Penly Grange School

The Place, the Regime and the Teachers

An Independent Boarding and Day School for boys and girls aged 7-13, Penly Grange is situated in delightful and extensive grounds and is well provided for, with its own chapel/lecture hall, purpose-built assembly hall, gymnasium/fitness centre and indoor heated swimming pool. The academic life of the school is fully supported by an attractive, well-stocked library and first rate ICT provision with controlled internet access. The school grounds provide ample space for a wide range of outdoor pursuits and the floodlit hard play area is used for netball, hockey, tennis, and basketball. Children come from all over the world to Penly Grange and the first thing that strikes you when you set foot in the school is the happy and homely atmosphere where everybody is encouraged to develop individual talents in a friendly but disciplined way.

So runs the description of Penly Grange on the school's website today. The school it describes bears only a passing resemblance to the one I attended in the 1950s and not just because of its modern facilities nor because the Penly Grange School of today is now a co-ed school whereas in the 1950s it was firmly a single sex, boys' school only.

Although *some* boys were happy at Penly Grange, extremely happy even, at least some of the time, I don't think it could generally be called a 'happy' place and it definitely wasn't 'homely', there was just too much fear in the air; fear of severe penalty if you stepped out of line, which was all too easy to do, especially when you were a junior and inexperienced in punishment evasion. There was some encouragement of 'individual talents', certainly in recognised fields of endeavour in schoolwork and sport, but the emphasis tended to be on collective performance and team effort, doing well for the school or your Group ('Groups' were subdivisions of the school population, equivalent to 'Houses', and had their own separate identity).

'Friendly but disciplined', the website claims for the Penly Grange of today. Is it possible to be both? 'Disciplined' was certainly true of Penly Grange in the 1950s but the word 'friendly', like the word 'homely', could hardly be applied to the Penly Grange of those days and for the same reasons: one or two teachers were genuinely friendly, warm even, but their friendliness stood out from the rest.

One thing, however, in the above website description was perfectly true of Penly Grange in the 1950s: the school then as now – the first decade of the 2000s – was indeed set in 'delightful and extensive grounds'. Even though as young boys, taking everything for granted, we might not have been fully appreciative of the beautiful setting, we did take conscious pleasure in its park-like qualities and games fields, especially those of us who enjoyed the outdoor activities and sports which took up a large part of our school time.

Penly Grange was in the country. It was part of the Sellersby estate in the hamlet of Nablock and had been auctioned off separately in the 1940s when the owner of Penly Grange Hall, Sir Arthur Grimald, died. Together with Grange Farm, lodges, stabling, and gardens, in all some 90 acres, it had been bought by Major Drury, Headmaster, on behalf of public school Marby College, and had become the premises for the whole of the Preparatory Department of Marby College. Marby College was situated two miles or so west of the market town of Marby, which was five or six miles west of Penly Grange, so it was some distance away, and Marby College and Penly Grange operated as entirely separate schools. The only point of regular contact occurred through the sporting fixtures between the two schools. Penly Grange was, in fact, nearer to the small town of Tibdale than Marby, Tibdale being only three miles away to the east of the school.

Approaching the school from the direction of Marby where I lived, and most of the day boys, you would, if arriving by car, turn left off the rising Marby-Tibdale road into a gently winding, tarmacked drive which ran between a rhododendron-edged wood on the right, running parallel with the main road, and a beech hedge on the left. After about a hundred yards, a stony dirt track came in on the right through the trees from the main road – this was the direct route into school from the bus stop. Almost immediately after this junction, a grassy area with a stone bird-bath, bounded by a high grey wall, opened out on the left, and shortly after that your view opened up briefly on all sides. You could see ahead of you to the right more rhododendron bushes, deep purple in season, set well back on the right hand side of the drive (which continued towards the east exit from the school grounds), interspersed amongst taller, deciduous trees, including a wonderful copper beech; then, to the left of the drive, the distant games fields, sporting white H-shaped rugby posts in winter and close-shaven, narrow strips of grass – the hallowed greens – in the cricket season. These carefully-mown strips of grass at the centre of the cricket pitches, you could be sure, would be furnished with yellowy-brown cricket stumps if you visited on a summer's afternoon.

A fairly shallow ditch, just a few feet deep, on the left of the drive near the main school building, and known as the 'ha-ha', ran straight up towards the playing fields between two expanses of mown grass, quite smooth-looking to the eye but more mossy and less closely cropped than the grass of the cricket pitches. Beyond the ha-ha, overshadowing the long jump and high jump sand pits (in the summer), was a most majestic, wide-spreading, dark green cedar of Lebanon. And beyond the cedar tree, and even taller than it, towering up behind the green and white cricket pavilion, was a huge beech tree under which there always seemed to be beech mast. I remember crunching through it regularly on my way to the cricket pavilion or that region of the playing fields used for rugby or cricket, according to the season. Beyond the rugby/cricket fields was an area of thicker, coarser grass which bordered the east side of Penly Grange woods and was used on November 5th for the school bonfire and firework display.

However, though you would have glimpsed this most eye-pleasing part of the school grounds as you approached the school, you would in fact have turned left, out of view of it, to reach the main school building, and you would have found yourself on a raised, shrub-bordered, rectangular terrace in front of the former Penly Grange Hall: an imposing grey stone building with tall windows, leaded in the top quarter, and given an added stately home air by the abundance of ivy on its walls. Penly Grange Hall, which had become the principal building of Penly Grange School, dated back to the 1830s and included a high-ceilinged, oak-panelled hall, a polished wood staircase, the Headmaster's study, the school library, an office, and the staff common room which overlooked the ha-ha.

The north side of the school, situated to the left of the principal school building, was less distinguished. There was a dark and rather dingy cloakroom with a low roof, overshadowed by a large, sprawling shrub, after which there came an ordinary-looking tarmacked play area which might have existed in any school except that at the far side there was a high wall concealing the former kitchen garden of the Sellersby estate; we weren't allowed in there and couldn't get in anyway, the door into it at the side was always locked. At right angles to the kitchen garden wall was the school chapel: a converted barn, with only a few small windows, and bare, whitewashed walls and not much in it besides the altar with a couple of candles on it and a lot of wooden chairs in rows rather than pews. The only thing – apart from the altar and candles and the high ceiling with wooden rafters – which gave the building a religious atmosphere was its association in our minds with pious and grave music, both from our singing of hymns in it and from the music appreciation lessons given there. These lessons were given by the decrepit, bespectacled, white-haired Mr Tench, who expected us to sit quietly and listen reverently to classical works such as Mendelssohn's

Hebrides Overture (Fingal's Cave), and Handel's Water Music, which seemed to go on endlessly.

After the chapel and through an archway – a short brick tunnel – you came into a quadrangle where stables had been converted into classrooms and changing rooms, and where, at the far end, a semi-converted barn doubled as an assembly hall and gym. Outside the quadrangle, beyond the left hand corner, there was an outdoor, *un*heated, swimming pool, in a rather bleak, exposed setting, and behind the assembly hall/gym, there was a sawdusty field with meagre grass which had been a paddock. It was not much used, at least not for organised activities, and we sometimes messed about in it and played our own informal games there. I remember having piggy back fights there, for instance, and doing leapfrog. Next to the paddock and on the edge of the woods was a lily pond, a favourite haunt of naturalists like Spilwell and Radford. Actually, most of us plundered it for frogspawn and tadpoles at some time or another, either for our own amusement or, more often, as part of our Science lessons.

Beyond the paddock were some rather neglected playing fields, neglected as far as maintenance went, used by junior forms for soccer and also used for the start and finish of the senior and junior cross country races. Whilst the school facilities in this north area of the school might have been termed 'basic' or spartan (actually we were encouraged to regard the outdoor swimming pool as something of a luxury, despite its icy green water and its isolated position at some distance from the changing rooms and shelter), the country farm characteristics of Penly Grange which survived did lend a certain charm to the general ambience; or maybe this was only in retrospect after we'd left the school. In the hurly-burly of everyday school life in the quadrangle, I doubt whether we gave the farm-like qualities of the school a thought, except negatively, when freezing in winter in draughty classrooms with stone or brick floors and inefficient radiators which you had to sit on, or wrap yourself around, to have any hope of getting warm, and how many boys can get round a radiator at any one time?

There was one rural feature of the Penly Grange grounds, however, which we couldn't fail to be aware of and for which we were truly grateful. So far I have only mentioned this feature or component in passing – the woods. The woods were on the north east side of the school. They were separated from the playing fields by a small orchard and a magnificent high, thick, beech hedge, far more substantial in my memory than the beech hedge along the drive. Mostly, when we went out to the games fields we passed along this beech hedge, on the woods' side, so its exterior became very familiar to us; and when the craze for keeping cockroaches in tins came in, we got to know the inside of the hedge too as we searched for cockroaches and for suitable leaves to feed them on.

21

The woods might have extended over no more than 30 or 40 acres but they seemed large enough to us to hide in, or get lost in, without ever being found. They were deciduous woods with broadleaved trees like oak, ash, elm, beech, sweet chestnut, and silver birch, and lots of brambles and bushes; so there was plenty of tree foliage in the summer and undergrowth in all seasons, to provide secret, hidden places and dens, and an abundance of leaves on the ground to kick, dive in and roll around in, especially in late autumn. We weren't allowed in the woods when we felt like it, it was one of several attractive areas on the school site which were 'out of bounds' except at stipulated times, but that made them all the more special when we were allowed to go in them.

Burton, then, was quite wrong when he called Penly Grange 'a dump'. From the point of view of grounds and setting he couldn't have been further from the mark; perhaps he just wasn't capable of appreciating them at that age or, in his eagerness to transfer the blame for his destructive, anti-social behaviour to the school itself, he was blinding himself to its merits. However, he had also accused Penly Grange of being 'old fashioned, antiquated and Victorian' and the teachers of being sadists and bullies. These accusations had a little more substance to them, but how much substance?

The Star Book and Group System

I have already said that the school's regime was disciplined but hardly friendly and I must add that its implicit moral philosophy did contain a Victorian 'spare-the-rod-and-spoil-the-child' element, still common in the 1950s, but as well as having no scruples over the use of corporal punishment, the ethos of the school also included a strong emphasis on the reward of good behaviour and achievement. In other words, its educational approach was a simple 'carrot and stick' one. Unfortunately, the 'stick' element was often very literal, and I will be giving examples of the all too ready use of the cane shortly. Both sticks and carrots – punishments and rewards – however, operated within a disciplinary framework governed by a 'star book'. This star book ruled our lives at Penly Grange in a number of ways, and since it plays a part in several incidents to come in this memoir, both serious and comic, I need to explain its nature and workings fully.

The star book was a small, soft-cover personal record book. We never questioned its existence nor the judgemental concept behind it. It was part of the school's routine life and moral fabric; it was always there, always with us, like the milieu and the buildings of Penly Grange. It wasn't something we could weigh up or evaluate then. Only looking back *now*, am I conscious of what a neat, if rigid, idea the star book was: in the way it bound together assessments of academic endeavour and moral behaviour in one compact place.

Each boy had his own star book and carried it around with him, like an identity card, and any of the teaching staff could add one or more stars to it whenever they liked. Stars could be awarded for good things or bad things in both work and conduct. Red stars were good, blue stars were bad. The book was the size of a narrow notebook top to bottom, but was a little wider than its height, and each page was divided by a black horizontal line. Above the line were the *red* stars and below the line were the *blue* stars. You could be awarded one, two or three stars at any one time. Three red stars awarded in one go was excellent and came with a special pat on the back and high dose of praise; three blue stars was disgraceful and demanded a visit to the Headmaster who would almost certainly cane you. A total of four blue stars in one week, whether acquired through bad work or conduct, also qualified you for a caning.

As well as offering a measuring rod for an individual boy's performance in school, the star book was also used to measure collective academic achievement and moral behaviour. This was done through Group competition. The total population of the school was about 120 and its division into four Groups vertically (i.e. each Group contained boys from the whole of the school age range) meant each one consisted of about 30 boys. Since Penly Grange was a Christian, Church of England foundation, the four Groups were named after Christian saints of long ago, dating back to the Middle Ages and earlier. There was E Group (St Edmund's), F Group (St Felix's). G Group (St Gilbert's) and H Group (St Hugh's).

The Groups were in continual competition in sport and other activities, and the star book system provided a means of their competing in schoolwork and standards of behaviour too, since each boy's red and blue stars in each Group could be totalled up at the end of term. Red stars, of course, counted as credits and blue stars as debits. It was not difficult to do a balance sheet for each Group and to discover which Group was most in credit. The Group most in credit would then win the Work and Conduct Cup for that term. It was another incentive for each boy to acquit himself creditably in his schoolwork and behaviour, and I suppose it was intended, as with the sporting competitions, to foster team spirit and counter-act an 'every man for himself' outlook on life. I don't remember, however, the Work and Conduct Cup being taken as seriously by us boys as the rugby, cricket, athletics or cross country competitions, or the Chess Cup for that matter.

To award red or blue stars, all the teacher had to do was write down any number from one to three against a capital 'I'(for Industry – schoolwork) or capital 'C' (for Conduct – behaviour) in the red or blue star section of a boy's star book and then initial it. You can imagine you felt some trepidation when handing your star book over to a teacher, following poor work or some lapse in behaviour. How many blue stars would you get, you wondered? You couldn't be sure. The teacher could see how many blue stars you already had and was well aware that four blue stars in one week meant reporting to the Headmaster and a probable caning. (You wouldn't normally expect to be given three blue stars at once, which guaranteed an especially hard caning, unless your misconduct had been particularly bad). This gave the teachers power over you, an ultimate sanction for them to wield, and ensured that you showed them the utmost courtesy and respect.

It was respect based on fear, of course, but unquestionably effective in maintaining discipline with most pupils. It also caused you to live on a knife edge. Messing or fooling about, which we called 'chossing', meant living dangerously if there were any teachers in the vicinity. Some teachers, moreover, seemed very arbitrary in their awarding of one or two blue stars or more, so you became particularly wary of them. I can now see more clearly that the sanction of blue stars must have been particularly helpful for the women teachers because the temptation to give them cheek was almost irresistible at times. When they asked you to place your star book on the teacher's table at the front of the class, it was a clear warning not to overstep the mark, and it usually worked. How we found a blameless way of ragging Mrs Nogg, the English teacher, I will be describing later.

The star book, however, as an instrument for the maintenance of discipline and as a deterrence to bad behaviour, did not work for every pupil. Some boys were quite incorrigible, totally impervious to all attempts to discipline them or keep them under control. The school bully Burton got away for ages with his intimidation and thuggery before eventually being expelled; blue stars, therefore, which of course he naturally acquired, obviously didn't make much impression on *him*. Then there were characters like Webley-Brown, not a bully though a bit of a ruffian, who was persistently in trouble and accumulated enormous numbers of blue stars. He would often need a new star book either because the blue star section would rapidly fill up – there was only one page for each week – or because he was always losing it through accident or design. Once, he tried to reduce the number of blue stars in the lower half of the book, the blue star section, by moving the line between red stars and blue stars down so that blue stars near the top of the blue star section became red stars! Suffice it to say, this desperate ploy, which didn't fool any teacher, and his frequent losing of his star book, exasperated the teaching staff no end but amused us immensely.

Some of us were a little sad when he eventually departed to another school

– I think somewhere in Ireland – where we were told he would fit in better and be happier. We were relieved, though, that he wouldn't be nicking our games kit anymore from our string bags in the changing rooms whenever he lost his, which was most of the time.

Teddy Eldin and the Cane

Teddy Eldin did a lot of caning. In addition to the routine canings meted out to boys with too many blue stars – always a steady supply of these – Headmaster Teddy Eldin would also find occasion for other canings. He would, for instance, at times, issue angrily from his study and drag in any boy making too much noise or committing some other alleged offence, such as loitering around his study area which was also the library area, and would summarily cane them. This was done 'pour encourager les autres', and to preserve the peace, but Teddy Eldin's sorties were quite unpredictable and his victims chosen quite arbitrarily so the only certain way to avoid these irregular canings was to steer clear of the area altogether which was not always possible. Even so, being boys we couldn't resist the urge to run the gauntlet, to flirt with danger and, once, such living dangerously led to a most amusing incident which I still chuckle about today.

However, I shall defer relating this incident for the moment because generally speaking Teddy Eldin's canings were not in the slightest bit amusing and it would be misleading and dishonest to laugh them away as if they were just a big joke or as if they 'hurt him more than they ever hurt us'. How much they hurt him we shall never know, not a lot I suspect, but they certainly hurt us and a few of us suffered a great deal.

Caning was on the backside in true Protestant public school tradition. You bent over and received any number of strokes from one to six across your buttocks. The usual allocation was two to four strokes. I can't remember anyone ever getting 'six of the best' at Penly Grange, though I do recall that happening at Marby College. The caning was excruciatingly painful for a short time. It stung and it stung and it stung, how it stung! I remember the usually self-controlled Rigby Smith jumping around once, in the cloakroom, after a caning, rubbing the seat of his pants furiously to ease the pain. I would have laughed out loud had I not known how painful it was myself. However, the pain would then subside and eventually any lingering soreness would fade away. I was caned four or five times (mainly for 'chossing' or being late), Rigby Smith only once or twice, as far as I can remember. Parker and Thorpe, both big swots, bigger swots than me, probably never. I imagine that over 80% of boys 'enjoyed' the experience of being caned at least once in their time at Penly Grange. Perhaps it did no lasting damage to some of us, perhaps in that era of strict discipline and inculcated respect for teachers it could have been justified for some offences; perhaps it was more effective than drawn out alternative punishments.

Perhaps. But for some wretched boys the caning was too harsh and totally misplaced. By and large we accepted canings for bad behaviour such as rudeness to staff, lying, cheating or stealing, or excessive 'chossing', but canings for bad work were less easy to accept. Whilst canings might have done something to curb unruly behaviour, it was doubtful to most of us whether they did much to improve academic standards, though they were certainly a spur to take more care over your homework, or rather worry about it much more. The trouble was, the boys who were academically weakest always ended up being caned most for their supposed lack of industry and those of us who did pretty well in our schoolwork, and were smug about it, realised the unfairness in punishing boys who simply found the schoolwork more difficult than us; we knew they usually tried just as hard as us, often harder. The allegedly idle boys, moreover, seemed to come in for more savage canings than those guilty of misbehaviour.

I remember both of the Hodgeson brothers being caned for bad work; the younger one, about the same age as me, I remember in particular. The Hodgeson brothers were quite large and flabby boys. Perhaps Teddy Eldin thought their flabbiness required heavier beating to be effective. One break, whilst in the library, I could hear the crack, crack, crack of Hodgeson Junior being caned. I had heard canings before, we all had. This time the caning sounded sharper than ever. Hodgeson said nothing, though his eyes were very red when I saw him later, and I didn't know what damage the caning had done to him until two or thee days later in the plunge.

The plunge was a large, square, deep bath in the changing rooms into which we all 'plunged' after Games. It was everyone together, especially after Group or School matches. I don't remember the term 'bonding' being used much in those days but that's what it was all part of; we played together as a team and we washed together as a team. It was good wholesome fun to us and did play its part in strengthening team spirit, and when I saw Hodgeson in the plunge after his caning I felt an increased bonding and sympathy I would never have felt if I had not seen him naked. There were deep red and purple weals across his buttocks and also across the back of his leg. The weals on his buttocks were bad enough but I was especially sickened by the sight of the weals on the back of his leg. Admittedly, these marks were near the top of the leg, where the leg was more fleshy, but even so it seemed all wrong it deliver blows in that area. Caning was always meant to be strictly on the buttocks, it

26

was supposed to be more humane, less harmful there; injections were administered there for the same reason. Was this deliberate or was it merely careless aiming on Teddy Eldin's part? Whatever the explanation I was shocked to see signs of Hodgeson's beating still very much in evidence after three days, whether a botched job or calculated. This was no quick punishment which did no lasting damage. It was hideously excessive and for what? Insolence to a member of staff? Stealing? Cheating? Bullying? No. Just for poor work, failing to revise properly or prepare for a test!

What I must say, however, made as great an impression on me as the brutality of Hodgeson's caning was his response, his stoic response. He made not one word of complaint, he just accepted it. He got on with his life at school almost as if it had never happened. He continued to struggle with his academic work but also continued to enjoy his rugby and play with great fervour. I looked at some team photos recently. I reckon that the one I saw of him in the Under 12s rugby team must have been taken the same term he was caned so ruthlessly. There he is in the team photo, with his round spectacles on his chubby face, grinning happily at the camera. Of course I admired the successful boys at Penly Grange – Rigby Smith, Westford, Rickmack and Parker etc. – but looking back I admire boys of lesser talent like Hodgeson even more, in some ways, for their resilience and their courage in adversity.

There was more to caning, of course, than the physical pain, whether that was temporary or more lasting. There was the humiliation of the tears afterwards if you couldn't fight them back, and you usually couldn't, and perhaps worst of all there was the build-up of apprehension and fear beforehand as you awaited your meeting with the Headmaster outside, then within his study, the dragon's den. (Of course you didn't have to suffer any apprehension if you fell victim to an on-the-spot caning, there was a bright side to that!)

To begin to explain the extent of the terror of 'seeing the Headmaster in his study' it is necessary to describe his appearance and persona. Edward J. Eldin, the Headmaster, was known as Teddy Eldin by all of us. Whilst the name Teddy was obviously derived from his Christian name, it was in every other respect totally unsuited to him. He was not a cuddly character. If he'd had any resemblance to a bear it would have been to a grisly bear not a teddy bear. In fact, he had very little resemblance to any kind of bear at all being a very skinny and bony person and on the short side; not particularly short to us small boys but he was certainly shorter than Mr Mace, the young Maths teacher, and no taller than Mr Swales the Deputy Head whose tubbiness was much more notable than his height. Teddy Eldin seemed very old to us with wrinkly face and yellow skin and almost bald head save for some wisps of yellowy-white hair across the top of his head and round his ears.

What made him especially forbidding, though, was his hook nose and his brown-framed, thick-lensed spectacles. When he stooped over you to check your work in class, and you looked up at him as he spoke to you, you saw his eyes through these lenses and they appeared grotesquely magnified. It was a most disconcerting experience, especially when you were trembling in case he discovered some error in your work. Fortunately for me I was good at the subjects he taught – Maths, Science and Latin – and so had less to fear than others when he was inspecting my work, but I was still scared of him in class.

However, seeing Teddy Eldin in his study was an even more disquieting experience than encountering him in the classroom, for that was where he would cane you if you got into trouble and had to go and see him. Probably cane you. I say *probably* because unless you had three blue stars in one go it was not absolutely certain you would be caned, you might avoid it, which only increased the tension of a visit there. Heightening the tension further was the physical atmosphere in Teddy Eldin's study with its unique smell, which embodied the awesome aura of his personality, authority and power.

When summoned to see him, or sent to him, or when reporting dutifully with your star book containing four or more blue stars in one week, as you were obliged to do, you would knock timidly on the oak-panelled door of his study and nervously await his response. On hearing his voice, you would clasp the thin, grey, iron handle and push open the door. It was a solid, heavy door and swung open slowly and ominously – to reveal Teddy Eldin sitting facing you at his desk. When he asked you to close the door behind you, and you did, you knew your fate was sealed. But what was your fate? Was there any possibility you might escape a caning? You hoped against hope there was, speculating about what sort of mood he was in, and you tried to gauge it from his expression, difficult because of those thick-lensed glasses.

Your first *thought* might have been focussed on him but your first *sensation* on entering the room was the smell of thick pipe smoke, heavy in the air. Teddy Eldin was a great pipe smoker. There were stories circulating amongst us that you could tell from the way he handled his pipe what mood he was in. If, for instance, he put down his pipe in leisurely fashion when you entered the room he was probably in a good mood; if it was already lying firmly in an ash tray and fully extinguished, he was ready for action and you'd probably had it. I wasn't sure about this theory but, after glancing at Teddy Eldin's face, I would flick my eyes over the desk and then around the study, to see if the cane was already out in room, in readiness; then, if not visible, I would look towards the place where the canes were kept, in morbid curiosity and apprehension. There were two brown leather arm chairs on either side of the desk and bookcases on either side of the room. The cane might have been on one of these chairs or on the desk, but if not out and ready for use it would have been at the right hand side of the study, in a floor level cupboard with frosted glass below the bookcase. Whilst the frosted glass prevented you from seeing precisely what was in this cupboard, you could make out something in there, or thought you could, which naturally fed your imagination, for it was known that Teddy Eldin had several canes. And so, as well as waiting to see whether he would make a move towards the place where the canes were kept, you had the added grim speculation entering your head, unless you could control it, and you couldn't, about which cane he might be using.

In reality, Teddy Eldin probably had no more than two canes, perhaps three, but much mythology grew up about these canes and it was generally believed that behind that frosted glass there lurked a whole arsenal of batons, rods and canes of different lengths, thicknesses and springy-ness. The canes were given nicknames such as 'bender', 'stinger', 'knobbler' and 'whipper'. But whichever cane he eventually produced, the tensest moment was always that second after you bent over and waited for the first blow to fall and the worst moment was the searing pain of the first stroke which was always a shock however much you had braced yourself for it.

Being caned in Teddy Eldin's study was actually a richer experience than the mere combination of fear, tension and physical pain. This was because the French windows at the back of his study looked out on an ornamental garden, formerly the central part of the garden of Penly Grange Hall. It was enclosed by the commanding beech hedge on the left, next to the orchard; a high yew hedge on the right; and, at the end, a wall with a door which was usually shut, so that you couldn't see properly inside the garden except when you were in the Headmaster's study. In juxtaposition therefore with the stomach-churning experience of the build-up to the cane, you had also a view of flowers (I remember roses, irises and geraniums), small shrubs, an ornamental pond, a lavender bush, the inside of a dark green hedge and a creeper clad wall that no one else could normally see: you had the privilege of seeing a secret garden, that's what it seemed to me. And ever since my Penly Grange days, whenever I have read or heard about a secret garden, that garden outside Teddy Eldin's study is the one that comes to mind. Consequently, I can now recall those visits to the study with more pleasure than pain for the pain has faded and the archetypal hidden beauty of the garden has grown as it has become associated in my mind with other even more lovely secluded gardens.

There was also, as I have mentioned, a light-hearted side to Teddy Eldin's caning, 'getting the stick' as it was called. It was often talked about and joked about in classrooms, changing rooms and playground. There was much gossipy curiosity, for instance, about which canes Teddy Eldin was using on which boys and also the number of strokes he was giving to each boy he caned. At one time it became the vogue to quiz his victims about their caning as soon after they'd left his study as possible, and before long Teddy Eldin issued a warning about this practice, particularly the asking of the question about the number of strokes he had meted out. You could actually hear the number of strokes given if you took the trouble to listen, though not of course if you were outside the building, the wisest place to be. The story goes that one day, despite the warning, one boy, I think it was Nelson, had the temerity to ask Webley-Brown, who was often caned, how many stokes he'd just had when he was only three yards or so from the study. To his consternation, Teddy Eldin suddenly burst out of his room brandishing his cane and shouting, "He got two, you'll get three!" Nelson took to his heels and ran off, whereupon Teddy Eldin pursued him round the school with his heaviest cane, re-iterating his cry, "He got two, you'll get three!" The story also goes that he never caught Nelson, and Nelson never received the threatened three strokes. If true, it shows that Teddy Eldin thought he had scared Nelson enough and maybe showed he had a sense of humour, contrary to the impression I have given of his character so far.

Indeed, were I to end my portrait of Teddy Eldin here you would certainly have to conclude that he was nothing more that an ogre and a sadist. Ogre he certainly was to us in our first years at Penly Grange; less so as we got older and began to find him more laughable than forbidding, though we remained a little frightened of him right up until the time we left. (Well, I did). Sadist? As Burton claimed? I'm not convinced. To explain why we found him amusing and why I don't believe he was necessarily a sadist, I need to describe other facets of Teddy Eldin and the other arenas in which he functioned apart from his study. These other facets of his character and spheres of influence scarcely reveal him in a more flattering light but they show him to be an earnest and sincere man who was more of a comic figure than a tyrant, notwithstanding his compulsive caning.

Teddy Eldin in the Dining Room

The dining room was the place where Teddy Eldin chose to make announcements and deliver warnings, admonitions and homilies; the assembly hall/gym in the quad was used for special school events like play productions but not for regular assemblies. His favoured time for addressing the school was after lunch on most days. The dining room was a new building, an extension to the old manor house and quite an agreeable place with plenty of windows and therefore light, and it was presumably well heated because I don't remember ever feeling cold there, though it was draughty in the covered but open-sided area outside, where you queued to go into the dining room and had your hands inspected by a monitor to see that they had been scrupulously washed.

The food at lunch time was good, the stew and apple crumble being exceptionally good, especially the latter. And so, as long as you got to sit next to a friend and not someone like the bully Burton, lunch time was enjoyable, and we usually listened to Teddy Eldin in a fairly relaxed and sanguine state of mind. Of course, if he was in reproachful mood, denouncing disorderly behaviour and threatening blanket punishments, if, for instance, tidiness in classrooms didn't improve and general noise levels weren't brought down in the main building, the atmosphere darkened and you became uneasy. You felt particularly uncomfortable during those moments – and every school has them – when you were asked, in front of the whole school, to own up if you had committed some specified offence. There was always a deadly silence after these appeals followed by a threat of collective punishment for the whole class under suspicion if no one owned up. However innocent you were, you tended to feel guilty and you had to exercise as much self-control as you could to prevent yourself going red and, apparently, giving the game away.

Some boys couldn't prevent themselves going red; sometimes they might have been guilty, often they weren't and were in danger of becoming scapegoats, pressurised by the rest of the school to own up to the unsolved crime and remove the threat of collective punishment hanging over all. The threat of collective punishment was therefore a blunderbuss method of extorting the truth, which could cause 'collateral damage' to the innocent for a while. However, the blanket policy usually worked in the end, for a few days later Teddy Eldin would announce with a smile on his face that the malefactor had owned up and the collective punishment had been lifted, just before the deadline for owning up was reached. On rare occasions when no one owned up, a cloud might hang over the implicated class or sometimes the whole school for quite a long time before a collective punishment was imposed.

Teddy Eldin didn't seem to enjoy imposing collective punishments any more than he actually enjoyed using the cane (I don't think) but he had more faith in the latter than the former. If he had one obsession it was with how hard boys were working or playing games and he seems to have genuinely believed, as I have already indicated in regard to schoolwork, that caning a boy was the best spur to make him redouble his efforts and therefore the best way to promote his improvement. The worst thing a boy could be was to be lazy. Laziness was at the root of all academic weakness or lack of progress in any sphere, and the dishing out of blue stars to lazy boys, under-girded and endorsed by the use of the cane, was the most effective means of rooting it out, he believed.

Where the blue star/caning policy wasn't practicable, i.e. when the number of lazy boys who merited a caning was too great for him to deal with (though he once managed to cane all eleven members of the Under 12 cricket team for scoring only 14 runs in one innings), he was prepared to use non-corporal, collective punishments. On one occasion, at least, the whole school was compelled to have extra Latin lessons instead of a half holiday because Teddy Eldin decided that standards in Latin were slipping and this was due to the fact that Penly Grange boys, en masse, were just not working hard enough at their Latin. The huge irony of this will be understood when I give an account of his Latin lessons a little later.

Generally speaking, Teddy Eldin preferred to spread sweetness and light (especially the latter) to the boys in his charge rather than either caning them individually or imposing mass punishments on them; rather than instilling fear and dread, which is all he actually achieved, apart from the unwitting humour which he also afforded us. I came to this conclusion after observing his performance in the dining room for over five years. It seemed to me that he was more in his element standing up in the dining room, addressing the school, sharing his infinite wisdom with us, than he was anywhere else, except in so far as he used the classroom for the same purpose. Perhaps the dining room was the most appropriate place for him for he certainly made a meal of his talks to us there!

Once he was up on his feet, after everyone had finished eating, his body language immediately settled into the same routine. He would draw himself up, gulp once or twice with a slight jerking movement of the head, and then proceed with his oration at a measured pace, though every so often he would pause and repeat the same head movements. He tended to speak out of the side of his mouth, not very loudly, though when he became agitated or exasperated his voice not only increased in volume it shot up in pitch too, a fifth or a sixth. As he spoke, he tried to convey a sense of control and composure with his hand movements, by bringing the finger tips of each hand together to make a spherical cage, moving them back and forth, apart ... together, apart ... together, giving his words bodily emphasis and precision. This worked very well until the fingers did not come neatly together but slipped off each other or even missed completely. The effect, we found, was hilarious from someone trying to be so serious and dignified, and Rigby Smith and I often had to fight hard to smother our sniggers.

Verbal idiosyncrasies in Teddy Eldin's little speeches included reiteration of phrases or single words, spoken quite quickly, with one beat pauses and gulps between each repeat. For instance, he would say, "Keep your shirts tucked in: it's slovenly to walk about with your shirt dangling out. It is, it is, it is ... yes, yes, yes". Or he would say, "You should never run in the hall ... Never *pause* never *pause* never" *gulp*. The 'nevers' in triplicate did not have the force of emphasis, they came over rather as meaningless repetition, like the needle of a gramophone stuck in the groove of a record. When Mr Swales whispered in his ear, informing him of some matter of school discipline, Teddy Eldin would nod, and mutter agreement in similar fashion: "I know, I know, I know."

As time went on, we found the technique of his preaching or moralising, and its content, as comic or curious as his verbal mannerisms. When, for example, he attempted to enlighten us rather than merely deliver a harangue or warning, he liked to present his pearl of moral or educational wisdom to us with a flourish. He would ask us a riddle-like question, which we couldn't answer, and often couldn't even understand, and then produce the answer for us with a triumphant look on his face, like a conjuror whipping a rabbit out of his hat.

I remember one day he baffled us with the question, "What is it you can never do as a pupil?" We all scratched our heads, thinking of such things as looking out of the window when you should be paying attention, handing in homework late, copying another boy's work, not revising properly – the usual things we were always being reprimanded for – but we didn't realize that Teddy Eldin did not mean 'what *should* you never do but what *could* you never do? He wasn't disappointed with the silence that greeted his question. Not only did he expect it, he was obviously itching to tell us; it was as if he'd just read or heard the answer, it was like the latest sensational news which he had prior knowledge of and he was generously going to share it with us.

He smiled. "Shall I tell you ... shall I tell you ... shall I tell you?" he asked rhetorically, using the head and hand movements described above and twitching his shoulders too. Then, after a dramatic pause, he told us: "You can never stand still ... never ... you're either going forwards or backwards, forwards or backwards, forwards or backwards. You never stay in the same place". This amazing statement did make us think for a few seconds. Those of us who fancied ourselves as philosophers or scientists (oh yes, we did think about big questions sometimes: boys such as Spilwell, Westford and Thorpe, Rickmack, Rigby Smith and I, did sometimes talk about theories of time and space) were wondering whether Teddy Eldin was about to offer us some observations on the science of motion or perhaps something on time travel. But we shouldn't really have expected anything like this and probably didn't, to be honest. After another pause, Teddy Eldin became more explicit and proceeded to make not a philosophical or scientific point but a trite, practical point about schoolwork. A boy's level of achievement in schoolwork *never remained the same*, he insisted. If it wasn't getting better, then it would be getting worse. Since our work would inevitably get worse if it did not improve, we had to ensure that it *did* improve and that meant working even harder than we would have done had we not known the vital truth about only moving forwards or backwards. Brilliant! We were back to his old hobby horse again. Effort is everything, laziness a great error and sin. Therefore, work harder or else!

Another time, he did come up with something other than the overriding importance of effort when he asked us what was the worst thing a boy could do. A goodie-goodie promptly came up with the answer he thought Teddy Eldin wanted to hear, "Not try hard enough, sir." Teddy Eldin brushed it aside with some irritation, "No, no, no!" He paused. "It's mental bullying!" he said, with an even more emphatic jerk of the head than usual. "Mental bullying! Far worse than physical bullying. Far worse, far worse, far worse!"

We'd heard much condemnation of bullying before from Teddy Eldin and the other teachers, which was always physical as far as we knew (not that they were very successful in preventing it). Bullying always entailed being punched or having parts of the body, such as ears or arms, twisted or wrenched. The 'Chinese burn', for instance, where the skin of your wrists or your forearm is twisted in opposite directions was much favoured by bullies and most of us had experienced it. We knew what such routine bullying consisted of, but what was *mental* bullying?" We really weren't sure. Teddy Eldin elaborated on the cruelty of mental bullying for some minutes and on how we should never do it but we still didn't know quite what he meant.

Later, Westford, who was to become Captain of School, told us what he thought mental bullying was. He gave us that modest smile of his and said he thought Teddy Eldin meant *teasing* by mental bullying. Teasing! This caused those of us who were listening to his explanation to burst out in unrestrained laughter. Teasing happened all the time. We all did it and we all got it from others; it was part of school life. To designate teasing as the worst offence of all was ridiculous. If teasing became tiresome we all knew the mantra to recite to dispel it –'Sticks and stones may hurt my bones, but words will never harm me!' And we half believed it; it was a defensive mechanism which sometimes worked. If it didn't, you just put up with the teasing.

Westford was a thoughtful boy and continued in his mild-mannered but firm way, "Maybe if the teasing goes on and on, and the teaser gets others to gang up on the victim it can be pretty horrible. Remember Burton. He kept on and on at you and never let up, and got bigmouths like Jakeman to join him."

"Yes," retorted Rigby Smith, "but he backed up all his taunting with his fists! And if Burton was a good example of *mental* bullying as well as real

34

bullying why didn't Teddy Eldin get rid of him sooner?"

"Because," chipped in Rickmack, who was a bit of a cynic, "he's only just thought of it. He's only just read about it or heard about it at some headmasters' conference."

"What? Teasing?" said Westford with a flicker of humour in his eye.

"No, even Teddy Eldin knows what teasing is," returned Rickmack dryly. "He's only just heard, though, that it's called 'mental bullying' and is a really BAD THING."

Normally, Teddy Eldin would name and shame boys for bad behaviour or lack of effort, just as he would also name and praise boys who did well and won prizes or teams that did well and won matches, but there seemed more of the former than the latter during our early years at Penly Grange. Then he went through a more compassionate phase – at least in the dining room – which didn't seem like him at all. Rickmack would claim again that he was only following educational trends here. I have already mentioned his use of euphemisms for boys who had been expelled. Burton was 'asked to leave' and other troublesome boys were going to be 'happier in another school', for instance. But he then surprised us by being even more magnanimous towards a boy called Saunders.

Saunders was a notorious thief. He would pinch pens, rulers, compasses, books, games kit, anything, as well as money if he got the chance. As soon as Teddy Eldin cited him in the dining room, I expected to learn he'd been caned and warned for the last time. But no. He hadn't been caned or even warned because he was clearly ill. He was ill, he was ill, he was ill! He couldn't *help* stealing things and we should all be sympathetic towards him. Maybe he would have to go to another school before long but in the meantime we should bear with him and we shouldn't put temptation in his way. This was the first but not the last time in my life that I learnt that stealing was not the thief's fault. Oh no! Stealing is the fault of those who allow their possessions to be stolen. If we all locked everything up or nailed everything down there would be no stealing. It was as simple as that. How you were supposed to do this in a school where you kept your books and pencil cases in unlockable desks and your games kit in string bags in the changing rooms which were easily accessible during the day was never explained.

Then there was the case of Mitchell who was always running away. Teddy Eldin or Swales would go after him in their cars and bring him back to school. Give him a free ride back! He was never punished, as far as we could tell, and we were supposed to be sympathetic towards him too.

"I wouldn't mind having time off school," said dark, handsome, frail-looking Loretti, who was good at English and close friends with Rickmack (also good at English), "but I bet if I took the afternoon off, or you did, and we wandered off somewhere, we'd be dragged back here along the ground – no car rides – and caned mercilessly." We all agreed with him.

Another time Teddy Eldin surprised us by announcing there was a new school prize being awarded, a different sort of prize. It was 'The Most Improved Boy in the School' prize. He positively shone with pleasure when he singled out Hanley, one of the thickest boys in the school, as the winner of the prize this year. We weren't sure whether this prize was Teddy Eldin's idea or a parent's, since school prizes were usually donated by parents. There was no doubting, however, the sincerity of Teddy Eldin's enthusiasm for this prize; though, as Rickmack pointed out, the best chance of winning it was to be as thick as thirty planks at the beginning of the year so that any improvement later on would be all the more notable.

Not satisfied with lecturing and advising on academic work and general behaviour, Teddy Eldin also stuck in his oar on physical education, school sports in particular. He was a great authority on sport (he thought); he was coach, guru, and pontificator on all aspects of it. He would remind us of the importance of watching the ball in cricket (that's a new one, we thought), playing with a straight bat, throwing in the ball above the stumps; but also whiting boots properly, keeping laces tied up and cricket bats well oiled. He had a few 'what do you never do?' pearls of wisdom for cricket too which included 'never hang around on the boundary when fielding, picking daisies: run towards the wicket, keep on your toes!' and 'never change the bowling in the last over of a match'. This latter pronouncement stemmed from one school cricket match in which a new bowler had been brought on in the last over of the match, had bowled a couple of loose balls because he wasn't warmed up (supposedly), and been smashed for four twice, giving the opposition the runs they needed for victory, much to Teddy Eldin's displeasure.

In rugby and hockey, he stressed the importance of playing in position, supporting the captain and keeping going till the final whistle. And, of course, he mentioned team spirit and being a credit to the school. Much of his talk about sporting practices was platitudinous, it was only what we heard from the teachers in charge of the team sports. We tolerated it, though we didn't feel grateful for it because it was superfluous, but he also had his authoritarian opinions on playing *skills*, coaching advice to individuals, which irritated boys like Rigby Smith and Porter, both fine batsmen and hockey players. It was his insistence that there was only one correct way of hitting the ball which they didn't like.

"He tells me I'm 'slogging' and using too much bottom hand," Porter complained one day when some of us were discussing batting techniques, "but Rocky doesn't mind too much; he likes the way I hit the ball." (Rocky

Craggs was the First team cricket coach and a former minor county cricket player). "Rocky wants me to develop a natural style which suits me, not one that just follows the old manuals." Teddy Eldin's criticism of Porter's batting technique must have been before his historic stand with Rigby Smith against Rostock Manor. After that superb batting display, Teddy Eldin hadn't a single word of criticism for Porter's batting technique; he held him up as a model of how to hit the ball for all young cricketers.

Rigby Smith, captain of hockey as well as cricket in his last year, was annoyed with Teddy Eldin's dogmatism over the handling of a *hockey* stick. Yes, Teddy Eldin could play hockey a bit, he conceded. In fact, it was the only sport we ever did see Teddy Eldin play – in a staff/boys' hockey match once – and it was the only thing which made us realise that Teddy Eldin was not quite as old as we thought. He didn't cut a very handsome figure with his skinny build, thick spectacles, thin wisps of yellowy grey hair and knobbly knees, but he played in a brisk manner and distributed the ball quite efficiently round the field. However, his ability to play a bit didn't give him the right, Rigby Smith contended, to dictate to everyone the right way, the only way, to handle a hockey stick. Rocky Craggs was our coach, as for cricket, not him, and Teddy Eldin's banning of the wearing of gloves for hockey no matter what the weather conditions – not Rocky Craggs' advice – was particularly gratuitous and silly.

I remember the little hockey stick talk on wearing gloves that filled Rigby Smith with such contempt. Teddy Eldin had a hockey stick in his hands and he was moving it around in the air as he addressed the school, this time well clear of the top table where he ate. He was doing a hockey playing mime with spoken commentary: "What is it you should never do when holding a hockey stick? Answer: Never wear gloves! Why? Because if you wear gloves you can't feel the stick properly and can't use it to full effect." He moved the hockey stick in his hands, up, down and roundabout, as if flicking the hockey ball to imaginary players in his imaginary team, here, there and everywhere. He was demonstrating perfectly, he thought, how supple and flexible bare hands on the hockey stick were, but he was indoors in the dining room not outside in the wintry air. "None of the top hockey players ever use gloves,' he asserted, "so don't let me ever see anyone using gloves on the hockey field. Ever, ever, ever!"

We played hockey in February and March. Sometimes it was mild in February and March, often it was freezing. When bitterly cold, your hands, without gloves, became totally numb. It was almost impossible to hold the hockey stick, let alone *feel* it in the way Teddy Eldin advocated in the nice warm dining room. To insist that you should NEVER wear gloves was absurd and it exasperated Rigby Smith, not only for his own sake but also for the rest of his team. Still, that was Teddy Eldin's firm belief, so you had to let your hands freeze up if he was stalking the touch line and watching you play. On days of hard frosts, Rigby Smith actually preferred away matches when Teddy Eldin was unlikely to be watching. Teddy Eldin sometimes came on away cricket trips in the summer but wasn't so keen on away matches in the winter.

Teddy Eldin's Academic Teaching

Teddy Eldin's teaching ability ranged from the reasonably competent to the abysmal. He taught Maths, Science and Latin; and, to the oldest boys, Sex Education, which was natural history with a few furtive, brief references to human reproduction.

He was a moderately good Maths teacher, in so far as he knew the subject fairly well (or seemed to) but he was very pedantic in his approach. Perhaps this wasn't an entirely bad thing for it instilled some discipline into our learning. I was good at Maths and usually did very well. On one occasion, however, I reached a solution to a sum by taking a short cut and I was mortified when, far from praising me, he awarded me two *blue* stars rather than the two red stars, which I'd been expecting, for not following instructions. Perhaps it taught me to be more careful and less complacent; I've certainly never forgotten the shock I got.

Science was not taught methodically as it is today. We didn't do it at first, aged 7-8, and then we had only two lessons of Science a week. It consisted mainly of biology, topics such as photosynthesis and pollination and the study of pond life. We were sometimes taught in a makeshift lab (in the right hand corner of the quadrangle) which had a folding, sliding door. It had formerly been a garage, I think. The room was quite long and narrow and rather dark.

I seem to remember looking at things under microscopes in this lab. Our gasps of amazement at the magnified dots, circles and squiggles we saw through the microscopes clearly pleased Teddy Eldin, though I don't remember actually learning anything about what we saw. Teddy Eldin enjoyed teaching Science and seemed quite confident and relaxed about it. He liked to surprise us with unusual scientific facts. As with his post-lunch, wisdom-imparting talks, he liked to see the puzzlement on our faces when we tried to grapple with a question he'd asked us and was quite happy seeing us wander off in the wrong direction before pulling us back on track with the correct answer. This he would provide in dramatic disclosure style, like the celebrity announcers of Oscar awards plucking out the winners' names from an envelope and reading them out to their captive audience.

One good illustration of his question-and-answer technique in Science would be the memorable occasion on which he asked us what cockroaches ate. This came in the context of learning about the eating habits of various animals: whether they were carnivorous, herbivorous or omnivorous, but not all of us had grasped that. Apparently there was only one answer to the question: 'What do cockroaches eat?' He listened patiently to our proffered answers which included such things as insects, seeds, bark, leaves and grass, smiling all the while and shaking his head knowingly. Then he gave us the answer. Actually, it was really a trick question because although no answers given were completely wrong, none was *completely* right and only the complete answer would do. What do cockcroaches eat? The answer was 'Anything ... Anything ... ANYTHING!' Teddy Eldin grinned ear to ear as he made the revelation. At which point Norton, not known as a leading thinker in the form and normally very reticent, raised his hand and enquired:

"Please, sir, do they eat *glass*?"

There was a split second's silence whilst we wondered whether Teddy Eldin would react badly to this question as a piece of cheek or plain provocative stupidity but we needn't have worried. Norton was no smart-aleck Spilwell, and Teddy Eldin was not without a sense of humour. He burst out laughing and when we realised it was all right to laugh we all roared with laughter too. Poor Norton was totally humiliated and of course it didn't end there. For ever afterwards he would have boys taunting him with, "What do cockroaches eat?" and then, "Do they eat glass, sir?" Some teasing became a little more subtle: "Anyone seen the glass-eating cockroach round here?" or "Anyone got any broken bottles for the cockroaches?" Fortunately, Norton was not an unpopular boy and it mostly bounced off him harmlessly because it was just fun and he didn't bother to react. I can safely record, I think, that he never became victim to that terrible thing 'mental bullying'.

I do not recollect doing any Physics with Teddy Eldin but on one occasion we did what I suppose was meant to be Chemistry in a similar 'Bet you didn't know this!' sort of way. I'm not sure what he called his experiment but one afternoon (Science lessons always seemed to be in the afternoon) he started to show off, like a magician performing in front of an audience. He was playing with a test tube over a Bunsen burner and he chortled as the liquid within the test tube changed colour. He was having great fun and we were enjoying it too, but, for us, for me certainly, it was alchemy not chemistry; I don't remember learning anything scientific from it.

Teddy Eldin also taught Latin. He was not good at Latin and was a very poor teacher of it. It was something of a mystery why he elected to teach the subject at all. There were two or three possible explanations. Possibly, the school was short of Latin teachers and he couldn't obtain them so he had to teach the subject himself to make up the deficiency. Or, perhaps, since he attached such great importance to Latin, he believed he should lead from the front by teaching it himself; no doubt he also believed that his zero-tolerance of laziness would help to raise standards, that the natural difficulty boys had in learning Latin required his special 'direct' teaching methods.

Latin lessons, for the first few years at least, consisted principally of working through Kennedy's Revised Primer. I remember this text book as a drab, brown-coloured book with heavy type for headings and main topics, and lots of boxes with lists of words. From it we learnt about cases and how to decline nouns and conjugate verbs. We were regularly tested, sometimes in written tests and sometimes orally in class. Teddy Eldin would fire off questions at us, choosing boys at random, apparently, to answer them, and woe betide you if you got a question wrong after being given a homework to revise.

When he had the Kennedy text book in front of him, Teddy Eldin managed to do all right but looking down at the book hampered his preferred method of raking the class through his thick-lensed glasses before targeting his selected pupil with a question. Sometimes, in the heat of a grilling oral test, he abandoned the book and threw out questions from the top of head. At these times he was liable to make mistakes because he really had very little Latin at the top of his head (or anywhere else for that matter). He was aware that quick-fire questions left him open to mistakes so he adopted a simple policy – he used the form's brainbox to provide the answers whenever necessary, which was often. The form's brainbox was Parker. Parker always got full marks in all the tests so what Teddy Eldin did was quiz boys in the class and then say, if he was in any doubt about the answer and he'd lost his place in the book,

"All right, tell them, Parker!" and Parker would dutifully supply the answer. Whereupon Teddy Eldin would nod and say, "That's right, Parker, well done!"

Using Parker as the first authority on all questions whilst pretending that he, Teddy Eldin, was the ultimate authority didn't deceive anyone, but he got away with it (just) until one day his elementary system went badly wrong. Of course it was the fault of the Latin itself. Nouns are divided into different declensions. The first two declensions follow predictable patterns in which the genitive case is always different from the nominative case (when the noun is the subject of the sentence). However, some nouns in the third declension do not follow this pattern and actually have the same form for the genitive as for the nominative. All those who have studied Kennedy carefully know this, but those who haven't and who blindly follow the rules for other declensions are liable to assume the genitive is *always* different from the nominative.

That is the background to what happened one day when the 'Tell them, Parker!' ploy backfired. Teddy Eldin was shooting off questions and he aimed one at a boy he suspected of not having revised thoroughly for the oral test on cases.

"Radford!" he snapped what is the genitive of ignis?" Ignis is the Latin for fire, and it is mentioned in Kennedy as an example of a *third* declension noun.

"Er, ignis, sir," Radford replied, with some confidence.

"Ignis! No, no, no!" Eldin exploded. "That's the nominative!" He went over to Radford to sort him out. Sometimes he would bang his pencil on the head of the duffer who could not answer a question or who had given the wrong answer. This was supposed to help him think more clearly. Sometimes he would repeatedly prod him with his pencil. His method of attack this time was the latter, the prod.

"You don't know the genitive of ignis, do you, Radford?" Prod. "You're not thinking, are you, Radford?" Prod, prod. "And you haven't revised for this test, have you?" Prod, prod, prod. Give me your star book, boy! Two blue stars! Two blue! Two blue! Two blue!" Radford, quailing, obediently handed over his star book, and Teddy Eldin scribbled a 2 in the bottom section of a page next to a capital 'I' (for Industry) and wrote his initials underneath: E.J.E. Those fearsome initials. Two blue stars! We were all scared now especially those of us who would have given the same answer as Radford. Fortunately, Teddy turned straight to Parker –

"Tell him, Parker!"

"The ... the ... genitive of ignis, sir?" Parker was stalling.

"Yes, yes!" Teddy Eldin was getting impatient.

Parker went pale and looked terrified. He was somewhat timid even when not especially frightened, so now he had the greatest of difficulty getting his answer out. But get it out he did, after a second or two:

"It's ignis, sir."

Teddy Eldin stood stunned. All eyes were on him. Would he savage Parker? Would he grab Kennedy's Primer to check Parker's answer? Would he climb down? He'd never doubted Parker's answers before. He turned to Radford,

"Ignis, of course," he said in conciliatory tone. "Well done, Radford!" Two *red* stars. Give me your star book back!" Radford dutifully handed his star book back and Teddy Eldin speedily made the necessary amendments, changing the blot on his record to a mark of commendation in an instant.

We were too taken aback to react much at the time, fortunately, but afterwards, in the playground, we collapsed. Westford, Rickmack, Loretti and Rigby Smith were rolling around in mirth unbounded; Parker, still shaken, was less amused. Radford's response after the lesson I don't recall.

41

The only thing worse than Teddy's Latin teaching was his Sex Education which I will be giving a full account of when I describe the extraordinary boy Spilwell who played a leading role in the unofficial promotion of that subject, much to Teddy Eldin's discomfort.

Mr Swales and Other Teachers

If I have given the impression that Teddy Eldin was the sole and absolute power in the school by dwelling on his overbearing character, his pontifications and his regular, uninhibited canings, I must now correct that impression. Teddy Eldin was indeed the ultimate power in the school, his study the seat of that power, and the dining room his almost exclusive organ or mouthpiece for the promulgation of his narrow views and opinions, but he was not in charge of the day-to-day running of the school. That was the role of Mr Swales, the Deputy Head. And just as Teddy Eldin deferred to the authority of Parker in Latin questions, so he deferred to Mr Swales on questions of school behaviour and the operation of the school day.

Mr Swales taught History and French but I can remember almost nothing about his teaching, only his deputy headship. He was an astringent sergeant major in his approach to discipline, a rigid enforcer of every school rule from the sensible and necessary to the petty and pointless. In the exercise of his authority he always got his way and plainly manipulated Teddy Eldin who would regularly cite what Mr Swales had said on some matter, as if quoting the oracle – 'Mr Swales says this, Mr Swales say that'. What Mr Swales said was normally about misconduct of one kind or another so Teddy Eldin's comments on boys' behaviour were often prefixed by 'I'm sorry to say, Mr Swales has just told me that ...' Some misdemeanour was then reported and the punishment that went with it; or it was an appeal for a boy to own up to something.

Generally, Teddy Eldin liked to report good news rather than bad, and he was very happy to announce a half day holiday from time to time. Afternoon lessons cancelled in such a strict school? Yes, it did happen! And not just because of snow or epidemics. There were sometimes genuine extra half day holidays, 'merit' half day holidays as they were called. But we did not get nearly as many as we might have done. In my memory there seem to have been numerous occasions on which Teddy Eldin would beam round the school after lunch and tell us that there was going to be a merit half holiday, only to have Mr Swales whisper in his ear and stem his beneficence in full flow.

"Ah, ah, ah!" Teddy Eldin would nod and mutter, and then alter his announcement: "I'm sorry to say, Mr Swales has just told me that the changing rooms are in a shocking state. They'll be tidied by everyone and then lessons will be as normal." Or, "Mr Swales has just told me that no one yet has owned up to the throwing of ink in N2 (one of the junior classrooms) so the half holiday is cancelled."

Had Mr Swales just been a collective punishment man whose only concern was for law and order in the school, his killjoy methods might have been excusable, even if often extreme and unpopular. After all, someone has to enforce daily discipline in any school and it's usually the Deputy Head's responsibility: he or she must ensure school rules are observed and bear the load of unpopularity that comes with the enforcement of them. Unfortunately, Mr Swales was not just a collective punishment man who favoured detentions for all and cancelled half holidays as standard punishments for the whole school.

He was also a ruthless punisher of individuals and even in those days when corporal punishment was normal – from light clips round the ear or back of the head to heavy canings in the Headmaster's study – his personal forms of physical chastisement, which he employed at will without any checks whatever, as far as we could tell, were open to question. Despite the harshness of Teddy Eldin's canings, I have delivered an open verdict on whether he was a sadist; I would even tilt towards acquittal of this charge, if by sadist is meant someone who actually enjoys inflicting pain. It seemed to me that Teddy Eldin caned in an unfeeling but dutiful fashion. He put a lot of energy and commitment into it, he had faith in its effectiveness. That's why he did it.

The same could not be said for Mr Swales who had the nickname 'Slasher' Swales on account of his manner of encouraging boys to get out quickly onto the playing fields. He would run behind us in his games kit in a fierce earnestness as we were trotting out to the rugby pitches and swipe at the back of our legs with the cord attached to his whistle. Naturally to avoid the sting of the cord on our legs we would run faster. No doubt he found our acceleration entertaining but it served no constructive purpose. There would always be boys who came later, for whom we had to wait anyway before we could start our game, and they would escape the leg chafing, so Swales' goading was mis-targeted and ineffectual, if getting the game started quickly was really his intention.

There was something grotesquesly comical, it has to be said, about this short, chubby man with his podgy legs, bobbing along with his whistle and cord, cutting a most un-athletic figure, exhorting us to get a move on and start playing our guts out on the rugby field as if he were a great leader and champion of the game. Once on the field and refereeing, he would actually use the whistle for its intended purpose, but far too often. He was altogether too fussy and officious, and his coaching, such as it was, always seemed to concentrate on what we were doing wrong. It was niggly and negative and took the fun out of playing.

In the classroom and changing room, he devised his own punishments rather than using blue stars, though he might use those too on occasions. In the classroom, he called his own form of corporal punishment 'Tickle Tibby'. This entailed getting the offending boy to stand on the teacher's table with his socks pulled down. He would then tap the boy's exposed calf muscles with a wooden ruler in a circular rubbing motion which would gradually increase in intensity. Tickle Tibby could last for some time and was intended to: it was quite different from the shorter, sharper shock of the cane. I never had to undergo Tickle Tibby but I saw it happen a few times and it didn't look particularly painful to me, though I noticed on one occasion it brought tears to Timpson's eyes. I wondered, though, whether his tears weren't just tears of boredom from standing on the table so long.

In the changing rooms, Swales used another form of corporal punishment if you transgressed in the plunge. Before you got changed, you had to report to him with your towel draped round the lower half of your body and he would lift up your towel and smack the back of your upper leg. It didn't hurt much, at least it didn't hurt *me* much, because your skin was still moist and slippery, and the blows Swales delivered never seemed to make a telling contact with your leg. Furthermore, his fat, podgy hand, made a very ineffective instrument of chastisement. What made this spanking punishment rather suspicious, though, apart from the nakedness involved, was the ease with which you could become liable for punishment when Swales was on duty in the changing room.

Whatever you did in the plunge you were in danger of breaking some rule or committing some offence or other. If you swam around in the water (and if there weren't many boys in the plunge it was possible to do this) you were mis-using the plunge because it wasn't supposed to be a swimming pool. If you remained almost motionless and washed with restrained movements to avoid the charge of messing about in the water, you were accused of being half-hearted and not getting on with it. If the bar of soap shot out of your hand as you grasped it, as it could easily do, you were charged with messing about on another count, and if you didn't use the soap at all you were in trouble for not washing properly. You just couldn't avoid transgressing in some way.

Was Swales a sadist? Oh, yes. On all the evidence above, I think we have to conclude that he was and that Burton was right in his allegation of sadism at Penly Grange, in respect of Swales, at least. But he had asserted that all the teachers were sadists. I have recorded an open verdict on Teddy Eldin as a genuine sadist. Were there any other teachers who could have been charged with sadism?

Another teacher who might well have been charged with bullying or sadism – on the face of things – was the PT teacher Mr Lampton. Mr Lampton had a mop of dark hair, streaked with grey, and a droopy, black moustache. He was middle-aged, of medium height, slim but not skinny, and he stood up straight in a firm, military manner. Despite his athletic build and strong posture, he was, however, in other respects, not a model of good health. His fingers were nicotine-stained and his fingernails cracked or bitten down, and his eyes were bloodshot as if he rubbed them a lot, or cried a lot, or was a little mad. Since his eyes usually had a wild look about them also, the last of these explanations seemed the most likely, though maybe he had had cause to cry a lot in the past and this had contributed to his mad look too.

We boys were not given to thinking or caring much about the private lives of our teachers, we just judged them on what we saw and the way they treated us, but in Mr Lampton's case we could not help seeing that he carried a lot of 'baggage' with him. His wild look had a faraway quality to it as if he had come from a very different life and world. We knew there was definitely something military in his background because he talked of his experiences in the Commandos, and there were rumours he was divorced, but that is all we knew about him. We feared him as much for his unknown, shadowy background as for his ready, irregular use of corporal punishment.

Lampton was a stickler for perfect posture and precision in movement. He was also obsessive about gym equipment being used properly and the mats at the far end of the horses, for instance, being exactly in the right place, inch perfect. This was more important than the vaulting exercise itself, as was landing properly on the mats rather than merely getting over the horses. He told us that landing properly on your feet was the key to all physical movement, that his training in the Commandos had made it possible for him to jump from the highest of buildings without harming himself and that we could acquire the skill too if we followed his instructions. He never demonstrated this skill to us nor, happily, asked us to practise it either. However, to enforce gym discipline as he understood it, which was the carrying out of his instructions to the letter, he used any implements on us which came to hand in the gym.

Table tennis was played in the gym in our free time so there were table tennis bats in cupboards or lying around on windowsills. The crudest form of table tennis bats, and the one provided by the school, had sandpaper surfaces and could inflict a lot of pain on a boy's buttock when wielded with a slicing action, as you can imagine. So could a rope, of course, and there were plenty or ropes in the gym. He used both table tennis bat and rope as it suited him

45

but didn't invent flimsy pretexts to use them as Swales might have done. Even so, his standards of behaviour and gymnastic performance were unreasonably high for junior school boys so it was not difficult to incur his genuine wrath and get beaten for one thing or another.

What is strange, however, is that I can't remember him being particularly disliked, and, though he was feared, he was respected too. There was a certain mystique about his knowledge and experience and we tried hard to carry out his orders and not upset him, and not simply because we were frightened of the table tennis bat or rope (and we were!).

I remember being terrified during the last week of one spring term when Mr Lampton was arranging for a gym display to be given to the school on the grassy area alongside the ha-ha. Terrified, because he had chosen *me* to lead a column of twelve boys in a sort of military tattoo; there was going to be music involved too. It was more like fancy drill than gymnastics. We didn't have to vault over horses or do somersaults, we simply had to jog on and off low benches, moving in single file formations, making figures of eight, diagonal lines and squares. It was simple in so far as it wasn't physically or athletically demanding but it wasn't an easy exercise from a mental point of view because you had to co-ordinate with another column of boys, merging and separating in a pattern. This was no problem for the majority of boys since all they had to do was follow me or the leader of the other column, Nevan. And Nevan could always imitate me if he forgot what he was supposed to be doing: he could do a mirror image of my performance.

The trouble was the whole thing was under-rehearsed and I didn't know what I was doing. I was amazed Mr Lampton was putting so much faith in me. I wasn't particularly good at gym but I was light-framed and nimble, which he seemed to like, and he said I was brainy so I would understand better than most what to do. But I *didn't* understand what I had to do and was wracked with fears of wrecking the whole of the display and consequently making a fool of myself (which I could cope with) and ruining the day for Mr Lampton (which I could not cope with). I didn't sleep for two nights and on the day of the display I was seriously tempted to be off sick. I felt sick with nerves anyway, there'd be nothing false about a day off sick.

However, not turning up would have created problems for the other boys as well as enraging Mr Lampton so I went to school and awaited my fate. It was worse than a visit to the Headmaster's study.

As I walked up the drive to the school, I cast my eyes anxiously over the area where the gym display was to take place. There were no benches in sight and no seats for spectators, as I expected. I was puzzled. The gym display had been arranged for the late morning so maybe there was still time to set everything up but not that much time. I went to my morning lessons feeling very tense. No one said anything about the gym display. I was desperate to speak to Nevan and ask him how he felt. He was the only one, apart from Rickmack, who had something special to do in the display like me, the only one who would have the foggiest idea how I felt. I saw Nevan in the morning break; he was in a different class from me and had been somewhere else the first three lessons. I put on a brave face and forced a smile:

"Are you ready?" I asked him.

"What for?" he replied. Nevan could be like that. Awkward at times or was he just trying to appear cool?

"For the gym display!" I said with some exasperation.

"The gym display?" he said airily. "Haven't you heard? It's been cancelled."

Cancelled? Cancelled? CANCELLED! I could hardly believe it! I felt a wonderful sense of relief flowing through my body and soul. I was like a man condemned to die a horrible death reprieved at the last moment. I could have jumped up and punched the clouds, embraced everyone, even Teddy Eldin. I didn't give a hoot why it had been cancelled but naturally I was curious and wanted the blissful fact confirmed by some explanation. I asked Nevan if he knew why it had been cancelled.

"Oh, they said something about the weather not being dry enough, but we've not had much rain, have we? And it's all right now. I think I know the real reason it was cancelled."

"Well it wasn't ready, was it? Lampton must have realised. It would have been a shambles," I said.

"Speak for yourself, Mouse! *I* was ready," Nevan retorted.

Oh, yes, Nevan, I thought, you're full of confidence now you don't have to do it, and you could have just copied me anyway. "So what was the real reason?" I asked him.

"Ah, well, you should be able to work that one out yourself, shouldn't you?" This was typical of Nevan's caginess; he was always full of vague, cryptic suggestions. He liked to pretend he knew something, he loved to get us guessing, he loved the puzzled look on our faces when he threw out a hint of something secret or unmentionable. But I wasn't playing his game.

"No doubt Teddy Eldin will tell us sometime," I said, in a firm, dismissive 'why speculate?' way.

"Ah, but will he tell us the truth?" Nevan replied in his sly manner.

"Why shouldn't he?"

"Ah!" said Nevan tapping his nose and smiling enigmatically.

Teddy Eldin told us the next day that they'd decided the end of term

47

wasn't the best time for a gym display and it had been postponed. So that was another reason for its cancellation: not the right time for it. Nevan gave me one of his knowing looks as Teddy Eldin was making the announcement.

We never had the gym display. Mr Lampton did not reappear next term and Nevan felt fully vindicated for suggesting there was some scandal surrounding him which had forced him to leave. All Teddy Eldin said was Mr Lampton had been 'unable to continue teaching'. I thought, and Westford and Rigby Smith agreed, that Lampton had left because of ill health. Maybe he also had some mental problem that Teddy Eldin didn't want to reveal. We weren't surprised, anyway. There had always been that crazed look in his eyes, and now I think about it, I don't remember ever seeing him in the Staff Common Room or talking with other teachers. He was an outsider, a loner; we often saw him pacing round the edge of the playing fields on his own, with a distracted, troubled air, in his long, faded, belted, yellowy-white mackintosh. There was something in his past, it seemed evident to us, which he couldn't share with anyone, and he would never have settled at Penly Grange.

He wasn't a sadist, I don't think, certainly not in the way Swales was. He meted out his corporal punishment as if he didn't know what else to do. He may have had some gymnastic qualification but it was most unlikely he had any teaching qualifications. Although I felt some sympathy for him, which remains to this day, as did some of the others, it has to be said that he should never have been let loose on a class of boys. He was too unstable. But should Teddy Eldin and Slasher Swales have been let loose on boys, whether in groups or individually? Just because they were at home at Penly Grange, in their element, and he wasn't?

None of the other teachers I knew at Penly Grange used corporal punishment except, perhaps, for the odd clip or cuff, or rap on the knuckles or head with a pencil or ruler. Anyway, I don't associate any of the others with corporal punishment, though one or two would award blue stars quite readily, knowing full well they might lead to canings by Teddy Eldin.

One such teacher was the Rev. Arnold Nailsworth. He had silvery-white hair, quite a long nose, walked with a limp and had a speech impediment which caused him to speak in a guttural way as if his tongue was swollen at the back of his mouth. It was said he had been a prisoner-of-war in Burma but it was never confirmed, at least I don't remember ever being told the facts about his war experiences. He was probably the most scholarly teacher we had at Penly Grange. He taught Latin and, as you might expect being a clergyman, Divinity.

He taught us when we were a bit older, aged about 11-13. He clearly knew his Latin well and would doubtless have been horrified if he'd sat in on one of Teddy Eldin's Latin lessons. He had little patience with the duffers in the subject and could be harsh when work was poor. I remember him giving Nevan three blue stars for getting under 30% in his Latin exam. That meant a visit to the Headmaster and an inevitable caning. Teddy Eldin gave Nevan two stokes of the cane which had really hurt him. This may sound heartless but at the time I'd wished he'd been caned harder because he still came second in the Junior cross country run, ten places ahead of me. (Rigby Smith won, as expected, and our group, E Group, won the Junior cup).

I remember Nailsworth teaching us Divinity in the library which doubled as the classroom for the top form of the school, so we must have been 12-13 years old then. His Divinity teaching consisted primarily of studying passages from the 'Little Bible', a selection of abridged extracts from the Authorised Bible, mainly stories. The extracts we read were mostly from the Old Testament, as far as I can remember. Although we tended to find the Little Bible rather boring – it had a very boring plain blue cover too and no illustrations – I was impressed with some stories, especially the story of Daniel in the Lion's Den, partly because I'd seen a picture somewhere else of Daniel with an angel by his side surrounded by very hungry and realistic-looking lions. I also recall being very moved by David's lament over Saul and Jonathan which we were asked to learn by heart and which I enjoyed doing when I realised I could learn it. I can still remember much of it, especially the famous lines about David's love for Jonathan 'passing the love of women' and the concluding sombre pronouncement – 'How are the mighty fallen and the weapons of war perished!'

One day we studied the story of Moses on Mount Sinai and the tablets of stone (on which the Ten Commandments were written) and the Israelites' idolatrous worship of the golden calf in Moses' absence. Nailsworth wrote the word 'immorality' on the board and tried to go through the Ten Commandments with us in a more adult way than we had done when we were younger. There were some suppressed sniggers because it was assumed that the word 'immorality' referred only to sexual immorality. Maybe that was Spilwell's fault for he would bring the topic of sex centre stage whenever he got the chance. He wasn't given many opportunities but on this occasion he seemed to be offered a great one. Nailsworth had difficulty pointing out to Spilwell that only *one* of the Ten Commandments related to sexual immorality. When Nailsworth did finally get this point across, having spent a disproportionate amount of time on the sixth commandment (adultery), Spilwell asked about the Tenth Commandment, about coveting your neighbour's wife. What precisely did it mean?

Nailsworth was caught in a dilemma. He didn't want to get bogged down with questions of sexual immorality, especially with a precocious boy known to be excessively interested in the topic of sex. On the other hand, he believed all boys should explore important moral questions before leaving Penly Grange (the chaplain, Henry Hewey, seemed less concerned about this) and wanted to make the moral case for the Ten Commandments. He took his Divinity teaching very seriously and believed Divinity was primarily concerned with imparting knowledge, understanding and acceptance of the moral and spiritual values enshrined in the Bible. So he was quite happy to explain the meaning of the word 'covet' in the Tenth Commandment: 'Thou shalt not covet' etc., etc. To do that, however, he had to acknowledge Spilwell's question about not coveting your neighbour's wife.

You will learn later how Teddy Eldin dealt peremptorily with Spilwell's attempt to ask a question in his Sex Education lesson; Nailsworth, to his credit, used a shrewder, less desperate ploy.

"Spilwell," he said, in his slow, guttural whir. "For next time, read chapter eleven of the Second Book of Samuel and find out about coveting your neighbour's wife there. Tell us about it, next time. Now we'll consider coveting other things mentioned in the Tenth Commandment."

For once, Spilwell was outmanoeuvred. He knew a lot about Science and Maths, quite a bit about History and Geography, but not much about the Bible. He certainly wasn't very good on Bible texts. He was silenced for the moment. I didn't realize just how clever Nailsworth had been here because I didn't know my Bible very well either. Nailsworth, I realized much later, was referring to King David's sin with Bathsheba, the wife of Uriah, which involved more than adultery. I don't remember, though, ever doing this topic with Nailsworth. I seem to recollect that he asked Spilwell to write an essay on what he'd learnt and that postponed the topic further until it faded from Nailsworth's lessons altogether. The next week, in fact, we were doing more boring topics like stealing and 'bearing false witness'. They gave Nailsworth his opportunity to bang on about honesty and integrity and truthfulness: subjects he much preferred talking about with 12-13 year old boys. The task of Sex Education had, anyway, been taken over by the Headmaster – Teddy Eldin himself. Nailsworth always implied that Teddy Eldin would deal thoroughly with any questions we had about sexual matters, whether scientific or moral, and we should wait until then. It proved a long wait and his treatment of them wasn't exactly thorough when it finally came.

Mr Carrow taught some Latin but his main subject was English. He was a fairly short, plump man with red hair, high-stacked on his head, and a bushy, ginger beard round his face and under his chin. His chubby face, or what you could see of it, went quickly red when he was aroused. Although fairly agreeable much of the time, he could become easily agitated about his pet concerns and you soon learnt what they were. He was a stickler for tidiness of work and a boy's appearance, particularly his shoes. Untied laces and unbrushed shoes were anathema to him. He insisted on work being presented in a correct manner, with dates and headings being laid out in exactly the same way every time. On layout, unfortunately, his advice conflicted with Mr Bracken's, the French teacher. Bracken liked us to use plenty of space and always begin a fresh page for each new topic. Carrow wanted the exact opposite. He hated blank lines which he regarded as a waste of space. All that was necessary, he said, was to draw a line in pencil under the completed work and then begin again on the next line. I thought the work looked too cluttered doing this but I didn't argue, of course; you didn't argue with Carrow on matters of presentation. One thing he was insistent about, and was quite right about I eventually came to see, was crossing out neatly. All that is required, he used to say, is a single line drawn clearly through a word. Don't scratch the word out, don't try to obliterate it, he would say, you only create a mess on the page; you're trying to remove the word with as little fuss as possible not draw attention to it.

I remember very little of Carrow's Latin teaching except that it was very fussy and finicky but certainly more competent than Teddy Eldin's Latin teaching (not difficult).

Some of his English teaching, at least what he taught us or got us to do, I remember quite well. He expected rather a lot of us in our essay writing, giving us generalised and abstract essay titles like 'Travel', 'Happiness', 'Time', 'Law and Order', 'An Ideal World'. He also liked to use proverbs as essay titles, such as 'fools rush in where angels fear to tread', 'a stitch in time saves nine', 'it's an ill wind that blows nobody any good', 'still waters run deep'. We were supposed to write witty, reflective, discoursive essays on these titles, not stories, and we weren't much good at it except for Rickmack; sometimes Spilwell and Loretti came up with something quite good too. Fortunately, Carrow did give us the chance to write stories occasionally, something which we were much better at and which we enjoyed much more. Jock Clayton (who was the seconder of my patrol when I first joined the Scouts and who did his First Class Journey with Rigby Smith) was a particularly good story writer and Carrow used to get him to read his stories out to us in class. Rigby Smith used to tell gripping stories off the top of his head, ghost stories, but that wasn't in class, that was at lunch in the dining room and I'm not sure whether he ever wrote them down.

As part of our English language work we learnt 'parsing'. This was similar to the 'clausal analysis' which we did later at Marby College. It entailed breaking down a sentence into its component parts and labelling each part. It was an advanced or developed form of the study of parts of speech. We were supposed to know already what an adverb or adjective was and other parts of speech. Now we learnt what an 'adverbial' or 'adjectival' phrase was and how it related to the other parts of the sentence in which it appeared; we also learnt the difference between mere phrases and the more structurally important *clauses*. I'm not sure whether parsing helped me at all to improve my written English but it did help me later in studying other languages and gave me some vocabulary and terms with which to describe or discuss written English.

Carrow also taught us 'figures of speech' to help us discuss or analyse poetry. Knowledge of figures of speech did make me more aware of devices of language which poets use to convey their meaning and feelings, but it tended to promote a rather mechanical approach to poetry appreciation. We learnt about figures of speech such as metaphor, simile, alliteration, onomatopoeia, apostrophe and personification from a green textbook which included examples of each one from famous poets. Then we were tested on them, usually in a written test.

Memorising the definitions of figures of speech and examples of them I found rather tedious, but I loved some of the poems we read in The Dragon Book of Verse, our poetry book, and enjoyed learning them off by heart. I had a good memory and found I could remember lines almost as well as Rigby Smith, Parker, Rickmack and Loretti, who usually got full marks whenever we had a memorising poetry test.

The poems I remember best from The Dragon Book of Verse were classics of English literature: The Listeners by Walter de la Mare (about a mysterious traveller visiting a deserted house in a forest), Ozymandias by Shelley (about a tyrant's fallen statue in the desert), the fragment Kubla Khan by Coleridge (based on a dream he'd had), Shakespeare's Sonnet LX –'Like as the waves make towards the pebbled shore' and Jacques' Seven Ages of Man soliloquy ('All the world's a stage'), from his comedy As You Like It; also, poems by Tennyson – The Eagle and 'Break, break, break'. The latter poem was about the loss of a close friend and didn't hit me particularly hard until after I had left Penly Grange and applied it to my own personal loss (not through death, as in Tennyson's case, but through the process, I suppose, of growing up and changing). Another memorable poem in The Dragon Book of Verse was a short, eight line poem in two verses called Heraclitus. This poem – by William Johnson Cory, according to the book – was my favourite:

They told me, Heraclitus, they told me you were dead,
They brought me bitter news to hear and bitter tears to shed;
I wept as I remembered how often you and I
Had tired the sun with talking and sent him down the sky.

And now that thou art lying, my dear old Carian guest,
A handful of grey ashes, long long ago at rest,
Still are thy pleasant voices, thy nightingales, awake:
For Death he taketh all away, but them he cannot take.

This poem of lament for the death of a dear friend has obvious similarities with Tennyson's 'Break, break, break', in its subject matter at least. At the time of reading the two poems, Heraclitus made more of an impact on me than Tennyson's poem. I think because it's more abrupt and dramatic: you learn straightaway, in the first line, of the death of the poet's friend – 'They told me, Heraclitus, they told me you were dead' – whereas in Tennyson's poem you don't know he is grieving the loss of his friend until the third verse. Also, the speaker in Heraclitus is talking directly to his friend who's died; Tennyson is only talking *about* his friend who's died, and he uses the word 'vanished' for his dying, less stark than the abrupt word 'dead' in Heraclitus. I can't remember whether Carrow told us, or whether I discovered it later, but the poem Heraclitus is in fact a free translation from the Greek. At Penly Grange, I regarded it as any other English poem, it was there on the page like the rest of them, a 'given', I didn't question its origin, I only know it moved me deeply and spoke directly to me.

I particularly loved the best known lines – 'I wept as I remembered how often you and I/ Had tired the sun with talking and sent him down the sky'. I could easily apply these lines to my own friendships, particularly to my friendship with Rigby Smith. We didn't 'tire the sun with *talking*', as such, not the first years of our friendship, though we talked quite a lot when doing Scouts together when we were older, and on the buses, but we certainly 'tired the sun' with *playing*. In the woods at school and even more so at home (Rigby Smith's home) because we were back at home in the evening and more likely to see the sun go down at home. Not in the winter, of course, it was always dark when we got home then, but certainly in the summer, spring and early autumn. Before Nevan appeared on the home scene and even after that, when the frequency of my visits to the Rigby Smiths' diminished somewhat, I would play football or cricket with Rigby Smith in the field at the end of their road or in their back garden till the light faded and after.

Colin and James Rigby Smith might play too and perhaps one of the

Wheeler or Barley brothers, occasionally Toffee, who went to a different school, might be there; Nevan, once he'd befriended the Rigby Smiths, was nearly always there. In the summer or Easter holidays, especially, when we could stay up late, we played on and on and never felt tired, just paused for breath occasionally and carried on. It would grow darker and darker. When we were playing in the garden, Mrs Rigby Smith would come outside tell us to come in. "How can you possibly see in that light!?" she would exclaim. It was extraordinary how we *could* manage to see in the darkness – more or less. Somehow our eyes adjusted to the fading light and we played on till it was pitch black: till when you kicked or hit the ball it did actually vanish totally from your sight, swallowed up in the darkness, and your game had to end. The sun would have long since gone to bed when we reluctantly gave up and came inside. Rigby Smith and I certainly did 'send him down the sky', the poem expressed that perfectly. I have never had such energy since that time nor such unthinking enthusiasm. It was partly my age: boys of eight, nine and ten, are not noted for their moderation and thoughtfulness but it was also because I was so happy to be at the Rigby Smiths' which became a second home for me.

Carrow and School Plays

Carrow also produced the occasional play. I remember doing *Hamlet* with him in the gym/assembly hall, which had formerly been a barn. The stage, at the far end of the gym, was fairly small, and every inch of space counted. We just did the final scene of *Hamlet*, which includes the duel between Hamlet and Laertes and four deaths, the deaths of Queen Gertrude, King Claudius, Laertes and Hamlet. For most of this final scene I was off stage, waiting to come on with Rickmack. Rickmack was playing Fortinbras (Prince of Norway), and I was one of his captains, and one of us, me, I believe, thought of something very funny we might do when Horatio, played by Loretti, was delivering his farewell speech to the just-deceased Hamlet.

At this point in the final scene, the four above-mentioned deaths have all taken place and there are four dead bodies lying supine on the stage (the victims might have chosen to die face down but for some reason in this production, and I remember it distinctly, they were all lying on their backs). This is a grave, solemn, and profoundly tragic time in the play. Nevertheless, during one costume rehearsal, Rickmack and I, because we were getting bored with waiting (I suppose), had a brittle stick backstage, all ready for an unscripted sound effect, and at the beginning of Horatio's elegiac speech, "Now cracks a noble heart ..." one of us snapped the stick.

It wasn't all that loud but, in the confined space, it was quite audible upstage, and immediately the legs of one of the upstage corpses began to twitch, then its stomach could be seen moving up and down. Soon the legs of the other three corpses began twitching and the stomachs of all four corpses were heaving up and down with ever-diminishing restraint. Life had returned miraculously to the vocal chords of the corpses too, as semi-smothered snorting noises could be heard issuing from them. The bottled up laughter then exploded from the now fully animated corpses and spread to everybody on the set, and even Carrow began laughing. The rehearsal completely disintegrated for several minutes.

Rickmack and I were very pleased with ourselves as the authors of such rich mirth but we made the mistake of doing it again (well, we were boys, weren't we?) and Carrow wasn't amused this time. He made Rickmack and me write an essay for him entitled 'Once Funny, Twice a Bore'. One punishment, at least, at Penly Grange thoroughly deserved. (Rickmack, I remember, quite enjoyed writing his essay).

My most vivid memory of Carrow, however, is not of him in school at all. He once came on one of the Lake District walking holidays, led by Mr Bracken, our scoutmaster. I'm not sure whether he stayed with us for the whole holiday but he was certainly with us when, based at Patterdale Youth Hostel, we climbed Helvellyn, for I remember the beginning of that walk very well. We were standing on the bridge in Glenridding, and Carrow was in his walking gear and all ready to go. He was glancing up at the hills in anticipation of the walk. It was a lovely sunny day, and the breeze was playing in his ginger beard and hair and rippling through his clothes. He was looking very relaxed, smiling a warm smile, a warm, radiant smile. I have never seen a more buoyant man.

Could this be Carrow the schoolmaster who got so upset if your shoes weren't presentable or you put the date in the wrong place or started a new page of your exercise book rather than rule off and continue on the next line? It was an amazing sight and suddenly I found it was easier to talk to him too. From that moment onwards I stopped seeing only the petulant, censorious side of his character and began to like him; I realised he could be happy and enjoy life just like us. A lot of other good things came out of Mr Bracken's walking holidays, but that is part of Bracken's portrait to come.

Mr Mace was a young teacher who taught Maths. He was tall, with black frizzy hair, receding at the front, and thick, protuberant lips. Like Carrow, the slightest provocation could cause his face to redden and in his case the red would spread to his neck too. He was a little effeminate in his movements and seemed more so in his games kit which exposed his slender, willowy legs. He was quite a good Maths teacher, by reputation, but he seldom taught me and I cannot remember any details about his lessons. His youthfulness and unease with us, at first, caused us to fear and respect him less than most of the other teachers but one incident I witnessed one summer's afternoon led me to change my opinion of him as a bit of a drip.

The buzz was going round the school that a rat was loose in the grounds and the groundsman Arthur Embury – who was from Lancashire and who, if you were lucky, would recite the famous monologue about young Albert and the lion – was going after it. Mr Mace had joined the hunt with him and they were scouring the beech hedge up towards the great beech tree by the pavilion. I was going down that way because I was due to score for the cricket match beginning at two o'clock. I didn't see them there but when I arrived at the pavilion they were gathered round the side of the pavilion peering at the ground with sticks in their hands. There were some other boys with them but keeping a discreet distance. As I got closer, I saw that Mace was, in fact, not carrying a stick, as such, but a cricket stump. It somehow added drama to the occasion, as if Mace had grabbed the cricket stump from the pavilion in a moment of urgency and panic.

After a minute or two, the rat appeared, large and brown, scurrying along the edge of the pavilion. Mace and Arthur Embury closed in, perhaps a little too hurriedly because the rat suddenly froze and then sprung at Mace who was stooping down closer to the ground. Mace straightened up, but didn't retreat one inch, and caught the rat in mid air with a terrific blow from his cricket stump which sent the rat tumbling into the beech mast by the pavilion. The spectating boys scattered and Arthur went over and finished the rat off with his heavy stick. Mace had gone very pale but he was still composed enough to tell the boys to clear off and get ready for playing or watching the afternoon's cricket.

It was a cool performance from Mace and ever after I looked at him with different eyes; he was not as weak and ineffectual as we thought. Not only had he stood his ground but he'd delivered a well aimed blow: that was courage combined with skill. Mr Mace eventually won general respect, if not always affection, through the number of school trips he used to run and his help and involvement with Scouting activities and camps, as well as his competence as a Maths teacher.

The Reverend Henry Hewey was the school chaplain for Marby College, and Penly Grange, being its prep school, came under his spiritual auspices and care too. Marby College is a member of the Purseywood Foundation of schools, an Anglican Foundation established by the clergyman James

Purseywood in the latter part of the 19th century to educate pupils 'according to the principles and moral standards of the Christian faith'. To assist this purpose, Purseywood had ensured that each of his schools had a chaplain.

Someone had chosen Henry Hewey to be the school chaplain for Marby College and its prep department in our time, presumably the Headmaster of Marby College and its governors and, on the face of it at least, he was not a surprising choice. The Purseywood Foundation is, or at least was then, somewhat 'high church' and Henry Hewey was certainly a 'high' churchman. He was the sort of clergyman you call 'Father', and some staff would call him that, though we always addressed him as 'sir' like the other teachers, and referred to him as Mr Hewey or, amongst ourselves, as Hewey or H.H., his initials, which he seemed to like. He was a bachelor and remained so throughout his life, I believe. (It was rumoured he had once been engaged to a young lady but had backed out of it, a story I can neither confirm nor deny).

In appointing him as chaplain, the Headmaster and governors might also have been impressed with his sporting credentials. He was a keen sportsman and good at cricket in particular. He would often play for clergy cricket teams, and most clergy cricket teams, it might be noted, are known to play to quite a high standard. The Headmaster and governors might also have been struck by his neat, dark hair and good looks, his tall stature and, above all, his genial, jocular air. He was full of fun, full of bonhomie and amusing, throwaway remarks. He was indeed quite a 'character'.

Whether, once in his post, the Headmaster and governors were equally impressed with his actual performance as a teacher and inculcator of the 'principles and moral standards of the Christian Faith' is less certain. His lessons were very light-hearted in style, also very undemanding and lacking in educational substance, to put it mildly.

Henry Hewey would breeze into the classroom with a big, avuncular smile on his face, carrying a copy of The Church Times and perhaps the Prayer Book or Bible. After making us stand for some time in silence to establish his authority, he would get us to sit down and would then read us something from the front page of The Church Times, in a very grave manner. This might last a minute. Then he would smile impishly and turn to the back pages and start to read out the cricket scores. He spent much longer on this. Sometimes he had The Daily Telegraph with him and read out the county cricket scores and Test Match score card, if there had been a Test Match. From time to time he would jump up and recite the Hail Mary. If it happened to be midday he would make us all stand up and recite it too:

Hail, Mary, full of grace,
The Lord is with thee!
Blessed art thou among women
And blessed is the fruit of thy womb, Jesus!
Holy Mary, Mother of God,
Pray for us sinners,
Now and at the hour of our death.

Hewey never offered us any elucidation of the meaning or significance of the words. It was enough, it seemed, merely to reiterate them. At first we found the recitation of 'Hail Mary' rather awkward and forced but as we got used to it we accepted it as one of Hewey's mantras, like his favourite, colourful expletive, which he might utter at any time on the slightest of pretexts – 'Hells, bells, and buckets of blood!' Hewey's mantras were meaningless to us but they were part of his personality and became great fun to hear or recite loudly in the classroom where the atmosphere for most lessons was normally formal, solemn and somewhat repressive.

Whilst Hewey was very easy going about school rules and discipline in general, he laid great store on courtesy and being polite. His favourite saying was 'Manners maketh man' and if he thought you were being insolent or rude, even in the smallest way, he was filled with righteous indignation and might punish you with his own misconduct marks which he called 'black marks' – he didn't use blue stars. Using his own misconduct marks (though he was known to award *red* stars sometimes for good behaviour or work), together with his eccentric, cavalier attitude to lesson content and his rare setting of homework, set him apart from the other teachers but in no way weakened his authority. On the contrary, he had an arrangement with Teddy Eldin that made his punishment code more rigorous than the blue star system used by the rest of the teaching staff. In the blue star system, four blue stars acquired per week or three blue stars awarded for a single heinous offence earned you a caning. Hewey's system was more astringent. Three black marks per week and two black marks awarded at one time earned you a visit to the Headmaster and an automatic caning. Fortunately, Hewey rarely gave black marks, but from time to time he would remind us that they were at his disposal. It was like laying a cane on the table to warn boys not to get out of line. It worked. We were usually relaxed in his lessons but did not take liberties with him, never more than once anyway.

I learnt very little Divinity from him but picked up a few churchy things from the Prayer Book which he would sometimes read from, or refer to, when he got round to doing some proper teaching. I remember going through one or two psalms, such as the famous 23rd Psalm, and learning some definitions from the Catechism when we were preparing for Confirmation: three things in particular. (Divinity lessons and Confirmation classes with Hewey are completely merged in my mind and I can't distinguish between them now).

Grace – a gift of God.
Sacrament – an outward and visible sign of an inward and spiritual grace.
Our purpose in life – to know, love and serve God here on earth and be happy with him forever in heaven.

It all seemed rather simplistic and Henry Hewey's faith somewhat formulaic but looking back I think he did pass on to us a little more than the importance of good manners. The fact that I remember those three definitions to this day, though they didn't mean much to me at the time, and they now give me some food for thought, is a sign he perhaps planted some spiritual seeds in me. And although I was not of a religious disposition, Hewey did something once in a lesson, a small, simple thing, which I've never forgotten, and which certainly made me think more deeply about the purpose of churches. He showed us a picture of a church with a spire and said to us, "You know what that is? That's the finger of God pointing to heaven."

His life style, however, for 'a man of the cloth', remained a questionable matter throughout our time at Penly Grange and at Marby College. I don't remember him smoking, he may have done, though no one attached a great deal of importance to it in those days – most adults smoked, it was quite normal, and they smoked almost anywhere – but he certainly liked a social drink, less common in respectable clergymen, and it was said he had taken underage boys into pubs with him, believing the law against under 18 year olds having a friendly pint of beer in a local tavern most unreasonable. As well as being a cricket lover, he enjoyed horse racing too and was known to bet on the horses. Not only bet himself but, at Marby College, he would place bets on behalf of the boys too. So, a controversial figure, especially at Marby College.

At Penly Grange he did little harm but also contributed little to the curriculum. However, he gave us a refreshing break from tests, exam results, homework and the constraints of some petty school rules; in psychological terms, he was probably equivalent to a relaxing leisure activity. And we mustn't forget: he kept us well informed about cricket in the outside world, surely a socially useful, mind-broadening experience for us!

Mr Timmerton, who taught PT and Science, was not an outstanding teacher but he was above average for Penly Grange and the least disliked of all the teachers I have mentioned so far with the possible exception of Henry Hewey. He was fairly short and of slim and wiry build. His hair was closely trimmed and he had clear-cut, well chisled features. His eyes had a benevolent twinkle in them. He was generally good-natured and he never raised his voice and was seldom angry. We liked his calm manner and the twinkle in his eye and were not afraid of him, though we respected him and usually listened to him closely.

As with Mr Swales and Mr Mace, it is his extra-curricular activities for which I remember him rather than his teaching – his games supervision and coaching. He supervised and coached both cricket and rugby (we tended to call it rugger) but I recall best his rugby coaching and refereeing. As a rugby coach, he was a good tutor of rugby skills and strategy and a quiet encourager rather than a nagger and critic like Swales. He gave the pack and three-quarters equal attention and was well balanced in his approach to the game. The same could not be said for his refereeing which was not as impartial as it should have been, certainly not in school matches.

In some ways this didn't bother us, quite the contrary for he was always biased in our favour, but there were times when the bias was so blatant it became embarrassing for us. I played once for the Second Fifteen – I was a reserve for the wing and came on at half time – but otherwise I didn't get into any of the school rugby teams. However, I became a touch judge for the First Fifteen and so I witnessed quite a lot of Timmerton's refereeing. He wasn't consistently biased. If we were winning or if the school we were playing against was not one of our arch rivals he might actually be reasonably impartial in his refereeing. But when the chips were down, or the opposition school was one we had to beat for school pride, he felt it incumbent on him to tip the scales in our team's favour.

Two schools we always had to beat were Rostock Manor and Conninghurst. On one occasion we were playing Rostock Manor at home and losing by a couple of points. Rickmack, our scrum half, put the ball into the scrum after Rostock Manor had infringed in some mysterious way and almost immediately Timmerton blew his whistle and awarded us a penalty for an even more mysterious offence. By sheer good fortune (ha! ha!) the scrum was under the posts of the opposition, and Pelham, our goal kicker, after recovering from his astonishment at being awarded the penalty, slotted the ball over between the posts with ease and we acquired three valuable points, putting us in a winning position.

In another match, Conninghurst School had a powerful three-quarter who played inside centre and was unstoppable once he got the ball. Yet he only got over the try line and scored *once* in the entire game. Whenever he had the ball or was about to get the ball, there would be some sort of foul given against his side. They're always plenty of infringements to chose from in rugby, so sometimes it was a forward pass, sometimes it was offside, sometimes it was a 'knock on'. (To this day referees still seem to blow for a 'knock on' if the ball is dropped whether the ball goes forward or not). And if a Conninghurst player did make it over the try line, Timmerton, as referee, always had the final expedient up his sleeve. He would allege that the ball had not been touched down, not 'grounded' properly. But even *he* couldn't make this refereeing decision if the player, having crossed the try line, lay on top of the ball for a full minute, and that's how Conninghurst did actually manage to score one try, when their star three quarter did just that.

There were protests of course, sometimes, from boys in the opposing school teams and very occasionally from their staff but, as far as I could tell, Timmerton ignored them. In any case, the best opportunity of balancing the score and exacting revenge for Timmerton's biased decisions came with the return match which would be an away match for us and one which would refereed by one of their teaching staff. Timmerton could do nothing then to influence the outcome of the match and he was in no position to object to any refereeing decisions they might make after his own refereeing performances.

According to Porter, the Rostock Manor rugby teacher was a reasonably fair referee, nevertheless, but the Conninghurst teacher was as biased as Timmerton. The bias shown by both schools was usually reflected in the match scores. The same team encounters would produce totally different scores according to whether they were playing home or away. If we won 20-3 at home, we would probably lose 27-0 playing away. Obviously this was a very silly situation and couldn't go on indefinitely. I believe the two schools did eventually call a truce, but it was after our time. When it came to cricket, the really frosty relations existed between us and Rostock Manor. How we came out on top in our bitter cricket rivalry, without any help from our umpire, you will learn in the chapter on sport at Penly Grange.

I recollect two female teachers: Mrs Leyton and Mrs Nogg. Mrs Leyton was the widow of an erstwhile Maths teacher at Marby College and Mrs Nogg was the wife of a History teacher there. Since they taught us only in the first two or three years, I can only hazily recall their appearance but I can remember quite well some of the things we did with them.

Mrs Leyton taught art which we enjoyed but didn't take altogether seriously because we didn't get marks for it and it wasn't therefore included in our term order. We painted pictures in her lessons which involved splashing paint on pieces of paper in an attempt to represent the sky, sea and clouds. Mrs Leyton didn't insist on our painting these things but she encouraged us to experiment with colours and we tended to choose these subjects for our experiments. I don't remember learning much about painting technique from her, probably my fault, but she also taught us how to make things, such as oven gloves and stuffed toys. Making things was much more fun than painting, I found, and you had something at the end you could use, maybe even sell.

I remember making a stuffed rabbit toy under her supervision which I was very proud of, and a kettle handle holder which I gave to my mum, made by weaving threads of coloured wool through a frame of tiny, empty squares. The colours of the wool had a gentle pastel quality and for the first time I became fully aware of the delights of different shades of colour and colour tones and the texture of materials; I enjoyed working *with* the colours rather than just looking at them. We also made things out of papier maché. We made papier maché objects and then painted them. I made a bowl. Rigby Smith made a papier maché head. This papier maché head – following Mrs Leyton's suggestion – was made into a glove puppet head. With Mrs Leyton's help, the head became the head of a stern, superior-looking, middle-aged lady. When Rigby Smith later wrote his puppet plays he called this particular puppet the Proud Lady. When I saw what Rigby Smith had achieved, I had a go at one too. I made quite a striking, evil-looking puppet head, which he happily used in his puppet plays too.

Mrs Nogg taught us English. She tried to improve our spelling, punctuation and vocabulary, with only limited success in the case of spelling. She helped me, I think, to get apostrophes sorted but can't have been very successful with curing me of some common spelling errors. Recently, I read again a diary I'd kept for a few months in 1957. I noticed that I consistently confused the spellings of 'there' and 'their' in my entries.

Mrs Nogg was moderately good at maintaining discipline in class; she had quite a strong voice and had the star book at her disposal to restrain unruly behaviour. However, she had a problem with her name. Like all keen junior school children trying to gain the attention of a female teacher, we loved to shout, "Miss! Miss! Miss!" with our hands thrust up high when asked a question. Since women teachers were few and far between at Penly Grange, the opportunity to shout "Miss! Miss!" was rare and we therefore made as much of it as we could. Mrs Nogg, like every other married female teacher, tried to put us right on the use of 'Miss' from the very beginning:

"I am not 'Miss'!" she firmly corrected us. "I am married, I am *Mrs, Mrs* Nogg. Kindly address me in full as Mrs Nogg." Unfortunately, because of her surname, she only made matters worse for herself for then we shouted,

"*Mrs* Nogg! *Mrs* Nogg! *Mrs* Nogg!" and as our excitement grew in our eagerness to be picked to answer her question, we spoke faster and then we began to gabble. The 's' in 'Mrs' began to elide with 'Nogg' until the first two letters of 'Mrs' were swallowed up altogether and what came out was, "'Snog! 'Snog! 'Snog!"

Mrs Nogg, declining the mass invitation from her pupils, would cut in,

"Do not say 'snog'! 'Snog' is not a nice word." (She didn't tell us what 'snog' meant, though). "I am Mrs ... Nogg. Two *separate* words." So for a time we said 'Mrs ... Nogg' very carefully, as two words, but enthusiasm would mount again, 'Mrs Nogg' would be spoken faster and faster until it became 'Miss Nogg', then 'Snog' again. Of course the uncontrollable enthusiasm on the part of many boys was feigned so that 'Snog' could be said, apparently, unintentionally. It was impossible for her to pick out amongst all the shouts who was saying 'Mrs Nogg' too carelessly and hastily and who was deliberately shouting, "Snog! Snog! Snog!" (most of us).

Mrs Nogg was very annoyed for a time, as you can imagine, before hitting on the only solution, which was a sensible rule anyway. When offering to answer a question which she had asked the class, she was not to be addressed by name at all. This measure got rid of the 'Snogs' but led to lots of 'Yesses' ... "Yes! Yes! Yes!" so that she then had to insist on no words at all. We were to raise our hands in silence until she decided which of us should answer her question, but this led to inarticulate noises and extreme facial appeals, sometimes quite grotesque, in our endeavours to be chosen.

Eventually Mrs Nogg got us under control and things settled down. She taught us English language quite effectively – I don't remember doing much literature with her – and didn't need to use blue stars too often. She was fairly generous in the awarding of red stars too. We liked her for that and generally found her an agreeable, though not particularly inspiring, teacher.

There were two teachers at Penly Grange, however, who were quite exceptional and were both inspiring in their own way – Charles Bracken and Robert Barnet. They were schoolmasters in the widest and best sense of the word and they merit a separate chapter each. Robert Barnet's story is a tragic one and needs to be told separately, anyway.

Charles Bracken

'Soft man, hard man'

Charles Bracken was not at Penly Grange when I first went there at the age of eight. By the time he taught me, when I was about ten, I had become used to the inflexible, traditional teaching we normally received, with its emphasis on rote learning, the regurgitation of knowledge, and the stamping out of small factual errors before general understanding, so his new approach to schoolwork was a very pleasant surprise.

It was his attitude rather than any teaching technique that made him so different. He taught French, a subject in which it is possible to accumulate enormous numbers of errors in written work no matter how careful you are. Many English schoolchildren aged ten, or older, are still having difficulty in spelling English words properly, let alone the words of another language, so written French has hardly got a chance!

I remember one of my very first French lessons with Bracken. He set us a written exercise and asked us to bring our exercise books up to the teacher's table at the front of the classroom for marking when we'd finished it. I brought my exercise book up thinking I'd not done too badly and found my heart sinking as he proceeded to cover my work with red biro corrections. He'd spotted masses of errors. I started to apologise, trying to muster an excuse, wondering whether I'd be receiving any blue stars and if so how many. Imagine my amazement, then, when he smiled and told me not to worry, it was good to make mistakes.

Good to make mistakes? Where had this one come from? Certainly not from Teddy Eldin's stable, nor had I ever heard it from any other teacher. He saw my bafflement and explained. It's good to make mistakes because you learn from your mistakes; in fact, the more mistakes you make the more opportunity you have for learning. What would be the point of producing perfect work? You would learn nothing when it was marked. But he was quick to point out you should make sure you *did* learn from your mistakes; not simply do your corrections mechanically, but try to understand why you had made the mistakes in the first place.

Bracken's approach was liberating, maybe too liberating. The main difference it made was to remove the fear of handing in poor work. For conscientious boys like me (conscientious over schoolwork, anyway) there was no danger of becoming lax. On the contrary, I began to like French more and wanted to do well, to please him by showing I was learning from my mistakes. I cannot say whether the less conscientious boys took advantage of Bracken's more relaxed attitude (they probably did) but, I must admit, his alacrity in awarding red stars by way of encouragement, and not just for high achievement, did slightly devalue them. Once he gave me two red stars for a mark of 13 out of 20. It was very nice but I remember thinking, 'Did I really deserve that?' Still, his generous approach was a welcome counterbalance to the tendency of some teachers to be niggardly over awarding red stars and too free in the awarding of blue stars. I don't remember Bracken, actually, ever giving blue stars. He may have done for bad conduct but I don't think he ever gave them for poor work.

Though a very different kind of teacher from the others, Bracken, as a character, was not an eccentric, he was not 'odd', but he did have some unusual personal characteristics. Or perhaps it was just the combination of his personal characteristics, physical and temperamental, which was unusual. He had dark, olive brown skin, deep dark brown eyes, short dark hair which lay fairly flat and thin on his head, though with a low wave at the front, and narrow lips. He was unquestionably good looking but was somewhat overweight, surprising for the energetic scoutmaster he was. Or it would have been surprising had he not also been both a smoker and eater of sweets. His fingers were as badly nicotine-stained as Mr Lampton's and he didn't look particularly fit. Clearly, he did not have an entirely healthy lifestyle and yet he was an enthusiast for sport. He was in charge of the Under 12 rugby and cricket teams and, as a Scouter, he was a great advocate and practitioner of outdoor life; he was, in fact, highly experienced in outdoor pursuits, such as camping and fell-walking.

It should be mentioned, perhaps, since I am going to praise him almost unreservedly, that though popular with most boys, certainly in comparison with Swales, Carrow and Nailsworth, he was not universally popular in our form. Rickmack didn't like him: he found him smarmy and too familiar and accused him of having favourites. Whether his attitude changed when Bracken made him Captain of E Group, a great honour since there were only four Group captains in the whole school, I don't remember. He was certainly liked by parents because he would talk readily to them when they came to school events about how their offspring were getting on. Teddy Eldin and Mace would talk about the new school swimming pool or some other improvement to the school site; Timmerton was often discreetly elsewhere, and Carrow would take evasive action if he saw a parent approaching him. Bracken, though, would go out of his way to talk to parents. (There were no regular Parents' Evenings in those days, not at Penly Grange, anyway). Rigby

Smith's mum told me once that she liked the way he worked his way round the boundary during a school cricket match, speaking to as many parents who were watching the game as possible.

Bracken the Scoutmaster ('Skip')

I have said that Mr Bracken was a French teacher and have mentioned that he was also a scoutmaster. What I should really have said was that he was a scoutmaster who also taught French. Although I'm certain he did much good as a French teacher, through his more humane and enlightened approach to his pupils, it was as a scoutmaster that he made his biggest impact for good, certainly on me and other boys, like Spencer and Honeyman, Westford, Thorpe and Rigby Smith. He actually introduced Scouts into the school by setting up the First Penly Grange Scout Group and built it up into a strong, thriving Group. It was evidently what he enjoyed doing most and he put his whole heart and much of his strength into it.

We had Cubs and Scouts on Friday afternoons, the only afternoon we didn't have Games, and if you didn't want to be in the Cubs or Scouts you had to join a work band and do odd jobs around the grounds. For this you had to don a boiler suit, so those who took this option were known as the Boiler Suit Gang or the Boiler Boys. (We all had to wear boiler suits, though, if we went into the woods when not doing Cubs or Scouts). The Boiler Suit Gang were in the minority and certainly when we were in the Scouts we looked down on them; we thought of them as skivers since they wandered around the place doing very little, apart from ambling about with wheelbarrows and messing about with spades, and they weren't learning how to be Scouts, of course, and working hard for badges like us. They used to knock off early too and have a swim whilst we were still doing Scouts.

I couldn't wait to join the Scouts. I had joined the Cubs at the age of nine and found it childish and undemanding. Swales was in charge of the cubs, he was Akela, and he bossed us around and told us lots of rules. He enjoyed himself but we didn't. I remember doing the Wolf Cub howls with Swales: squatting down on our haunches with the other Cubs in a circle around him as he played the part of Akela, and chanting, "Dyb, dyb, dyb! Dob, dob, dob! We will do our best!" and then leaping in the air with forefinger and third finger on both hands in a 'v' shape placed either side of the top of our heads, representing wolves' ears, and shouting, "A-ke-la!" I put lots of energy into it, I jumped up as high as I could, but not much of my heart into it. I found it difficult to take the ritual entirely seriously, though I loved most make-believe games. It was probably that I just didn't like Swales as Akela.

We learnt other Cub salutes and rituals and played games but not much else in the Cubs. The Scouts learnt lots of interesting things about living and surviving out of doors and finding your way around the countryside, and they made dens in the woods and went camping and walking. The Cubs made dens too but they weren't up to much. The Scouts also had demanding tests which led to badges on a graded scale: there was a structure, a stairway to climb, goals to achieve. I remember the excitement I felt when I first received my Boy Scout Membership Card and Record of Progress, when I was not quite old enough to join. I was nearly eleven. I opened the card and saw all the tests on the left of the card, over thirty of them, leading to the award of the First Class badge which every Scout was encouraged to attain. On the right were spaces for Special Proficiency badges if we aspired to further achievements. The whole card looked quite daunting but I felt the challenge of it and couldn't wait to get going, like a fledgling mountaineer eager to conquer the first peak and then all the rest, or a novice sailor looking forward to the first solo trip as a first step to winning the Olympics or The Americas Cup!

Rigby Smith, being a bit older than me, had joined the Scouts already and had passed all his Tenderfoot tests. It was the usual story of me trying to catch up with him. As I was still a month or two short of my eleventh birthday, I could have had a problem with catching up since you couldn't become a Scout until you were eleven. Fortunately, however, Bracken allowed me to do the Tenderfoot tests and begin preparation for the Second Class badge before my eleventh birthday and my investiture as a Scout; he knew I wanted to do my Scout tests alongside Rigby Smith and others, such as Thorpe and Westford, and I was grateful for his flexible attitude. Swales said he'd make me a Sixer (a group leader) if I stayed on in the Cubs for a few more weeks but I declined his offer. I'm not sure, actually, whether he really wanted me to stay on in the Cubs or not. I don't think he liked me much. He thought I messed around too much in Cubs and was too much of a joker. Swales didn't like jokers.

We learnt lots of useful, practical things for the Second Class badge in Scouts. Things like First Aid and the Highway Code, and camping skills such as fire lighting, hand axe and cooking. Some things, like knots and lashings, signalling, and compass and map, were quite difficult at first. Rigby Smith got on better than me at knots and lashings (at first) and hand axe (slightly); I got on better than him at compass and map; and we were both about the same when it came to signalling – semaphore and morse code (later dropped from the Second Class badge) – and to fire lighting (we both fancied ourselves at fire lighting). I think I was better than him at identifying trees, in the test called 'six common trees', but he would have disputed this. He thought he was good on trees and at bird spotting too. Actually, like hand axe, he wasn't as good at either as he thought he was.

Passing all the tests took time, effort and commitment, and we worked hard for them, at weekends too. We were extremely proud of ourselves when we completed our Second Class badge tests in only a few months, just six weeks after my eleventh birthday, and received our Second Class badges which got sown on the left sleeves of our uniform. We wanted to begin working at once on our First Class badge tests but were told we needed to wait for the summer when real camping could start outside school. We had always wanted to go off camping somewhere instead of just playing at camping in the school woods during the day, and now we were even more eager.

Bracken, as you might expect, showed a different side to him as a scoutmaster. I was never entirely comfortable switching from 'sir' in the classroom to 'Skip' in Scouts but I accepted that he was in a somewhat different relationship to us when he was our scoutmaster. Surprisingly, you might think, he was less easy going as a scoutmaster outside the classroom than he was as a French teacher inside the classroom. He remained more affable than most other teachers but he was far more earnest about Scouting than French and he drove us on in our Scout tests with much more rigour. He was also far less tolerant of lapses in Scout discipline and good Scouting practice than he was of carelessness in our French homework or inattention in class. For him, Scouting provided character training as well as useful practical knowledge, and the experience and skills you acquired from Scouting would see you in good stead for the rest of your life; they might even save your life one day. Rigby Smith told me some years ago that one of the skills he learnt in Scouts really did save his life once.

Although Bracken ran our Scout troop in an efficient and purposeful way on Friday afternoons, and guided us well through our various activities and tests, we didn't see the full extent of his Scouting dedication and expertise until we went away camping with him and on his Lake District walking trips. The situations in which we found ourselves on these Scouting holidays, sometimes dangerous situations in the case of the walking trips, revealed his mettle and spirit and really tested ours. Those camps and walking trips were unforgettable and truly character-forming experiences, and I also had conversations during them which I would never have had at school or home. I learnt more about Rigby Smith from them, though he didn't open up entirely, and I must say it was great to be able to talk to him without Nevan being around. (Nevan always tagged onto Rigby Smith whenever he got the chance). Nevan had one bad experience of camping at Nablock and opted out of camping thereafter; nor did he go on any of the walking trips. I didn't shed a tear.

68

We went on weekend camps to the woods at Nablock near Tibdale, where there were rhododendron bushes galore as well as oak and elm and beech and silver birch and other deciduous trees. There were lots of clearings in the woods at Nablock. I remember there being many thick-trunked felled trees lying on the ground, and logs and wood chippings scattered around large areas. We developed the basic camping skills at Nablock which we'd learnt in the woods at school, putting them into more prolonged practice; and we learnt some new things too. We learnt such things as setting up a patrol's camping area and digging latrines, and pitching tents and keeping them in good shape *in all weathers*. And it was at Nablock, because we there for two days and two nights, sometimes longer, that we had our first real taste of the agreeable and disagreeable sides of camping.

It was agreeable, indeed exhilarating, to wake in our tents in the morning, to smell the soil and dewy grass and, moving aside the front flap of the tent and thrusting out our heads a little, feel the morning breeze on our faces and glimpse the woods and fields outside and the sky above; and, sometimes, if we were lucky and it was a clear day, see the sun winking through he trees.

Each Scout patrol had its own fire in a staked out area we called a 'kitchen', though it also included living and eating areas and sections for wood and water etc., and it was good to get up and get your patrol's fire going in the morning, boil some water, and have that first cup of tea of the day. Bracken introduced a competitive element to the making of the first cup of tea. He awarded extra points to the first patrol to bring him a cup of tea in the morning. (Points were awarded for all sorts of good camping practices and the patrol with the most points won an award at the end of the camp: this was a great motivator).

It was a cunning ploy on Bracken's part since he ensured he had at least one cup of tea every morning without lifting a finger or issuing an order; sometimes he might have several cups of tea as keen Scouts in other patrols brought him further cups in their rush to be first. Bracken pre-empted being woken too early in the morning by over-zealous Scouts by having a rule that no Scout should get up and move around before 8am and that included making cups of tea. 8am may seem very late to be getting up when camping, especially in the summer, but Bracken had a very good reason for laying down this rule apart from the personal one of not wanting his cup of tea too early! He explained it to us:

We were out of doors all day when camping, doing energetic and often strenuous things and then we stayed up quite late round the Scout troop's communal campfire. If we also got up early in the morning we would soon run out of steam and become exhausted. We all needed a good night's sleep as well as him. He was right, and we saw the common sense in his rule. That doesn't mean to say that we all kept the rule about not rising too early (very difficult on a fine summer's day in July) but if we did get up we were very quiet about it and made sure we didn't disturb him or any other Scout who wanted to sleep or doze on, so we all benefited from his sensible regulation.

Actually we did not always succeed in being quiet when getting up before 8 in the morning. I remember one occasion when I heard noises 'in the night' not far from our tent and I got up to investigate. Although it was only about 5 o' clock in the morning, being July it was broad daylight and I had no difficulty seeing what was making the noise. It was a couple of cows who were nosing around our kitchen. One of them was knocking against our patrol's tea chest, at one corner of our kitchen, which contained our food and most of our camping utensils. To understand what happened next I need to explain the simple construction of a Scout patrol's kitchen.

Each patrol's kitchen was marked out with string attached to wooden stakes, running round a rectangular space of some ten square yards and at a height of about three or four feet (a metre or so). Each corner of the kitchen usually had a thicker, stronger stake, and in our case we were using the above-mentioned tea chest as one of our corner stakes. I didn't like the cows being so near our kitchen, they were trespassers as far as I was concerned, and I wanted them to remove themselves immediately. They no doubt felt they had every right to be there and thought *we* were the trespassers (I don't know where they'd come from, though) and they ignored my explicit hand movements suggesting they go elsewhere. I approached a little closer and endeavoured to make my message even clearer with further demonstrative gestures. Still no response from them. So I clapped my hands: just one sharp clap, not very loud, I didn't think.

It certainly worked, for both cows retreated speedily. All would have been well had it not been for the position of one of the cows when I clapped my hands. She had her horns under the string round the kitchen and, tossing up her head in a reflex action as she backed away, she caught the string on one of her horns. The string was attached to the tea chest, you will recall, and the tea chest was lifted peremptorily into the air with some force. It flew through the air several yards before crashing to the ground and spilling its contents.

Since the contents included such things as spoons, enamel plates and mugs and metal dixies (large cooking pots), the jangling noise when the tea chest hit the ground was considerable and woke half the camp site. Since, also, the tea chest contained food such as sugar, salt and tea, and sliced bread, and jam, porridge and cornflakes, there was a great deal of clearing up and restitution of stock needed later that day. That made me very unpopular with those in

70

my patrol who were not inclined to believe my version of events which, naturally, blamed the cow entirely for the devastation.

Fortunately, Bracken did accept my account of what had happened and was actually sympathetic, though I may not have mentioned clapping my hands, I think I just said I had tried to shoo the cows away. Mace, however, who was helping out at this camp, as he often did, tried to made a bad joke out of it by commenting that my practical joking and horse-play of the past had finally caught up with me, only it had turned out to be cow-play, rather than horse-play. Ha, ha!

But to return to agreeable things about camping which we enjoyed at Nablock and elsewhere. Some were things we'd done at school but only briefly owing to limited time available. They included ranging the woods in search of wood, chopping it up and sorting it into different categories of size and thickness, and feeding the fire with the right kind of wood to keep it going economically and to cook on. Cooking was enjoyable when the cooking was reasonably quick and resulted in food neither burnt nor undercooked. It's commonly believed that ordinary food tastes best when eaten out of doors, in the open air, and it's true. That's why we particularly liked doing toast and a simple thing you could do with flour and water which Bracken showed us and didn't take long. You mixed the two together to make a thick paste and then spread the paste round a green, v-shaped stick, a clean stick with the bark scraped away (and green so that it was less inflammable) and you stuck it into the tips of the camp fire's flames, turning it round and round until it was brown and cooked all round. It was delicious eaten fresh, straight off the fire in the smoky air, and we called it a 'twist'.

Making furniture, such as makeshift seats, and gadgets for the kitchen, such as racks and dressers, with sticks, branches and logs, string and rope etc. was good fun too, and just being in and around the woods was a delight when the weather was good. After all our camping chores were complete, we also enjoyed wide-ranging games in the woods which invariably entailed plenty of chasing around, exploration and hiding: the sort of thing we did in the school woods, but the Nablock site was bigger and the games could go on for much longer than they did at school.

The most pleasurable thing of all about camping, certainly for me, at Nablock and at all the other camps I went on with Bracken, was the communal campfire round which we all gathered most nights. We drank cocoa, ladled from large dixies on the fire (I liked doing the ladling out into the assembled company's enamel mugs and I did it whenever I could) and we listened to stories told by Bracken and to jokes or recitations of verse from anyone plucky enough to give them, took part in communal chants, choruses, yells and parodies, and in pieces of comic dialogue (sometimes taking the mickey out of the Girl Guides); and, on special occasions, we performed, in patrols, sketches and party pieces we'd prepared.

What we did most, and I enjoyed best round the campfire, was singing songs and simple rounds together. I remember a brown Scout song book and a green YHA (Youth Hostel Association) song book. We began with singing the words from one of these two books but we soon learnt many of them off by heart, picking them up from Bracken or from older Scouts and then we didn't need the books any more. This was just as well since it wasn't easy reading books round the camp fire as darkness descended; firelight was good to look at but not very good to read by.

We sang a wide range of songs – British and Irish folk songs and ballads, sea shanties, children's songs, patriotic songs, and some modern popular songs; songs from America, such as Home on the Range, Battle Song of the Republic, Marching through Georgia and Polly Wolly Doodle, and American negro spirituals (Camptown Races and Poor Old Joe were my favourites); one or two from Europe, and also, from Australia, Waltzing Matilda, because it was about camping, I suppose, as well as being a terrific, rollicking melody.

The subject matter and mood of these songs was as varied as their origins. There were the silly, farcical, absurd, macabre or nonsensical songs like Michael Finnagen ('who grew whiskers on his chin-agen'), Ilkla Moor Baht'at, 'I know an old woman who swallowed a fly', 'Found a pea nut'; and action songs like 'I'm a little teapot' and Head and Shoulders; and songs which could be extended or adapted as much as you wanted, like Old MacDonald Had a Farm and She'll be Coming Round the Mountain, and circular songs which could repeated ad infinitum, like The Bear Went Over the Mountain and They were Only Playing Leapfrog. We particularly relished Old MacDonald Had a Farm because it encouraged us to make the loudest animal noises we could possibly make, something definitely not permitted when we were at school.

In our repertoire there were quite a large number of sad and tragic songs. A very mournful song which we sang regularly was the well-known ballad 'Clementine', which tells the tragic story of the death by drowning of a dainty little girl called Clementine, in the words of someone who loved her. I always imagined this was her mother not her lover and felt her maternal grief increasing with every reiteration of the refrain:

Oh my darling, oh my darling,
Oh my darling Clementine!
Thou art lost and gone for ever,
Dreadful sorry, Clementine.

I found 'Clementine' more poignant than any other song we sang, even though it became so familiar to us that many of my fellow Scouts used to sing it in a jokey, facetious way; perhaps they were embarrassed by the deep emotion in it too. The last two verses I found especially moving and even now I don't feel they can easily be dismissed as mere sentimentality:

In my dreams she still doth haunt me,
Robed in starlight, soaked in brine,
Though in life I used to hug her,
Now she's dead I'll draw a line.

How I missed her, how I missed her!
How I missed my Clementine!
But I kissed her little sister
And forgot my Clementine.

I never understood why these two verses touched me so much, particularly the last line of the song but I think I now begin to understand why. Several other songs we used to sing which relate tragic deaths do not let go of the tragedies or deaths they recount, for their tragic victims survive in some form after their deaths and persist in haunting the people or places they loved; songs such as Cockles and Mussells about sweet Molly Malone, Waltzing Matilda and Widdicombe Fair. But in 'Clementine', the bereaved mother (as I believed) lets go of her dead daughter at the end of her lament, in the very last line – she 'moves on'. It seemed almost callous to me, so hard on Clementine to be forgotten by her mother but so commonsensical, I can see now.

Many of the songs we sang round the campfire were romantic love songs and although one or two of them were happy, or held out the promise of happiness, like Bobby Shaftoe, Strawberry Fair and 'O! No, John!', most of these love songs were sad too, sometimes bitter. An adult bystander would have been amused to see and hear eleven, twelve and thirteen year old boys singing these melancholy, rueful love songs quite sincerely and earnestly, apparently, especially the ones about separation and longing and broken hearts, inconstancy and infidelity in love. Songs such as My Bonnie, Early One Morning, A-Roving, There is a Tavern in the Town and Barbara Allen. What could these young boys have known about such things, the grown-up observer might have wondered?

Rigby Smith seemed to like the last two songs, songs of jilted or unrequited love, quite a lot, for I often heard him singing or humming them, and not just at Scout camps. I came to my own conclusions about why he liked them (he would insist, incidentally, on singing 'I will hang my *heart* on the weeping willow tree, in the chorus of There a Tavern in a Town, instead of 'I will hang my *harp* on the weeping willow tree) but they weren't my favourites, I wasn't all that keen on songs of heartbreak, though I must admit I did like, and still do, the Welsh air, The Ash Grove, which has a bereaved man mourning the loss of his sweetheart. I think it's the setting of The Ash Grove, the mention of the blackbird's singing and the bluebells in the green valley which is particularly appealing to me.

In some ways, I enjoyed the short, simple rounds (canons) which we sang round the campfire in different groups, usually our patrol groups, even more than the longer songs we all sang together as one. This was because rounds by their very nature are more involving and musically interesting to sing. When you are singing against, yet in time with, someone else's line, as you are when singing a round, you are caught up in an interplay of voices which requires more concentration and attention than when merely singing along with everyone else, and there is a competitive element too, as you seek to hold your own against those singing a different part of the round from you.

The rounds we commonly sang were Frere Jacques, London's Burning and Three Blind Mice. Two rounds we also sang quite a lot, which I particularly liked, were the rougher, more physical and primitive sounding Gin Gan Gooli and 'Hold him down, you Zulu warrior' (In some versions it's 'Swazi' warrior). The former contains a variety of vowel sounds and consonants, and a rise in pitch in the chorus, perfect for rending the night air; and the latter has a great end line, 'Chief! Chief! Chief! Chief!' etc. which sounds terrific when rippling round the campfire in counterpoint to the main lines of the round – 'Hold him down, you Zulu warrior/ Hold him down, you Zulu chief!' Both these rounds give plenty of scope for stamping feet, shouting or grunting, or smacking or thumping your thighs or the sides of the log or box you're sitting on.

My favourite round of all, however, was not a noisy one, redolent of community chanting and tribal dancing in African jungles, but a quiet, very English round:

From out the battered elm tree, the owl's cry we hear
And from the distant forest, the cuckoo answers clear:
Cuckoo, cuckoo, tu-whit, tu-whit, tu-whoo,
Cuckoo, cuckoo, tu-whit, tu-whit, tu-whoo.

Sung in a forest setting where our campfires usually were, or at least close to trees, on a spring or summer night, this was the perfect round to sing. There was the firelight, with sparks leaping up into the darkness, there were the dark shapes of the trees where an owl might well have been perching, and one of them might indeed have been a 'battered elm'. And there was the call of the two birds, the owl and the cuckoo, conveyed onomatopoeically by the sung phrases 'tu-whit, tu-whit, tu-whoo' and 'cuckoo, cuckoo'.

Sung contrapuntally as a round, the words would create a wonderful echoing effect round the campfire and through the night air, and when the last phrase, the last 'tu-whit, tu-whoo', was sung by the last group to sing, maybe no more than a handful of voices, the dwindling, thinning sound would emphasise the vastness of the surrounding darkness. The silence which followed when the round ended and the singing stopped altogether – with only the sound of the crackling of the fire and its wood smoke in the air and maybe one or two nocturnal noises audible in the background – was enchanting and thrilling. That moment was the best camping moment of all for me, especially when it was a fine night and we were round the fire by moonlight or starlight; perhaps starlight was best of all because it was darker then and the greater darkness gave more power to the sounds of the singing and the night.

There were many *disagreeable* aspects of camping, of course. One thing I remember about the Nablock camp site was singing of a different kind which was as maddening and disturbing as 'From out the battered elm tree' was calming and serene. That was the pigeons in the woods. On one weekend camp, the wood pigeons kept me awake all night with their persistent, monotonous cooing and I hated them intensely. For a long time I imagined these birds were called night jars, not pigeons. What else could they be called?

Other unpleasant sides to camping applied to all camps wherever they were. They included such things as sleeping on particularly hard or bumpy ground on groundsheets alone (no air beds allowed in those days); creepy-crawlies, like earwigs and spiders getting into your hair or sleeping bag or down your shirt, along with bits of grass or twigs or little stones (I never understood where they all came from); midges and mosquitoes in the summer evenings; having to keep your tent tidy and kit sorted, a tiresome, never-ending task; many camp chores, like washing up, especially when the water was cold and greasy and all the tea towels were wet; and fetching water, which was sometimes quite a long way away. At the same site where the cow tossed our tea chest in the air and caused such pandemonium, we had to walk half a mile up a hill to get water and the handles of our buckets cut into our hands after just twenty yards because we filled them to the brim each time we collected, to reduce the number of journeys needed.

Cooking wasn't always fun either. It could be tedious and boring when it took too long – boiling potatoes always took ages – and eating could be disappointing and depressing when the food wasn't cooked properly or was served with bits of wood and dirt on your plate because someone in your patrol hadn't done his kitchen duties efficiently and kept the plates clean and away from the ground. Some Scouts, like Colin Rigby Smith (who came on my last camp), declared they didn't mind bits of dirt in their food: it was all part of the pleasure of camping in the great outdoors, he maintained, but I must say I never cared much for foreign bodies in my food. Strangely, I did not believe they did anything to improve the taste of the food nor did they enhance the experience of outdoor eating for me.

The worst side of camping, naturally, reared its ugly head and brought gloom and misery when the weather was rotten: when it was wet and windy and cold, and remorselessly so. Short spells of bad weather were usually tolerable but not prolonged periods, unrelieved by even the smallest breaks in the rain and glimpses of the sun. Camping during prolonged bouts of bad weather brought out Bracken's dual approach to us, his soft and hard sides, very markedly.

Bracken had instilled into us the need for efficiency and economy when camping: to conserve wood, for instance, and not to let the fire roar away needlessly when it served no function, nor use more fuel than necessary by boiling more water in a dixie than required. Lighting the fire in the first place was a skill, of course, one we had to acquire for our Second Class badge and we were allowed only two matches to do so in the test. Rigby Smith and I usually managed to light a fire with only one match and we were very proud of this, especially as we normally managed it without any paper or fire-lighting aids. It was perfectly possible to light a fire without paper or firelighters if you collected the right kind of kindling wood (dead nettles were very good as well as dry leaves, the thinnest of twigs, and birch bark) and if you laid the fire properly, had intermediate wood between the light, flimsy kindling stuff and much thicker sticks, and the wood was dry. We were strongly advised to maintain a good supply of wood so that the fire never ran right down and to keep the wood dry by constructing proper shelters for it and keeping it covered when it was wet.

On one of our summer camps in North Yorkshire one year, our woodcraft was put to a severe test by incessant rain and, at first, Bracken wasn't at all sympathetic when some patrols started to have difficulties keeping their fires alight. He accused them of falling down on their fire-lighting skills and being careless in their provision and supervision of their wood stocks. In those days you could go off into the woods and gather up as much dead wood as you liked and there was always a plentiful supply. It was up to you to make the effort to collect it, sort it into quick, slow or medium burning wood piles and store it somewhere accessible and dry; in true Scout fashion, 'to be prepared'! On this particular North Yorkshire camp, the first two days were dry, warm and sunny. There had been plenty of time to build up stocks of wood but the fine weather had made many Scouts complacent and they weren't ready when the rain came on the third day despite warnings from Bracken.

He was not prepared to help on the first day of rain when some patrols couldn't cook their food; he simply spoke to the patrol leaders and told them to sort themselves out and learn their lesson. Our patrol was all right the first day or two: we felt quite smug. On the second day of rain he suggested that patrols who had used up their matches and couldn't light their fires should borrow fire from patrols who still had fires burning or borrow matches from them. This met with only limited success. On the third day of rain, a food poisoning bug spread round the camp and still Bracken remained unsympathetic, but he did take action of a kind. He summoned every Scout in the camp to an emergency meeting and lectured us on the importance of hygiene, particularly washing up. He held up a frying pan and pointed to a hypothetical speck stuck in one corner. That speck, he said, might be food that contained bacteria which could spread germs. It shouldn't be there, he said, and wouldn't be if the frying pan had been washed up properly. It was no doubt shoddy washing up which had led to the tummy upsets, he suggested. We should learn our lesson, he said. No sympathy then for those with tummy upsets, quite a lot of us by then.

During the third day, the rain still hadn't relented and was becoming, if anything, worse. The stream at the edge of the camp site, which had at first been no more that a pleasant little gurgling brook you could easily hop over, had become a raging torrent which you couldn't even take a running jump over now and were advised to keep well away from. The rain had got in everywhere, even the best organised patrols hadn't managed to keep it out. Everything was sodden, not only the wood and things in the kitchens but everything in the tents too: all our kit, our rucksacks, our sleeping bags, our clothes, and our towels, so we had nothing to dry ourselves with. It was a wretched time, especially for /of us who were sick too. I remember having cold, wet feet all the time and longing for a dry towel.

When we first moaned about wet tents, kit and clothes etc., Bracken accused us of not following good practice over tent care: not 'trenching' the tents properly (digging a channel round the tents to take the water away), not checking the pegging down of the tents, nor keeping the guy ropes at the right tensions, and allowing our belongings to touch the sides of the tents and therefore letting the rain soak through the sides into the tent and onto them. (We didn't have fly sheets then to prevent this). If we or our belongings were wet, it was our fault, he said. However, sometime on the third day, Bracken, seeing that the rain was not relenting, relented himself. And he did not do it in a grudging, niggardly way but, following his softer, essentially benevolent nature, he did it wholeheartedly.

He visited every patrol with splints of wood soaked in paraffin (it was the only time he ever gave us paraffin to aid our fire lighting) and helped them get their fires going properly and provided them with dry logs to keep them going if they had run out of longer burning wood. Any patrols who were still having problems cooking food he allowed to come and cook on his stove which was protected from the elements under a well secured awning. He helped sort out the tents of some patrols who were in a desperate state and supplied, from somewhere, fresh dry towels. With Mace's aid, he extended the sick tent and put up more camp beds for Scouts who were not recovering quickly from their sickness.

Above all, he did not make us feel guilty any more about our camping inadequacies and failures, and at the communal campfire at night, when the rain eventually abated enough for us to meet round it again, he raised our spirits with some new songs or yells, as well as some old favourites, and told stories, and encouraged us to do our own turns or little sketches. The rain didn't really stop, just eased a little but with Bracken's changed attitude we felt a lot better and somehow survived until the end of the ten days. (Our summer holiday camps usually lasted ten days).

Looking back on it, we were glad Bracken had not gone soft on us too soon because we'd learnt lessons from our discomforts and deprivations and now had a bottom bench mark for unpleasant camping conditions. However bad camping conditions were henceforth we could compare them with that North Yorkshire camp and say, 'They're not as bad as that!' And it proved true. Some of our Boy Scouts were put off camping completely by that particular camp but those of us who went again found it really *was* the worst camp we had to endure; other camps, even ones with above-average wind and rain and not much sun, were paradisal by comparison.

The Lake District Walking Holidays

On our Lake District walking holidays during the Easter break, Bracken again showed his hard and soft sides. We used to stay at Youth Hostels and do our own cooking, and although we occasionally visited a shop to buy a postcard or an ice cream we didn't buy our food each evening in shops – the shops wouldn't have been open when we ended our day's walking – we carried nearly all of our food with us on our backs in rucksacks, several days' supply at a time sometimes. We didn't have our own separate food (except for sweets); food was provided and organised on a collective basis, and carried in only a couple of rucksacks. Since food was needed for about ten Scouts, being the approximate number in our party of Scouts on each expedition, and much of our food was in tins, the two rucksacks which contained the food could get very heavy, especially when we were walking up a mountain.

We took it in turns to carry the food rucksacks and it gave some Scouts an opportunity to show how tough they were by carrying them with apparent ease and offering to take them longer than their turn: Scouts like Spencer and Rigby Smith and Spiky Silcock. On the other hand, some Scouts struggled to complete their stint and might try to pass on their load to someone else before their turn was up. Bracken was rarely sympathetic towards them, especially if he suspected them of laziness or lack of guts, and he was particularly unsympathetic if the rucksack was onerous because it had not been packed properly. He had taught us to pack tins and sharper-edged objects near the front of the rucksack and to put a sweater or towel at the back of the rucksack next to our backs to act as a buffer or cushion to prevent these objects cutting into our backs as we moved. If the Scout carrying one of the food rucksacks got a tin or sharp object sticking into his back and consequently had to stop and hold everyone up whilst he repacked the rucksack, Bracken was withering in his criticism.

It was a similar thing with boots. Sometimes one of our party had to stop because of a blister or some foreign body in his boot or both. If Bracken thought the blister or unwanted object in the boot were the result of careless preparation for the day's walk – not checking first every nook and cranny of the boot for bits of wood, thorns, bracken or small stones etc., not checking the socks for similar things or not putting them on properly, or not tying the boot straps tightly and securely – he reproached the Scout in question in no uncertain terms.

And he was a hard taskmaster. We had to walk up to thirty miles a day sometimes and often over very hilly terrain. He encouraged a steady, brisk pace and allowed us very few breaks. At the Youth Hostels where we stayed he imposed strict discipline on us. We had a cooking and washing-up rota and he made sure we all did the chores the Youth Hostel required of us, with no skimping, and they were real chores in those days. He also made sure we went to bed at a sensible time and got up early in the morning. He insisted on silence in the dorms at night so that we all got a good night's sleep. We accepted all this because we knew we'd come to walk, to see the Lake District, not to waste our energy talking through the night or dawdling over our chores in the morning.

On the other hand, he wasn't dour and stony-faced about everything all the time. He could often be light-hearted and easy-going; in his manner, at least. He was aware, for instance, that 'all *walk* and no play makes a *Scout* a dull boy'. When we were moving on more level terrain and had some breath to spare he would sing songs as he walked along, some of which were new and which we soon picked up from him, and they would raise our spirits and help to put a spring in our step.

I remember learning from him whilst we were walking, 'My girl's a corker/ She's a New Yorker', a comedy of the grotesque song, in which the speaker of the song compares parts of his girlfriend's anatomy, from head to toe, to outlandish and ugly things, then adds humorously, 'Gee, that's where my money goes!' For example:

She's got a head of hair just like a grizzly bear ...
She's got a pair of lips just like two greasy chips ...
She's got a great big nose just like a garden hose etc.

The song has a springy rhythm and a simple chorus of meaningless but catchy sounds (Ta, ra, ra, ra/ Ta, ra, ra, ra, ra/ ... umpa, umpa, ump, pa, pa/ umpa, umpa, ump, pa, pa etc.) which made it very suitable for singing whilst you were bouncing along a track. (Better therefore near the beginning of the walk when you were in buoyant mood).

We also learnt, whilst walking with Bracken, Under the Lilac Tree, a song which has all the ingredients of a Victorian melodrama and cautionary tale: the young, innocent, trusting lady, the dastardly, deceitful villain, the reward of virtue (heaven) for the former and the punishment of wickedness (hell) for the latter, with the moral spelt out at the end –'Don't tell a lie!' I was surprised to discover recently in a reprinted YHA Song Book that the two best verses of this song had not been included. In these omitted verses, which Bracken didn't omit to teach us, the villain gets his comeuppance in a punishment-fitting-the-crime way, even before he goes, as a matter of course, to hell. Having married the innocent, trusting lady for her money (this is implicit), the villain in the song is delighted when she conveniently dies and, as the words of the song tell it, 'He sat on her tombstone and laughed till he cried'. But his punishment comes instantly in the next verse: 'The tombstone fell over and that's how he died'. This is comedy, farce and melodrama, all rolled into one, and another contribution, of a kind, to our cultural education; though we didn't know it, of course, it was pure fun to us.

We also sang, inevitably I suppose, 'I love to go a wandering along the mountain track/ And as I go I love to sing with a knapsack on my back'.

Although the song became too familiar and somewhat corny, I found it very pleasurable to sing it whilst walking, not only because of its cheerful, tripping rhythm, but because it was most satisfying to be doing the very thing you were singing about – words, music and action all blended together.

Although we had very few stops once we started walking at the beginning of each day, when we *did* stop for a break Bracken made sure it was a good one and he handed round generous slabs of Cadbury's fruit and nut chocolate to all of us with a cheery smile. It was rarely hot in April when we had the walking holidays but it was for a couple of days one year and when we came across a rock pool up in the hills on our route one afternoon, he stopped cracking the whip and allowed us to swim or paddle in it at leisure. He also endeavoured to give us a day's break from walking on each holiday, if possible. We went shopping then, of course, in places such as Grasmere and Keswick, (buying Kendal mint cake and having cream teas etc.) and went rowing on Lake Windermere. The latter activity wasn't always plain sailing as I recount in a later chapter.

We had a walking itinerary to keep to, even so, for we had to get from one Youth Hostel to another each day, usually a long distance apart, and we couldn't take days off if the weather was bad. Bracken wasn't prepared to alter his schedule, anyway, so we walked in all weathers; and he took us into some rugged areas and in very harsh conditions sometimes. During the three walking holidays I went on with Bracken, we climbed most of the high peaks in the Lake District, including Scafell Pike, Great Gable, Bowfell, Fairfield, Dolly Waggon Pike, Helvellyn and Siddaw. He took us along narrow ledges, had us clambering up rocky slopes and tentatively edging our way across scree near the tops of valleys with steep drops below. We walked through driving rain, blizzards and mists and were often buffeted by powerful, icy winds. And all the time we carried rucksacks on our backs with all our stuff in; even rucksacks without the food tins could be quite heavy after 15 or 20 miles walking. So Bracken expected a lot of us but he wasn't reckless in his leadership.

He made sure we followed fell walking codes, took care and behaved sensibly, looking out for each other and staying close together, especially in the mist. Mist was the thing that most concerned him. I remember on one occasion, I think it was in the vicinity of the Langdale Pikes, he was very worried when the mist descended and he insisted we made sure we could always touch the person in our group who was in front of us. "Put your hand on his shoulder now," he said, "and make sure you know he's always there and never moves beyond the length of your arm!" The gravity with which he viewed the mist was one thing, in particular, that rubbed off on me, and subsequently I have always been wary of the mist when walking in the hills, which has been no bad thing, I'm sure.

There are two incidents that stand out most distinctly in my memory which illustrate, once again, how he could be both a hard man and a soft man. One is from those Lake District walking holidays and one from my camping memories.

The Lake District incident can be simply related. It was my third Lake District walking holiday and we'd had one of the toughest hikes I could ever remember, up and down more peaks than usual and on the roughest terrain. We could have coped with that in average circumstances but by midday the weather had turned particularly nasty and we were walking in unrelenting, driving wind and remorseless, penetrating drizzle which continued all afternoon. By evening we were not only footsore and exhausted but soaked to the skin, drowned, and utterly dejected. Our spirits were already rock bottom when we arrived at Keswick Youth Hostel and learnt that there was no hot water in the hostel.

Up to this point, Bracken had not commiserated with us in the slightest, he'd just driven us on doggedly in silence. Now, having spoken briefly to the rather gruff warden and learnt about the lack of hot water, he turned and looked at us in our despondent, battered and dishevelled state and uttered just two words: "Follow me!" We followed him without question, though we thought him crazy for taking us away from the Youth Hostel where there was at least shelter. We followed him blindly into the centre of Keswick, astonished when he walked into a very large and grand hotel there. He told us to wait in the lobby whilst he went and had a word with someone at Reception.

He returned a few moments later with a smile on his face. "We're in luck," he said. "They've got room for us. We're staying here tonight and the rooms are on me!" It was brilliant! We all had hot baths, dried out completely, had a four course meal and slept in comfortable beds with proper sheets that night (not sheet sleeping bags). And it was, of course, all the sweeter for the austerities and hardships we had endured that dire day of the foulest weather I ever could remember. Bracken was true to his word. I don't know how much it cost him to put us up in that splendid hotel and pay for our evening meal but he never asked us for a penny of it back.

The camping experience occurred after I had left Penly Grange, the following summer. Rigby Smith, Spencer and I had been asked to go and help Bracken with the running of the summer camp. He used to invite Old Boy Scouts to come and help him at the summer camps and one or two who had left Penly Grange had come to help him the previous years whilst we were still at Penly Grange. It seemed to me they had a pretty cushy time: standing around chatting, eating food cooked by someone else, organising a few games and joining in the singing round the campfire, perhaps ladling out some cocoa occasionally, but not exerting themselves unduly apart from that. I hadn't noticed them doing any washing-up, for instance. I was expecting to enjoy the same sort of easy-going camp lifestyle but I was in for a shock.

When I arrived on the site, somewhere in South West Scotland, Bracken explained he had formed an extra patrol of just four Scouts who were leftovers from other patrols. They were a loose bunch of fairly inexperienced Scouts who needed an experienced Scout to be their patrol leader. There were no other patrol leaders available from the current Penly Grange troop so he was going to ask me to take on the job 'for a while'. I could hardly refuse and got down to the task, resolving to do as good a job as I could. It shouldn't prove too difficult, I thought; I had, after all, been a patrol leader my last year at Penly Grange.

It did prove difficult, however. Very difficult. The Scouts I was put in charge of were a useless bunch who had no concept of the common good, of pulling together, of rotas or of sharing the work load of the patrol. One of them, Meadows, was always complaining he was being picked on, and it was never his turn to do anything, it seemed. He was always going off in a huff, probably a fake huff, though I was never sure of that. Peterson offered to collect wood but that's all he did. He would disappear for hours and although he would return with a reasonable quantity of wood he was never around when anything else needed doing. Wainstone Junior and another boy, called Cranfield, spent most of their time messing about. Their favourite pastime was throwing their Scout knives into the ground; sometimes they played a game in which you aimed to narrowly miss the other person's foot. It was flirting with danger and inevitably one of them eventually got a knife in his foot – Cranfield – from a miscalculated throw from Wainstone (I think it was miscalculated) and required first aid. Thereafter he nursed his injured foot and did even less to help than before.

I tried instil some discipline into my patrol but to no avail. I found myself doing all the work: keeping the tents tidy, keeping the fire going, cooking, fetching water, and often washing up too. After a couple of days I made it clear to Bracken that I was working very hard, in case he hadn't noticed, and suggested one of the other Old Boy Scouts might like to help but he didn't seem very sympathetic to my request, said the other Old Boy Scouts were doing other things and asked me if I wouldn't mind continuing. I did mind but nevertheless I did continue and by the end of the week I was thoroughly exhausted and utterly fed up.

At the end of six days, Bracken, on a wet, cool evening, invited me to his tent to share a meal with him and the other leaders: Mr Mace, Spencer and Rigby Smith. He told me to leave my patrol to its own devices for awhile which seemed to me to be rather a rash thing to do but maybe I wouldn't be staying long in his tent so it wouldn't be too rash. I thought he would probably give me some curt advice on how to handle a bunch of lazy, good-for-nothing Scouts and then send me back to my patrol, supposedly enlightened by his wisdom, to carry on with my recalcitrant charges. I was in a very pessimistic mood as I made my way to his tent.

When I entered Bracken's spacious bell tent, the first thing that struck me was the smell of cooking. It was a very pleasant smell of proper cooking, a spicy, exotic smell. Bracken was sitting there, behind two calor-gas-supplied rings emitting a steady blue flame. Something good was cooking in a pot on one of the gas rings and, on the other, a kettle was steaming away quietly. Next to Bracken was Martin (Rigby Smith) and then from left to right came Spencer and Mr Mace. They were all looking happy and relaxed, and seemed tickled when I entered the tent somewhat diffidently. I had never had time to visit the bell tent before on this camp, except to pop my head in briefly to see if Bracken was there for a quick word. He seldom had been.

"Do I see a mouse creeping into our lair?" Bracken enquired jokingly. He corrected himself quickly, "Sorry, Tim, I know you're not Mouse any more, no more than Martin here is Berry [Rigby Smith's nickname at Penly Grange] but I couldn't resist saying that: the way that you came in so timidly. Come and sit down. Make yourself at home. You deserve a break and you're going to get it." Hitherto on this camp he'd seemed quite indifferent to the disagreeable plight he'd pitched me into when asking me to be patrol leader to the worst collection of so-called Scouts I'd ever had to deal with. Now he had nothing but praise for my efforts and was full of appreciative comments. And he had good news for me. I was to be released from my patrol leader assignment. Martin was going to take over from me for the few remaining days. Martin smiled at me. His smile was special; it went back six years, to my first day at Penly Grange when I was eight. "You'll have to give me a lot of advice, of course," he said. This amused me for he had rarely taken advice from me but he was laughing anyway.

"So long as it is only advice," I said, "you can have as much as you like." I was laughing too, the laughter of immense relief. A great load had been lifted off me and I was beginning to feel good, very good inside. I liked being in the tent with the other leaders too; they seemed especially civilised and congenial after all that time with the immature, uncouth members of my patrol.

And things were to get even better as I experienced even more of the softer side of Bracken. He handed me a fork and a flat, rectangular billy, replete with a helping from the pot on the gas ring. I looked in the billy and saw something yellowy mixed with rice. It didn't look particularly appetising but I accepted the dish from Bracken's hand and took a mouthful of the food with the fork I'd been given. It was a curry, I soon learnt, and absolutely delicious. It was the first time I'd had a curry and I have never tasted a better one since. Good news, good company and good food! It was the best moment of that Scout camp by a long chalk (admittedly there hadn't been very many good moments to rival it so far) and one of the best meals with friends I've ever had. And Bracken, hard man, soft man, was at the centre of it. He had helped to create that great moment of unity, camaraderie, relaxation and social cheer. He had been demanding of me and astringent, aloof even, leaving me out in the cold for a time, yet, finally, he'd been kind, warm-hearted and welcoming, his true nature.

There was something else for which I will always be grateful to Bracken. Something which was a component of the Lake District walking holidays but which I have not spoken about yet. So far I have mentioned only the physical and adventurous aspects of all the Lake District hiking we did. It is certainly true that the physical challenges and occasional dangers entailed in walking many miles over all sorts of terrain, and the climbing up peaks in all kinds of weather, dominated our minds at the time and tended to be what we talked about most afterwards. However, we were not unconscious of, or insensitive to, the aesthetic side of the Lake District, we just didn't separate the beauty of the scenery in our minds from the overall adventure of wandering in the hills, being up on the peaks and close to the tarns, working our way through valleys and woods, and alongside lakes and streams, and beside rocks and sprawling grey-stone walls.

As boys aged eleven to thirteen, we were, I believe, even more awestruck then by the towering crags and peaks, the valleys and gullies and the majesty and grandeur of the earth, sky and water landscape than we would have been seeing it all for the first time as adults. Furthermore, we did not detach ourselves from the beauty of the landscape and scenery by taking photographs of it, as we probably would have done when older. Some of us took snaps of friends outside Youth Hostels but we were too young to be serious photographers, certainly at that time, for amateur photography was not so easy and so commonplace then. Cameras were not so technologically sophisticated in those days and you had to be an accomplished photographer to produce good photographs of scenery. In any case, there was no colour photography of any quality available then for the ordinary person with an ordinary camera – photographic prints were generally black and white. So, in true Wordsworth fashion, quite unwittingly of course, we simply let the images of nature and their colours impress themselves directly on our *minds* till a suitable time came to recall them.

That time came when Mr Jeffers taught us at Marby College. Mr Jeffers, a forceful, somewhat overpowering schoolteacher, taught us English at

'O' level, and before we made our choices for 'A' level he introduced us to some poetry which we had not done as part of the set books for the 'O' level Literature exam. I'm not sure whether he taught us this to encourage us to choose English 'A' level or whether he simply had time to fill in after the 'O' level exams (no going home after exams in those days), but he certainly threw himself into his task of instilling into us some love and reverence for great English poetry, Wordsworth in particular.

Mr Jeffers was not a question-and-answer man; he did not try to tease things out of us like the quieter, milder Mr Stuart who also taught English at Marby College. Mr Jeffers liked to *perform* English literature, to introduce us to selected authors by reading their work aloud in class with passionate gusto and intensity. Whilst he was reading literature to us there were to be no questions, we just had to listen attentively and drink it all in. Apart from some Shakespeare, which went largely over my head, it is only his Wordsworth performances, in fact, which I can now remember. He read us Wordsworth's 'Immortality Ode', the narrative poem Michael, Lines Written Above Tintern Abbey, and some lines from The Prelude. Mr Jeffers had a small body but a very powerful, resounding voice, and his recitation of the 'Immortality Ode' as he paced round the classroom was an extraordinary and unforgettable experience. I still remember clearly his impassioned delivery of the opening stanza of the poem, particularly the way he hammered out, with heavy staccato, each monosyllabic word in the longer last line.

> There was a time when meadow, grove and stream,
> The earth and every common sight,
> To me did seem
> Apparelled in celestial light,
> The glory and the freshness of a dream.
> It is not now as it hath been of yore;-
> Turn wheresoe'er I may,
> By night or day,
> The things which I have seen I now can see no more.

At fifteen years of age I certainly did not have the mature adult perspective on childhood which Wordsworth had when he wrote his poem in his thirties; I was not old enough to experience fully an adult's nostalgia for times long past, for the early years when life was sharper and more vivid. Nevertheless, I recognised even then that some glow and wonder had gone from my life, and so the lines meant something to me. Even had I not suffered my own disillusionment in the woods at Penly Grange during my last term, I would probably have known that had I returned there two years later, the childish spirit of adventure, the excitement generated by the woods, would have waned.

Actually, though, as I listened to Mr Jeffers reading Wordsworth and I read his poetry afterwards to myself, the woods at Penly Grange were not prominent in my mind; they were at the back of my mind, in shadows. Knowing Wordsworth was an inhabitant of the Lake District, what his poetry principally conjured up in my mind was the scenery I had witnessed on our Lake District walks. The 'meadow, grove and stream', and 'the earth and every common sight', alluded to in the 'Immortality Ode' were the meadows, groves and streams, and the land and sky of Cumberland and Westmorland, just as they were to Wordsworth. The light which 'apparelled' them was the sunlight I'd seen clothing the green hillsides on the lower part of the fells or glinting off the face of the lakes spread out beneath us when turning to view them halfway up a mountain.

Wordsworth's poetry also helped me to recall the *sounds* of the Lake District, especially the sound of the streams, the sound of running water. On every walk we ever made there always seemed to be a brook, a stream, a burn, running alongside our path or not far away. That's why Wordsworth's narrative poem Michael made almost as strong an impression on me as the 'Immortality Ode'. I was particularly struck by the 'tumultuous' and 'boisterous brook of Greenhead Ghyll', mentioned in the opening and closing lines of Michael, when I realised we had actually walked by it on our ascent of Fairfield. Greenhead Ghyll brook is an especially powerful and noisy stream, as Wordsworth's adjectives suggest, and I recollected how you could still hear it when it was a long way below you, sounding like the far off roar of distant traffic. Other lines in Michael which stand out for me because of those Lake District walking holidays are lines describing the shepherd Michael's regular life on the hills –

… he had been alone
Amid the heart of many thousand mists,
That came to him and left him on the heights.

I understood those lines. We'd had that experience of the mist suddenly descending when we were up a mountain and almost as suddenly clearing, all fell walkers have had it. Being plunged into mist could be alarming or disconcerting when you could see no more than a yard ahead but, equally, the clearing of the mist, the reappearance of the path ahead and the view around you, lifted the spirits no end.

And then there were the famous lines in Book One of The Prelude where Wordsworth describes the dramatic occasion when he was rowing on Lake Ullswater on a moonlit summer evening, and a crag appeared above him out of nowhere, when ...

> ... a huge peak, black and huge,
> As if with voluntary power instinct
> Upreared its head. I struck and struck again [rowing strokes],
> And growing still in stature the grim shape
> Towered up between me and the stars, and still,
> For so it seemed, with purpose of its own
> And measured motion like a living thing,
> Strode after me ...

I could respond to those lines in a personal way, having sometimes seen rocky crags, hitherto out of view, suddenly looming up above us, seemingly with a life of their own, during our walking amidst the Lake District fells.

I could, of course, quite possibly, have visited the Lake District some other time, apart from Mr Bracken's walking expeditions and read Wordsworth's poems for myself, quite independently of Mr Jeffers' recitations, but *would* I have done? And even had I done so, at what age would it have happened? Surely much later in my life. And would the impact on me have been as great? I think not. Both Bracken and Jeffers undoubtedly made an important contribution to my appreciation of Wordsworth, but it was Bracken who laid the foundations for it by giving me the opportunity to experience the grandeur and beauty of the Lake District at just the right age, the same sort of age Wordsworth was when many of his key encounters with the natural world occurred.

So, all in all, Bracken played a very important part in my education, in the widest sense of the word: as a French teacher and scoutmaster, but particularly as a scoutmaster, as 'Skip'. His highly positive influence on me was unequalled by any other teacher at Penly Grange. Except, perhaps, Robert Barnet, who contributed greatly to my mental, social and intellectual development, though over a much shorter period of time than Bracken.

Robert Barnet

'Man for All Seasons'

If Penly Grange School were ever in the dock, charged with poor teaching standards and mistreatment of its pupils, Robert Barnet, who taught there in the late 1950s and then again in the mid 1960s and beyond, would, like Charles Bracken, be a leading witness for the defence. Not only because he was an excellent teacher in every respect, but because he chose to come back and be part of the school again when he might easily have gone elsewhere. If Penly Grange really had been a 'dump', an antiquated, Victorian, Dotheboys Hall, as the bully Burton alleged, why would the lively, liberal and humane Barnet ever dreamt of returning? (I have shown, admittedly, that Teddy Eldin's Latin teaching was almost on a par with Squeers' English teaching in Nicholas Nickleby, but it was not typical of most teaching at Penly Grange).

Robert Barnet had been a pupil himself at Penly Grange and must have been amongst the first to go there. Like many other boys he went on to Marby College when he was 13 and like most, but not all, boys at Marby College he stayed until he was 18. When he was about 20 he went to university where he read History and Politics. Between Marby College and university, in what we now call the gap year, he came back to Penly Grange and that was when he taught us – in our last year. How lucky we were!

His physique and appearance was not particularly impressive or distinguished. He was not very tall, his figure was quite spare and he had rather pale skin. His short, dark hair had a little quiff sticking up at the front of his head on one side which he couldn't control; he was continually pushing it down but it kept popping up again. The strength of his personality, however, came through his facial expressions and his tremendous energy. His eyes were full of vitality and he never stood still. In lessons he was always moving about, up and down and round about, in his well-worn cavalry twill trousers, speaking or challenging us to answer his questions. He was quick to see if you were day-dreaming or in a bad mood and would involve you with a teasing question or simply ask you what you were thinking. Yes, he would get at you to draw you in, rag you, if he thought it necessary, but it was always benign and it was always between you and him: he didn't get the rest of the class to gang up on you and subject you to mob mockery as some teachers did. He would even wink at you sometimes. No other teacher ever did that, except for Timmerton, who once, according to Rickmack and Rigby Smith, winked at them when he had awarded them a surprise penalty in a school rugby match.

Robert Barnet encouraged us to have opinions and express them. He did not merely impart important information to us and then tell us what to think, nor did he try to get us to guess what *he* was thinking, the one and only answer, which was Headmaster Teddy Eldin's way. He wanted us to think for ourselves and think about wider issues than we had hitherto been asked to think about. Although he taught some French and English, I remember him mainly for his teaching of Current Affairs. This was in the library which doubled as the classroom for the top form in the school, the scholarship form. The library, which was next to the Headmaster's study in the old manor house part of the school, looked out over the grassy stretch leading to the splendid spreading cedar tree and the playing fields beyond, and we felt privileged to be there for all our lessons but especially for Current Affairs which gave us a sense of being grown up and mature. Current Affairs was in our curriculum to prepare us for the General Paper in the scholarship exam. Fortunately, Barnet used the subject not just to prepare us for an exam but to prepare us for life beyond school.

Through his Current Affairs lessons, Barnet introduced us to the art of debating. Of course we had touched on important topics before with other teachers, and engaged in some class discussion, but had not explored them before in a systematic way. At his instigation, we learnt the formal structure of debating, with 'motions', 'proposers' and 'opposers' and 'seconders', and 'questions from the floor', and 'summing up' etc. Rigby Smith, Rickmack, Spilwell and Loretti were always keen to be one of the main speakers; Westford liked to act as Chairman. Barnet liked everyone to say something and urged the more reticent to speak 'from the floor'. I was fairly reticent but didn't mind saying something from the floor because there was usually time to work out what you wanted to say and you didn't need to say much. When Barnet explained that you could interrupt speakers at any time – through the Chairman – on 'a point of information', Spilwell seized on this pretext and would interrupt with some pedantic correction whenever he got the chance.

The topics we debated were the familiar ones: Capital Punishment (still on the statute books then), Pacifism, Communism, and the Decline of the British Empire. Also a topic which was becoming more and more popular – Space Exploration. The Soviet Union had fired the first satellite into space in October 1957 – Sputnik 1 – and it raised many questions. Did we need to explore space? Was it worth the money? Did we, in the West, have to keep up with the Soviets out of necessity or pride? Of course, the topic was linked with the Arms Race and the H-Bomb and the question of Deterrence.

The question of nuclear deterrence was the most hotly debated topic because we all felt threatened by the Atom Bomb, or the H-Bomb – what later came to be subsumed under the broader heading of Nuclear Arms. It's easy to forget, having made it to the 21st century, the extent to which we lived under the shadow of the H-Bomb in the 1950s and the real fear that existed of total destruction in a Third World War. Not that the fear of global catastrophe has ever gone away since then, but its envisaged cause has broadened considerably; it was just World War we feared then as the trigger of Armageddon. Being wiped out in a matter of minutes by the mere pressing a button always seemed a strong possibility in those days. The Cold War was very cold then and might have exploded into sudden heat at any moment. Never mind the 45 minute warning of Saddam Hussein's WMD, we were led to believe we might have only 11 minutes, at the most! The only reason why we weren't entirely paralysed by the thought was the extremity of the possible scenario and the feeling we could do nothing about it. We were still children, minors, with no power or influence in politics (though we liked to think our generation was highly significant socially), what could we do? What could anyone do? Most of us were fatalistic. If it happens it happens: que sera sera (in the words of the pop song), let's get on with life anyway, it might not happen. That was probably my view, which many of us held, but I wouldn't presume to speak for everyone. Some of my peers wouldn't think about it at all; some believed, the more bellicose, that we should do a pre-emptive strike against Moscow for self-preservation; some supported the CND (Campaign for Nuclear Disarmament).

On the whole, though, we didn't pay much attention to politics outside our formal debates. We knew, of course, about the Suez crisis in 1956 but hadn't the faintest idea of its lasting gravity and significance. All we could grasp of it was the slight to Britain's pride and the damage it caused to Britain's status in the world. The resignation of Prime Minister Sir Anthony Eden over Suez we regarded as merely an embarrassment for the nation not a turning point in Middle Eastern and world politics. It was generally thought that Eden had been foolhardy in ordering British Forces, in alliance with France and Israel, to seize control of the Suez Canal, but Forrest, the oldest boy in the form (and a good batsman, incidentally) who left at Christmas, said there was more to it. Forrest was a keen historian with political awareness, and he said the Americans were partly to blame for not supporting Britain. I don't remember actually debating this question at all, most of us were very ignorant of Foreign Affairs and incapable of discussing it in any depth. If the truth be told, if it hadn't been for Barnet, most of us would have thought very little about world politics, and cared even less, except for the immediate threat of the H-Bomb and the spread of Communism.

Whilst Barnet's impact on us in the classroom was considerable, he

91

probably made an even greater impact on most of us through his extra-curricular activities. He became involved in a whole range of pursuits beyond academic schoolwork and packed an enormous amount into the school year. He went on school trips whenever he could and helped out at Scout camps. His contribution to sport at Penly Grange was immense and his influence inspirational. He brought with him a great reputation as a sportsman from his former days at Penly Grange and also his time at Marby College, where he had won his colours for cricket and rugby, and we'd seen him playing with great verve and panache in Old Boy matches at school. Rigby Smith, who stood in awe of his sporting prowess, remembered seeing Barnet win the senior Long Jump on Sports' Day just before he left for Marby College. Rigby Smith was aged seven then and visiting Penly Grange before attending the school that autumn – a very impressionable age.

Barnet helped with the training of the school rugby and cricket teams and I remember him being great fun on the coach on away fixtures. (I went as touch judge for the First Fifteen rugby team and then as scorer for the First Eleven cricket team). He got us all singing lustily, but not the usual rude and ragged songs of schoolboys on buses. He taught us to sing parodies of well known songs, adjusted to fit Penly Grange School or its pupils. His favourite was his adaptation of Gilbert & Sullivan's 'He is an Englishman' (from *H.M.S. Pinafore*): we sung Sullivan's tune to Barnet's modified words. We soon picked it up and even those who couldn't sing would join in the chorus and somehow make the word 'Penly' or 'Penly Grange' fit in with the tune:

> For we ourselves have said it
> And it's greatly to our credit
> That we're from Penly Grange,
> That we're from Penly Grange;
> For we might have been from Conninghurst
> Or Rostock Manor or Shirebrook,
> Or a girl from St Cath'rine's
> Or a girl from St Cath'rine's;
> But in spite of all the other fools
> Who belong to lesser public schools
> We remain Penly Grange boys,
> We remain ... ai ... ai ... ai ... ai ... ai ... ai ... ain ...
> Peh, heh, heh, heh, heh, heh ... hen ly boys!'

We knew it was very silly but it still felt good to sing it and raised our morale and self-esteem as members of Penly Grange School.

Barnet adapted another famous Victorian song to poke good-natured fun at Phil Westford, the Captain of School, which we all sung merrily once we'd got the hang of it. The tune was the Eton boating song:

My name is Philip Westford,
Commonly 'Phil' for short,
I'm a jolly good worker
And I'm jolly good at sport;
Pray silence, boys, listen to me
And you'll find it not hard to see
How I came to be
Captain of School at Penly!

All this singing was good preparation for the school revue Barnet organised for the summer term. He got us performing sand dances, feeble, funny sketches – which included parodies of Shakespeare – and pantomime turns like 'There's a hole in my bucket'. I seem to remember indulging in a bit of slapstick too, Laurel-and-Hardy type stuff.

But there was more to his dramatic and creative side. He loved music, jazz in particular, and he shared his love of jazz with us, or attempted to. There was a loft above one of the classrooms in the quad where we were given more freedom and could listen to records, but it was our own pop records we usually listened to there. Barnet used to arrange events in the loft which often included music but what was more special for us was going round to his caravan in the paddock, near the pond, and listening to his jazz records. I seem to remember doing this only once or twice. The boarders, I knew, did it frequently in the evening. Apart from Spilwell's lectures or racy readings in dorm after lights out, these visits to Barnet's caravan were the only things for which I envied the boarders.

Barnet's jazz records were of Chris Barber mainly and, to a lesser extent, Humphrey Littleton (traditional jazz). Our music was pop music, 'rock' music, but we found jazz fascinating, not only the sound of jazz but its associations for us. Jazz, rightly or wrongly, was linked in our minds with the Roaring Twenties, night clubs in American movies, big bands and jiving. But that was only one side of it. It was definitely not as accessible as rock 'n' roll and pop songs. There were few simple tunes to sing or whistle in jazz and rarely any words to latch onto; it was all, as a rule, just brassy instrumental music. But therein lay its attraction, for we were convinced it must be quite intellectual. Classical music was intellectual, we assumed, but classical music was boring, and listening to jazz was a much more exciting way of being intellectual in our music listening.

We didn't understand in what way jazz was intellectual but older brothers listened to jazz, students at university listened to jazz, clever young people and older mavericks listened to jazz. It was obviously quite subtle, and people who loved jazz had been initiated into some mystic art; they knew something we didn't know. We were intrigued and wanted to experience whatever it was. For a time, probably only the time we knew Barnet at Penly Grange, jazz represented for us something exotic beyond pop music, something to be tried and tasted to see what it was like, though we weren't sure how much we really liked it. At home, at parties, with most of our friends, we still listened to pop music and hummed or sang pop songs, and paid special attention to the pop charts, the Top Twenty, which rarely included jazz numbers. Very few of us became lasting converts to jazz.

You might ask, indeed I often wondered at the time, how it was that Barnet's mould-shattering, unconventional pedagogy could have been tolerated in the traditional, hidebound, restrictive regime of Penly Grange. Charles Bracken was liberating in his *attitude* and went against the heavy-handed, disciplinary grain of the average Penly Grange teacher but he still kept within the spheres of classroom, games field, and Scouting codes and practices. Barnet did what he liked, it seemed, he accepted no confines or conventions, other than the laws of the land and common decency, of course!

One simple explanation why Teddy Eldin tolerated Barnet's freewheeling, 'anything goes' teaching style was that he knew Barnet wasn't staying long. Teddy Eldin knew that, after a year, Barnet would be going to university. And Teddy Eldin might have thought that his influence would quickly fade once he had left. But this explanation doesn't, in fact, wash, because he was allowed to come back after university and teach permanently, so Teddy Eldin wasn't reluctant or afraid to have him back. Why was that? Clearly he realised Barnet's worth, which was a point in Teddy Eldin's favour, but he doubtless saw him too as an essential upholder of public school traditions and values, despite his dangerously liberal approach; he recognised that although Barnet was a rocker of the boat, he was still on the boat and still believed in the boat. So although Teddy Eldin took a risk having him back, it was not that much of a risk for him since it was obvious Barnet was not against the system, not fundamentally. He was a reformer not a radical, Teddy Eldin must have decided, and he, Teddy Eldin, could contain or temper his reforming zeal.

Yes, Barnet returned to Penly Grange in the middle of the 1960s. It was the time when my contemporaries and I at Penly Grange were starting at university or doing our gap year. We moved on then quickly into the late 1960s. We paid little attention to what was happening at Marby College and even less to Penly Grange, soon ten years behind us. But snippets of news, pieces of hearsay, gossip, did come through to me occasionally and I also picked up some information about Penly Grange's progress from the Old Marbian magazine which kept tumbling through my letter box each year. Whenever Barnet's name was mentioned he was still doing great things for the school. On top of his teaching, he was continuing to run trips and camps, and coach school teams. He was still producing plays and revues too and he was also promoting pupils' creative writing, by publishing, for instance, a selection of their poems. He was, indeed, as tireless and brimming with life and enthusiasm as ever, for all sorts of things. (And still a bachelor, it seemed).

A few more years passed. One Easter, in the early 1970s, I came home to see my mum – my dad was away on a business trip – and heard there was a message for me from Martin: Martin Rigby Smith. I hadn't seen him for about five years and that occasion had only been a brief meeting somewhere in Oxford. I was glad to hear from him again but clearly this wasn't just a social call. According to the message, there was some bad news about Robert Barnet, 'that popular teacher at Penly Grange', my mum called him. She didn't really know him, she'd not visited the school much, but she knew of his fine reputation and seemed troubled by the news.

My mum told me Martin was staying with his parents and she gave me the number to ring. I recognised it immediately. It was the same number he'd had in the Penly Grange days. Evidently his parents hadn't moved in the last fourteen years or so. I rang the number and got Rigby Smith's mother who put me quickly on to Martin.

"Glad you got the message," said Martin. "How are you?"

"Fine," I said, and not wanting to beat about the bush, I added, "I gather you rang about Robert Barnet?"

"Yes," said Martin. "Have you heard the news about him?"

"I've heard almost nothing of Penly Grange in the last few years but the last I heard of Barnet he was doing fine. As active and inspirational as ever."

I once again pictured him moving round the library-classroom, awaiting our responses to his challenging questions, scanning our faces to make sure we were really engaging our brains; waving his arms round on the coach to start us singing; hurrying out to the rugby pitches to get our games started, ahead of us not behind us like Swales; leading the way, not goading and harrying us like him.

"Well, I'm afraid he's quite ill. In fact," Martin paused, "... his illness is terminal." I remember being struck by the word 'terminal'. It sounded mundane and innocuous. In the context of school, it suggested he was going to be, or had been ill, for just a term, a school term. But, no, of course, it didn't mean that, it meant he wasn't going to get better, he was going to die.

"What's he suffering from?" I asked.

"Cancer."

"What sort?"

"I don't know where it started but according to my dad [his dad was a surgeon] he was riddled with cancer when they admitted him back into hospital last week. He's been ill for over two years but now it's at an advanced stage. He hasn't got long."

It seemed incredible. Barnet of all people! He was the youngest, healthiest and most energetic of all the staff we had known at Penly Grange. Surely he still had the longest and brightest teaching career ahead of him. Even the ancient Teddy Eldin, retired now, was still going strong from what I'd heard. All I could say was: "Poor chap, it doesn't seem possible."

"No, it doesn't, does it? Anyway, James is going to see him," Martin continued. "He's visited him already. He thought I might like to come too this time and suggested I might ask someone else from our school days who remembered him. I thought of you and tried you on the off chance you might have come home for Easter. Obviously you have, which is lucky. Would you like to come with us?"

I met them at the hospital the following afternoon. Barnet was in Marby hospital, in a side ward. There was someone else in another bed, a very old man, but he was asleep the whole of our visit. James Rigby Smith, Martin's older brother, was a clergyman now. I remembered him being a considerate and conscientious person who was academic and musical, and, like his brothers, good at cricket. He had gone to Cambridge to study Classics. As he was a very serious and thoughtful person and from a religious family (all the Rigby Smiths were religious), I wasn't surprised to hear he'd gone into the church.

Since he had already spoken with Barnet, and was a priest, it was natural for James Rigby Smith to take the initiative in our conversation with him. James had a direct manner, neither too impersonal and detached, nor too sympathetic and condescending. I said very little and let the Rigby Smiths do the talking. I expected Barnet to remember Martin but not me, but I shouldn't have done, for he'd always paid attention to each of us individually and he certainly did remember me. He asked me if I were still doing cricket scoring or was I perhaps *playing* for a cricket team now? He gave me that teasing smile of his I remembered so well.

Actually, apart from that question I remember nothing of what we spoke about during that hospital visit. My distinct and lasting recollections are all visual. Half sitting up in bed, he was a small, slight figure, and there wasn't much colour in his face. Apart from his paleness, however (and he'd always been a little pale), he didn't look ill. He was very calm and didn't seem in any pain. There was something strange about the whole situation. One could imagine he was *convalescing* from an illness because of the stamps on a tray on his lap, the Punch magazines (supplied by Mrs Rigby Smith), the glass of water by his bedside, and the cards and flowers, but dying? Definitely not. It didn't seem real. There was a bible there too but there are often bibles in hospitals; it didn't alter the impression that here was man who could be out of hospital quite soon.

I will never forget those stamps. There were masses of them. He was sticking them into an album and I noticed they were stamps from all over the world. I remember thinking 'why cast your net so wide'? Why not just concentrate on Europe or the Commonwealth as we used to do? Would he ever complete the work? It seemed he'd given himself a Herculean task. Did he know that? Was he trying to stretch himself, set himself one last challenge?

We went back to the Rigby Smiths' home for tea. Martin was sombre and silent. James Rigby Smith was sombre too but strangely buoyant at the same time and wanting to talk. He turned to me as we drank our tea and spoke in that clear, crisp manner of his, "He's a committed Christian, you know, a firm believer. It's amazing! I've talked and prayed with him a few times and I'm deeply impressed with his faith."

I had not been particularly conscious of Barnet being a committed Christian when we were at Penly Grange – it was not something he had put on display – but I wasn't surprised, somehow, to learn that he was, or had become one. James paused and put his cup down on its saucer. I didn't know whether he was waiting for me to say something, but I thought I ought to speak, so I said something like, "Well, that's good", trying to sound positive but not really feeling it.

"Yes," continued James, "he's at peace with God, he's ready to go."

I remember thinking, 'That *is* amazing: there are many people twice his age who are not ready to go. How can he be so resigned?'

So when I heard from Martin that he'd died just three weeks after our visit, I tried not to feel too sad. If he was at peace and ready to go then that was more cause for rejoicing than grieving, surely? To live so well and die so well was truly a great thing, was it not?

And yet I couldn't get those stamps out of my head. Did he get all those stamps into his album before he died? Unlikely. Did he think of them representing countries all over the world which he would never visit now and experiences he would never have? Had he not felt some injustice that the worlds he'd opened up for so many children were closing down for him so prematurely?

I thought of what he'd done for us, and been for us, that last year at Penly Grange, and doubtless for many pupils who had come after us. What he'd

97

given us: encouragement and inspiration, liberation from rigid thought, the spirit of fun, initiation into so many good things in life; and his personal touch, an appreciation of us as individuals, including me. Thinking of all this, and the memories of him so very much alive, I could only see, and feel, the tragedy of his early death. He was only thirty-four.

Sex Education and the Amazing Spilwell

'Cometh the hour, cometh the man'

Sex education at Penly Grange was almost non-existent. It might have been better, though, had it been entirely non-existent since we were told just little bits of information in a guarded, cryptic way, which left us confused and tantalised. The unspoken policy for the subject seems to have been to tell us as little as possible for as long as possible.

That is not to say that there was no provision for Sex Education in the curriculum. On the contrary. Headmaster Teddy Eldin, who took full responsibility for it, had decided to deal with it methodically within the context of his Science lessons. The plan was to run a course on reproduction and life cycles which would culminate in a study of human reproduction, at which point the 'facts of life' would be taught. However, this would not occur until the last year at Penly Grange, when the boys were aged 12-13, because boys weren't ready to learn them, or didn't need to learn them, until then, it was implied. We were led to believe, furthermore, that learning 'the facts of life' was a privilege granted only to the oldest boys in the school, that we were going to be initiated into secret knowledge withheld from younger boys and we would then pass through another archway into senior school and on into adulthood.

Naturally, we were eager to become initiated into this secret knowledge, to pass through that archway, especially since we were becoming increasingly curious about sex anyway. By the age of 12, when we entered our last year at Penly Grange, we were more than ready to learn 'the facts of life', and we became increasingly frustrated by having to wait, even then, until the *end* of the Science course before we could learn them. Not that we respected Teddy Eldin as a guru or the ultimate authority on any subject – quite the reverse – nor that we knew nothing at all from books, magazines, films, what our parents might have told us or what we'd picked up from older siblings and school-friends (gossip, grapevine, the jungle telegraph etc.), but we'd learnt nothing formally about sex and we believed Teddy Eldin to be the keeper of the *official* secrets, the classified information in this sphere of knowledge, and were very intrigued to know what he was going to tell us.

The Science course on reproduction began. It seemed to us unnecessarily thorough and on topics which had been studied before or were of little immediate interest to most of us. We learnt about binary fission in amoebas and, I think, touched on multiple fission too. We learnt about such things as mucor, 'pin mould' and spores. We were given some idea of life cycles and external and internal fertilisation. There was something about sperm swimming to eggs, attracted by chemicals, which I found quite bizarre, a mixture of space fiction and a Walt Disney animated cartoon. We then spent a lot of time on parts of flowers and their structure. Words like 'pistil', 'ovary', 'stigma', 'stamen', 'petal' and 'sepal' and 'calyx' flooded our brains. Rigby Smith, who could decline Latin nouns and conjugate Latin verbs better than anyone apart from Parker, got them all totally muddled and began muttering, "Why do I have to learn all this anyway? I'm not doing Science for my scholarship exams. Why doesn't Teddy Eldin just get onto what we all want to know?"

He didn't. After considering regularly-shaped, symmetrical flowers and irregularly-shaped and composite flowers – such as buttercups and roses, sweet peas, daisies and dandelions – we did self-pollination and cross pollination again (I'm sure we'd done it when we were nine or ten). We gave some time to wind pollination and the dispersal of seeds. I remember being interested in the stinging nettle example and the design of sycamore seeds in assisting wind dispersal. Even Rigby Smith was interested in sycamore seeds because of their aeroplane-style wings which seemed to make them sentient beings. Dandelions fascinated him too because of their 'clocks' which gave a tangible sense of the passage of time, and plucking their stalks and blowing their fragile forms away, which we both liked doing, gave us a satisfying 'hands on' experience. But in Rigby Smith's case it was matter for poetry and philosophy not science. I suppose I was more interested in how it all worked, the scientific side, not merely what it could evoke in the imagination which was what appealed to Rigby Smith.

After learning the different life cycles of flowering plants: ephemerals, annuals, biennials and perennials (I remember grasping the meaning of the word 'ephemeral' – short-lived – by seeing how it applied to flowers, and was therefore able to use it later for other things in life), we considered evergreen and deciduous trees and tulip and daffodil bulbs. Only then did we move onto animal reproduction, beginning with insects and the phases of the butterfly's life cycle: with larvae and pupae and metamorphosis and so on. All amazing stuff, of course, but time was running out and we still hadn't even got to reproduction in mammals. But we couldn't move on to that yet because we still had to give time to reproduction in fish and amphibia, frogs of course being the classic example.

We'd done frogspawn before, seeing samples in the lily pond, watching their progress into tadpoles and metamorphosis into frogs. We now looked at the topic again. Birds came next and their mating practices, which seemed to be bringing us a little closer to human mating with the birds' habit of jumping on each others' backs, but no parallels were suggested. We were told to wait for sexual reproduction in mammals before real comparisons could be drawn, but we weren't there yet.

Eventually we did get on to mammals and we reached the mating of dogs. Teddy Eldin seemed reasonably happy to tell us about the manner of sexual reproduction in dogs and became as explicit as he was ever going to be. Not before time, because we estimated it could well be the last lesson of the course, the last chance we had to learn about the 'facts of life', human sexual reproduction, in the classroom. Teddy Eldin explained to us the mechanics of dogs copulating. He did a little drawing for us on the board and even demonstrated the actions involved with his hands. Then he paused, took a deep breath and said, "Sexual intercourse by humans is really very similar. In fact –"

At this point I must break into my account of this climactic sex lesson and provide some important narrative background.

To begin with, the reader needs to be aware that in addition to the Science lessons, supposedly dealing with the essential facts about sexual reproduction in humans, Teddy Eldin had been giving us separately some moral advice in matters relating to puberty and sex. This moral advice, most of which was pretty baffling or useless, had usually been delivered in his after lunch slot when the rest of the school had been sent away. I remember him telling us never to look in a lady's handbag and not to comment if we ever saw blood on the toilet seat. Perplexed at the time, I only realised much later that this was his way of warning us about possible embarrassments over women's periods and menstruation. On masturbation his advice was beautifully simple – 'Don't'. What he actually said was, 'Don't play with yourself: leave your privates alone!' On wet dreams, if they occurred, he said, 'Don't worry about them, they happen', without attempting to explain why they occurred. His catch-all moral guidance for all behaviour, including all sexual activity, was 'Never do anything your mother wouldn't like you to do.' Together with your conscience, your mother's approval or disapproval would settle all 'should I or shouldn't I?' questions about sexual behaviour.

There wasn't a lot more to say, it appeared, except to warn us about the possibility of our witnessing animals having sex. (Teddy Eldin always seemed anxious to spare us any possible embarrassment over sex). 'If you see two dogs stuck together in the street, look the other way,' he said, and then added, 'or you might perhaps throw a bucket of water over them.' How we were supposed to get hold of a bucket of water if we should see two dogs stuck together, he never said. Rush into the nearest house, shop or café and request one for the specified purpose? Which brings us back to the copulation of dogs in that final Sex Education lesson. However, I am not yet in a position to return to that lesson because further, even more vital, narrative background is still required. This indispensable background relates to one person, our classmate Spilwell, to whom I must now turn.

Spilwell

Simon J. Spilwell who was in our form – the top form that last school year – was one of the most extraordinary boys I ever knew, in a number of ways. He had bright yellow hair, almost white, combed straight down to the front of his head and a tuft of hair that stood up at the back; the tops of his ears stuck out too. He had piercing green eyes, and freckles on his face and the backs of his large hands. His feet were large too and he was on the tall side for a boy of his age. He was something of a mad scientist and a fanatic in every interest or hobby he pursued. He loved playing with mechanical gadgets, such as single-bladed, petrol-fuelled propellers which you could flick-start with your fingers, though it sometimes took a lot of effort, concentration and determination to do so.

I remember he once sported a pair of goggles with little windscreen wipers he'd made himself and walked around the school in them to display them to everyone, until ordered to take them off immediately by Swales who wasn't amused (but then Swales was hardly ever amused except by his own unamusing antics). At Marby College, Spilwell rigged up a circuit between his radio and the door of his study so that the radio went off as soon as the door was opened; a useful device when listening to the radio was banned during prep time and there were spot checks and surprise raids by the master on duty. He was equally interested and capable in natural history and he chased and collected butterflies, for instance, with passionate intensity.

Spilwell's preoccupations and abilities were not perhaps so remarkable in themselves, they simply indicated an intelligent mind with an aptitude for science and technology, but they were combined with an exceptional precocity in knowledge of adult things and a forceful and audacious character. He was totally uninhibited in self-expression, full of confidence in himself and quite irrepressible: impossible to put down, discourage or deflate for long. His physical energy and drive (no weedy scientist, he) stood him in good stead in most sports and he powered his way into the First Fifteen rugby team through his reputation as a tireless forward and ferocious tackler (At Marby College he broke his own leg in a reckless attempt to bring down the thuggish Crawford from an impossible position).

As a scientist and growing boy, he had become extremely interested in the subject of sex and, aware of the deficiencies in sex education at Penly Grange, he had decided to provide his own instruction for the benefit of the ill-informed, which was most of us. Of course he wanted to show off too. He was a real showman, though he never showed much desire to act on the stage, just on the stage of life, a stage which was vacant when it came to adequate presentations on the subject of sex. In that area, as we have seen, there was a real 'gap in the market'.

Spilwell began his sex instruction in the dormitory at night after the duty master had left. His main teaching method was through a set of text book or exam style questions. He would ask such questions as: What are the male sex organs called? Name the female genitalia. Name the scientific term for sexual intercourse. What is premature ejaculation and what are its drawbacks? What is coitus interruptus and what are its dangers? What is a more common term for onanism?

Since the answers to his questions from the boys in the dorm ranged from inarticulate sniggers, to the articulated but totally incorrect, by way of the flippant and facetious, he ended up answering the questions himself which he wanted to do anyway. According to Thorpe (as a day boy I had to rely on his information), the reaction of the boys to Spilwell's Sex Education course was mixed. Some were intrigued and some amused and entertained, but others were soon bored and irritated and would shout, "Oh, shut up, Spilwell! You're obsessed! We want some sleep!" ... "Tell us a story or wrap up!" said Porter who was probably thinking of tomorrow's cricket match or practice in the nets and wanted to be fresh for whichever it was.

Rigby Smith and I, though day boys and therefore not in the dorm at night, didn't escape altogether from Spilwell's endeavours to enlighten the ignorant on sexual questions. One morning in break, Spilwell caught us doing nothing in particular and sat us down on the window seat in the library.

"Now then," he had said, fixing us with his zealous, penetrating eye, "you day boys need to be quizzed too. How good is your knowledge of sexual matters and the 'facts of life'? Let's see, shall we?" And he proceeded to ask the same sort of questions he'd asked the boarders in the dorm. I remember two related questions he'd asked us, because they did seem to be, well, very 'adult' questions. What is the 'missionary' position in sexual intercourse and what are its disadvantages? As he expected, we were quite unable to answer either question and he was more than willing to supply us with the answers. I was amazed as well as amused that he should have pondered the second of the two questions, at his age, but when he explained his answer I could see it was a genuinely thought-provoking question, from a physical point of view, anyway.

We found Spilwell's sex instruction hilarious, as well as informative, but not in the slightest bit rude because of the way he delivered his questions and answers. He did it all straight-faced and in a strictly formal manner as if he were a zoology lecturer. There was no smirking or smuttiness, no crudeness or coarseness. He used the proper scientific language, the correct technical terms. If he ever used a rude or obscene word he would make it clear he was just quoting the language of the plebs, the uneducated and unrefined, he was utterly disdainful of swear words. His way of speaking, however, wasn't entirely expressionless and colourless, he did 'play things up' a little. He spoke in an affected, precious manner, in a sort of parody of official language, and he lingered over words which included the letter 's', wrapping his tongue round them, giving them a sensual resonance. Words such as 'orgasm', 'sexual', 'detumescence', and 'masturbation' came in for exaggerated enunciation and sibilance. But it was always controlled, and like a good actor he never laughed at his own performance, it was all done with the utmost seriousness, and that was what made it so very funny. And don't forget, this earnest sex education instructor was only just thirteen.

How much Teddy Eldin knew about Spilwell's sex instruction is uncertain but he definitely knew what everyone knew: that Spilwell was excessively interested in sex and extremely well-informed about it too. He may also have been beginning to suspect that Spilwell had put his brother up to asking a question which had caught him off his guard the previous year. Teddy Eldin had been teaching some ten year old boys about the life cycle of chickens and had got onto the hatching of their eggs; a safe enough subject, he must have thought, but then a hand went up. It was the hand of Graham Spilwell, Spilwell's younger brother.

"Please, sir, you know when mothers have babies, a doctor has to be present?"

"Yes," said Teddy Eldin, tolerating the digression from chickens for the moment, perhaps because Graham Spilwell was a bright boy who usually asked intelligent questions, "that's usual."

"And," continued Graham Spilwell, "conception is where it all starts?"

"That's right," said Teddy Eldin, doubtless hoping he wasn't going to be asked what led to conception in humans because that was only for the older boys.

"Well," Spilwell Junior pressed on, "does the doctor have to be present at the conception as well as the birth?"

According to Colin Rigby Smith, Teddy Eldin had laughed, muttered 'no, no, no', taken off his glasses, breathed on them, polished them, rubbed his eyes, put his glasses back on again and changed the subject back to the hatching of the hen's eggs. That incident, as I've said, had been a year ago. Now Teddy Eldin was teaching the top form in the school about what led to conception in humans. It had been a long time coming in his biology course but it *had* now come and he couldn't change the subject, and the older Spilwell, the highly knowledgeable Spilwell, was sitting in the classroom waiting to hear what he had to say. More importantly, he was waiting to ask his questions, for Teddy Eldin had promised that when he had finished his exposition of 'the facts of life' questions would be allowed.

So now we return to the point in the lesson when Teddy Eldin is telling the class that sexual intercourse between humans is very similar to sexual intercourse between dogs. He continued, "In fact, it's virtually the same." He nodded, "The same, the same, the same." Then he drew himself up and, with somewhat gritted teeth, asked, "Right, are there any questions?"

Spilwell's hand shot up, but, in a pre-emptive strike, like a gunslinger shooting from the hip, Teddy Eldin gunned him down before a single word could come out of his mouth.

"Get out, Spilwell!" he blazed, "we don't want to hear any of your questions!" (Oh yes we did, we did want to hear his questions, we very much wanted to hear his questions. And we wanted to hear the answers to his questions even more). There was a pause during which Spilwell failed to react. For a second I wondered whether he was going to be defiant, to protest in some way. But then he got up without a word and swiftly left the room. After the library/classroom door closed, there was a prolonged silence. Teddy Eldin knew he would have to say something. Even by his standards he had been excessively peremptory and unreasonable. All Spilwell had done was to raise his hand to ask a question and Teddy Eldin had just asked if there *were* any questions. He gave us a very forced smile and tried to justify himself:

"Spilwell," he said, "only wants to show off, he's trying to be clever. He'd be wasting our time." (Who'd been wasting our time, I wondered?). Then he added, "I'll see him later in my study. Then he can ask me whatever questions he wants, and I'll answer them, if they're genuine." Teddy Eldin was trying to reassert his authority and sound fair to Spilwell at the same time, but to us, certainly to me, the 'seeing him later in my study' sounded ominous and threatening.

Nothing much happened in the lesson after Spilwell's expulsion from the room. No one dared to ask much, in case their question was deemed a clever, Spilwell-like question. There were some innocuous questions about fertilisation and pregnancy but nothing about sexual intercourse itself which we'd heard so little about from Teddy Eldin. Then the lesson ended. Anti-climax. We did not feel we had been initiated into any secrets. We had not been taken through 'the facts of life' archway into the mysteries of adult life, as we'd hoped; we still thirsted to know fully what grown-ups knew about sex.

Spilwell visited Teddy Eldin's study after Games in the afternoon and spent a long time in there. We did not hear the sound of the cane nor Teddy Eldin's raised voice which could often be heard through the study door when he was particularly irate about something. Spilwell emerged eventually. He was subdued and expressionless and made no statements to anyone.

We did have one more biology lesson but it was about pregnancy and then the rearing of cubs and puppies (dogs again!). The 'facts of life' seemed to have been left behind. Spilwell was back in the classroom but he said nothing and asked no questions. Teddy Eldin was more relaxed. We had no idea what he'd said to Spilwell but he clearly felt he'd dealt with him and he'd snuffed out his dangerous, subversive influence. In one respect he was right. Spilwell stopped offering his sex education to interested boys in their free time. His question and answer sessions were dropped and he made no attempt to advertise his expertise as he had done hitherto.

But in another respect, Teddy Eldin was quite wrong to think he'd silenced the irrepressible Spilwell. Two days later, Thorpe told me, smiling, that Spilwell had begun to read a story to the dormitory after lights out. (Maybe he'd remembered what Porter had said). The story was a novel by D.H. Lawrence, an 'adult' book, and it was called Lady Chatterley's Lover (a foreign edition presumably, it was still banned in our land). Spilwell was reading out selected highlights. This time *everybody* was listening, and drinking up every word!

Sport at Penly Grange

'It's fun to win ...'

Sport was of huge importance at Penly Grange, as it was at Marby College and, as far as we could tell, at all the other prep schools we played and their senior schools. Of course I am talking about school sport, team sport, particularly rugby and cricket. (Football – soccer – was played only up to the age of eleven and then superseded by hockey and rugby).

The importance of sport was reflected in the school timetable. The normal school day consisted of lessons in the morning, Games in the afternoon, and lessons again after tea until a quarter to six. On half days, Wednesdays and Saturdays, there were no lessons after tea but we still had Games in the afternoon. Friday was the only day of the week we didn't have Games in the timetable – we had Cubs/Scouts instead. Even so, those in school teams might have a practice or training session squeezed in during the afternoon on Fridays. Attendance at Games was always compulsory, like lessons, but sometimes it entailed spectating rather than playing sport.

When the First School Team was playing at home on Saturdays, sometimes on Wednesdays too, the rest of the school who were not playing in matches were expected to watch them: to line themselves up in an orderly manner along the touchline line, if it was rugby or hockey, or around the boundary if it was cricket. If it was a First Eleven cricket match, boys were also expected to record the score in their own little score books. That meant recording every ball bowled, every run scored, including 'extras' (runs not scored from the bat) and every wicket taken. I don't remember many of us objecting to this; some did, but I quite liked doing it. It helped us to concentrate on the game and relieved the boredom a little when there was not much excitement on the pitch. The compulsory watching of school matches was intended to foster school spirit, give the school team support, provide examples to the younger boys of how to play the game, and underline its importance.

Achieving a good standard of play in school matches was important at Penly Grange not only for its own sake but also because it also provided an opportunity to raise the reputation of the school, especially helpful when the school's academic reputation was still in the making. The presumption was that if a school was doing creditably at sport it must be a good school. But what did doing creditably at sport mean at Penly Grange? Did it mean winning all one's matches all the time?

No, apparently not. Not officially. According to Teddy Eldin, when it came to sport, what mattered was *effort*, as with work, and the *spirit* in which you played, not success. He impressed this upon us time and time again in the dining room after lunch. In his attitude to sport, Teddy Eldin ostensibly subscribed without reserve to the sentiments of the American sportswriter, Grantland Rice, with whose famous lines in Alumnus Football (1923) he was probably familiar:

For when the One Great Scorer comes
To mark against your name,
He writes – not that you won or lost –
But how you played the Game.

When we were thrashed by another school, those who had been in the school team waited in some trepidation to learn Teddy Eldin's judgement on their effort. Sometimes he pronounced that the school team had done its best and not been disgraced, at which pronouncement there was naturally much relief, and it helped to mitigate slightly any sense of humiliation felt. Sometimes he adjudged that effort had been inadequate and gave the team a severe talking to: they had let the school down etc., etc., and the players would have to pull their socks up in future. Usually he just made the players feel bad about their defeat and did nothing further but there was the famous occasion when he caned all eleven boys in the Under 12 Cricket Team for being bowled out for a very low score, alleging it had been an utterly spineless performance. As far as I could tell, our teams usually tried their best, especially when the opposing school was strong, and Teddy Eldin's pronouncements on the degree of effort shown by them when they lost seemed quite arbitrary. As a matter of fact, I don't ever remember our teams being criticised for lack of effort when we won, even on those occasions when the opposition was so weak only a token effort was made to achieve victory.

'How you played the game', of course, also involved the question of sportsmanship. Teddy Eldin was as keen on losing gracefully, in gentlemanly fashion, as he was on pure effort and commitment. On one occasion, following a defeat in an Under 11 soccer match, Eldin hauled one player into his study and gave him a tongue lashing for alleged bad sportsmanship. Since that player was my close friend Rigby Smith, he told me all about it. He said Teddy Eldin was so angry he was surprised he hadn't caned him, just lectured him at length. Rigby Smith was mightily relieved not to be caned but surprised and indignant that he'd been accused of bad sportsmanship because he hadn't disputed any decisions nor quarrelled with the final result, as far as he was aware. He admitted he'd been bad tempered towards one or two of his own players and frustrated by the whole team's performance but that had been understandable, he felt. They hadn't played well. When he tried to make this point to Teddy Eldin, he'd brushed it aside contemptuously and declared it was immaterial with whom he'd been bad-tempered; he should not have shown any bad feeling to anyone. If you lost, you had to rise above it, stay calm and composed, look happy, be polite and friendly to everyone, that sort of thing.

"Like a Boy Scout?" I suggested, "Smiling and whistling under all difficulties?" Or I might have said showing a 'stiff upper lip', if I'd known the expression then.

"That's right," said Rigby Smith, "exactly. Or not show any feelings at all. It's all about self-control, apparently, and 'holding your head high'."

Some years later, at Marby College, we encountered a more realistic view of losing from Mr Galland, the rugby coach there. Mr Galland stressed the importance of effort and commitment too (he was actually a superb motivator and could really fire you up for any game) and he equally encouraged good sportsmanship but he also recognised that losing was not a pleasant experience and did make a difference. If he felt that we hadn't done ourselves justice he would say so, but if we'd tried hard and lost he wouldn't simply say, 'Never mind, you did your best, you weren't disgraced, that's all that counts'. He might say we weren't disgraced but, looking at our despondent faces, he wouldn't offer us further moral comforts, he would say frankly, 'I know how you feel. Let's face it, boys, it's fun to win and it's not fun to lose!'

As the years went by at Penly Grange, and we saw more and more of Teddy Eldin's responses to our winning and losing, his persistently proclaimed principle that how you played the game was the only thing that mattered looked increasingly flimsy and unconvincing. Finally, his reaction to two cricket matches one summer term, against the same school, Rostock Manor, the home fixture and then the away match, blew it away completely.

It was our last summer term, and the first of these two matches came fairly early on in the cricket season. Rostock Manor brought its First Eleven cricket team to Penly Grange. They had come some distance and were our arch rivals. Having failed to get into the Under 12 Team and then the Second Eleven, I had turned to scoring for the First Eleven. I think I was good at it and I certainly enjoyed it. I felt involved in the matches and it gave me a sense of authority and importance. During the match I was the one who always knew what the score was and I might send messages for the score board outside the pavilion to be altered if it was wrong; and the umpires would consult *me* if they lost track of how many balls had been bowled in one particular over. In the tea interval, and after the match, people would crowd round me to look at the score book and might ask me questions about statistics or the finer points of the final score.

I rarely kept score at Marby College, in fact I ended up doing swimming there rather than cricket, so the scoring I did for the First Eleven at Penly Grange stands out quite distinctly in my memory and I can still remember a few of the scores I recorded, in some detail, especially the matches against Rostock Manor that final summer term.

The first match, on our ground, was on a Saturday afternoon in May. It was a fine, dry, sunny day. Rostock Manor batted first straight after lunch. They had quite a good batting team and we had rather a weak bowling team and they knocked up a very good score of 146. In those days a score of 100 was reckoned to be quite a solid total and 120 probably a match winner. The target to win of 147 looked very daunting indeed, if not impossible. Rocky Craggs, our cricket master and coach, who was one of the umpires, and Teddy Eldin who was watching the match, came into the pavilion for tea looking glum, especially Teddy Eldin who was muttering things about our team's loose bowling and sloppy fielding. On the other hand, the master in charge of Rostock Manor's team, who was the other umpire, looked very happy. I remember he was quite a broad man with black curly hair going bald on top and gold-rimmed glasses which glinted in the sun. I don't remember his name, it was something like Mr Smethwick so I'll call him that. I didn't like Mr Smethwick. He was fat and smug and smiling. I got the impression he couldn't wait to get back to the game after the interval, to his umpiring and his presiding over our inevitable defeat.

Tea finished, our two opening batsmen, Nelson and Wainstone, went out from the pavilion to 'climb a mountain' and disaster struck early on. Nelson was bowled the second over, which brought Rigby Smith to the crease with just one run on the board. Rigby Smith was our captain and Rocky Craggs rated him highly but he hadn't notched up many good scores in matches to date and his ability to build a substantial innings had yet to be proved. He got off to a good start hitting a loose ball for four straightaway but the last ball of the next over Wainstone was given out caught behind by Mr Smethwick: his finger went up without hesitation after an appeal.

Even from my position in the pavilion I could see it was a dodgy decision. The ball had gone down the leg side nowhere near Wainstone's bat. He and Rigby Smith agreed afterwards that the snicking noise the ball had made was caused by the buckles on the straps of his pads. Be that as it may, Wainstone, our best opening batsman, was out (whether he should have been or not). We were now two wickets down, and only five runs towards a total of 147 had been scored. Mr Smethwick looked very cheerful and his gold-rimmed spectacles seemed to glint even more brightly in the sun as he strode confidently to 'square leg' to take up his umpiring position for the next over.

Porter had come in, at no.4, to take Wainstone's place. Porter was a good batsman and had a wide range of strokes. He was particularly good off his legs and, once he had his eye in, anything on the leg side was liable to get short shrift whether it was pitched up or not. The trouble was he was erratic and you never knew how he was going to perform. We soon found out, though, that day.

Rigby Smith got a single which brought Porter down to the bowler's end and brought our total to six runs. Mr Smethwick, looking relaxed and untroubled at square leg, was quite surprised when the second ball bowled to Porter came whistling past him. He obviously expected Porter as the new batsman to take his time settling in and getting his eye in. Unfortunately for Smethwick, and Rostock Manor's First Eleven, it took Porter only one ball to get going. He began hitting the ball with tremendous power. I remember the ball made a sizzling noise as it flew through the air and a zipping noise as it struck the ground and ricocheted off to the boundary, quite unstoppable or un-interceptible. No other batsman in our team hit the ball in quite the same way. Rigby Smith struck the ball well but he stroked or clipped the ball, he didn't smash the ball like Porter.

Which was immaterial, because Rigby Smith soon got his eye in too and he, too, began to score freely in his own stylish manner. After just three more overs we had reached 50 and then it was 60. I could see from his body language that Mr Smethwick was becoming worried. I don't think he had given up hope at that point because Porter's hitting was becoming more and more uninhibited and he must have thought, as I feared and he hoped, that Porter would get over-confident, overreach himself and give his wicket away. If Porter was out with 60 or even 70 runs on the board there would still be over 70 more runs for Penly Grange to get. His bowlers were capable of taking wickets, he doubtless believed, and, as he knew Penly Grange had no other batsmen of the same calibre as Porter and Rigby Smith, with Porter out they could still probably polish off the new batsmen before Rostock Manor's total was reached. But Porter didn't play an injudicious stroke and he was seeing the ball better and better, and Rigby Smith was playing with increasing boldness, almost matching Porter's scoring rate and doing some beautiful cover drives and lake cuts and strokes off the back foot. The hundred mark was soon reached and then the score raced on to 120.

With the score at 120, I was now pretty confident that even if Porter or Rigby Smith were out at this point, the rest of our batting line-up could surely get the remaining runs. Mr Smethwick obviously thought so too. He looked a defeated man as he made his way with drooping posture to his umpiring positions, from square leg to the bowler's wicket, from the bowler's wicket back to square leg again. There was nothing he could do. He couldn't influence events, in the Timmerton fashion, with umpiring decisions favourable to his side because there were no more appeals to respond to, there were no appeals for LBW (Leg Before Wicket), or catches, because Rigby Smith and Porter weren't missing any balls or giving any catches, except for balls hit so hard they couldn't be held; and run-outs were never a possibility, the batsmen were just strolling between the wickets as the fielders were run ragged round the field. Although the sun was still shining (very much so for us), Mr Smethwick's glasses didn't seem to be glinting any more.

Rigby Smith and Porter did not, in fact, lose their wickets. They stayed in and coasted home. Two overs later, with score on 145, Porter hammered yet another ball to the midwicket boundary and it was all over. Rigby Smith and Porter were mobbed as they came off the field. They had just achieved a third wicket victory stand of 144 in well under two hours. Surely some kind of record. I was so excited I wanted to rush out and pat them on the back too but I had to complete the score book. I don't remember the names of the Rostock Manor bowlers but I remember that the basic scorecard of our innings read like this:

Nelson	bowled	0
Wainstone	caught	1
Rigby Smith	NOT OUT	71
Porter	NOT OUT	74
Extras		3

TOTAL (for 2 wickets) 149   Result: Penly Grange win by 8 wickets

Teddy Eldin was not surprisingly 'over the moon'. *His* glasses were definitely glinting, gleaming in the sun! He was full of praise for Rigby Smith's and Porter's batting, commending Rigby Smith's measured strokes and skilful placement of the ball and Porter's sheer power, variety of shots, and swashbuckling approach to his task. He made no reference to our team's loose bowling and sloppy fielding which he'd mentioned at tea; he seemed to have forgotten all about it.

I didn't see Mr Smethwick after the game. He didn't come into the pavilion to look at the score book as the opposing school's umpire often did, though one or two of the Rostock team did want to check the score card of their innings. I didn't, in fact, spare Mr Smethwick a thought then, I was just basking in the triumphal glow of our great victory. Later, I remembered his over-confidence at tea time and gloated over the total reversal of his team's fortunes. Then I put him out of my mind.

I couldn't, however, put him out of my mind indefinitely because there was the return match to come, the away fixture at Rostock Manor. It was about a month later. I was keeping the score again for Penly Grange and as soon as I saw Mr Smethwick, in his white umpire's coat and wearing his gold-rimmed spectacles as before, poised to go out onto the pitch to umpire with Rocky Craggs, with a very determined look on his face, I realised he'd be desperate for revenge and wondered whether he'd be tempted to give any dodgy umpiring decisions in his team's favour. But I don't actually remember anything about his umpiring decisions in this match nor his reactions during or after the game; only what Teddy Eldin told me of him on the coach going home. I remember Teddy Eldin's reactions, though, very well.

Our team's attitude going into this return match with Rostock Manor, and the game itself, were very different this time. Our confidence was high. We'd won two or three matches since then and had a draw. We were in form. Though our bowling attack continued to lack bite because we had few bowlers with real penetration, we had a strong batting side and Rigby Smith and Porter had been continuing to score runs, particularly Rigby Smith who was establishing himself as a reliable and successful no.3 batsman. Having beaten Rostock Manor already this season, we were sure we could do it again even though it was an away fixture and it had been a long and quite tiring journey to Rostock Manor by coach.

So, when they batted first, as before, and scored 105 runs all out, over forty runs less than last time, we couldn't see any problem in getting the runs. Rigby Smith and Porter would soon knock them off, we thought. Of course nobody said that. You wouldn't have done, that would have been tempting providence and unlucky. But I could tell that's what everyone was thinking; even Rigby Smith, I think, who tended to be a bit of a pessimist despite his increasing self-assurance in his batting.

Our bowling hadn't been particularly good but had sufficed. Rigby Smith had put himself on to bowl because Rocky Craggs had insisted he did after seeing him bowling with venom in the nets at school, but he had quickly and wisely taken himself off when he lost his line and started bowling wides. Rigby Smith had had the good sense to persist with Nelson and Thomas (quick bowlers) and use Rickman's off spin and Porter's away swing sparingly (Porter was a genuine all rounder but lacked stamina in bowling) and, together with fairly tight fielding, Rostock Manor's final total had been kept down to that above-mentioned 105, making a reasonable target of 106. Teddy

Eldin, watching as before from outside the pavilion, seemed quite relaxed at tea time and was looking, I thought, almost as pleased as Mr Smethwick had looked at tea time during the home fixture.

Unfortunately, Teddy Eldin's good mood did not last very long. When we batted after tea, our innings ran into deeper trouble than it had in our first game against Rostock Manor. After about ten overs we had just 10 runs on the board with three wickets down. For a while things didn't seem too bad because Rigby Smith and Porter (who had come in at no.5) were both still in and the score moved forward to 40. However, Porter was not seeing the ball as well he had done in that glorious previous innings and in one mad moment he took a wild swipe at a well pitched ball on his middle stump, missed it, and was bowled. Not very good for us. But worse was to come.

Rigby Smith, who had been building a solid innings and had reached 24, suddenly did a very rash thing when his usual common sense and good judgement went AWOL. He chased an innocuous ball outside his off stump, which he didn't need to play, and snicked it. Since the ball was from a slow bowler and travelling at a slow pace it was an easy catch for the slip fielder behind the stumps. At this point our total was just 45 and we were five wickets down with all our best batsmen out: Nelson, Wainstone, Loretti, Porter and Rigby Smith.

Shortly after this, Teddy Eldin, who had been pulling ferociously on his pipe with darkened countenance (I could see him out of the corner of my eye as I marked the score book), came into the pavilion to look at the score book between overs. He was extremely agitated. As I looked up at him, he expostulated in his higher pitched voice, a sign that he was particularly vexed.

"I've never seen such reckless batting! Trust Porter to slog out, he's got no patience, but Wainstone and Nelson just played across the ball, and what happened to Rigby Smith? I've never seen him play a stroke like that before, it was sheer madness! And his bowling was all over the place! I'll have to have a word ... with all of them afterwards!" He threw his eyes up to heaven, he just couldn't credit what he'd seen. "Who's coming next?" he asked, and peered over my shoulder at our batting line-up in the score book. Silcock and Honeyman, nos 6 + 7, were already batting, and he read the following names to come in after them: no.8 Nevan, no.9 Timpson (wicket-keeper), no.10 Rickmack, no.11 Thomas. He grunted. He didn't seemed reassured and hurried out to watch Honeyman's and Silcock's performance. It was a very critical time in our innings.

Honeyman and Silcock didn't do too badly. They pushed the score onto 70 before Silcock was given out LBW by Rocky Craggs (yes, Rocky was no Timmerton: if he thought you were out he gave you out whether you were in his team or not). Nevan came in next. At the time I thought Nevan was lucky to be in the First Eleven but I have to be admit he was probably a better batsman than I gave him credit for, and on this occasion he certainly played with great character and no little amount of skill. He wasn't of the same calibre as Rigby Smith and Porter but he could defend well and pick out the bad balls, and with Honeyman, a sound batsman too once he'd settled in, they put on 20 runs before Honeyman was run out through a mix up with Nevan who wasn't so good at running between the wickets.

Seven wickets down now. We had 90 runs on the board, only 16 runs short of our total, but when we lost two further quick wickets (Timpson and Rickmack) – for only three more runs – we were on the brink of defeat. Teddy Eldin was shaking his head and looking decidedly disgruntled. He was not a happy man. Not a happy man at all.

We only had Thomas and Nevan left now, and Thomas was an inept batsman who rarely laid bat on ball and had only ever scored one run before for the First team. I expected him to be bowled almost immediately. Somehow, though, he snicked the ball through the slips and got three runs because all the fielders had closed round his bat. That brought Nevan to the striker's end and he cracked two fours in quick succession, then scored two more runs. We'd reached 103. Even then, Rostock Manor must still have believed they could win the match because Thomas had to face the bowling again, when Nevan failed to get a run at the end of the over, and they brought on their best bowler to despatch him.

He bowled hard and fast and direct at Thomas but somehow, somehow, again, Thomas got the edge of his bat to make contact with the ball and it flew in the air over the slips, reaching the boundary in double quick time. We'd done it! We had 107 runs. We'd won by one wicket, scoring one run more than the total we needed!

On the coach going home, Rocky Craggs was very satisfied with his team's performance but Teddy Eldin was positively bubbling! He was radiating sweetness and light. He personally congratulated every member of the team. It looked like the harangue against the careless batting of the top five players, which he'd threatened when we were five wickets down and facing defeat, had been put on permanent hold, cancelled even. To underline how special the team's triumph was, he told us of Mr Smethwick's feelings about the game:

"Oh he was disappointed, he really was!" said Teddy Eldin. Especially after they'd done so well to get Rigby Smith and Porter out who scored all the runs in the last match; he really thought they'd be getting their revenge this time. But he didn't know how strong our batting was in depth; I told him we had good batsmen throughout the team. He didn't expect that. Yes, he was disappointed, he was, he was, he was!" Teddy Eldin was trying to be sympathetic towards Mr Smethwick but he couldn't disguise his overweening pride and delight at our second consecutive victory over our arch rivals Rostock Manor, an away victory too. His eyes were sparkling behind those thick-lensed glasses.

I knew then for certain what I had really known all along. Teddy Eldin's avowal that *how you played the game* was what truly mattered, not the result, was humbug. And having been at Marby College, I can now see that he actually agreed entirely with Mr Galland – 'Let's face it, boys, it's fun to win and it's not fun to lose!'

Jakeman

'The Napoleon of Crime'

When Burton left, having been 'asked to leave', his chief henchman, Vic Jakeman, took his place as the leading bully of our age group or cohort; actually he was a little bit older than most of us which gave him the edge physically and in terms of general maturity, though not academically.

Jakeman was very different from Burton in almost every respect: in appearance, character, intelligence and all round ability. Whereas Burton was stocky and solid-looking, with a round, flat, expressionless face, except for the ever-present glare of hostility in his eyes, Jakeman was tall and fairly slim, with a narrow, pointed face and ears, and lively eyes, filled with foxy cunning and, often, amusement. Whereas Burton always seemed restless and troubled, Jakeman was much more relaxed and seemed to enjoy life. He was not averse to physical bullying and had backed Burton up when he was throwing his weight around physically but Jakeman's *mental* dominance was much stronger; he usually got his way through his forceful personality and the use of his tongue rather than his fists.

For instance, when Burton lost the race to 'bag' the snooker table after lunch or tea, he would usually grab the cue off whoever had it and punch them hard if they protested. Jakeman was more subtle. He would get someone else to bag the table for him and if that failed he would spoil the game for whoever was playing by scoffing at their performance and challenging them to play him. You could either ignore his taunts or try to silence him by taking up his challenge. In the former case he would usually succeed in getting you to curtail your game and he would then take over with alacrity and play for as long as it suited him; in the latter case he would humiliate you by beating you easily, for he was a very good snooker player, and then he would have gained the right, he would claim, to continue playing till someone could beat him. No one ever could, except Porter occasionally. Unlike Burton who was a poor player and held the snooker cue in a clumsy fashion, Jakeman was an elegant player who played with style and flamboyance which made losing to him even more annoying – it's particularly galling losing to a swank and a show-off.

Jakeman was good at all games and sports, in fact. He gained his colours in the school teams for all major sports, eventually winning the Best Sportsman of the Year award in his final year. There was no question therefore about his sporting ability, but not satisfied with his success in school sports he wanted to be top dog in all games and every recreational activity that had a competitive element or could be given one. He wanted to be the best, or thought the best, not only at snooker and billiards and table tennis, boxing and general fighting, but also at all the other schoolboy activities or pastimes.

If we were collecting sweet cigarette cards or stamps, he wanted to have the best collection and he usually did, and would go looking to make up gaps in his collection with an aggressive determination. Anyone who tried to rival him in any pursuit or pastime he would find some way to put down or deride. And he was very good at mockery, teasing and insults and provocation. He was, indeed, the perfect exponent of mental bullying which Teddy Eldin so roundly condemned, and yet Teddy Eldin seemed completely unaware of it, or overlooked it, because Jakeman had a jokey, persuasive, genial way with him.

As top dog, he was always at the fore with both regular schoolboy pursuits and the latest crazes. Most classrooms were lodged in Penly Grange's converted quadrangular stable block, the 'quad'. Though we were not allowed on the grassy patch at the centre of the quad, we were allowed to play round its outer circle and this had become the main area for games such as marbles and the racing of dinky toy cars. The racing of dinky toy cars was a passion for many of us for a year or two. Some spent hours polishing their cars and lubricating the wheels to enhance their performance.

Racing a dinky car was a manual skill and required, in particular, strength of wrist and forearm. With a pushing, thrusting motion of your hand and arm, you propelled your dinky car along the asphalt ground round the circle of grass with as much force as possible. Whoever got his car round the quad first would win, though quite often you would race over several laps to spin out the race, since it didn't take long to get round the quad just once if you had a good car and could direct it accurately.

Apart from your own strength and skill, a lot depended on the car you were racing too. I remember three makes of dinky car in particular: the Maserati, the Ferrari and the Hillman. I liked the look and feel of the Hillman best and always wanted to race it, and my next favourite was the Ferrari, but for sheer speed, the red Maserati (it's always red in my mind) was the best with its low-slung design and spread out wheel base, though it was the least attractive in looks, I thought. Jakeman, of course, had a Maserati and would invariably win his races, never failing to pour scorn on my green Hillman which I stuck to out of pure sentiment, though it wasn't very streamlined and never won a race.

When yo-yos were all the rage, Jakeman had the most sophisticated

118

(coloured hardened plastic rather than tin, with a silky cord rather than an ordinary piece of string) and could do the slickest things with it. I was happy enough just getting the yo-yo to go straight up and down for awhile and maybe passing it over the back of my hand a couple of times. Jakeman would get his yo-yo to go between his legs and up over his shoulders; then he would throw it out horizontally and whisk it round in a circle like a lasso. His greatest skill, which I could never master, was to keep the yo-yo going, though looking motionless, an inch from the ground, and then get it to shoot up his leg and over his arm and back to the ground as if it were a live creature. That was impressive, I have to say.

During the conker season he always seemed to have the conker with the highest score, a ridiculously high score which no one could hope to match and which took the fun out of trying to improve your conker score because whatever you achieved it would be way below his total. Moreover, if you did build up a good score, he would come and defeat your conker in some sneaky way and then claim your score and add it to his already grotesquely overblown total. His alleged totals for his conkers would reach figures like 870 or 960. According to the broadly accepted methods of building conker scores, he might genuinely have reached the totals he claimed, but it was the conkers he used and his ways of winning that were dubious.

When you displayed your nice, round, shiny brown conker for a conker contest, sometimes dulled a little in sheen through having been soaked in vinegar to toughen it, but still looking very much like a conker, he would produce a small, shrivelled thing on a piece of string and declare it to be a champion conker with a massive score which could take on and defeat all-comers. Though its boasted victories were not so easy to credit because it was so small, it was certainly possible to believe the so-called conker was invincible. Its miniscule size made it extremely difficult to hit and, furthermore, it looked and felt more like a jagged pebble from the beach or a lump of grit than a conker.

Jakeman, and indeed others, also had tricks for destroying rival conkers. One was to draw you near to a wall for a conker contest and smash your conker by hitting it against the wall, or, if it was your turn to hit his conker, then he would move it slightly to one side so that you would miss and hit the wall behind. Moving your conker wasn't allowed and the rule was that the striker had another go if this happened but that wasn't much good if your conker was in pieces on the ground.

When you got wise to this ploy of Jakeman's and insisted on conducting your conker battles in the open, then he had another underhand device to eliminate your conker. That was to miss your conker when supposedly trying to strike it but manage to wrap the string of his conker round yours then pull it away sharply with a downward tug so that your conker was torn off its string. Once acquainted with these devious methods and also his habit of searching out and competing mainly with those who already had good scores, it became possible to believe that he really had accumulated an enormous tally for his so-called conker.

Other crazes and pursuits which Jakeman was determined to dominate included cockroach collecting and the fad for mini tanks made out of cotton reels. I don't know who started the cockroach craze but one summer some boy had shown off his captured cockroach in a tobacco tin to a few friends. To keep it alive, he was feeding it on beech leaves and had punched holes in the tin's lid to give the cockroach air. Soon everyone wanted a pet cockroach and started doing the same thing. It became competitive. There was kudos gained in finding large cockroaches and putting them in large tins with plenty of leaves and keeping them there the longest. Not surprisingly, Jakeman managed to acquire the largest specimens and the longest survivors (he claimed). He would look at your specimens and belittle them by revealing his. "Is that all you've got?" he would say sneeringly. "Look at this!" and then with a flourish he would produce a tin out of his pocket and display his superior cockroach, with the same ostentation he exhibited when potting a ball in snooker or smashing a winner in table tennis.

The mini tanks were great little homemade contraptions and almost anyone could make one. All you needed was a used cotton reel, a match stick or two, a piece of candle wax and a rubber band. You then constructed a miniature, self-moving machine: the kinetic energy was supplied by the rubber band unwinding. Jakeman's tank was more impressive than most but even he couldn't match Spilwell's. Spilwell produced an enormous specimen, using a bigger drum than a cotton reel for his tank, which towered over other mini tanks and climbed up slopes twice as fast as all of them. In this particular area of prowess Jakeman had to concede he was not the best, but losing out to Spilwell didn't seem to bother him, no doubt because everyone regarded Spilwell as something of a freak against whom it was unnecessary or pointless to measure yourself.

I have said that Jakeman was good at mockery, teasing and insults, and I used the word 'good' advisedly. He had a definite talent for 'taking the mickey'; he made fun of people with natural ease, picking out and pinpointing distinctive characteristics or physical mannerisms in other boys with a telling phrase or lampoon. His mimicry or 'skitting' was not very subtle but he had an undoubted knack for inventing nicknames for people which caught on. Some of these nicknames were a little obvious. 'Flab Man' or

'Porky' for fat boys; 'Scraggs' or 'Skin Bag' for thin boys; 'Wooden Top' (after the TV programme The Wooden Tops) for boys not noted for their intelligence. I didn't think much of my nickname from Jakeman, though I suppose it had a clever element to it. Rigby Smith hated his nickname, though I didn't think it so bad really or inappropriate.

Jakeman called me 'Mouse'. The clever bit about this nickname was that my surname was Moss so it was simply a play on words. However, in so far as it suggested I was small and timid I didn't think it was so good. All right, I was a bit on the small side but no smaller than some boys, nor was I a lot shyer than most, though obviously I didn't have the same amount of confidence as Rigby Smith, Rickmack or Porter, or someone like Westford who became Captain of School. So I wasn't very happy with the name Mouse but I suppose it was preferable to being called Timothy, my first name, rather than Tim. I didn't mind Tim, I quite liked Tim, but I hated Timothy and I always dreaded the possibility of being called Timothy at school. I was relieved when I realised that it wouldn't happen at Penly Grange for Jakeman's nicknames always stuck so henceforth I would be known as Mouse and nothing else. In the end I got used to it.

Rigby Smith never got used to his nickname. Jakeman called him 'Berry' and it was soon taken up by others. Eventually many of the teaching staff were using it too; Mr Bracken, for instance, used it. I remember Rigby Smith protesting to me:

"Berry! It's a stupid nickname. It's got nothing to do with me. No connection with my name or what I'm like."

" Well," I said, "you are dark-skinned, a bit, and they do say 'brown as a berry', don't they?"

"I'm not as dark-skinned as Loretti and, anyway, 'brown as a berry' is daft! Have you ever seen a *brown* berry? Berries are red or black or green or yellow, or blue, even, but how many *brown* berries have you seen?"

I don't know why the supposed meaninglessness of his nickname should have irritated him so much because in itself it was an innocuous name with no pejorative connotations that I could see. I think, though, he simply resented the fact that everyone called him by a name that Jakeman had coined and when Jakeman used it there was always a note of derision in his voice.

We both agreed, however (somewhat reluctantly), that some of Jakeman's other nicknames were very apt and in one or two cases were quite brilliant. Although Mr Swales was called 'Slasher' by the senior boys, Jakeman called him 'Bristles'. This suited admirably his stubby moustache and his prickly character. Silcock, Jakeman dubbed 'Spiky' on account of his hair, some of which stood up stalk-like on his head; Spiky Silcock also made a catchy alliterative phrase. A boy called Trelford, a year older than us, who was very tall with thin spindly legs, Jakeman named 'Stilts' which was visually spot on.

Perhaps his most humorous and creative nicknames were those he coined for Sledge, a boy in his own form, and Parker in ours. Sledge was a round, heavily-built boy who walked with a slow, rolling gait. Jakeman did not dub him 'hammer' (as in sledgehammer) as some of the staff did. Much more subtly he called him 'Sludge'; with just one change of letter to his name capturing him physically quite perfectly. Parker was the form swot, the biggest brain in our form. He had a small body and quite a big head and Jakeman called him 'The Mekon' from the Dan Dare strip in the Eagle comic. The green-coloured Mekon was Dan Dare's arch enemy. He had a grotesquely large head and small body; he floated ten feet above the ground on a small seat, and he was an evil genius. As a caricature of Parker's appearance and superior intelligence, 'The Mekon' was a truly inspired nickname.

Yes, Jakeman had a way with words and he also had a way with people, a certain power over them, borne of his immense self-confidence and strong self-assertiveness. Most of us belonged to some gang or another, it was just another form of play, but he was certainly in charge of, or manipulated, the strongest and most intimidating of them.

When there was a half holiday and an opportunity to go in the woods, it was almost standard practice, at one time, to join a gang and have a mud-ball slinging contest against another gang or try to ambush them. I remember a gang of slightly older boys than us, who called themselves the XR gang and who would waylay smaller boys in the woods, carrying out mock kidnappings and holding them in their HQ until ransomed. The XR gang were a fairly benign bunch, on the whole, who treated the gang warfare in the woods as a make-believe game, not a lot different from Cowboys and Indians or Cops and Robbers.

Notwithstanding the essential innocuousness of most gang conflict, however, some of the gangs of older, bigger boys did sometimes go too far and began frightening the younger, smaller boys. Jakeman was implicated by hearsay in this sort of thing but what exactly he was doing wasn't clear; nor was his precise relationship with the XR gang, though some of his mates were in it. There were stories circulating of the XR gang holding younger boys against the electric fence on the west side of the woods and tying them to trees. Half these stories were made up but eventually Teddy Eldin got wind of them and decided to have a crackdown on gangs and gang leaders.

He summoned certain suspects to his study and meted out canings and dire warnings to them and then told us all about his tough action one day in the dining room after lunch. He gave the names of the boys he alleged were the ringleaders of a bullying gang. I remember his use of the word *ring* leader because it made it all sound so sinister and yet it was so inappropriate for the two boys he cited – Crawford and Rook. Though Crawford and Rook were large boys who did bully in a hamfisted sort of way, they didn't warrant the name 'leader' and certainly not 'ringleader'. If they had been bullying or pushing younger boys around, and if their behaviour had been orchestrated in any way, then we knew Jakeman would have been calling the shots: he was the true leader, their mastermind. Yet Teddy Eldin did not mention Jakeman. He had not been hauled in, he had not been caned, and, as far as we knew he had not even been warned.

So Jakeman, highly crafty and influential in the various ways I have described, had something of T.S. Eliot's *Macavity: the Mystery Cat* about him. Whenever the evil deed took place he wasn't there and he always had an alibi, yet he controlled the 'operations' of all the criminal cats. He was the 'Napoleon of Crime'!

Jakeman and Rigby Smith

There was usually tension and rivalry between Jakeman and Rigby Smith, and for several reasons. I have said that Jakeman liked to be top dog in everything and described how he *was* in many ways but, in fact, in one or two things Rigby Smith matched or even bettered him. Jakeman ruled the roost in snooker and billiards but Rigby Smith could give him a very good game of table tennis and sometimes beat him and without the advantage of Jakeman's superior, sponge-thickened table tennis bat. Being older than Rigby Smith, Jakeman was in the main school teams before him and gained success sooner than him but Rigby Smith could run faster and was way ahead in track events in athletics and cross-country running. Rigby Smith could also get to the snooker table first, through being fleet of foot, though that didn't do him much good for reasons given earlier.

Academically, in schoolwork, there was no contest. Rigby Smith was always in the top stream and was in the scholarship form in the last year; Jakeman only did the Common Entrance exams for Marby College. It's difficult to say whether Jakeman was really bothered about this, in itself. There was a tendency for boys who were good at sport but not work to dismiss the brainy boys as swots and convince themselves that the real glory was gained through sporting achievement; certainly being good at sport brought you popularity from the other boys and plenty of praise from the teaching staff too who liked to see the school's prestige being raised by successful sporting performances. Jakeman may well have been unhappy that Rigby Smith was successful at both work and sport – though he wasn't the only one who was good at both – but something he would have found even harder to take was the fact that Rigby Smith was better than him at chess too.

Chess was not regarded as just the preserve of the intellectual and the academically bright. Most boys liked to play chess and the chess sets and boards provided by the school were in great demand; it was one of the most popular board games. Some had their own chess sets and quite a few carried small 'travelling' chess sets around with them and would bring them out and challenge anyone to a game before a lesson, perhaps, or when waiting in a tuck shop queue. It was one of the ways in which boys not regarded as academically gifted could prove they were nevertheless clever, mentally adept; indeed our chess team included two boys at least who were very good chess players yet who were not in the scholarship form. Jakeman, I know, would like to have been top dog at chess; he would like to have been able to beat Rigby Smith in particular. I can understand that. I tried really hard to beat him myself but normally failed. The only consolation was that nobody could beat Rigby Smith at chess, not even Parker. Rigby Smith was a slow player but he invariably came out on top, both in internal school tournaments and in matches against other schools.

Whatever Jakeman thought of Rigby Smith's intellectual prowess compared with his, and the extent to which it troubled him, he was more discomforted, I think, by a certain quality in Rigby Smith's character or temperament than he was by his mental abilities. Rigby Smith was his own man, he went his own way (except that he was influenced unduly by Nevan at times but that's another story). He refused to have anything to do with Jakeman's gang, though Rook and Crawford wanted him to join them, and he even had a gang of his own of sorts, as I've already mentioned, which I was a member of, naturally. Rigby Smith's gang, which was no more than a few boys who tagged along with Rigby Smith when he went into the woods looking for mock battles and the odd skirmish or two with the XR gang, was no threat to Jakeman and his crew but Jakeman didn't like to think there was a group of boys he didn't control, that they were *any* boys following somebody else. At root, it was Rigby Smith's independence, his freelance air that Jakeman found was the real challenge to him.

For his part, Rigby Smith didn't like Jakeman's commandeering of the snooker table, his showing off in all games, recreations or pursuits, and his generally bossy and boastful manner. Above all, he was irritated by Jakeman's continual scoffing and his use of that nickname 'Berry' to spearhead his taunts. Jakeman would frequently approach us with that provocative grin of his and ask quite unnecessarily,

"What yuh doing, Berry?" As I've commented already, the name Berry seemed, to me, quite inoffensive but Jakeman always managed to make it sound like an insult and Rigby Smith always took it as such. Jakeman would then go on to find something about Rigby Smith to disparage, such as how he'd tied his shoelaces, wore his tie or combed his hair.

In this context something else should be mentioned which became a source of rivalry between them, for a time, certainly as far as Jakeman was concerned. It was something that both of them would probably be embarrassed to admit to today, and even then they might not have been keen to acknowledge, because it boiled down to pure vanity. Vanity is for girls not boys, surely. (Or used to be).

Jakeman and Rigby Smith both cared a lot about their hair. Their hair*style*, to be more precise. In the 1950s (and beyond) the fashion for rock and film stars was to have as high a wave of hair as possible at the front, with the rest of the hair swept back smooth and flowingly over the top and sides of the head. Our pop idols were Elvis Presley, Marty Wilde and later Cliff Richard. They all had hair styles like this. Of course you usually needed brylcreem to keep the hair in place but if you trained it you could eventually get it to stand up in a smooth wave without the use of haircream, with just a hair spray or a little water.

Jakeman was constantly whipping his comb out of his pocket and slicking back his hair over the top and at the sides and shaping the wave at the front of his head with his hand. He did it for only a few seconds at a time and managed to achieve an impressively high wave but he did need to keep combing it to keep it in place. The trouble for him was that Rigby Smith spent ages, at home, *brushing* his hair in front of the mirror and he eventually achieved a higher wave than Jakeman's and one that stayed in place better and with less maintenance in public.

I must say, I thought that Rigby Smith was better looking than Jakeman, anyway. You might have called him handsome, and Jakeman might have been jealous of his looks. I can't be sure of that but you could tell Jakeman was jealous of his amazing wave; it became clear when Jakeman persisted in mocking Rigby Smith's hair with a string of derogatory remarks. Since Rigby Smith's hairstyle was basically a better version of Jakeman's own hair style, his gibes were hollow and ineffectual and didn't bother Rigby Smith in themselves, but I knew that, as ever, Jakeman's reiteration of his nickname nagged away at him. I remember 'an exchange of views' between Jakeman and Rigby Smith over their hair which went something like this:

Jakeman: What yuh doing, Berry? What's that stuff stacked up on the top of your head? Have you got nowhere to put it, Berry? [*Rigby Smith, trying to stay calm, remains silent*]. Have you looked at your head in the mirror today? Did it crack?

Rigby Smith: At least my head can be *seen* in the mirror. There isn't a mirror big enough for yours.

Jakeman: Oooh, what a cutting comment, Berry! Very cutting! Pity you can't cut your hair with it!

Rigby Smith: Pity you have to keep *combing* yours, Jakeman. Let's face it, you're just jealous!

Jakeman: Jealous, jealous! Jealous of your hair! It's not real. It's joke hair. What's it for? Is it some kind of fly catcher?

Rigby Smith: (*Looking narrowly at Jakeman*) No. I don't catch flies, I swat them!

Jakeman: Talking big, are we, Berry? Can you *act* big? I doubt it.

Rigby Smith wouldn't be drawn into a fight. For some reason he was holding back. I didn't think he was afraid of Jakeman (or not much), so I didn't know why he was holding back, but it was obvious that sooner or later there had to be a showdown between them. Jakeman was itching to prove he was better that Rigby Smith, stronger at the very least, and Rigby Smith wanted to shut Jakeman up and get him off his back. I wanted Rigby Smith to take Jakeman down a peg or two. But could he do it? I wasn't sure.

The tension and animosity between them was building all the time; Jakeman stepping up his provocations and Rigby Smith ready to snap. I was very uneasy about this inevitable fight because I had no idea who would win nor how it might affect the rest of us, me in particular.

Rigby Smith

Rigby Smith (forenamed Martin George) was the first boy I remember meeting at Penly Grange, along with Bookworm Beddoes. It was Mrs Leyton who, having led me through the archway into the quad on my first day, had pointed out my classroom to me at the far end of the quad, near the gym/assembly room, and had told me to go in and 'make friends with the boys in there'. It must have been during the lunch break. I don't know what I'd been doing in the morning; perhaps being shown round the rest of the school. I walked with trepidation into the indicated form room, thinking it extremely unlikely I would make any friends, just hoping I would be accepted. I was, in fact, trembling, shaking all over and feeling sick with apprehension.

I was just eight years old. Rigby Smith, as I was to learn, had started at Penly Grange when he was seven, at the beginning of the school year. He had already been there for two terms and had an elder brother there called James. He had friends, was now established in the school, and was doing well.

It was very different for me. I had come from a local authority primary school, a mixed school therefore, and I had no idea what a private all boys' school would be like. I was excited by the prospect of attending an all boys' school but afraid at the same time. I was a complete stranger and I had no brother or friend at Penly Grange. I had heard that the teachers would be strict and that you had to learn Latin and French. That was daunting. It was the summer term and I was also worried about joining Penly Grange so late in the school year and being behind all the other boys in my form. On top of that, I was going to be a day boy in a boarding school. I had been told there weren't very many day boys in the school so I was a bit anxious about being different from the majority of boys in the school. Above all, I felt the panic and isolation of *not knowing anyone*.

Things were soon to change but I had no idea of that when I ventured into N3's classroom for the first time. There were only two boys in the classroom, as it happened. They were sitting at desks at the far end of the room, one behind the other, but were turned to face each other, and appeared to be rehearsing some lines together. In fact, they were revising for a test on the conjugation of the verb amo, to love, as I understood later: the future and imperfect tenses.

'*Amabo, amabis, amabit, amabimis, amabitis, amabunt!*' is what I heard, and then, '*amabam, amabas, amabat, amabamus, amabatis, amabant!*' Then they repeated the lines in turn. I guessed it was Latin; I didn't think it was French. I noticed that the boy in front, who was the darker of the two, was the more animated. He was waving his arms up and down as he spoke as if he were conducting a piece of music, and he appeared to be having great fun. He broke off his recitation when he caught sight of me, and the other boy, a light-haired, pasty-faced boy, stopped too, and they both looked at me. I thought I must say something so I stammered, "Mrs Leyton told me to come in here," but obviously too quietly.

"What?" said the darker boy, "I didn't catch that. Are you new?" Is it so obvious, I thought, feeling even more like a fish out of water. Is it my school uniform? Does it look right? Though I don't know how I could possibly have thought it wouldn't be obvious I was new.

Fortunately, the boy didn't wait for an answer but started to do the talking. "You'll love it here," he said, giving me a grin I could only describe as wicked and ironic, "especially if you like Latin. Have you done any Latin?" I shook my head. "Well, it's not too bad, is it, Beddoes?" he remarked, involving the other boy in the conversation.

"It's not bad," replied Beddoes, "but it gets a bit boring at times."

"That's Beddoes," said the dark, brown-eyed boy. "We call him Bookworm Beddoes because he's always reading books. All the time."

"And that's Rigby Smith," said Beddoes – this was before Rigby Smith got his nickname 'Berry' – "and he's the form swot. He's always top of the form."

"I am top of the form but I'm not a swot!" Rigby Smith rejoined. "I do other things. Not like you: you've always got your nose stuck in book. Never do Games until you're forced to, do you?" He turned to me. "Do you like Games?"

"Yes," I said, and meant it, though I didn't know what games he had in mind.

"And what Group are you in?" Rigby Smith enquired.

"I think it's G Group," I said, speaking a little more loudly now, I thought.

"That's a pity, I'm in E Group."

Rigby Smith sounded disappointed as if he *wanted* me to be in the same Group as him and my spirits rose accordingly. He had already put me more at ease by turning attention from me as new boy to Beddoes, Bookworm Beddoes. I don't suppose he had done it deliberately but, in any event, things got even better for me when I answered his next question.

"And are you a day boy or a boarder?"

"A day boy," I replied, a little fearfully. But I needn't have worried. As far as Rigby Smith was concerned it was the right answer.

"Super!" he enthused. "You're one of us!" But he wasn't referring to himself and Beddoes, for Beddoes moaned and put his head on his desk lid in mock agony, then raised it and groaned,

"Not another day boy. What do you want to be a day boy for?" (It certainly was an exaggerated, disproportionate response because out of a school of 120 boys there were only about 20 day boys, so they made up only a sixth of the school's population; one more was hardly going to swell the ranks of the day boys).

"Day boys are much better than boarders and you know it!" Rigby Smith retorted. And an argument started between Beddoes and Rigby Smith, Beddoes extolling the advantages of boarding school life and how it helped you to make friends and grow up quicker – I don't know where he got that one from – and what fun it was, pillow fights and things, and how you didn't have to waste time travelling each day; and Rigby Smith was going on about how day boys could do lots more things at home in the evening and what fun it was travelling to school each day. The sad thing about Beddoes's declared point of view, as I learnt later, was that he wasn't really happy as a boarder. He was a bit of a loner and didn't mix well with the crowd, and life probably *would* have been better for him as a day boy. I don't know, though, because I never learnt what his home circumstances were. He left Penly Grange early, before he was twelve.

All that really mattered to me at the time, anyway, and well into the future, was Rigby Smith's wonderfully affirming words "You're one of us!" And when I told him my name – Tim Moss – he didn't bat an eyelid; he didn't snigger or make any jokes about moss or laugh about the fact that my full Christian name was Timothy, he just told me everyone would call me Moss, which I expected would happen. Later on, when we'd been friends for quite awhile he started to call me Tim and I called him Martin but this was usually at home not school. By then, though, Jakeman had attached his nicknames to us which stuck and which we sometimes used ourselves, when we didn't think about it, because everyone else did at school.

My fears about being behind the rest of the form did turn out to be justified for a time. I had a lot of catching up to do, especially in Latin and French. However, the teachers were quite sympathetic, at least at first, and after my second or third Latin lesson when I was still clearly struggling, Rigby Smith said to me, "It's really not that difficult, you know. I'll help you learn. We'll revise for tests together, like you saw me and Beddoes doing when you first came in. It'll be fine, you'll see!"

So Rigby Smith took me under his wing for some schoolwork, as well as keeping a general eye on me and getting me in with other day boys, like Barley, Scales and Edland. Soon we were sharing our marbles – our best marbles – and then it was sweet cigarette cards. By another stroke of good fortune, I was moved sometime during my first term from G Group into E Group, so I was then in the same Group as well as the same form as Rigby

Smith. (I was moved into E Group probably because I was a day boy and E Group tended to take the day boys).

As far as work went, Rigby Smith used to encourage me by saying that I'd soon catch him up and certainly I did make very good progress once I'd settled in, and I got into the top four in the form but I never did catch him up in Latin, French, English and History. I eventually overhauled him in Maths because although he was pretty good at arithmetic and algebra, he didn't find geometry so easy and when we started to do geometry his marks fell below mine. Science was another subject I did better at than him, though we didn't do it much at first. Geography was a subject he found boring and he didn't try very hard in it so I used to end up, as rule, with better marks than him in Geography too. As I closed the gap on him, we developed a friendly rivalry but it remained friendly because he never felt his pre-eminence in the classroom was seriously threatened by me. He remained top of the form overall by some margin. That was until Parker entered the school about four terms later.

Rigby Smith led the way for me in many other school things too: some of them educationally, artistically or culturally worthy, some of them of more dubious worth, though I didn't think so at the time. From him I learnt, or was introduced to, such skills as pea shooting, using a water pistol, flicking pellets with a ruler, and making and throwing paper darts. Actually he wasn't very good at making paper darts, only at throwing them. I remember he said to me once when we were having a dart fight with some other boys in the form, "Look, why don't you just make the darts, and I'll throw them, I can throw better that you!" I couldn't agree to that. I didn't mind playing second fiddle to him on some occasions, especially if we did any close contact physical fighting, but I wasn't going to let him have all the fun in a paper dart fight. Actually, I got quite good at dart throwing and at using a pea shooter too. He became quite impressed with me.

I remember we spent a lot of breaks playing tag – we called it 'tig' – where one person is 'on' and has to chase the others. Being a very fast runner Rigby Smith always did well in tag and was always keen to initiate a game when it was 'every man for himself' tag, but I came to prefer chain tag where once you were 'caught', by being touched by whoever was 'on', you joined hands with the others who had been caught and swept across the playground in a line. If there were enough boys playing the game you could eventually cover the entire playground so that it was almost impossible to evade being caught. However, you were supposed to keep the line together and not relinquish your grip on the next person's hand in the line so that only the people at the end of the line could make the required touch. This meant that although the chain could surround you, you could escape by ducking under the arms of those who didn't have a hand free. They could try to prevent you of course by lowering their arms but if you were on the small side it was easier to burrow under the lowered arms. I got quite good at evading capture in chain tag and consequently came to like it. I think I was better at it than Rigby Smith, in fact. I suppose I remember the chain tag mainly for that reason for we played plenty of other games which I remember less well. There was really nothing else I was better at than him. Except swimming.

Yes, I was better at swimming than him (or was more successful at swimming than him, anyway, because he didn't try very hard at it). I got the Master's Certificate for swimming, for which you had to swim about two miles, dive for bricks on the swimming pool floor, swim under water for the length of the pool and perform various tasks in the water fully clothed. Rigby Smith didn't care much for swimming and only got the Senior Certificate which entailed less demanding swimming feats. However, in all other sports he outstripped me completely; but then he was always more gifted than me in sport and games and, indeed, more gifted than most, eventually winning the Best Sportsman of the Year award in his final year.

As well as being good at schoolwork and sport, also chess, which he taught me to play, incidentally, Rigby Smith had other interests which he pursued with almost equal enthusiasm. Drama, for instance, that is to say, acting in plays: we didn't have drama lessons as such at Penly Grange, separate from English lessons. He liked to perform in plays whenever he got the chance and was a very confident and competent actor. We had form plays, Scout plays and school plays. He took part eagerly in all of them. Being a day boy, he did well to get principal roles in school plays because many school play rehearsals occurred in the evening after supper which meant he either had to stay very late at school or miss the evening rehearsals and work harder in the rehearsals he could attend.

I liked to be involved in play productions too but never wanted a big part so I didn't normally envy him his leading roles. The only plays or shows I can now remember doing were a Dick Turpin one, an evening of sketches and monologues, and the last scene of *Hamlet*. Rigby Smith played the title role in Dick Turpin and I played a walk-on part, an ostler or stable hand. Although Rigby Smith had most of the lines, naturally, the only line I can remember is the one *I* had about halfway through. I had to come rushing on and say, "He's gone, my lord, and the horse has gone from the stable!" In one performance I tripped over as I was saying my line and everyone burst out laughing. Thorpe said it was hilarious the way I went sprawling immediately after saying, "He's gone!" I could see the comedy in that but Rickmack commented dryly that no one had actually heard me say the line, they'd only laughed because I fell over. He called it 'banana skin' humour; all audiences were like that, he said. I daresay he was right.

The only other thing I remember about the 'Dick Turpin' play (I don't remember its title) is that Dick Turpin's sweetheart, called something like Esmerelda, was played by Rigby Smith's younger brother Colin. That was both odd and amusing, especially if you'd seen them quarrelling as I had! In the sketches and monologues show, Rigby Smith did a Macbeth send-up. The speech he was trying to burlesque was Macbeth's soliloquy, "Is this a dagger which I see before me /The handle toward my hand? Come let me clutch thee ..." I remember him standing on a chair and making mock grabbing movements around a dangling light bulb. We thought it was very funny and it may have been (unlikely, though, in all honesty). Fortunately, there were no video recordings in those days and there is no record of the performance to dispel any illusions we might have had about it being a marvellous piece of comedy.

Rigby Smith was prominent also in the last scene of *Hamlet* which I took part in too, at different levels, you might say. I have already mentioned in an earlier chapter how Rickmack and I disrupted one rehearsal by making the dead bodies on the stage come alive with laughter. Since I was merely playing one of Fortinbras's captains in the play, coming on only at the very end of the scene, I was able to create a humorous effect off stage while waiting to come on. But it wasn't just a silly distraction from the play. Well, it was silly and it was effectively a distraction from the *rehearsal* but it was related to the play, to Horatio's words: 'Now cracks a noble heart'. I emphasise this because although I was a bit bored with not being on stage when all the action was happening, I did feel I had some involvement in the scene before I came on because I had helped with the making of the two swords used in the duel between Hamlet and Laertes, and I had watched the two actors in all their fight rehearsals. Furthermore, I did find the death of Hamlet very moving.

Rigby Smith was playing the part of Hamlet, and Wainstone was Laertes. Carrow, who was directing, had decided to use swords made out of bamboo which we, the cast, would make. Somebody cut two bamboo sticks to the right length and then they had to be painted with silver paint to give them the look of steel. I offered to paint Rigby Smith's sword blade for him and make a protective guard for his hand. I ended up doing a protective guard for Wainstone too after a blow from Rigby Smith in rehearsal slid off Wainstone's blade and rapped him on the fingers. I remember him shaking his injured hand in agony and swearing uncontrollably.

Admittedly, from a purist point of view, it was a bit silly painting the bamboo swords silver because they were so obviously made of wood and the sword fight was far removed from the rapier fencing contest that Shakespeare clearly had in mind. Instead of a thin metallic sound of rapiers clashing and a light steely rattling, you had the much louder *thwack*, *thwack*, *thwack* of bamboo on bamboo. Be that as it may, the decision made to conduct the fight more like a medieval sword fight with swiping, sweeping, slicing actions and cross blows rather than jabs and lunges, as in a fencing match, enabled the fighting to be much more uninhibited and no eye guards were needed and other restrictive safety measures. Well, they weren't thought necessary then; no doubt the Health and Safety people of today wouldn't have agreed and would probably have closed the show down.

Rigby Smith and Wainstone certainly fought in an unbridled way. They practised their sword fight for hours in the gym, mainly in the lunch hour. Although they had to fight on the stage at one end of the gym for the performance, they rehearsed in the whole of the gym. I remember watching them hammering away at each other up and down and across the gym, using all the available space. They evidently loved every minute of it and when I saw what fun they were having I really did feel envious of them playing the parts of Hamlet and Laertes. It did seem unfair that those two alone should get to do all the fighting in the play. Even when I came on as a soldier I didn't do any fighting, I just stood there for awhile doing absolutely nothing while Fortinbras rounded off the play with some very formal, ponderous lines. It was all very static. I don't remember even carrying Hamlet off stage: that would have been something.

Still, I had played my part in making the swords and I was pleased that Rigby Smith was playing Hamlet. It seemed fitting somehow, and Hamlet's death became later, in retrospect, a sort of swan song, or epitaph, for our Penly Grange days and our special friendship. Despite my attempts to make comedy out of tragedy by that backstage prank on Horatio's line, 'Now cracks a noble heart', I have never forgotten the elegiac words which follow, and I can still see, in my mind's eye, grave, dark-skinned Loretti, as Horatio, speaking those words over Rigby Smith's, the dead Hamlet's, body:

"Good night, sweet prince, and flights of angels sing thee to thy rest."

The Woods

Rigby Smith and I loved the woods at Penly Grange equally, though I might qualify that statement by saying that I think he loved them more than me at first and I loved them more than him towards the end of our time at Penly Grange. There were many good things about the woods, which we shared, and which overlapped and reinforced each other.

133

At ordinary times, the school woods were out of bounds so when we were allowed in them it always felt like a treat, a real privilege. We were allowed in the woods for Cubs and Scouts, and on half days or special 'merit' half day holidays. In Cubs we mostly played games in the woods, but in Scouts we learnt serious woodcraft as well as playing games. We learnt how to lay a trail and how to track; how to construct and light fires and cook; how to dig and chop; how to use string and rope to make gadgets and, when we were older, how to make proper shelters. Nearly all of these involved trees, or wood or leaves from the trees, or woodland plants. We used twigs to make arrow shapes on the ground when leaving a trail, or snapped a thin branch of a tree to indicate the route we had taken; we collected wood of various thicknesses and sizes for our fire, discriminating between kindling wood and the more solid and longer burning wood, and learning which types of wood burned best; we wielded handaxes, later felling axes, on the cuttable wood, learning how to split wood vertically as well as horizontally, and we sharpened the ends of thicker, taller sticks with our Scout knives to make stakes for posts, and whittled sticks down or skinned them, sometimes for cooking or other purposes, sometimes just for fun: to see how far we could pare them down or how smooth we could make them.

Stick whittling or skinning was a fairly harmless activity but less creditable was the practice of hacking bark off trees which we sometimes indulged in, in our early Scouting days, together with attempting to throw our Scout knives into tree trunks, practices which would be condemned today as ecological vandalism. But so would some of our other practices, such as breaking and hewing down branches with foliage for camping or other outdoor pursuits, and creating open camp fires, including digging square turfs out of the ground first to make an earthy hollow to set them in: all perfectly acceptable back in the 1950s, provided the trees weren't saplings or in copses, the fires were supervised and kept under control, we didn't make a mess, and we cleared up afterwards.

We experienced our greatest pleasure in the handling of wood and being close to trees, bushes and leaves, when we were making dens, sometimes as part of our Scouting activities, sometimes done separately from Scouts on our own. Actually, when done separately from Cubs or Scouts, it wasn't usually a matter of building dens but of discovering places where we could hide in comfort. We would burrow into a piece of dense undergrowth where no one else had been or was likely to go, and eventually find a slightly more open space, usually close to a tree, clear a little more space for two or three people to move around a bit yet stay hidden, cover our tracks, and then regard our hiding place as our secret den.

The feeling of being separate from the rest of the world, except for one or two friends, safe and cocooned, and in control, because it was our own place which no one knew about (so it seemed) was a true joy. And, yes, there was something else: with the green foliage and branches of the trees around and above us and the dead leaves and soil beneath us with their earthy smell, as we lay close to the ground in our dens, we did feel very close to nature. I'm not sure whether I would describe it as a spiritual experience, it might have been for Rigby Smith, knowing him, but for me it was simply the thrilling experience of another kind of life, an independent life, a feeling of being a separate individual with my own sensations, free from the social pressures of school life and school rules and the crowd. Not that I shunned collective life. I liked being part of a larger group or community in many ways, Scouts for instance, but I appreciated a little private space too and I liked being with just one or two friends best.

Dens were seldom part of our woodcraft learning, though, even when done in Scouts. They were bound up with our games and it was the games we played in the woods which we enjoyed most of all, together with that sense of freedom we felt when we were in them, whatever we were doing.

There were two broad categories of games in the woods. There were organised games, usually organised by Cub and Scout leaders, and there were our own games on half holidays or merit half holidays which were haphazard, off-the-top-of-our-heads and usually shambolic, especially anything involving gang warfare.

The organised games were mainly 'hide-and-seek' type games, treasure hunts and stalking and capturing games. The most popular game was French and English, which was my favourite too, but Rigby Smith had a particular liking for a Robin Hood and Sheriff of Nottingham game because he had an obsession with Robin Hood.

The French and English game consisted of trying to capture the enemy's flags from their HQ whilst endeavouring to defend your own flags in your own HQ. The flags, perhaps four or five, were normally our Scout neckerchiefs, and they were supposed to be tied loosely round the branches of trees, spread out, and perfectly visible. There were a limited number of Scouts or Cubs who were allowed to defend the flags and they were supposed to keep at a distance of five yards or so from each flag. Obviously, if you stood right by the flag it was impossible for your enemy to dash in and snatch a flag without being touched which would eliminate you from the game, at least for a time. As Rigby Smith was good at hiding and being patient in hiding, like me, and was also very quick, he did well in the French and English. He would creep up on the enemy HQ and wait until the defenders lost concentration, then dash in and snatch a flag or two. Sometimes he would use me as a diversion. I would crack a stick or something (I liked cracking sticks!) and whilst one or two of the enemy were investigating, Rigby Smith would swoop in from the other direction.

He would understandably get annoyed if the enemy didn't play fair: if they tied the neckerchiefs too tightly to the trees or stood too close to the flags. Another thing that annoyed him was when the game was called off before it was finished; he might have been carefully manoeuvring himself into an ideal strike position and his patience would go unrewarded. He would be very angry then for he took all organised games very seriously; mind you, most of us did, though most of us lost interest in a game before Rigby Smith did.

The Robin Hood game was a hunting, hiding and escaping game. It overlapped in Rigby Smith's mind with his own games in the woods which, in turn, merged with the unorganised games we played separately from Cubs and Scouts. These unorganised, usually *dis*organised games, happened at times when anyone was allowed in the woods, and since these times also occurred when there were no school sports or matches being played (certainly when we were younger), any boy was free to get involved. That's when gangs formed and overran the woods, though no one was supposed to tamper with dens or special places used by Cubs or Scouts.

Rigby Smith positively wallowed in the unorganised games because they gave free rein to his imagination and his love of make-believe adventures. I could go along with him in this; in fact, my enjoyment of make-believe play lasted longer than his. He would turn a tussle with the XR gang, in his mind, into a Robin Hood/Sheriff of Nottingham battle. After all, we were in woods, weren't we, and that's where Robin Hood and his merry men lived and thrived.

We all enjoyed ambushes, which invariably took the form of hiding behind trees or in the bushes and then leaping out on the usually *suspecting* enemy with shrieks and waving of arms, holding real or imaginary sticks, water pistols, or catapults (normally useless because the ammunition went wildly wide of the mark or never left the catapult owing to the overstretched elastic snapping). For Rigby Smith, the ambushes we made were nearly always Robin Hood and his outlaws ambushing the Sheriff of Nottingham and his cronies, and if he ever captured one of the Sheriff of Nottingham's men – a real boy in the XR gang or in another gang, or just an imaginary person – he would be taken to our HQ which he called The Major Oak. It didn't really matter a great deal to him if all this was accepted by others because it was all happening in his head anyway. Even so, he did need at least one other person to endorse his Robin Hood fictions and he relied on me to be that person.

Any tree which had a branch you could climb on, preferably a high one, became a look-out post to warn of the approach of the Sheriff of Nottingham's men and the danger of the whereabouts of the Major Oak being discovered. He had this fantasy about one day finding the real Major Oak and also the place where Robin Hood was buried: the spot where Robin Hood, when dying, had requested burial, the spot where Little John's arrow, shot into the air at Robin's command, had landed. He cast me in the role of Will Scarlet (he was Robin Hood of course), telling me I wasn't big enough to be Little John but assuring me Will Scarlet was a very important member of Robin Hood's band. I was quite happy to accept this until Nevan popped up one day and started playing Little John without any apparent objection from Rigby Smith; and Nevan was barely an inch taller than me! I was not pleased.

As I say, I did go along with Rigby Smith's make-believe situations (most of the time), but the Robin Hood stuff was a bit overdone, I thought. I was more enthusiastic about his spying, mystery and secret places make-believe which wasn't Robin Hood centred or tied to any set of characters or stock situations, so you could imagine or invent anything you liked. Rigby Smith loved woodland mysteries, in particular. Whenever he hadn't seen me for awhile, when I'd been absent from school, he would tell me he had discovered some *secrets* in the woods. It was all deliciously vague but not totally vague for he would take me to a certain spot in the woods and point out some hidden place where the secret could be found; fortunately, he would rarely spoil the secret by revealing it to me. That was always going to come later. As part of our imaginary secrets together we would concoct passwords and secret codes. I was quite good at inventing codes, better than him, I think. Sometimes he liked mine and accepted them gladly, sometimes he insisted on using his, but we agreed on our passwords and codes most of the time. We didn't argue much, we got on well.

His most substantial secret, and one which came to acquire a great deal of significance later on in our changing friendship, was his make-believe about a network of tunnels in the woods. I say 'make-believe' but he really did believe it for a time, or seemed to, and he came to convince me of it (almost). It was, after all, based on some external, objective facts, it didn't all come from his head.

There were a number of small craters and narrow pits scattered around the woods, and there was a ditch which ran along part of the north side of the woods at a depth of about four or five feet. Most of the ditch was exposed but where it ended there was a fallen tree across it, overgrown with a wide spreading creeper, and when you dived underneath it you discovered there was a hole in the right hand side of the ditch about two feet from the ground. It didn't penetrate very far into the side of the ditch, no more than a foot but it wasn't difficult to believe, if you wanted to, that it had at one time gone further in, much further in. Although the small craters looked natural they might have been the result of digging, perhaps, and maybe those narrow pits – most of which were overgrown, so you really couldn't tell – were the remains of long trenches. Maybe these trenches had a secret purpose and used to lead somewhere. Maybe they went far deeper and eventually turned into underground tunnels. And maybe these tunnels were all linked and included all the pits in the woods and the ditch with the concealed hole in its side. It was perfectly believable. All it required was a little imagination and Rigby Smith was not lacking in imagination!

According to Rigby Smith, the XR gang knew about one hidden tunnel but didn't know about the rest. He was going to discover all the other tunnels and crack the secret network which he was sure existed. He took me to a couple of the pits which were overgrown with brambles and said he had a strong hunch they led to tunnels deeper down. And he wasn't all talk. Not long after this, he produced a map of the tunnels in the woods which he had worked out from all the 'evidence' and his own intuition.

For a boy not so keen on geography, geometry or drawing, he had done a surprisingly good job. The map was well designed. There were a number of lines criss-crossing diagonally. Each line was a different colour and drawn very neatly and every area of the wood was carefully labelled. He had also drawn on compass bearings. He must have spent some time on it. It was top secret, he told me. He kept it folded in a special little red and green wallet and every so often he would show it to me. One day we would fully investigate the tunnels, he said. But not just yet. When the time was ripe. He said I was the only person who had seen the map or who would ever see it. It was going to be our secret alone. This map consequently bound us together in a new way and became crucially important to our friendship in our last year at Penly Grange. Rather too important to me, as it turned out.

Ghosts and Puppets

Though I was happy to take part in them most of the time, I have to admit that Rigby Smith's make-believe games tended to be too subjective, too Rigby Smith-centred. That was inevitable I suppose. He did, however, manage to find a less self-centred and more socially useful channel for his powers of invention. If that sounds too pretentious, let me put more plainly: he told ghost stories, and wrote plays for puppet shows, for others to listen to, take part in, and watch. And in both cases – ghost stories and puppet plays – he showed some awareness of the material he was working with and his audience; perhaps as much as you could expect from an eleven or twelve year old boy.

I can't remember exactly when he began to tell ghost stories at lunch time to the younger boys on our table. He must have been at least eleven because he began his ghost story telling by repeating the tale of an evil judge which

Bracken had told us in Scouts round the campfire, and we couldn't join the Scouts until we were eleven. Bracken called the story King Rat but I have since learnt its real title is The Judge's House and it's a short story by Bram Stoker, author of Dracula.

The story concerns a young maths scholar who takes up lodgings in an isolated, dilapidated Jacobean house in the country which used to be the home of a malignant judge, notorious for sentencing many to death by hanging. The maths student is preparing for an important maths exam and at first welcomes the isolation of the house because he wants somewhere quiet to study away from people. So, at first, he doesn't object to the rats scurrying around his room, but then a giant rat appears which he can't get rid of and which becomes increasingly threatening. This giant rat, he discovers, comes out of a picture on the wall. The picture is a portrait of the hanging judge who used to live in the house. What is equally sinister and ominous is the fact that the rat sits on the high-backed, carved oak chair in the room, a judge's chair, and casts a baleful look over him.

There is a bell rope in the corner of the room on the right hand side of the fire place, attached to a large alarm bell on the roof. Its purpose, since the house is so isolated, is to call for help from the village some distance away in an emergency. However, the bell rope has an evil history: it's the same rope used to hang the judge's condemned victims, and the menace towards the student intensifies when the giant rat gnaws away a section of it, enough to hang a man. The malevolent rat eventually materialises into the hanging judge himself, dressed in his courtroom robes and seated on the high backed carved oak chair, and, in a moment of sheer terror for the student, the hanging judge places his black sentencing cap on his head. The next day the student is found hanged, swinging from the end of the bell rope.

It's a chilling tale of supernatural metamorphosis that can be drawn out effectively through slowly building up the stages by which the giant rat eventually turns into the hanging judge. Bracken had kept up the suspense well when telling the story by firelight and we hung on his every word. He had the advantage of the night, of course, and the barely known woods around us when he was telling us the story. Rigby Smith was re-telling the tale in familiar school surroundings and in broad daylight. He took his time over it but he still managed to make the story gripping and obviously enjoyed doing it, for he then had a go at re-telling another ghost story he knew. It was one which I think he had heard on the wireless as a play. Interestingly, this story also involved a painting with sinister, supernatural properties, on the wall of an old house. It also involved death by hanging.

The painting in this ghost story was a landscape painting and depicted a bleak moorland scene in north Yorkshire, with only one upright feature, apart from some human figures which were too small to make much impression on the observer of the picture. That single vertical feature was a withered oak tree, on the horizon in the background, which had just one bare, horizontal branch. The story was a sort of time travel story because in the play you learn about the human figures in the painting who lived about two hundred years ago.

One of the characters in the play, living in the present, finds a way of entering the picture and becoming involved in the lives of the people in the painting who are ancestors of his. When he comes back out of the picture and returns to the present, he tells his friend, who has not gone with him, that there is a bitter and unresolved conflict going on in the past which he has become part of. The conflict stems from an unresolved crime, a murder, for which no one has yet been convicted. Despite being warned by his friend not to do so, he is determined to go back into the picture, and into the past, to help resolve the conflict.

But he never returns to the present day and his friend wonders what has happened to him. Is he trapped in the past? One day he is looking at the picture on the wall again and he notices something different about the withered oak tree. There is something dangling from its lone branch. On closer examination, he realises with horror that the object dangling from the branch is, in fact, a person and that that person has been hanged from the end of a rope. He has a horrible conviction that it's his missing friend.

These two stories went down so well with the boys at lunch time that they clamoured for more. In order not to disappoint them and because he obviously enjoyed doing it, he began to make up stories straight out of his head. He would break off at a moment of suspense as the meal came to an end and then pick up the story and continue with it the next day. Usually, though, only if asked to do so and then with affected reluctance. This was a good tactic because it meant he was doing them a favour and made his audience more attentive and appreciative. His slowness to accede to the demands of the younger boys also gave him a little extra time to recall what he'd said the day before and develop his storyline.

Sometimes he'd get the younger boys to remind him where the story had got to, as a sort of memory test for them, which would put the ball back into their court for awhile and give him further thinking space. He made use of me too when his plot stalled or when questioned by one of the boys about an apparent inconsistency in his story. He'd turn to me and say, "Did I tell them about what was happening in the other dungeon all this while?" or "You can explain that, can't you, Mouse?" While I was struggling to cover up for him, producing some ingenious explanation or simply stalling, he would be scanning his brain for a quick twist in the plot to shore up his creaky or contradictory story.

As I remember, his favourite dodge to move the story on when it was going nowhere, or somewhere too predictable, was the sudden introduction of new characters or the invention of added history to the story's background.

"Of course, two hundred years ago," he'd say, 'the Manor House was owned by Sir Richard Tilsley who had died in mysterious circumstances." He would then digress from the main story and hope he might never have to return to it, if he could keep the digression going. Sometimes this worked because the digression became more interesting than the original story and provided him with fresh inspiration. Often the stories became more like shaggy dog's tales: they meandered on and on with constantly delayed resolutions. He did however manage to keep his audience listening and convince them that he did know the ending to the story. Usually.

The Puppet Club

Rigby Smith's written plays for glove puppets were, however, the product of greater creativity than his off-the-cuff verbal ghost stories. They grew out of his formation of a puppet club when he was barely eleven and therefore before his lunch time ghost story telling phase. His puppet club was not a school activity, it was home-based, but several day boys from Penly Grange were in it and one of the things that led him to form the club was the making of glove puppets in Art lessons at school. Mrs Leyton had showed us how to make puppet heads out of papier maché and paint them. Rigby Smith produced, with a fair amount of help from her, the head of a severe, haughty-looking woman, with a tight circular bun of hair on top. I also made a head, with rather less help from Mrs Leyton, which, when painted red and black, looked like the head of a wicked man or devil.

Rigby Smith then acquired some other glove puppets – one or two were given to him and one or two he bought – and then he decided it would be good fun to put on some puppet shows. To present puppet shows he needed a puppet theatre, and his parents got a handyman they knew to make a puppet theatre for him. It consisted of a wooden frame about 5-6 feet high and 4 feet wide, with an inner rectangular frame at the top, about 1 foot high by 4 feet, for the stage area. There was hardboard round three sides of this rectangular performance area and there was an inner ledge at the front of the open section for the placing of props or stage furniture. The rest of the frame, i.e. the part of the frame beneath the rectangular section at the top, was covered by curtain material. Those operating the glove puppets would be concealed behind the curtain material so long as they knelt, or crouched, and kept their heads down.

I suppose we might have made this simple puppet theatre construction ourselves but I'm not sure how precise our measuring and sawing of the wood would have been. We might have done it perhaps after a year or two in the Scouts for we became quite good at making camping gadgets. Well I did, I became quite handy with light tools, such as hand axes, small hammers, saws and chisels. However, we'd only just joined the Scouts when the puppet club began – in fact I might still have been in the Cubs – and I don't think we could have constructed it then by ourselves. Anyway, Rigby Smith, who was never particularly handy (though he was good at making dens and fortifications for our make-believe games), was quite happy to have the puppet theatre made for him; I doubt whether he even considered making it himself. He just wanted to perform puppet shows. Later, he wanted to create the scripts too for his puppet shows.

Rigby Smith knew he'd need other people to put on shows and so he formed the Puppet Club. His members were his two brothers, James and Colin (James, in fact, was only an associate member), Brian Barley, two friends of his who didn't go to Penly Grange – Ray 'Toffee' Denton and Nick Wheeler – Nevan and me. He got each member to pay a voluntary subscription and found them a job to do. Colin Rigby Smith was the secretary, Brian Barley was in charge of the stage, Nick Wheeler of the puppets, Toffee Denton was chief model and prop maker, and Rigby Smith got both Nevan and me to look after the lighting and scenery. This was not a very good idea because we didn't get on very well and disagreed about suitable scenery. When I pointed this out to Rigby Smith, he said he'd asked both of us to cover lights and scenery because Nevan wasn't very reliable and I wasn't always available. He was right on both points.

Nevan didn't seem to me to be all that enthusiastic about the Puppet Club. He took ages to produce any scenery and his subscriptions to the club amounted to little or nothing. I was very keen for the club to succeed (and, incidentally, subscribed as much as I could) but found it difficult to come to all the practices and rehearsals. Everybody else in Rigby Smith's Puppet Club lived either at his house (his brothers) or very near to his home. Toffee Denton lived the furthest away of the others, about a mile, but I lived on the other side of Marby, two to three miles away, and it wasn't easy for me just to nip round to the Rigby Smith's home, as the others could do on a regular basis, without any assistance from parents or public transport. I had a bike but it wasn't always in working order and I wasn't too keen on cycling, anyway, when the weather was really bad, which it sometimes was since the Puppet Club began in the winter.

In the end, Rigby Smith let me help his brother Colin with the music instead of clashing with Nevan over the usually non-existent or inadequate scenery. We played gramophone records before the show began, changing the needles on the 78 rpm records as swiftly and neatly as we could and turning down the volume of the music as smoothly as we could when the show began. The two pieces we played most of the time, I remember well, were The Nights of Gladness and The Cuckoo Waltz.

Operating a glove puppet didn't require a great deal of physical skill. You simply had to make sure that your arm remained hidden at all times below the level at which the glove puppet appeared, your fingers fitted properly into the hole in the puppet's head and arms, and you moved the head of your puppet in time with the words you spoke. A little more skill was required of you vocally for you had to speak in the appropriate tone of voice for the glove puppet character you were animating and speak loudly and clearly so that the audience could hear you. I think Rigby Smith would have preferred to have played all the characters himself. He couldn't, of course, but it was possible to play two characters simultaneously, with a different glove puppet on each hand, which he sometimes did. To be fair to him, he didn't exactly hog all the roles selfishly for himself. Sometimes, if not many showed up for rehearsals, he didn't have much choice, he had to play two parts or more. He did let the others have a role if they wanted one but he got impatient if anyone stumbled over their lines and made heavy weather of their parts; then he might take over.

He wasn't very happy about me having a part because he said I spoke too quietly and without enough expression. However, he let Nevan have a part sometimes and I don't honestly think he was much better than me. Actually, after he let me do the sound effects as well as the lighting I didn't mind too much about not having speaking roles and I used to enjoy devising ways of creating various stage effects. Making spooky or crackling sounds was probably the most fun. Unfortunately, in one performance I can remember, the one with the wizard and the rumoured ghost on the loose, I was supposed to light a sparkler to coincide with the wizard waving his wand and casting a spell, and I was very late getting it properly lit. By the time it went off, the policeman was saying, "Thank goodness, no more tricks from the wizard now: he's safely locked away." The timing couldn't have been worse. Rigby Smith saw the funny side of it but always suspected me, I think, of doing it deliberately.

The initial challenge facing the Puppet Club was finding suitable scripts to perform. The play books for puppets (both glove and string puppets) which Rigby Smith bought, borrowed or was given, were mainly fairy tales with well known, established characters. There were plays such as Little Red Riding Hood, Thumbelina and Puss in Boots. There was no great objection to their stories themselves, although as we grew older we tended to view fairy tales as being for small kids only. The main problem was that we didn't have the required puppets to perform these fairy tale plays nor the will nor the skill to make them all.

There were some Punch and Judy scripts available in puppet books or from the library, and Rigby Smith had a glove puppet of a very youthful-looking Punch which was a start, but things became complicated for him when an uncle of his gave him an older-looking Punch and Judy so that he had now two Punches and one Judy in his puppet collection. If he used the younger-looking Punch, he wouldn't match the older-looking Judy and he was rather fond of his young-looking, cheeky-faced Punch. If he used the younger Punch, nevertheless, because he preferred him, what would he do with the older-looking Punch? He couldn't use the older one as a different character because he looked more like the classic Punch character than the younger one did. Nor could he *not* use the older-looking Punch. He was a very striking and well made puppet and it would be very poor use of resources available for the puppet club if this puppet weren't used.

Rigby Smith soon realised what he had to do and was very happy to do it. He would have to ignore all plays already written for particular characters and write his own plays using the glove puppets he had and the props available. Making use of all the puppets he had, gave rise to some interesting scripts. Not perhaps at first because I remember the first play used just three characters. It wasn't one of his best but you have to begin somewhere, don't you? The script included Mr Plod the Policeman, the young Punch, and an evil wizard which was the puppet I had made under Mrs Leyton's guidance. Although the head was mainly red and black, the puppet's eyes had come out rather green so it was nicknamed 'Green Eye'.

As far as I remember, the play consisted of Mr Plod the Policeman on night duty being terrified by rumours of ghosts roaming about. The young Punch was cheeky to Mr Plod until the spookiness of the night frightened him too. There were lots of weird noises off stage, which I helped to make, and Mr Plod and Punch were frequently being tapped on the shoulder by invisible hands or were frightening each other in the dark by bumping into each other. Green Eye the Wizard was behind the faked ghostly phenomena and, when he showed himself, he was hit over the head by the young Punch who also hit Mr Plod by mistake (or maybe it was deliberate, I can't remember). The Wizard, thinking he'd been hit by Mr Plod, threatened revenge on Mr Plod with his most evil spell.

I've no idea how Mr Plod managed to lock the Wizard up at the end of the play. Apart from the last line of the play, the only other line I remember is the first one, also spoken by Mr Plod the Policeman, who was played by Toffee. Not because it was a particularly dramatic line but because it became a family joke amongst the Rigby Smiths. Whenever I was with them thereafter and the puppet plays were mentioned, one of the family would quote with mock gravity, "I CAN'T BEAR BEING ON DUTY AT NIGHT", mimicking Toffee's deep, booming voice, and everyone would laugh.

The next play was a lot better and much more ambitious. The Puppet Club soon acquired a grand total of nine puppets and Rigby Smith wrote a four scene play for seven of the nine puppets. The setting for the last two scenes – a haunted house – was not very original but some of the characters he created were quite cleverly drawn, I thought. He solved the problem of having two Punches in this play, and thereafter, by turning the older Punch and Judy into Punch's uncle and aunt. He then invented a sort of sitcom relationship between the two Punches, with the younger one, the nephew, being impudent to his uncle and generally mischievous, and his uncle, acting in loco parentis, constantly angry with his nephew for running up bills and being a nuisance in the house. But there was more to it than that because Judy (Aunt Judy), in her turn, was constantly 'having a go' at Uncle Punch for living in an extravagant way himself; and she liked to tease him too.

I think I remember the subtleties of this play better than the first not only because there *were* a lot more this time but because I copied out the script for the Puppet Club, in fact copying out lines became one of my jobs. Although it took quite a long time because I printed every letter, I rather enjoyed it. It made me feel more useful and it made up for the fact, I thought, that I couldn't come to all the rehearsals. I also felt more personally involved in the script through copying it out. In case anyone is wondering, I might mention in passing that I did not contribute to the composition of the scripts, I was only ever a scribe. Rigby Smith sometimes listened to my suggestions about the production of the plays but he wanted to write the scripts himself. That was fine by me, I didn't aspire to be a playwright and generally I liked what he had written, though occasionally I thought I could have improved one or two of his lines.

This second play was called something like 'Punch and the Haunted House' and was quite well plotted. The last scenes of the play were set in the haunted house and contained a lot of corny and predictable things such as mysterious tapping noises, bogus ghosts, and lots of creeping up, and jumping upon, the wrong person in the dark. In true Punch and Judy style, there was also plenty of beating of heads with truncheons or hammers, and big boasts and threats made about what was going to happen to an adversary or foe when finally caught or hunted down.

Despite the stock situations, however, in these last scenes, Rigby Smith's script had its positive points. It moved at a frenetic pace and made something colourful and lively out of the all the dramatic clichés. He brought in all seven of the glove puppets which had featured earlier in the play in separate scenes, working them into the plot somehow, and they bobbed in and out like characters in a farce. The eventual apprehension of the baddie, the criminal Slippery Sam, at the end of the final scene, and the arrival of a policeman to take him away, was hardly original, but the play also ended with a resolution of a conflict between Uncle Punch and nephew Punch set up in the first two scenes of the play. These earlier, much slower moving scenes contained some good dialogue and characterisation, some of which I can still remember.

In one of these scenes, the opening one I think, Uncle Punch tells Aunt Judy he has become a private detective and he intends to catch the notorious criminal, Slippery Sam, and gain the reward of £500. In the conversation between Uncle Punch and Aunt Punch which ensues, we learn that Uncle Punch lives in a profligate way, eating huge quantities of toast and using an excessive amount of electricity and gas; so much so that the Punch household is running short of money. The gaining of the reward for the capture of Slippery Sam is therefore imperative not merely something desirable. As Aunt Judy adds to the list of household bills which need paying, Uncle Punch becomes more and more agitated and repeats the phrase 'how annoying, how annoying!' and it becomes his catchphrase throughout the play.

In the following scene we learn that young Punch is also after the reward for Slippery Sam, so it becomes clear that the two people who don't normally get on very well anyway are on a new and bigger collision course than ever. Rigby Smith, however, does not reveal this fact immediately. He gives the young Punch a long soliloquy in which he explains to the audience why he's taken up carpentry. The inspiration behind the speech derived from a single prop – a small, pink, plastic saw. Rigby Smith hit on the idea of writing a comic monologue in which Punch tries to demonstrate how to saw a piece of wood when he knows very little about it. There is some obvious comedy as Punch bungles his attempts to saw the wood – a highly suitable piece of 'business' for a glove puppet since a glove puppet can hardly cut wood anyway – and makes feeble excuses for it, including quite a good joke about making a mistake with his sawing action because he's following a carpentry manual for lefthanders not righthanders.

There follows an argument with the next door neighbour, a rival carpenter, who becomes the other baddie in the play, and only then does Punch's friend

Ben (looking remarkably like one of the Flower Pot Men, because that was the glove puppet he was supposed to be) enter and tell Punch about the reward of £500 for Slippery Sam, who is hiding – very conveniently for dramatic purposes – in a haunted manor. Thereafter, the pace quickens and the plot thickens; there is more excitement but less humour. I would say it was a very entertaining play, though I'm not sure what our audience, made up mainly of parents, really thought of it. I remember them being very nice and polite about it, Barley's father in particular – a very gracious, white-haired man, somewhat older than the other parents, who had a limp and carried a thick walking stick.

The Puppet Club had glove puppets of a monkey and a dog, in addition to the seven puppets used in the Haunted Manor play, so Rigby Smith wrote another play which made use of them. The dog became Punch's dog Toby who bit Punch's enemies, and others, and stole sausages, in traditional fashion. The monkey, called Mitch in another play about the young Punch in a junk shop, appeared in this play as a mischievous character who's more impudent than Punch himself and who insults Toby as other characters do, but gets away with it (the others don't) most of the time.

Rigby Smith also wanted to use his Proud or Posh Woman glove puppet, the one which he had made at school under Mrs Leyton's guidance. He invented two parts for this glove puppet in one play (dressed differently, I suppose, though I don't remember how). First of all, the puppet becomes Uncle Punch's maid, and later the puppet was used to portray a snooty lady in the park with her spoilt, cossetted son, called something like Cecil or Clarence. The sitcom of Uncle Punch and Young Punch, in constant antagonism over Punch's unruly, irresponsible behaviour, continues in this play and is expanded. Punch gets into trouble and runs up bills which he attempts, by various ploys, to prevent reaching his uncle, but he is also cheeky to his uncle at home and wreaks domestic havoc through his simple, short-cut methods of doing the housework.

Punch's simple, quick method to do the washing up, for instance, is to pour water all over the plates and allow them to 'self-wash'. Clearing the table simply entails sweeping everything off the table. The Puppet Club had a set of plastic plates and it was easy for a glove puppet to throw them around. They could easily be thrown into the audience too, they wouldn't hurt anyone – not lightweight, plastic plates – and it suited Punch's character so it was dramatically justifiable and a good way, once again, of making use of the resources available.

Rigby Smith used another 'How To' book in his script (in the same series no doubt as the carpentry manual mentioned in the previous play) as the pretext for this buffoonery. The book has been written by Punch himself and is a self-help book called 100 Ways to Do Things Quicker. Punch recommends it to Uncle Punch's maid as well as to him and demonstrates examples from it. Miss Twitford, as she is called, eventually quits when Uncle Punch, driven to distraction by Punch's demonstrations from his book, bellows at her, not intentionally at her but she gets the full blast of his voice in her face when he shouts at his nephew. Some of the dialogue was very lively and quite incisive. I can't recall it well enough to quote it except for Uncle Punch's culminating outburst against Punch's idiotic book and its sure-fire recipes for domestic disaster:

UNCLE PUNCH: Oh, confound your rotten new book of '100 Ways to Do Things Quicker'! It only makes *me* do *one* thing quicker.

PUNCH: What's that, uncle?

UNCLE: Lose my temper!

The Puppet Club was a great success but only for a time. We put on two shows and then it fizzled out. Rigby Smith just couldn't keep up the enthusiasm and commitment in the others. Another home-grown project of his suffered a similar fate. He and his brother Colin, Nevan, Nick Wheeler and his brother Des, were part of a gang at home which sporadically skirmished with a local gang of somewhat larger and older boys known as the Gribley gang. At one time, Rigby Smith thought it a good idea to turn their own gang into a more disciplined unit which would train and develop physical skills. His model for discipline and organisation was more Scout or sport-based than military and he devised a number of tests for all members of the gang to train for, supposedly to improve their fitness and fighting capability. He called the newly-organised gang the Red Hand Gang and when the tests were completed the members of the gang were to have a badge.

The tests consisted of such things as running, jumping, lifting, throwing, archery and lassoing, though there wasn't much equipment for the latter two. For archery, Rigby Smith made makeshift bows from any bendy branches he could trim down and put a string on, and made arrows from bamboo sticks with the sharp-ended legs of broken geometry compasses shoved into the hollow ends of the sticks for arrow heads. These were never actually fired at anyone, only at tree trunks or pieces of cardboard marked out with concentric circles and attached to walls. For lassoing, any thin rope of ten foot or more would do. He tried to set high standards himself in these tests and to lead the way, and he was able to do this for all the athletic tests. I don't remember him showing exceptional skill in archery and lassoing, however. Not that I saw him doing much of either because I never really got involved in the Red Hand Gang; I was more of an associate member, like James Rigby Smith in the Puppet Club.

The Red Hand Gang, like the Puppet Club and many of the make-believe games in the school woods, faded away probably because they were too Rigby Smith-based or dependent, but also partly, I'm sure, because at that age – 10 to 12 years old (and younger, of course) – child-originated group projects and schemes often flare up and burn out quickly. I suspect Rigby Smith would not, in any case, have maintained his own enthusiasm for the Red Hand Gang and the Puppet Club as he continued to grow older and become more and more preoccupied with schoolwork and school sport.

Sport and Fighting

The fact that Rigby Smith should be so good at sport and so keen on it, when he was always near the top of the form in schoolwork and also possessed the creative abilities described above, should surprise only those who have limited, stereotyped views of human aptitudes and interests. Whilst it is true that Penly Grange contained, on the one hand, the small and weedy-looking Parker who was the cleverest boy in the form and not a great games player, also Thorpe who was very bright but not keen on sport (brains), and, on the other hand, the superbly built Latham brothers, who were weak academically but sensational swimmers and brilliant on the rugby pitch, also the solidly-built Porter who was an outstanding games player but not so good at schoolwork (brawn), there were a fair number of boys who did equally well both mentally/intellectually and in sport, so that the supposed 'brains and brawn' dichotomy just did not apply generally.

Rickmack, for instance, who like Rigby Smith ended up with a scholarship to Marby College, was a leading actor in most school plays, one of the best essay writers in the form, and also excellent at sport. Though not as successful as Rigby Smith at cricket, Rickmack still got into the First Eleven and was a top rugby player – a great scrum half – and the Captain of the First Fifteen rugby team. Captain of School, Phil Westford, who came top of the Common Entrance candidates and eventually went to Cambridge, did well in swimming and rugby; and the precocious and very bright Spilwell was equally successful at the same sports. Honeyman, along with Spencer, one of the best two Scouts in the school, was reasonable at schoolwork and a good sportsman too. Loretti was good at both work and sport: I remember him winning the English prize in his last year. And leading sportsman Jakeman, though not an academic success, was, as we have seen, streetwise and replete with native wit and intelligence and not short on verbal skills.

As far as I myself was concerned, there was no disparity between work and sport in terms of my interest and enthusiasm. Though not as successful at sport as I was at work, I was always eager to do well at sport; if anything, more eager to do well in sport than in work. As a matter of fact, I became increasingly annoyed with those who assumed that because I was 'brainy' and did not get into the first teams for any sport, except the swimming team occasionally, and was not athletically-built, to put it mildly, and also because when I was about eleven I started to wear glasses to read what was written on the board in the classroom, I was just a swot and therefore sport was of no importance to me. It was all right for Rigby Smith and Rickmack and others to be both good at schoolwork and sport but, in my case, the fact that I was regarded as academic and clever seemed to disqualify me in other people's minds from being seriously interested in sport. Perhaps that was another reason why I took up scoring for the First Eleven. Not only to be involved in some way in school cricket matches when I couldn't get into the team, and win some respect, but also to prove I was keen on sport and knew something about it. I was not *just* a swot!

Rigby Smith's passion for sport was, even so, greater than mine, no doubt because of his greater ability, and probably greater than all the others too. His passion knew no bounds, in fact, and showed itself in many ways. I shall mention just a couple of things here – over and above his normal, understandable elation or depression at winning or losing – to illustrate how much sport meant to him.

He kept a diary from time to time and sometimes showed me what he wrote in it. Alongside his record of marks in school tests and exams and his progress in Scout tests and what he did on half holidays, such as fighting the XR gang and discovering *secrets* in the woods, he noted down all the scores of the practice games he played every afternoon, even the most humdrum of practices. And not just the sport he played at school. If he played knockabout football at home with a few friends he put those scores down too. There was a real difference for him between winning or losing 5-4 or 4-3. I appreciated that too, of course, and maybe some other sports enthusiasts amongst us may have jotted down various scorelines at one time or another, but surely not as diligently as Rigby Smith.

Secondly, how many of us seriously thought of becoming professional sportsmen? We may have dreamt of it – I'm sure I did once – but who in our year would have said, in a firm 'I've-made-up-my mind' way, 'I'm going to be a sportsman when I grow up'? Porter, perhaps, but then Porter's talent was almost exclusively sports-based; I don't think there was any other boy, I can recall, who plumped for sport as a career choice before anything else as Rigby Smith did, whilst he was at Penly Grange at least. I remember him spelling it out quite clearly to me once when we were in his back garden at home.

There were just the two of us in the garden. He was prancing around, shooting out his fists as if he were boxing, delivering straight rights (he fought southpaw) and uppercut lefts, bobbing and weaving as he evaded imaginary blows from his imaginary opponent. He managed to throw out remarks as he moved,

"I don't know," he said, "whether I'm going to be a boxer ..." – at this point he changed his actions and started miming tennis strokes ... "or a tennis player." He did some magnificent mimed shots: forehands, backhands, serves, smashes and volleys. Although he spoke in a casual, offhand way, he was perfectly serious and seemed to be making a factual statement, not simply expressing an aspiration. The only question in his mind was which sport he would be doing, not whether or not he would be doing sport. I was struck by the fact that in narrowing his choice of sports down to two he'd eliminated his much-loved cricket (though this incident occurred, it must be said, before his hugely successful cricket season). So I asked him why not cricket? He broke off in the middle of a superb backhand cross court shot, stopped and turned to me in reply,

"Cricket is all very well," he said, "but you're not playing it all the time, are you? You're sitting out watching the others, aren't you, for some of the time, a *lot* of the time if you get a duck when you bat and go straight back to the pavilion in a couple of minutes. Whereas boxing ... or tennis ... you're at it all the time ..." and he resumed his boxing and tennis mimes, matching them to his spoken comments, which continued: "I love all the running and stroke play in tennis but it's not so physical as boxing, is it? When you're boxing, you're moving all the time, and you're fighting all the time, you're giving everything, it's total involvement!" And then he was shadow boxing again, pounding the air and dancing about with even greater energy.

His enthusiasm for boxing, doubtless stemming from what he'd seen on television or in films, was fantasy-based in part, I have to say. He had never taken part in organised boxing at school because it was done only by the boarders in the evening, but he had done some semi-friendly boxing with other boys which entailed delivery of blows to the chest and arms only, and he had done pretty well at that restricted form of boxing from what I'd seen, also at other kinds of ad hoc fighting. What struck me most about his declaration for boxing, though, was that it confirmed he wanted to be a successful *fighter* as well as being successful in school sport. Boxing, I could see then, was ideal for him because it was sport with a physical fighting element as well as an athletic one.

But how good was he, or could he be, at fighting when really put to the test? With Jakeman continually spoiling for a fight this was no academic question. The odds on him beating Jakeman in a fight were finely balanced,

I thought. Although Rigby Smith was fairly tall himself, certainly above average height, Jakeman was even taller and slightly older and probably stronger though not much; he didn't look much tougher than Rigby Smith because he was slimmer in build. What was compelling about Jakeman, however, apart from his height, and was the thing that would probably cause a neutral bystander to put his money on him after just looking at him, was his supreme confidence, his cocksure air. Moreover, as far as we knew, Jakeman had a good track record of fighting. Not that we had seen him fight a great deal. He didn't need to fight much, he usually got his way without fighting, other than the occasional thump or twisting of an arm.

Rigby Smith's track record of fighting was mixed. He'd been crushed and humiliated by the thuggish Burton who had defeated him with one vicious punch in the face, and he'd had some inconclusive fights with boys in the XR gang but these were only skirmishes, anyway. I had seen him, however, deal decisively once with an unknown youth in a field near his house. For some reason, Brian Barley, the younger Barley, quite a gentle character, not particularly strong and not given to fighting, had got into an argument with a really rough-tough boy nobody knew, and this boy had suddenly started laying into him. I didn't see what started it, I was with Rigby Smith at the front of his house, playing French cricket or something, when Nevan came running up excitedly.

"Quick! Someone's been arguing with Barley and now he's attacking him, he's in real trouble!" he shouted. We followed Nevan back to the field where Brian Barley was, not particularly excited ourselves because we knew about Nevan's tendency to sensationalise news, especially if he'd heard it first (and he usually had).

When we arrived at the field, the rough, aggressive boy was on top of a helpless Brian Barley and raining punches into his face. It was the unacceptable form of fighting, in our book, which the hated Burton had been guilty of. Rigby Smith was outraged. He liked Brian Barley and was very indignant about his receiving such treatment, which he was sure, knowing Brian's peaceful nature, was totally unprovoked. He bellowed at the boy astride Brian,

"Leave him alone! Get off him and fight someone your own size!"

The boy complied, and when he got off the supine Brian, and stood up, you could see that he was not particularly big, in fact he was slightly shorter than Rigby Smith. Even so, he was quite stocky and looked very determined and pugnacious, a definite fighter, prepared to take on all comers. I was glad Rigby Smith was going to take him on not me. Rigby Smith's anger spurred him on and he wasted no time in closing with the gritty, tough boy, and eventually wrestled him to the ground and pinioned his arms. As Rigby Smith held him down, Nevan squirted water in his face from a lemon squeezer (he used it as a water pistol) and Nick Wheeler, who had suddenly shown up, rubbed grass in the boy's face which I tore out of the ground and handed to him. The Puppet Club were working together spontaneously as a team, probably better that they'd ever worked together with the puppets!

Rigby Smith soon released the boy; it was hardly a fair contest now, and the boy showed no desire to continue fighting him. However, his antipathy and hostility remained and was now redirected towards Nick Wheeler who had subjected him to the indignity of having his face rubbed in common, earthy grass. "Let me get at him, let me get at him!" he yelled. Wheeler ran off with the enraged boy in hot pursuit.

Nevan, who had stepped aside to allow the boy free passage, was grinning broadly, revelling in it all. His smiles weren't normally expansive, he liked to keep his feelings hidden, but he loved incidents like that. Rigby Smith was asking Brian how he was, and examining the bruises on his face. Rigby Smith was more relaxed now, relieved he'd got rid of Brian's assailant, though still angry about what had happened to him. He knew the aggressive boy wouldn't catch Nick Wheeler, a past master of escapes, though he could fight if he had to, he had quite a steely, mean streak in him. Whilst the end of the fight had hardly been heroic – four or five against one – Rigby Smith had defeated the boy in a one-to-one fight to begin with, and that was definitely one up to him; he could notch it up as a victory of his own.

The manner of the fight between Rigby Smith and that belligerent young stranger (never seen again) was, in fact, not untypical of most fights we had at school. Hitherto, when I have spoken of fighting I have tended to talk in terms of boxing, fighting with fists. Actually, our usual mode of fighting, except for routine skirmishes, whether friendly or whether a clash of real animosity and strong rivalry, was wrestling. We were allowed to have *friendly* fights in the gym on the mats and we would challenge each other to wrestling bouts as we might challenge each other to a game of table tennis or billiards.

I say 'we' because many boys took part in these friendly wrestling bouts, though I gave them up after being defeated first by Rickmack, easily, and then, less easily, but still conclusively, by Scales at the back of a minibus. Rickmack wasn't much bigger than me but he had a grip of iron and was a fierce fighter, and he completely overpowered me. Scales looked like a choir boy with his fair hair and ruddy cheeks but fought like a terrier when we had recreational fights on the back seat of the hired minibus between Penly Grange and Marby (a mode of transport we used for a short time). I just couldn't summon up the necessary drive and determination to match Scales's tenacity and rigour: he fought as if his life depended on it, I don't know why, and I had to acknowledge he was probably stronger than me anyway (slightly).

The unsupervised wrestling bouts in the gym were very simple in format. You closed with your opponent and grappled with him, attempting to sling him on the floor and sit on him. If you achieved this with your arms round his neck, you held him on the floor and squeezed his neck until he submitted. It was a rudimentary form of judo, I suppose. It wasn't very nice having your neck squeezed, you could hear it cracking and you felt you must be suffering enormous bodily damage but once you were released your neck usually recovered quite quickly; I don't remember anyone ever being seriously hurt. What was worse, though, was being sat on and almost smothered as your opponent forced himself down on your head. You could turn your head sideways and still breathe all right for a time: some boys, like Rickmack, showed amazing resilience in this respect and hardly ever gave in. Rickmack would frequently squirm and twist and eventually get free from heavier opponents.

Rigby Smith did well too in the wrestling bouts, not only because he was quite strong but also because of his agility. He could slip out of his opponent's grip and engage him suddenly from another angle. If he couldn't wrestle the larger boys to the ground, he might dive at their ankles and uproot them, nimbly dodging to one side as they threatened to tumble on top of him, then falling on them with lightning speed when they fell. He wasn't the very best wrestler, he wasn't heavy enough nor ruthless enough, but he was pretty 'handy' and, certainly, as they say, able to 'give a good account of himself'.

I'd heard Jakeman was quite a useful boxer and won fights at school, but I hadn't seen him wrestle much and if he did fight Rigby Smith it was likely, as I have said, to be a wrestling encounter not a boxing fight. So, Rigby Smith might acquit himself well against Jakeman, especially if goaded, as he was when tackling that tough, aggressive boy on Brian Barley's behalf. If I'd had to, I would have put my money on Rigby Smith (or was that wishful thinking on my part?) but I don't think many other boys would have done. Nevan might have done, he had seen more of him at home, more than I had, but what Nevan really thought about Rigby Smith, or anyone else for that matter, was always a mystery to me.

The Fight with Jakeman

I can't remember precisely what sparked the eventual showdown between Rigby Smith and Jakeman but it must have been something to do with the billiard table in the main school hall because I remember a scuffle with a snooker cue and Jakeman making a remark which stung Rigby Smith into saying, "Right! You want a fight, you can have it! In the gym!" Rigby Smith then made his way to the gym, closely followed by Jakeman and the handful of others boys, including me, who had been standing round the billiard table.

It was almost superfluous to nominate the gym as the place for the fight. It was the usual place, both for friendly fights and serious trials between rivals. There was no question of a fight in the school hall where the billiard table was situated because it was not far from the library and the Headmaster's study, and no one would risk a commotion anywhere near there, it would be asking for a swift and savage caning from Teddy Eldin.

I remember clearly how rapidly the news travelled that there was a fight in the offing. Perhaps it was something to do with the fact that it was a fine summer's day, conducive to the spread of sounds, with warm air and windows widely open, although I daresay the news of a real fight would have got around pretty quickly whatever the season or weather, it usually did.

When we left the hall and followed Rigby Smith and Jakeman, there were about six of us. By the time we reached the quad there must have been another twenty, and, by the time we got to the gym at the other end of the quad, a further twenty or thirty had appeared from the four corners of the school site. In just two more minutes, the gym was crammed with over half the school's population of boys. So it seemed. The breaking news' cry had gone out in a flash and been taken up by an ever-increasing number of voices till it had become like a football crowd chanting just one word.

"Fight! Fight! Fight! Fight!" reverberated round the school.

I would like to be able to record that I held Rigby Smith's coat and acted as his second, but the fight wasn't as formal as that (In any case, he probably wasn't wearing his jacket: it would have been 'shirt-sleeve order'). There was some orderliness in the process of the fight, however, and a sense of an occasion, a sense that it was a big spectator event not to be missed, for I can remember Rickmack shouting at all the boys pressing into the fight area and ordering them to get back and give Rigby Smith and Jakeman a chance; also Rook and Crawford egging Jakeman on, and Westford directing two or three boys to pull another mat out to make a bigger fighting area.

Once in the gym, Rigby Smith began to look disconcerted. The confidence and resolution he'd shown a few moments earlier when issuing his challenge to Jakeman seemed to have evaporated. He appeared unnerved by the shouting and the mob of boys. He faltered. Jakeman noticed his apparent loss of nerve and made a taunt suggesting Rigby Smith wanted to chicken out. Rigby Smith responded by hurling himself at Jakeman and trying to floor him straightaway. This strategy surprised me because I assumed Rugby Smith would fight more cannily than that, allow Jakeman to make the running and use his agility to outmanoeuvre him and counter-attack when Jakeman made a false move and threw too much of his weight forward. Not a bit of it. Rigby Smith seemed to be in a hurry and was throwing caution to the wind.

Jakeman recovered from his initial surprise at his opponent's strong assault and outmanoeuvred Rigby Smith, bringing him down and almost succeeding in getting completely on top of him with a deft turn of his body. The fight was going almost the opposite to the way I had expected. Then Rigby Smith wriggled free and got back on his feet, looking quite fresh and strong and physically unruffled. He was doing okay, I thought, and Jakeman looked less sure than he had done at the outset. Rigby Smith may have looked untroubled physically but I could see he was troubled mentally. He seemed to have lost his appetite for the fight. He looked very uneasy and, in the sports commentator's jargon of today, 'unfocussed'. I didn't know why.

He closed somewhat half-heartedly with Jakeman again and they hit the mat together. They rolled a few feet and Rigby Smith ended up beneath Jakeman. Then suddenly it was all over. Rigby Smith capitulated. He hit the mat with his hand in a gesture of submission and Jakeman got off him and looked down contemptuously at him.

"That's fixed you, Berry!" he said. "You may be clever, you may *think* you're clever, but you can't fight! Not me, anyway."

He grinned smugly at Crawford and Rook and at his other supporters and admirers who seemed to have increased greatly in number the moment Jakeman won the fight. Most of the spectators had been neutral and were, in fact, disappointed the fight had ended so soon. It was free entertainment for them and they probably expected a much closer contest. When Jakeman left the gym, a few moments later, with his arrogant swagger, his supporters left with him and the day boys who might still have had some sympathy for Rigby Smith, and also Thorpe and Westford, followed them shortly after. Soon it was just me and Rigby Smith in the gym. Nevan was nowhere in sight. 'I bet he's slunk off,' I thought, 'not wishing to be associated with failure', though, I must say, I hadn't seen him at any time before or during the fight.

Rigby Smith, who had finished tucking his shirt in and straightening his hair, was looking sheepish and was avoiding my gaze. He was also looking relieved and more relaxed despite his abject surrender. I had to ask him of course:

"Why did you give in so easily? I don't understand. You were doing fine."

Rigby Smith seemed bored by the question. "I didn't think it was worth it. I didn't see the point."

"Didn't see the point?" I was incredulous. "You challenged him to the fight. You wanted to shut him up. You've always said that."

"There was too much noise. Too many people. I didn't expect so many to turn up. I couldn't concentrate. I wasn't fighting for their benefit."

Although Rigby Smith's playing of Hamlet in the school play was yet to come, I'd seen him perform in form plays and Scout plays and I hadn't noticed him being timid of audiences, quite the contrary. This alleged aversion to crowds of spectators didn't ring true. He was obviously aware of that because he added a further justification for calling off the fight:

"It was too close to lesson time. There wasn't time for a proper fight." That was half true. There was only about ten minutes to the first lesson after lunch (afternoon lessons were after lunch in the summer term not after tea as in the autumn and spring term) but how long would it take to fight Jakeman? A single fight didn't normally take more than about five minutes or so, even a closely contested one. And anyway he'd called the fight himself and I reminded him of that fact again.

"Look, I didn't know what time it was when I challenged him, did I? Only I saw Loretti's watch when we started the fight and I realised there wasn't long to go."

"But to give in so easily! You didn't need to do that. Jakeman will be all over us now. He'll be even worse!"

"Oh, I'm not worried about him. He doesn't bother me."

I was flabbergasted. "Not bothered about him! You're always moaning about him. Saying you want to shut him up and deal with him. And when you get the chance you throw it away. I don't understand. Are you really afraid of him? Did you really expect to lose that fight?"

This remark jolted Rigby Smith out of his apathy and apparent indifference. "Look!" he blurted out. "I've got two blue stars already this week. I don't want anymore!"

"You mean – "

"Yes, I didn't want to get into trouble. There was such a racket going on. The noise could be heard all round the school. How long before Swales or Teddy Eldin heard it? Or one of the teachers coming to take their lessons? Or some monitor reported us? It would have been two blue or even three."

He was right of course. Although friendly fights on the mats in the gym were allowed, as I've said, real fights were banned, partly because a boy was more likely to get hurt in a real fight but mainly because real fights caused a hubbub, were disorderly and undermined school discipline. Even the lenient Bracken might award two blue stars for serious fighting, though there was a slim chance you might get away with a warning from him, but all the others would have given at least two blue stars. (This was in the days before Robert Barnet, it should be said, who would probably have treated the fight as if it were a sporting event or part of a show and then organised a debate on the rights and wrongs of settling disputes through physical trials of strength).

Two blue stars, the minimum punishment probably, added to the two he already had, would take Rigby Smith to the dreaded four blue stars in a week which would qualify him for a caning from Teddy Eldin. Three blue stars at once, which was the more likely punishment, would qualify him (and Jakeman) for an immediate caning and one that would have been even more severe.

The revelation that Rigby Smith had given up the fight and surrendered to Jakeman through fear of the cane aroused mixed emotions within me. I understood his fear of the cane. I knew what it was like. In fact, I had been caned only the previous week and it was still burnt into my brain and body like the previous canings I'd had, though the marks were almost gone. This last caning had been the worst, I think, and been meted out to me for receiving three blue stars at once. I suppose the punishment was fair by Penly Grange standards, though the offence wasn't heinous in intention and was the result of bad luck, it seemed to me.

I was having a pea shooter fight with Norton in the form room and he was beating a retreat and heading towards the door. I sent a pea flying towards the doorway to intercept his escape and who should enter the very moment the projected pea reached the open doorway but Mrs Leyton, the Art teacher. The pea pellet hit her smack on the forehead. She was not pleased. I had no idea she was in the vicinity and was not expecting any staff to be around. Unluckily for me she had chosen just the wrong moment to come into the form room to get a piece of paper from the drawer in the teacher's table at the front of the room.

She demanded my star book instantly – once she'd recovered – and remarked how fortunate it was that the pellet had not gone in her eye. My offence was compounded, she said, by the fact that she had already warned me about using a pea shooter in the form room. I had been warned, that was true, and my heart sunk knowing I was going to get three blue stars. It was only after I'd been caned and more or less got over it that I appreciated how fortunate it was indeed that my pellet had not gone in Mrs Leyton's eye. I was relieved for her but even more so for me, knowing I might have had to bear the guilt of inflicting serious eye damage on someone, maybe leading to permanent damage to the injured eye, even complete loss of vision. The temporary pain of my caning then seemed slight in comparison with that frightening thought.

But I digress. The point I wish to make here is that I knew what it was like to be caned and could fully understand that Rigby Smith should want to avoid any possibility of being caned. He evidently still remembered his first caning and was eager not to have a repeat or worse experience. Yes, I understood that. But even so I was disappointed in him. I would have preferred him to have defeated Jakeman conclusively and put him in his place and then stoically accepted any caning which might have resulted from the feat. This would have been the noble, heroic thing to do.

Rigby Smith's humiliation at the hands of Burton I had accepted because Burton was some sort of invincible alien, a monster in our eyes, beyond the pale of civilised values, certainly beyond our prep school values, but Jakeman was another matter. Jakeman was powerful but not invincible and he had beaten Rigby Smith in a perfectly fair, ethical contest. If the circumstances of the fight had not suited Rigby Smith that wasn't Jakeman's fault. What's more, Jakeman hadn't been afraid of being caned for fighting, so it seemed, so why should Rigby Smith have shrunk from it? Shouldn't he have been a bit braver about it all?

Rigby Smith's failure against Jakeman was just one of a few things which led to him being dislodged from the pedestal I had put him on from the first moment I had met him. It is true that before we left Penly Grange he had almost climbed back onto it again through his later achievements but things were different then: I was older and more confident in my own abilities and he didn't seem so far beyond me then, so he never quite recovered the heroic status I had ascribed to him in the early days.

Important as it is in any boy's eyes, however, physical prowess is only one thing and, in any case, there was another round to come in the contest between Jakeman and Rigby Smith, and the outcome of that next round was rather different. But I recall other incidents which undermined further my admiration of his character and all round abilities. They were hardly serious failings for a ten, eleven or twelve year old boy, but, when you look up to someone, any lapses in that person's conduct or level of success always stand out more.

I remember being surprised, for instance, by his capacity for foolish or reckless behaviour. At first, when initiating me into the life of the day boy or into Games or schoolwork, I had been struck by his composure, self-possession and level-headedness, compared with many other boys. Later, I saw instances of more impulsive and less controlled behaviour which shocked me a bit, though they shouldn't have done really, it was only because of my expectations of him.

I recall two episodes when we were Scouts where he showed the rash, reckless side of his character. Once, when we were getting wood together for making a fire, he became impatient with me and my alleged slowness in chopping up wood. He loved chopping wood and took every opportunity to do it. Having taken and passed his felling axe test he became obsessed with using a felling axe and would use one on any type of wood, even when a felling axe wasn't the most suitable implement to use. On this particular occasion I remember, he had got his felling axe stuck in a block of wood and was very frustrated he couldn't continue with his chopping. Bracken had said not to struggle with an embedded axe blade but let him deal with it, but Rigby Smith didn't want to admit to any failure in his use of an axe and, besides that, he couldn't be bothered to wait until Bracken could help him.

I was in his patrol at the time and we wanted to be the first patrol to get our fire going and keep it going. Rigby Smith, as ever, was being especially competitive about the whole thing and when he saw me hacking away with a hand axe he wanted to use the hand axe himself, now that his felling axe was temporarily out of commission.

"Come on," he said, "let me have a go. You're too slow!"

"I'm doing all right," I said, and I honestly thought I was. A neat pile of carefully hewn sticks was gradually accumulating a few yards from the log I was using as a chopping block.

I continued my chopping and ignored him. This angered him. "No, you're not!" he cried, "We've got to speed up!" And he grabbed the axe from me, pushed me to one side and began chopping the piece of wood I was in the middle of slicing up. He made quick work of that piece and proceeded to pick up and attack another piece of wood, saying, "You see!" But this time the axe blade slipped off the wood, and then the log, and grazed his ankle.

"Damn!" he said, "when was this blade last sharpened?" It was the axe's fault of course. He wasn't bothered about his grazed ankle, it was only a slight wound, but he was jolly lucky he hadn't done himself or me more harm.

This may seem only a small incident of not much significance but for a patrol leader it was an appalling example to give. Not only had he grabbed the axe from me while I was using it which was obviously dangerous, he had broken nearly every rule concerning correct use of the hand axe. He had not checked that there was no one within at least an arm's length plus two axe lengths of his axe. He had started chopping away assuming I had moved to this safe distance, he hadn't checked to see that I *had*. He had not positioned his feet properly, well away from the point of impact of the axe or the path of its follow-through, an important safety precaution should he miss the target or deal it only a glancing blow. He had not checked the firmness of the ground himself nor the steadiness and evenness of the log being used as a chopping block; and if he was at all uncertain about the sharpness of the axe's blade, he should have checked it himself before using it and sharpened it himself.

Actually, he was normally quite a good patrol leader and very scrupulous about following the rule book, especially over questions of safety: he wouldn't have let anyone else in the patrol carry on the way he had. He had just been completely blinded by his passion for chopping wood and by the spirit of competition.

A related weakness of his was that he would rarely admit he wasn't good at something if it was something he wanted to be good at or thought good at. Since he was good at most things we boys did, it was some time before I realised he couldn't actually do some things as well as he thought he could and would refuse to acknowledge his shortcomings. It was debatable just how good he was at pitching a tent, for instance, certainly he wasn't as proficient at it as he liked to think, but there was one thing he claimed he could do, on one of our Scouting holidays, which he could barely do at all, with near disastrous consequences. And that was rowing.

It happened on one of our Lake District walking holidays with Bracken. Although we spent most of our time walking over twenty miles a day, sometimes thirty, we usually had one day off near Lake Windermere, in the middle of our hiking schedule. One year, on our day off, some of us went down to the Lakeside at Bowness and considered hiring a boat and going for a row on the lake. Rigby Smith didn't *consider* it. As soon as he saw the rowing boats bobbing at the lakeside he was itching to take one out on the lake and he'd made up his mind he was going to do it; I could tell from the look in his eye. I was standing by a rather timid boy called Mortimer who seemed tempted by the rowing boats but was very cautious about taking one out on the water. He turned to me and enquired,

"Can you row?"

Before I had time to answer, Rigby Smith cut in with – "Don't worry, come with me, I can row."

"Are you sure?" asked Mortimer.

"Course I can!" said Rigby Smith, brimming with confidence. "Come on!"

Mortimer and I were persuaded that Rigby Smith knew what he was doing and we quickly hired a boat. The boat hirer gave us some instructions but Rigby Smith didn't seem to be paying any attention to them. He made us sit down at different ends of the boat and he sat in the middle and took the oars. He got the boat moving all right but seemed to be rather heavy-handed about it, I thought, for someone who was supposed to be an experienced rower. The wind was blowing off the shore and we made good progress for a time but Rigby Smith soon discovered, and so did we, that he couldn't control the direction of the boat. We were soon drifting out towards the centre of the lake and when Rigby Smith tried to change direction all he succeeded in doing was make the boat go round in circles.

We had started out in high spirits, enjoying the breeze and the movement of the boat and the thought of being away from the land, and scorning the landlubber Scouts who had stayed there, too scared to venture out onto the lake. We trusted Rigby Smith's rowing ability and we assumed we were going to have a great time. But after fifteen minutes of drifting more and more helplessly, our mood changed and we began to question our trust in Rigby Smith. Mortimer's doubts were much stronger than mine; I was still hoping he did know what he was doing, that maybe he knew something we didn't know, that he had some awareness of where we might be drifting to, perhaps, and that we would get back to the shore eventually, somehow. Actually, we were getting further and further away from the lakeside we'd left, yet seemed no nearer the other side of the lake.

"I thought you said you could row!" Mortimer started shouting.

"I didn't know the wind would be so strong," Rigby Smith responded. He looked worried but he wasn't panicking. "Come and help me," he said, "instead of whining, I'm getting blisters."

Mortimer seemed frozen to the spot and didn't move, so I moved next to Rigby Smith and took one oar and tried to manipulate it. We both struggled with one oar each but totally failed to co-ordinate our efforts, turning the boat half one way and then half the other. The only thing that was actually affecting the movement of the boat in any significant way was the wind, which was carrying the boat, and the three of us in the boat, where it willed. We were now a long, long way, it seemed, from civilisation. In those days there weren't nearly so many craft on the lake as today and there were no nearby boats to signal to for help.

It started to get very cold. We hadn't thought about the cold, we only had shirts and shorts on, no coats. Mortimer started to screech, "What are we going to do? What are we going to do?"

"Start waving," I said, "stand up in the boat and wave towards the people on the shore we've come from," but the shore was a long way off and it was difficult to see anyone on the shore. Mortimer stood up and tried to wave and then fell over. He became hysterical.

"You're going to get us all killed!" he shrieked. "We'll never get back now!"

A moment later, a sudden ray of hope, I saw a speedboat approaching us and I waved frantically at it. Rigby Smith abandoned his futile rowing efforts and waved too. The speedboat drew up alongside us and a middle-aged man wearing goggles leaned over and asked us if we were in a spot of trouble.

"Yes," squealed Mortimer. "That boy," he said, pointing at Rigby Smith, "said he could row and he can't. None of us can row."

162

"Can't row?" said the speedboat man. "Bit rash coming out here, isn't it? Even if you can row, it's hard work out on the lake in the wind. Where are you from?" Rigby Smith muttered to me that he *could* row but said nothing to the man and was clearly reluctant to tell him the name of our Scout troop. Mortimer, on the other hand, let it all gush out. He was entrusting himself entirely into the hands of the speedboat man who was an adult and would be our saviour, he was sure, if we were nice and polite to him.

"Never mind," said the speedboat man, "you've learnt your lesson, I'll tow you back." And he did. As for learning our lesson, well, yes, Mortimer and I did, but not Rigby Smith. As soon as we got back to shore, he remarked, much to our astonishment and consternation, "I think I've got the hang of it now, I'm going to have another go."

"You're mad," said Mortimer, "you can count me out," and although I was Rigby Smith's friend, his closest friend, I declined too. The adventurous, romantic challenge of a boat on the open water of the Lake District's largest lake had lost its appeal. Rigby Smith found someone else to go out with him a second time and needed help yet again to get back to shore, an ordinary motor boat this time. Even though I thought him a fool and blamed him for getting me and Mortimer into the rowing boat under false pretences and giving us quite a fright, I suppose I did feel a sneaking admiration for his determination to try again even after his total failure the first time, but I think my feeling that he was an idiot to do so was even stronger.

Something else that shook my confidence in his capabilities occurred in the field of sport where I believed him to be unmatched and unmatchable. As a matter of fact, it shook him much more than it shook me for he took it to heart much more than I did. It was the annual school cross country race. The Junior Cross Country Race. He had won the race the previous year and he was still eligible to run in the Junior Race the following year, though he was over eleven. His rivals in the race were mostly a year or so younger than him and his winning the race again was regarded as a formality. Rigby Smith was looking forward not only to winning glory for himself again but also helping our Group, E Group, to win the Junior Cross Country Cup again.

Out of a field of about 50 runners, my aim was to be in the top twenty and maybe the top six in my Group. After the start of the race I didn't expect to see Rigby Smith again and, sure enough, by the time I'd crossed the first two fields to the north east of the school he had disappeared from view with Scales, Nelson and Timpson. (I think Nevan was in the leading group too). Following them, there were perhaps another dozen or so boys ahead of me. Imagine my surprise then when, about a mile and a half later, I found myself drawing level with Rigby Smith near the Backgammon Inn which was

163

situated along the route of the race, close to the Marby-Tibdale road. He was some way behind the leaders and I was amazed.

My first thought was that it was a shrewd ploy on his part, perhaps to make the race more interesting. He had fallen behind deliberately and intended to go up a gear or two before long and storm past the leaders in the last hundred yards of the race. There was still time for him to catch up since there was still another mile or more to go. That was his plan, surely? But when I came past him and saw his face I realised he was not holding himself in reserve, quite the contrary, he was straining every muscle just to keep going. He was in agony. When he saw me come past, he tried to match my pace but couldn't. He looked shattered and humiliated. I just didn't know what to think or what to say to him. I took no satisfaction in going ahead of him because he looked so miserable but I ran on to the finish, in a daze, on 'automatic pilot'.

I finished nineteenth and Rigby Smith was twenty-fifth. Nelson won the race and Scales was second (Nevan was fourth or fifth). Rigby Smith was inconsolable. He felt ashamed. He had been expected to win and hadn't even come in the top ten. He felt he had let E Group down and he went to apologise to Mr Bracken, the master in charge of E Group. He needn't have been so worried about letting his Group down because his Group, our Group, had Scales, Timpson and Nevan in it and other good runners so we still won the Cross Country Cup.

I did what I could to cheer Rigby Smith up. I reminded him that our Group had still won the Cup, since he seemed to need reminding of it, but he went on about how he was expected to win and what a bad example he'd set. How was it a bad example, I asked him, if he'd tried his best? He didn't like the question. He tried to tell me that the race was the greatest of humiliations for him because he had indeed tried his best. He'd tried like hell. And if he'd tried like hell and still not even come in the top twenty what a bad runner he must really be. He couldn't get over the fact that he was older than most of the other runners in the race, and his age advantage, together with the fact that he'd won last year's race, gave him no excuse whatsoever for losing the race.

When I pointed out to him that it was only one race after all, he retorted by saying that particular race would never happen again and that was the one he wanted to win and should have won. And there were no excuses. He really thought his failure to win showed some weakness of character on his part, even though he admitted he'd 'tried like hell'. I couldn't change his mind and he was sunk in a deep gloom for a couple of weeks. He never lost another race as far as I can remember and swept the board for all the track races in that year's athletic track events but he never fully recovered his self-esteem in sport after that cross country race; not until his last year at Penly Grange when

164

he proved one of the best three-quarters in the First Fifteen rugby team, was Captain of hockey, and enjoyed his outstanding cricket season.

The debacle of the Junior Cross Country race was probably the lowest moment for Rigby Smith since the days of Burton and possibly marked the lowest level he ever dropped to in my estimation, in sporting prowess anyway, but thereafter came a revival in his status and esteem and it began with another encounter with Jakeman. Quite a different encounter this time with quite a different outcome.

The Re-Match

It happened literally out of the blue, a day of blue skies: some months after Rigby Smith's short-lived fight with Jakeman in the gym. I remember it being a fine, dry, autumn afternoon in the woods. It must have been a 'merit' half holiday because we were not in the woods as Scouts and it was our free time. We were in our boiler suits and had been making a den in a very casual, lackadaisical sort of way. It wasn't a secret den, we were making no attempt to keep it hidden and weren't keeping a lookout or anything. The sun's rays were slanting through the trees and Rigby Smith, in one of his reflective moods, was lying on his back amidst the crisp, yellowy-brown leaves, enjoying the sun and the woods and the leaves and the mild autumnal air. I was tinkering with one of the branches of our den. He was very relaxed and so was I.

Into this quiet, peaceful world of ours, Jakeman, boiler-suited like us, suddenly blundered. Why he appeared there and then I have no idea. He was on his own, unusually, and seemed taken aback to see us. Perhaps he was on his way to join his cronies in another part of the woods, perhaps he was expecting to see them and not us. In any event, he soon recovered from his surprise and adopted his familiar, sneering manner and mocking tone of voice.

"It's Big Wave Brownie Berry and his little Mouse! Mickey Mouse! What are you two doing in your little hidey-hole? Afraid to come out and play with the others?"

"We were enjoying a bit of peace and quiet until you came along," Rigby Smith retorted. And I chipped in,

"Yes, so leave us alone! Go and join your gang. They're not here, are they? Can't you see that. Or are you blind?" Jakeman came over to me, grabbed one of my arms and began twisting it and forcing it up behind my back, standard treatment from a bully.

"Don't give me that and don't tell me what to do! I'll stay here if I want to, you little runt!"

"Leave him alone!" said Rigby Smith, in a very firm and resolute voice. I'd heard that command and that tone of voice before, when Rigby Smith had challenged the rough-tough lad punching Brian Barley, but this time it created a curious, almost comical effect, because Rigby Smith hadn't moved and had spoken from his lazy, supine position on the leaves. Jakeman stopped twisting my arm, but didn't let go of it altogether, and turned towards him.

"Oh, yes, and what are you going to do about it? Do you want another fight, Berry? Do you want to get thrashed again?"

"All right," said Rigby Smith, still in his recumbent position, though he did raise himself slightly on one elbow. "See if you can do it again."

Jakeman faltered for a moment. Perhaps he was surprised by Rigby Smith's casual manner, as I was. But then it dawned on me why Rigby Smith was so easy-going, so relaxed, so different from the way he'd been at their last fight. Here in the woods there were no baying crowds and Jakeman had no supporters. There was little likelihood of Teddy Eldin or any other staff hearing any sounds of a private fight in the woods, so Rigby Smith's fear of being caned for fighting, which was genuine, I believed, was not a factor, nor was shortage of time which Rigby Smith had used as an excuse before, though I was less sure about that excuse. Above all, the stage for the fight, if there was to be a fight, was the woods where Rigby Smith was perfectly at home. The re-match, if it was to happen, would be like a home fixture for him.

Jakeman sensed, I think, that he was facing a more confident Rigby Smith this time. And he realised that whereas Rigby Smith would have my full moral support, he was on his own this time. But he pressed on. After all, he had beaten Rigby Smith once before in a straight fight, as he saw it, and he may not have known, or believed if he *had* known, what had inhibited Rigby Smith on that occasion.

"Get up then," said Jakeman to Rigby Smith, releasing me, "this won't take long." He was still as sure of himself and arrogant as ever.

"No," said Rigby Smith. "You want to fight, you come and get me. Why I should get up for you?" Jakeman hesitated only a second before replying,

"All right, you've asked for it!" And, from a couple of yards away, he hurled himself onto Rigby Smith. Except that he didn't. That was his intention. What actually happened was that as he was in mid air over Rigby Smith, Rigby Smith raised his right leg, momentarily caught Jakeman's flying body on the sole of his foot, and propelled him over his head into the undergrowth. It was a beautifully executed movement and astonished me in its precision. I had never seen Rigby Smith pull off anything so effective in any fight before, though I had seen him do some nice manoeuvres. Had he been saving that up for Jakeman, I wondered? Fortunately for Jakeman there were dense heaps of leaves in the undergrowth where he crash landed so he wasn't hurt much, even if he was shaken, and after a couple of seconds he got up and returned swiftly to Rigby Smith who was now standing on his feet looking ready for anything. Jakeman was still antagonistic but a new note had come into his voice: a note of admiration, envy even.

"Bloody hell, Berry!" he exclaimed, "how did you manage that?"

"I got it from a book," replied Rigby Smith.

"A book, what book?"

"What's the point of telling you? You don't read books, do you, Jakeman?"

"Watch it, Berry! You think you're so damned clever, don't you? I can read any book that matters. Not just schoolbooks, which is all you read, you bloody swot!"

"Is it? Well this is a book about judo, which I got from a sports shop, and it's not a schoolbook. So put that in your pipe and smoke it!"

Jakeman changed tack, he clearly wasn't comfortable talking about books with Rigby Smith. "I don't believe you," he said, "I think what you did was just a fluke. I bet you can't do it again."

"Try me!" said Rigby Smith. Jakeman and Rigby Smith then had an eyeball to eyeball confrontation for four or five seconds. Jakeman was probing for any weaknesses in Rigby Smith's resolution and confidence. Clearly he found none because he suddenly dropped his contemptuous manner and laughed. It was not a laugh entirely without mockery but it was a real laugh and eased the tension a little.

"Why should I fight you?" said Jakeman. I've beaten you once. What would be the point?" At this moment I sensed the chances of a fight were ebbing away unless Rigby Smith was determined to have one.

"You've beaten me once, Jakeman, yes, once only. There won't be a second time." Rigby Smith was making a stand but he wasn't exactly throwing down the gauntlet. Jakeman could walk away from that and he did.

"I'm not wasting any more time with you two," he said, "I've got better things to do," and he turned and walked away. I muttered under my breath 'good riddance to bad rubbish' and I thought he'd heard me for he turned round to say something, but it wasn't a hostile remark and was aimed at Rigby Smith not me. There was no scorn in Jakeman's voice, in fact it was almost conciliatory in tone.

"Will you lend me that book on judo sometime? I'd like to see it." There was a pause. Rigby Smith was weighing up how to respond. He clearly detected the friendly note in Jakeman's voice for he replied in a much more aimiable tone himself,

"Maybe, if I can have some of your swaps." Rigby Smith was referring to Jakeman's stamp collection. He had shown it to us once or twice, together with his collection of spare stamps or swaps. Rigby Smith had noted them well and wanted a couple of them, preferably without offering anything in return, but he hadn't wanted to ask any favours of Jakeman so he'd said nothing. Until now that is.

"Sure," said Jakeman, "maybe one or two. You can swap them for some of yours, anyway." And he turned again and walked off into the woods.

That was the beginning of the end of the rivalry and conflict between Jakeman and Rigby Smith. Jakeman stopped baiting him, and me too, fortunately. I was afraid he might turn his attention exclusively to me now that he had made peace of a kind with Rigby Smith but he evidently regarded us as a unit when it came to choosing his targets for mockery since he dropped his jeering and bullying approach to me too. That is not to say he changed completely. He was still cocky and facetious, he still found things to laugh at about Rigby Smith and me, but his laughter was much more good-natured; when he laughed at one of us he seemed to be genuinely amused by something, it was not entirely uncharitable, doing-down laughter.

The next term Rigby Smith and Jakeman were both playing in the First Eleven hockey team and had to get on together and I believe they did, up to a point. That year Jakeman won the Best Sportsman of the Year Award and the following year, after Jakeman had left and gone to Marby College, Rigby Smith won it. Would Jakeman have been pleased to know that Rigby Smith won the same award as him, that they had a major achievement in common? That they really were equally matched, in sport, at least? I don't suppose Jakeman could have cared less but it's nice to think he might have done. As I've conceded already, although a show-off, bully and tormentor, Jakeman had his good qualities or, at least, his enviable ones.

Incidentally, Rigby Smith got the swaps he wanted from Jakeman but he never showed Jakeman the book on judo. He told me that he had never actually promised to lend Jakeman the book and he seemed to suggest that getting some stamps from Jakeman in exchange for nothing amounted to putting one over Jakeman. At the time that pleased me and didn't strike me as being ethically dubious, and in any case I wondered whether the real reason for Rigby Smith not lending the book to Jakeman was that it didn't exist. I never saw it. That doesn't mean anything, though. His house was full of books. The only room in the house where there weren't books was the bathroom, and I was never likely to have seen every book he might have read.

Had he really mastered some judo skills by studying them in a book or was that brilliant throw of Jakeman in the woods merely an instinctive, spur of the moment action? He'd done it, though, that was the important thing, and he'd levelled the score with Jakeman in his eyes and mine. Actually, what caused him to go back up in my estimation was not so much his proven fighting ability as his self-possession and self-confidence. That was the quality that had impressed me from the beginning, when I first met him in the classroom when I was eight.

One thing I must stress here is that the ups and downs of Rigby Smith's stature and esteem in my eyes did not fundamentally affect our friendship. They certainly affected our *relationship* in that I looked up to him less when I realised his fallibility and learned of his weaknesses, and when the gap between us narrowed, in schoolwork anyway. But we remained firm friends. We still spent a lot of time in each other's company and we enjoyed each other's company. We travelled to school together on most days, we were in class together daily and in the same Group and we were in the Cubs, then Scouts together. We usually spent Games time together and even when Rigby Smith was in the school teams and I wasn't, I often took part in practice games with him.

So the knocks that Rigby Smith suffered to his standing and reputation did not threaten our friendship. There was indeed a threat to our friendship as we grew older but it came from a different source, outside ourselves. It came from another boy. And that boy was Nevan.

Nevan

Nevan and the Rigby Smiths

Bernie Nevan was not at Penly Grange School the first two years I was there and he could do nothing to prevent the establishment of my firm friendship with Rigby Smith during that time. Like us, Nevan was a bus-travelling day boy from Marby, and as soon as he appeared on the scene he started to wriggle in on our journeys to school each day, sitting by Rigby Smith on the bus whenever he could. As a matter of fact, though, even before Nevan came on board, I had to get used to sharing Rigby Smith's company with someone else when travelling to and from school, because a year or so after I started at Penly Grange, Rigby Smith's younger brother Colin joined the school and tagged on to his older brother, which was a bit of a nuisance, I found.

Even by the standards of most seven-year-old boys, Colin Rigby Smith was a scruffy, untidy individual, with his shirt regularly hanging out, the knot of his tie halfway round his neck, socks round his ankles and shoe laces invariably loose if not completely untied. The only boy who was scruffier than Colin Rigby Smith, apart from Webley-Brown, was his cousin Terry who started at Penly Grange two years after Colin. Although we all found it difficult to keep ink off our fingers from the ink wells in our desks and from the dripping metal nibs of our crude, old-fashioned wooden pen holders, Colin Rigby Smith seemed to attract ink to his hands as if it belonged there; they were always ink-stained and he hardly seemed to notice. His form mistress Mrs Nogg used to call him Inky Paws.

He was unaware of, or indifferent to, other physical factors such as the weather or temperature. We all had to carry a rain coat with us to school which Colin Rigby Smith managed to do but he never wore it. He carried it on the top of his satchel, inside the shoulder strap, and that's where it always stayed no matter how hard it was raining. Rigby Smith, Martin, who was supposed to be looking after him, was always telling him to put it on, and Colin was always 'going to, in a minute' but he never did, and then Martin got into trouble with his mother when they got home if Colin was soaking wet. Colin miraculously managed not to lose his cap, at least not very often, but that too was attached to his satchel in some precarious fashion and seldom, if ever, worn. There was an amusing side to all this of course, and his scruffiness and carelessness didn't really bother me, but I was bothered about other things associated with him.

170

For instance, the way he always wanted to join in our games when he was far too young to do so at the age seven or eight when we were nine or ten, and the way he affected our walking home together from the bus station in Marby. Before Colin was around, Martin and I used to linger in Marby town centre and look in shop windows and buy sweets in a leisurely fashion. Occasionally Martin would walk part of the way back to my home or I would walk some way with him to his home, even though we lived in opposite directions and it might add half an hour or so to the time it took us to get home. We never thought twice about it, we were friends, but once Martin became responsible for getting his younger brother home we spent less time hanging around the shops and seldom if ever walked towards each other's homes from the bus station.

So Colin Rigby Smith was a bit of a drag on us, especially when he first started at Penly Grange, but less so as he got older, and eventually I came to like him and we became quite good friends. He had a sense of humour similar to mine and liked practical joking and the odd prank. He was quite a good cricketer (like both his brothers), a spin bowler, and about the time I was scoring for the First Eleven cricket team he also scored for the Second or Third Eleven, when his Under Eleven team weren't playing. To take the mickey out of boys scoring for the opposition, he would make up comical variations on the names of our team members. Webley-Brown (who was not bad at sport, incidentally) would become Web-Belly Pot-Brown; blond-haired Spilwell would be *Spin*well White Head; and a name like Simpson would become Simpering-Pimpleton. Colin used to be highly amused when the opposing scorer really believed boys at Penly Grange had such preposterous names and gullibly wrote them down in their score books and put official scores next to them.

Colin Rigby Smith may have been an irritant when he was younger but he was hardly ever a serious obstacle to my friendship with Martin. He was very much Martin's younger brother, there was over two years between them and they quarrelled a lot, so there was never any question of them uniting against me as brothers. I suppose I took Martin's side if I had to take sides, though I don't remember any disputes involving just the three of us, and I don't remember Colin ever resenting my presence. The same could not be said for Nevan. Colin was frequently in some sort of conflict or argument with Nevan, and since I found Nevan a rival from the beginning, Colin and I tended to have something else in common as well as our sense of humour – opposition to Nevan.

However, the situation wasn't straightforward because as time went on Nevan came to regard himself as a friend of Colin's as well as Martin's and deigned to play with Colin even if Martin wasn't around. This was pure expediency, of course. Nevan was always round at the Rigby Smiths' and would play with whoever was there, even Colin if need be, if no one else was there. But to be fair, there *were* times when Nevan and Colin got on all right. According to Mrs Rigby Smith, Bernie (she never called him by his surname Nevan, like us) was fine with just one other boy; it was only in the company of two others or more that he fomented trouble. It seems he couldn't resist it.

Nevan was about the same age as me, i.e. about three months younger than Martin. He was shorter than Martin and very slightly taller than me. I used to assert he was the same size as me, no bigger, but to be honest I suppose he was perhaps half an inch taller than me when we first met at the age of ten. I was a slow developer physically and I think he might, in fact, have become another half an inch taller than me before we left Penly Grange.

He was small-framed and slim, with thin, light brown and shiny hair; smooth, pale brown skin; small nose and unremarkable facial features. What was special about him was his eyes, his narrow, greeny-brown eyes. Actually, his eyes may not have been narrow in themselves: they just seemed to be because his regular look involved a narrowing of his eyes in a sly, knowing expression. It was a guarded, secretive, sometimes probing, inquisitive look. The look said either 'I know something you don't know but I'm not telling you' or 'You know something I don't know, don't you? Why don't you come clean?' It seemed it was all right for him to tease us with secrets he was keeping to himself but we had no right to keep any secrets to ourselves. He fed on intrigue and gossip from any source.

Nevan had met Martin Rigby Smith in a street near their homes, and the Rigby Smiths used to jest that he and Martin had only become friends because of Nevan's television. Nevan had invited Martin round to watch his TV, and since the Rigby Smiths did not have television at the time, Martin had jumped at the chance and had immediately become hooked, especially on the Monday Western (Hopalong Cassidy, Tex Ritter, Roy Rogers etc.). Later, when the Rigby Smiths acquired television but had only the BBC channel, the Nevans had ITV or 'commercial' TV as it was known then, so Nevan maintained his hold on Martin through his TV set. He had other inducements to lure Martin to his place as will become apparent when I tell you more about his home.

So, when I said Nevan was always round at the Rigby Smiths' it was only a half truth. The full truth was that Martin was either hosting Nevan at his home or round at Nevan's home. When I went round to see Martin at weekends or in the holidays, which was not a regular occurrence because I lived on the other side of Marby, Nevan would nearly always be at the Rigby Smiths' or Martin would be round at his place. I liked being at the Rigby Smiths', even when Nevan was there, unless he was being particularly obnoxious. Apart from Martin, I came to like Colin too as time went on, as I've said, and I also appreciated the fact that their older brother James did not look down on me as many boys of his age group did but would treat me respectfully and pay some attention to me (at times).

Mrs Rigby Smith, a well spoken, highly educated but not posh lady, with long dark hair, was also nice to me and would sometimes engage me in thoughtful discussion. In fact, that's what I particularly liked about the Rigby Smith household in general: it was a place where you could have an intelligent conversation. The house being full of books helped to make it a natural place for serious conversation but since it wasn't a highly ordered and rigorously tidy house, you could still feel relaxed there and talk freely.

Martin's father, a very hardworking surgeon, I saw very little of, but I discovered he was a good sort because he would sometimes play football on Sunday afternoons with his sons and their friends in Belcombe Park, a National Trust property near Marby. Once or twice I joined in, and I discovered Mr Rigby Smith was a pretty good player and a very considerate one. He would pass you the ball when you were in his team to keep you fully involved, and he'd spread the ball around the pitch, not just do through-passes to the players most likely to score. I was comfortable therefore with all the Rigby Smiths, the parents and all three brothers, and with being in their home. I didn't find Nevan's home so welcoming, though.

Unless I was needed to make up the numbers for a game, Nevan did not seem pleased to see me when I went round to his place, which I only did if Martin had gone there. He didn't make any explicit comment and never tried to send me away (directly) but he used to give me a look of grudging welcome, as if to say, 'Oh, it's you, is it?' and he made me feel an intruder into his and Martin's company, an intruder whom he was graciously tolerating. This was infuriating since I felt *he* was the intruder into our friendship.

Nevan had an elder brother, quite a lot older than him (though not as old as my brother and sister), who regarded him as an uncivilised little pest (like Robert Brown's view of his younger brother William in Richmal Crompton's William books) and who seemed to view Martin and me in the same light, in contrast to James Rigby Smith's attitude to me. Nevan's father, a solicitor, who was seldom at home, was taciturn and uncommunicative when there, a world apart from us, though he was never unpleasant to us.

Nevan's house was very neat and tidy, and we were usually confined to one part of the house – downstairs in the back living room – to keep it that way. In the Rigby Smiths' house there was only one room we were expected to leave undisturbed, apart from their parents' bedroom, and that was Mr Rigby Smith's study where he kept his photographic equipment and his medical books and papers. So I much preferred the Rigby Smiths' house to the Nevan's and, sometimes, if I came round to see Martin and he wasn't at home but round at the Nevan's, I would go straight back home. That's if I was feeling in a particularly anti-Nevan mood and not up to the mental sparring that inevitably went on between us when Martin was present.

But I mustn't be unfair on the Nevans and their house and hospitality. Although I didn't feel entirely at home at Nevan's, and his large, tidy and immaculate mock-Tudor house wasn't as homely and lived-in as the Rigby Smiths' (it didn't, after all, have three boys traipsing all over it all the time), it did have an agreeable touch of grandeur about it, especially the pillared verandah overlooking their tennis court, which impressed me and gave me a sense of privilege to be there. Moreover, Mrs Nevan was a gracious lady who was usually pleased to receive Bernie's friends at her home, and she certainly regarded me as a friend of his and not just Martin's friend; she accepted me willingly, she didn't just tolerate me.

Mrs Nevan was always very nicely dressed and her hair was beautifully arranged with a neat bun at the back of her head. She had a dark complexion and large, dark brown eyes, and she was always very courteous to me and kind and generous to all of us. She often gave us tea and would offer us round, chocolate mint biscuits, wrapped in green and silver foil, which were called Yo-Yos and were a real treat. Even so, although generally gentle and relaxed towards us, she was a bit of a stickler about correct speech and manners and would sometimes tell us off when our noisy or rough-edged behaviour became too much for her.

But she never shouted at us, she always spoke very softly and politely. Her favourite reproof was 'that's not to your credit', a delightful understatement, however strongly expressed, which matched Mr Rigby Smith's understated admonitions or reprimands, such as 'that's not very elegant', for bad table manners or uncouth behaviour, or 'that's not a very good idea', for reckless or stupid behaviour. Mrs Rigby Smith's big thing was consideration for other people's feelings. 'How would you like it?' she would say if she witnessed, or heard about, any teasing or unkindness or lack of consideration on the part of her sons. She was well aware of the power of words to wound and would exhort her sons, and her sons' friends, if the occasion presented itself, to think before making a comment about other people and ask three questions: 'Is it kind?' 'Is it true?' 'Is it necessary'?

Mrs Rigby Smith, though, didn't believe her sons paid much attention to her words, certainly not when they concerned tidying their things or coming home for a meal on time. Sometimes when I was going to have a meal with them and we were playing out first, down in the field with Martin and Colin, and we came home late, Mrs Rigby Smith would get very cross and say to them, 'There's no point in saying anything to you, is there? It's all in one ear and out the other' or she might say, 'It's water off a duck's back, isn't it!'

My own mother didn't correct me much or moralise with me a lot. I think she'd given up pep talks to her children after failing to have any impact (she thought) on my much older sister and brother. She was only concerned that I shouldn't get into trouble. She seemed happy about my fraternising with the Rigby Smiths and if I asked her if I could go to their house, she would simply say, 'Don't get into trouble and don't be back late'. My dad whom I saw little of because he always seemed to be away on business trips didn't say much to me about my behaviour but I remember when I was about eight or younger he would say, 'Don't do this or that', or sometimes it was, 'Don't upset your mother', followed by 'or I'll belt you!'. He did belt me once, with his slipper, but it made very little impact on me, unlike Teddy Eldin's canings.

Nevan the Agitator

Nevan's most notable behavioural trait, as already intimated, was his disposition to stir up trouble. Had my mother known this and known that a visit to the Rigby Smiths' was liable to bring me into contact with a natural trouble-maker, she might have been less free in granting me permission to go round to the Rigby Smiths'. Nevan could stir up disputes amongst any group of boys just by his mere presence sometimes. At the time I thought he was simply a malevolent person and I was convinced he spared no opportunity to undermine my friendship with Martin. Looking back now, however, I see things more psychologically and a little differently.

Nevan had no siblings to play with: his elder brother looked down on him and offered him no companionship. He liked being with other boys, he was a sociable type, and had a very low boredom threshold. He had an excessive hunger for excitement and sensation which was only partly assuaged by adventure comics and tabloid gossip about the misfortunes of movie stars or pop stars and by his watching of war films and his collection of war memorabilia. In other words, he wasn't satisfied with second hand, vicarious experience of war and hubbub, and, where they were absent in his own life, he thought he would create them or something equivalent. Not because he was malicious exactly but because upheaval and disruption were for him stimulating and entertaining.

When he was with other boys and nothing very much was going on, it was as if a subconscious voice within him said, 'This is all very dull, why don't you liven things up a bit. Get some arguments going, stir up some disagreements about something, anything. Boys are made for action, competition, conflict, not peaceful co-existence'. He was a bit like young Albert Ramsbottom in the famous Lancashire monologue which relates Albert's visit with his parents to the zoo in Blackpool. In this zoo, there's a great big lion called Wallace lying quietly in his cage, with his sleepy head leaning against the bars. The monologue goes on, as Lancashire folk will know:

Now Albert had heard about Lions,
How they was ferocious and wild –
To see Wallace lying so peaceful,
Well, it didn't seem right to the child.

So straightway the brave little feller,
Not showing a morsel of fear,
Took his stick with its horse's 'ead 'andle
And pushed it in Wallace's ear.

Nevan was frequently pushing a stick metaphorically into somebody's ear to get a reaction when nothing much was happening. Sometimes he would merely provoke one of us and there'd be bickering and perhaps a quarrel or two would break out. Sometimes he would single someone out, like Colin or me, and get the others to gang up on that person. The others would include Martin, Brian Barley, and one of the Wheeler brothers, and perhaps Toffee if he was there, though he might be the victim himself. Martin's attitude was ambivalent. If he was persuaded that the ganging up was just a game he would go along with it but if it turned acrimonious or cruel he would usually object. But there was one famous piece of ganging-up-on-one-person he was drawn into by Nevan which was extremely unkind and which he didn't object to at all. In fact, from all accounts, he joined in on it with relish.

I say 'from all accounts' because I wasn't there and I got the story from Colin, Martin himself and, briefly, from Mrs Nevan. Toffee was the victim on this occasion, a perfect target for Nevan. Toffee was the nickname of Raymond Denton who lived about a mile from the Rigby Smiths. He was a little posher than the Rigby Smiths because he went to a slightly better class of prep school and as well as playing sports like cricket and tennis he played golf and was learning to ride. He was no more of a snob than any of us were (and maybe we were all a bit snobbish through being at private school, though the Wheelers weren't, they went to the local state school) but he spoke in a deep, rather formal and pukka voice which, together with his more upmarket lifestyle, led to him being dubbed a 'toff' which then became 'toffee', a name which stuck. It was not one of Jakeman's nicknames because Toffee was not at Penly Grange and Jakeman didn't know him, though doubtless he would have ragged him given half a chance.

Toffee, who was nearer in age to Colin than Martin, started off as Colin's friend, became friendly with Martin and, eventually, the older brother James too. I think Nevan was jealous of Toffee, perhaps inevitably, since Mrs Rigby Smith made no secret of the fact that she liked Toffee too and so did Mr Rigby Smith, so he was well in with all the Rigby Smiths who, incidentally, always used his nickname with affection and never in a taunting way. To them he really was Toffee and not Raymond or Ray. The trouble with Toffee, certainly when he was about nine or ten, was that he had a short fuse and took himself very seriously. This made him an ideal object of provocation for Nevan. Nevan could easily wind him up and lost no opportunity to do so. Sometimes, when teased, Toffee would burst into a blazing rage and bright sparks would fly. So Nevan, who loved fireworks, incidentally, thought he'd make something of it. On one occasion, he set up Toffee's towering temper like a firework, lit the fuse and stood well back to watch the effect. Very well back.

Nevan had a shed in his garden, provided for him by his parents, which acted as an HQ for various activities and adventure games. There was no such shed in the Rigby Smiths' garden so Nevan's shed was one more enticement for Martin (and Colin) to Nevan's place. The shed was quite a solid construction and had a lockable door. There was a small window but it was just a pane of glass, it didn't open. One day, when Toffee was round at Nevan's with Martin and Colin Rigby Smith, Nevan had the idea of luring Toffee into the shed and then locking him in. Just for a bit of fun, he said.

Martin went along with the idea and so did Colin, reluctantly, when given a role to play in the game and assured it would be just for a couple of minutes … just to see what happened. So Nevan got Colin to tell Toffee there was a secret message for him hidden in the shed, and while Toffee was looking for this message that didn't exist Nevan whipped out the key of the shed from his pocket and turned the key in the lock. Toffee didn't cotton on for awhile what was going on, he thought it was part of the game, but when he realised he'd been tricked he came to the door and started to bang on it.

He was clearly not amused and at this point Colin thought they should let him out. But Nevan thought he should stew for a lot longer and suggested they all went off to the Rigby Smiths' for awhile. They played cards for about twenty minutes and then Colin and Martin began to feel uneasy and agreed it was time they went back to let Toffee out. They got back to an empty shed and a very irate Mrs Nevan. Toffee was gone. Mrs Nevan had heard Toffee shouting, kicking and hammering on the door. He'd hammered and kicked for a very long time apparently. Fortunately, Mrs Nevan had a spare key and she had unlocked the door and released him. Toffee had gone storming off home and wasn't seen again for a fortnight. He rarely went back to Nevan's house after that, except, when a bit older, to play tennis.

Rigby Smith told me he had never seen Mrs Nevan so angry. She was angry with them all but especially with her son Bernie because it was his shed and he was in charge of the key. When Nevan protested it was only a bit of fun and they were going to let Toffee out soon enough, she rebuked him with her usual reprimand 'that's not to your credit', only this time she actually raised her voice. She was really furious, and Nevan was banned from using the shed for three weeks. I don't think he was all that chastened, though, because I heard him laughing about it a week later with Martin. Martin himself wasn't very comfortable about it, especially since his own mother had been as angry as Mrs Nevan when she heard about it, brushing aside his excuse about it being only a game, saying, "How would you have liked it, would it have been a game for you? Always think of other people's feelings!"

Sometimes it wasn't enough for Nevan merely to stir up trouble amongst his friends or playmates. He looked for excitement beyond our group, to more explosive and dangerous targets than Toffee. Indeed, like young Albert, he sought to rouse sleeping *lions* (not just short-tempered puppies) and there were one or two in the vicinity. To begin with, there was the Gribley gang, made up of slightly older boys from other schools. They weren't really dangerous if you kept out of their way but they were dry tinder and could be ignited. Nevan didn't like fighting much himself, being on the small side and not very strong, but he liked to see other people fighting. Martin Rigby Smith's gang and the Gribley gang seldom came to blows, it was all posturing at the end of the road, a free exchange of taunts and insults, the usual sort of bravado. You know:

"We could batter you before breakfast, you little squits!"

"Come on, then, prove it, if you're so tough … you couldn't batter an egg!"

"Come 'ere and we'll show you!"

"No, you come 'ere! Prove it over 'ere."

"We don't need to. We could sort you out any place, any time."

"You and whose army?"

"Army? We don't need an army: we could beat you with our arms tied behind our backs," etc., etc.

Martin knew it would be madness to engage with the Gribley gang other than verbally because his gang weren't numerous or strong enough. But Nevan wanted some sort of action and some sort of victory over the Gribley gang, even a successful skirmish would be better than nothing, and he knew of someone who could prove to be a secret weapon to this end. His name was Gordon and he was the Rigby Smiths' neighbour. Gordon was quite friendly with the Rigby Smiths, especially James. He was a bit older than James and, more significantly, he was tall and massively built and he moved with a solid, menacing motion like a humanoid, two-wheeled tank. Just the sort of ally they needed in battle. If only they could get him to join the gang.

But it wasn't a realistic prospect, he was much too old to get involved in smaller boys' affairs, especially since James himself wasn't even a regular member of the gang (though Martin used to claim he was when questioned about the personnel of his gang). However, if they could make the Gribley gang *believe* Gordon was a member of the Rigby Smith gang it would do a great deal for their kudos and image. They could walk around the neighbourhood with just that little bit more confidence, maybe even a swagger.

One day Nevan orchestrated events so that Gordon did become involved in our gang conflict, although if only briefly. Nevan's machinations didn't always work but you had to admire his cunning, I suppose, when they did. He knew any plea to Gordon to join the Rigby Smith gang would fall on deaf ears, we were just little kids to him. What Nevan decided to do therefore was simply to get Gordon to come out into the road at a critical moment. The plan, over which he collaborated with Martin (not me, though I was there), was firstly to draw the Gribley gang up the road to the Rigby Smiths' home with even more insolent and provocative gibes than usual. As the Gribley gang approached the Rigby Smiths' house and we withdrew into the front garden, Nevan, as planned, nipped round to Gordon's house and knocked on the door which was answered by Gordon's mother, as expected. Nevan did not say, 'Can Gordon come out and play?' but 'Can Gordon come out because James wants to show him something in the road'.

Intrigued, Gordon came out and walked ponderously and purposefully towards the Rigby Smiths' house. He was somewhat bemused to see about six or seven small boys (small to him not us) retreating down the road at speed. Fortunately, he didn't seem to mind when he discovered he'd been used by our gang, after all he hadn't had to do anything, merely appear, his large heavy bulk had done the work, but he wouldn't be tricked into coming out again. Still, that didn't matter for quite a while. The Gribley gang were convinced Gordon was in the Rigby Smith gang, kept well clear of the Rigby Smiths' territory and showed us a bit more respect. They still hung around Nevan's home occasionally but that didn't worry Nevan too much. He knew how to take evasive action and, what's more, his Machiavellian instincts led him into making friends with one of the Gribley gang so that if he was cornered by the group at any time he would have an ally amidst them.

Nevan had mixed success trying to arouse another sleeping lion – Mr Hay. Gordon lived in a detached house on one side of the Rigby Smiths' 1920s detached home and Mr Hay lived on the other side of their house in an Edwardian semi-detached. Mr Hay was a crusty old bachelor who kept himself to himself and deliberately maintained an old-fashioned lifestyle; he resisted modern life as far as it was possible for him to do so. There were no labour-saving devices in his house, no washing machines, toasters, vacuum cleaners etc., and no TV, radio, or telephone. He preferred the frugal, fend-for-yourself way of life. He went to church every Sunday morning but that appeared to represent the full extent of his social interaction or, at least, fraternisation with others. He did have a car, a small van, which he needed for his hardware business at the other end of Marby town.

Mr Hay liked a quiet life and didn't welcome visitors. He had once been a teacher, but had clearly decided he didn't actually like children and he fully endorsed the Victorian maxim 'children should be seen and not heard' except that in his case he would rather they weren't seen either. His extreme unsociableness could be quite Scrooge-like. For instance, when there was a snowfall and the snow was suitable for sledging down the road he would try to prevent it by putting ashes down over the snow, and if he saw anyone with a toboggan he would come out and castigate them for making the pavement and road allegedly more dangerous for pedestrians. He hated ice cream vans with their vulgar, jingly music and if one ever came up the road, he would rush out and tell the man in the van it was a private road (which it was) and he should ply his wares elsewhere, if he had to ply them at all. So instead of a bright-eyed, eager child running up to buy an ice cream, the ice cream man would get Mr Hay's furious red face, upbraiding voice and finger-wagging reproach close to his windscreen, and he'd be obliged to kill the music and remove his van from the road posthaste.

Mr Hay's liking for a quiet life was unfortunate because he lived next door to three noisy boys who were always playing games in their garden and knocking balls over into his garden and then disturbing him again by coming round to ask for them back. He initially did return the balls, grudgingly, when requested, but after a time he refused to do so on each and every occasion and said he would do so only from time to time and when it suited him. If one of the Rigby Smiths *had* to go round to get a ball back when they had run out of balls to play with, or had to apologise for some minor damage they had caused to his property through a flying ball (hit or thrown), he would bite off their heads with a fierce, sometimes prolonged rebuke. Yes, he had quite a temper and going round to see him – I emphasise only done if you *had* to – was not a very pleasant experience.

Nevan had heard about Mr Hay's touchy temperament, of course, but rarely if ever seen him in a full flare-up. He tended not to be around (I can't think why) when one of the Rigby Smiths had gone to ask for a ball back or confess to the breaking of one of his greenhouse windows, which happened occasionally. Nevan decided he would very much like to see him stirred up. He was not going to break a window of course – Nevan was no vandal – nor was he going to go round and ask for a ball back and get a tongue-lashing. He proposed simply doing something which he and Rigby Smith normally did, but to intensify it, literally turn it up to a point which would catch the attention of Mr Hay and, he hoped, irritate him sufficiently to trigger his rage.

Nevan proposed playing their rock 'n' roll records as loudly as possible to annoy Mr Hay. Colin told me what happened when Nevan and his brother Martin tried it the second time. They had tried it once before, he told me, using Cliff Richard's records Move it and High Class Baby and got no response from Mr Hay next door or from anyone else. The idea had been a complete dud. Nevan was convinced this was because Cliff Richard's voice was not sufficiently raw and powerful. He insisted on playing Elvis Presley's Hound Dog, this time, and playing it at full volume over and over again. Inside the Rigby Smiths' house it really was very loud and at one point James appeared and ordered them to 'turn that racket down' and stop disturbing everyone. He was ignored. Hound Dog continued to blare out round the house:

You ain't nothing but a hound dog
Cryin' all the time.
You ain't nothing but a hound dog
Cryin' all the time.
Well, you ain't never caught a rabbit
And you ain't no friend of mine.

When they said you was high classed,
Well, that was just a lie.
When they said you was high classed,
Well, that was just a lie.
You ain't never caught a rabbit
And you ain't no friend of mine.

The words 'hound dog' and 'crying all the time' are certainly very audible and become very memorable after the record has been played a few times, even if the rest of the words of the song are somewhat indistinct and submerged in the general rock 'n' roll sound of this huge hit number.

Colin said his mother was out shopping or she would certainly have intervened. Anyway, Nevan's plan still didn't work, according to Colin. Mr Hay's house stood quiet and undisturbed, there was no sign of any movement or reaction from him. Perhaps he was out too? Or perhaps he just hadn't heard. The Rigby Smiths played their records in an upstairs room, and you could only open the top windows. This upstairs room was on the far side of the Rigby Smiths' house in relation to Mr Hay's house and being a detached house there was no question of the sound travelling straight through the walls into the adjoining house. Moreover, although gramophones could be quite loud in those days they didn't have the capacity for amplified sound that modern 'hi-fi' equipment has today. So Nevan's plan to rouse Mr Hay was a flop, but it didn't stop him trying again 'just to see'.

This third attempt roused James again, though not Mr Hay, but this time James tried a different tactic to stop Hound Dog being played at full volume. He started to practise his violin in the next room. I was in the Rigby Smiths' home on this occasion with Martin and Nevan, and I remember the incident well. (I don't remember Colin being there, but he probably was). I had heard James Rigby Smith playing the violin before and it was not a very mellifluous sound, to say the least, but he had played with some restraint so that the sound wasn't too penetrating. This time James scraped away ferociously at his violin strings, totally unconcerned about the quality of sound he was producing, and the effect on the ears was excruciating.

Nevan, Martin and I went into the next room and protested. James ignored us in the same way, I imagine, as they had ignored him when he had complained about Hound Dog being played too loudly before. They returned to the room where they were playing Hound Dog and left the door wide open so that the noise would sound even louder to James's ears. Whereupon, James played his violin even more loudly and screechingly. In the end we offered terms. We would stop playing Hound Dog if James would stop playing his violin. James agreed happily. He'd won.

Nevan did get Mr Hay to come out on one occasion in most spectacular fashion, though I've never been sure whether it was intentional or not. It happened in connection with another 'lion-rousing' enterprise which was very successful, too successful. It was positively dangerous, in fact, and I happened to be there. I liked a bit of mischief myself, especially if it was part of a collaboration with others, such as Martin or Colin Rigby Smith, but I wouldn't have supported this sort of mischief or condoned it if I'd had the choice. But I didn't have the choice. It happened too quickly, I just got caught up in it, with all the others. It was crazy, really, suicidal. But to Nevan it was just another entertaining experiment in human behaviour. What's more, he had made some provision for it, as I was to discover, and had anticipated what might happen.

As ever, he got someone else to spearhead his lion-rousing, and on this occasion it was the older of the two Wheeler brothers – Nick Wheeler. Nick, who wasn't at Penly Grange, was a tall, slim, tough lad who wasn't averse to a fight; as they say in the Westerns, he might not go *looking* for trouble but 'sure knew where to find it'. Nevan, who had got to know him through Martin, was only too ready to help him find trouble, if he was, unusually, having any difficulty doing so, and one Saturday afternoon he got Nick to provoke some lads who were playing football on the field at the end of the Rigby Smiths' road. Nevan suggested some taunts and insults he might use and Nick began hurling them at the football players who included some quite large lads. He was at a safe distance and the lads were so intent on their football that they continued to ignore Nick even when he raised his voice and made his insults a little more colourful.

"Lob a stone at them," said Nevan, and Nick duly complied. The stone fell harmlessly at the edge of the football pitch and, like the gibes, appeared to go unnoticed. At this point Martin became more aware of what was going on. He'd been talking to me about something and he turned and told Nick to stop it. Martin was alarmed and so was I. There were far more lads playing football than were in our gang and, as I've said, some of these lads were quite big. Nick, though supposedly a friend of Martin's, never liked doing what he was told by anyone, especially Martin, and he threw another stone.

"Look," said Martin, "you can't just throw stones at people! They'll retaliate soon. Just leave them." And he gestured to Nevan and Nick to come away.

"Oh, he's not doing any harm," Nevan responded. "He's only lobbing them. They're too far away to be hurt by a thrown stone. It's just a bit of a lark to see what they'll do."

"We know what they'll do," said Martin, "they'll come and get us. And they've done nothing to us. It's daft!"

"No, it isn't," Nevan replied. "It'll give us a chance try out that idea of ours. You know, the dustbin lids? I've told Nick and he thinks it's a great idea." I didn't know what he was talking about but Martin did and he answered with some surprise and anger,

"That was going to be used against the Gribley gang, not a load of people we don't even know!"

"Does it matter?" said Nevan. "We get to try it out, anyway. It's all ready." During this exchange between Martin and Nevan, Nick had continued lobbing stones and his aim was getting better. Eventually, and almost inevitably, one of his stones found a target, and then another one did. The first stone hit a player at the edge of the pitch on the leg and the next one fell right at the feet of the player with the ball. At last their concentration on their game of football was broken and they became aware they were under attack. There was a howl of furious protest from several of them as they looked around to see who was attacking them and from which quarter. Since Nick had made no attempt to conceal his whereabouts, though Nevan was hiding behind a tree, the players easily spotted him and ran towards him and us, picking up stones and anything else that came to hand as they did so.

"Quick!" said Nevan, "back to Martin's house." The Rigby Smiths' house was only about a hundred yards away but there was a long hedge in their road, running alongside the parallel footpath which led to the field where the lads had been playing, and Nevan, Nick Wheeler and the rest of us retreated as close to the hedge as possible which provided some cover and protection, at least for a minute or two. Nevan raced into the Rigby Smiths' drive, which was about ten yards long and led straight to the garage and adjacent shed, housing the dustbins, and beckoned us to follow him. And then I learnt what he meant by the dustbin lid idea. Martin had stopped arguing with Nevan. It was too late for arguments, and he was soon helping Nevan handing out dustbin lids from the shed.

"Use them as shields," Nevan instructed, and he brandished one in demonstration. The steel dustbin lids had handles on top so it was just a matter of grabbing their handles and holding them up with the insides of the lids facing outwards and you had perfect shields in your hands. Very conveniently, there seemed to be dustbin lids for all of us, and there must have been about six of us, and that's when I realised how Nevan had indeed prepared for this event. The Rigby Smiths had two dustbins and the Nevans perhaps three. But Martin and Nevan between them, I assumed, had gathered together at least half a dozen dustbin lids in readiness for a defence against a missile throwing enemy.

Nick, in a mood of bravado, went out into the road to draw the fire of the football players, to be briefly joined by Colin who seemed to gain courage with a dustbin lid in his hand. I went out too, relishing the excitement, feeling fairly safe with a dustbin lid in my hand, though I was careless for a moment and didn't hold my dustbin lid high enough and I took a glancing blow on my forehead from a small stone thrown by one of the footballers in the vanguard of their band. It didn't hurt much but it drew blood and I was suddenly pleased and proud to have been wounded in battle and hoped the others would be impressed, especially as I wasn't complaining or whimpering about it, but no one seemed to notice.

Having come through the hedge, the main body of football players advanced towards the Rigby Smiths' house, still full of righteous indignation, well armed with ammunition in the form of stones and bits of broken brick. The sound of stone and brick on metal, a clattering, chinking, chonging sound, depending on the size and weight of the stone and the force with which it had been hurled, could be increasingly heard as a hail of missiles hurtled through the air and bounced off the dustbin lids. Nick, Colin and I were soon forced to back off and return to the Rigby Smith drive, taking shelter of a kind behind the lilac tree which grew beside their gate.

"Shut the gate!" ordered Nevan and Martin together. This, like the dustbin lids, seemed part of a pre-arranged plan. I remember that in future years this green wooden gate stood permanently open until it finally rotted away and was removed. But at this time it was quite a solid and strong wooden gate which went across the full width of the drive and formed quite an effective barrier, in conjunction with the rest of the frontage of the Rigby Smiths' front garden which was protected by a brick wall surmounted by a green wire fence interlaced with thorny, rambling roses. So, shutting the gate, which was usually open, was like raising the drawbridge of a castle under siege.

Unfortunately, the gate was not as effective as a drawbridge. It might have prevented the infuriated football players from reaching us, but it offered little defence against flying stones and broken bricks. The dustbin lids protected our own bodies from these missiles fairly successfully but they couldn't prevent them from hitting the flowers or shrubs in the garden, the walls of the house and the windows of the Rigby Smith home. Martin and Colin Rigby Smith weren't too bothered about the flowers and shrubs and probably thought the walls could withstand a certain amount of pelting with hard objects – it was a solidly built house – but they were clearly worried about the windows.

And not without cause, because one or two missiles began hitting the windows. Miraculously, the missiles did not break any glass at first but it was only a matter of time before a window was broken, maybe several windows were broken, and that spelt serious trouble for Martin and Colin because they knew they couldn't plead innocence and allege it was an 'unprovoked attack'. *They* had started it. Well, Nick had started it, egged on by Nevan, but they were both their friends, they couldn't use them as an excuse, it was a matter of joint responsibility. Martin and Colin knew that. Martin told me afterwards he was just about to sue for peace, to avoid a huge damage bill and extremely irate parents – though he'd no idea how he would achieve a truce with Nick as defiant as ever and continuing to hurl abuse at the football players – when it happened. Salvation. In the form of Mr Hay!

Elvis Presley and Hound Dog had not roused Mr Hay. But he was roused now. Oh, yes! Mr Hay was not a very tall man, in fact he was on the short side, but he was quite wiry and very fit and energetic for a middle-aged man, and, with his red face, and his eyes blazing rage and indignation, he was a fearsome sight. Especially when wielding a stick, as he was now! He was also shouting with eloquent venom – as an ex-English teacher he had quite a good vocabulary and turn of phrase:

"You rascals, you ruffians, you louts, you rabble-rousers, you hooligans!" Fortunately, all his ire was directed against the football players, none of it at us. "This is a private road, a quiet road, a peaceful road." (He seemed to have forgotten that he lived next to the Rigby Smith boys). "Take your noise and your lawlessness and undisciplined behaviour away from here! I will have peace and quiet in this road. Get out, get out, get out!"

It wasn't clear to me whether his face, his stick or his words made the most impact, but the astonished football players were soon running for their lives back down the road towards the field whence they had come and out of sight behind the hedge. Mr Hay pursued them halfway down the road and then returned towards his house. We were mightily relieved, of course, but also, left high and dry, and still holding our dustbin lids (though lowered now), we felt rather foolish and wondered what he would say to us. He said nothing, in fact, just threw us a 'think yourselves lucky' look, and stalked back through his little gate and into his house.

We were surprised he'd said nothing at all about the stone throwing and that he'd only mentioned the noise; that, as ever, was the major offence for Mr Hay. He didn't appear to be blaming *us* for all the rumpus in the road which, let's face it, Nick Wheeler and Nevan had stirred up in the first place. But he didn't know that, and he may have thought we were innocent because we were behind the Rigby Smiths' gate and not out in the road, and we were clearly defending ourselves.

Mr Hay's intervention, which dug the Rigby Smiths out of a hole, was obviously a stroke of good fortune for them, and all of us, but especially for Nevan. Before Mr Hay intervened, Martin was furious with Nevan for encouraging Nick to provoke an attack on his home, with potentially serious consequences, but Mr Hay's sudden appearance on the scene changed his attitude entirely. It became a great story for him and Nevan to relate and to add to the folklore about Mr Hay that they were accumulating. Nevan was so crafty about it when he told the story! His clever idea to use the dustbin lids was always highlighted and he even went beyond that, hinting that *he* had got Mr Hay to come out, that it was part of his overall strategy; and it was difficult to deny this completely because he had got Gordon to come out. I didn't really believe it, nor, I think, did Martin, but he wasn't sure, and nor was I, to be honest. You just never knew with Nevan.

Rigby Smith's Friendship with Nevan

I always thought Martin's friendship with Nevan was a very odd affair and although I was biased I must point out that Colin thought so too and, from one or two remarks that she made, so did Mrs Rigby Smith. Superficially their friendship was easy to explain. They lived very close together, were about the same age, though Nevan was a bit younger than Martin, and after Nevan was ten they were both day boys at Penly Grange School. They each had things the other one wanted. Nevan, as already mentioned, had a TV, later a better TV when the Rigby Smiths acquired their first TV. He also had a shed for meetings, the latest style of radio or gramophone, and usually the very latest records, a wide range of comics, and a tennis court.

For his part, Martin made an almost ideal playmate for Nevan, not only because he was enterprising, full of ideas and game for almost anything, but also because he had two brothers within a two-year age range – one older, one younger – and there was always something going on at the Rigby Smith home, or out in the road or down the road in the field not far from the Rigby Smiths' house. Nevan and Martin certainly had many tastes in common too. Sport, pop music and a fondness both for playing make-believe adventure games and for gang warfare, mostly pretend gang warfare or 'shadow boxing' with other gangs.

They also enjoyed going to the cinema together – 'going to the pictures' we called it – and talking about the films afterwards and the trailers for movies to come, sometimes re-enacting scenes from the films. I often went with them to the cinema and Colin would come too on most occasions. We usually went in the afternoons, any week day in the holidays, especially Thursdays, and Wednesdays (a half school day) in term time, if Martin and Nevan weren't involved in any school matches. We sometimes went to the Saturday morning matinees at The Palace Cinema, which were jam-packed and noisy, swarming with every wild and uncouth kid from Marby. If you wanted an ice cream or drink in the interval, it was a real battle to get to the girl with the refreshment tray hanging round her neck. These Saturday morning matinees consisted of a wide variety of short movies, some of which were serialised. I remember films like Tarzan, Roy Rogers, Lassie and Bugs Bunny. The animated Bugs Bunny was in colour but most of the other films were black and white.

When we went to full length feature films during the week, the cinema was rarely full and the atmosphere was much calmer and more dignified. We tended to sit upstairs. I remember seeing films with the Rigby Smiths such as A Hill in Korea, The Square Peg (and other Norman Wisdom films), The Great Locomotive Chase, Battle of the River Plate, The Dam Busters,

Hollywood or Bust and quite a few Westerns. We loved Westerns and Norman Wisdom films especially but our favourite of all was probably the adventure film Twenty Thousand Leagues Under the Sea, a movie version of Jules Verne's fantasy novel, starring James Mason and Kirk Douglas. The Rigby Smiths and Nevan must have seen it at least four times and they looked down on me because I only managed to see it three times. Nevan always got the part-coloured movie magazine which featured the currently-shown film, and he would display it to all of us and allow us to look at it for a few minutes at a time (he was very generous like that). He let Martin look at it more than anyone else, to suggest that he and Martin were extra special friends. I tried not to let this bother me but of course it did.

Martin and Nevan were unquestionably close friends but they didn't get on perfectly together by any means. They disagreed quite a lot, in fact, and were not really compatible mentally – not in the way Martin and I were – and their undoubted rivalry over some things seemed quite deep-seated to me, not always just friendly rivalry. They may have been relaxed together when it was just the two of them on their own, but when there were others around there was some competition over who would exert the most influence over the others and get their way in choice of games they played.

In garden cricket or football, or cricket or football played on the field near the Rigby Smiths' home, there was a fair degree of collaboration because we all enjoyed those games equally, the rules were generally agreed, and those games couldn't be played at all if everyone didn't join in wholeheartedly. We would always be short of enough people for a proper game but we would get by somehow if we really wanted to: 'where there's a will, there's a way'. Problems would arise when we couldn't get two equally balanced sides but that's always a problem for any group of boys, it was not just a problem for us.

However, their make-believe games were much more problematical. They both enjoyed Cowboys and Indians, because this American make-believe game, based almost entirely on Westerns seen in the cinema or on TV, involved plenty of simulated action: riding, shooting, lassoing, running, jumping, crawling, swimming, wrestling, fisticuffs, and the use of a range of weaponry, including six-shooters and rifles, and bows and arrows, and spears and hatchets and knives, in a range of exciting stock situations such as pitched battles on the open plains, the attack and defence of waggon trains and forts, ambushes in passes, and, to add to it all, at critical moments of high danger and drama, Indian war cries and drums, and bugle-accompanied cavalry charges coming to the last minute rescue. They both loved re-enacting all that and being both Cowboys and Indians at different times but I think Nevan preferred being a Cowboy because the Cowboys tended to have the guns. So Cowboys and Indians was fine but as time went on, Nevan increasingly preferred more modern war games, Second World War games, involving machine guns and much more powerful armaments.

Martin preferred more ancient, time-honoured forms of fighting and smaller scale conflicts, entailing hideouts in remote places and ambushes in passes which had boulders and bushes where small bands of outlaws could hide before pouncing; and, following his cowboy hero the Range Rider, as seen on TV, he loved leaping on his enemies and engaging them in imaginary fist fights rather than shooting them. He also wanted to play Robin Hood, as at school, but Nevan said there weren't suitable woods nearby and he regarded bow and arrows as rather limiting and primitive. Nevan liked full scale military engagements with tanks, artillery and aeroplanes and huge explosions causing craters and collapsing buildings and utter devastation. Anything less was too tame for him.

So there came to be disputes and arguments over which make-believe game they were going to play. Colin and the others (who might have included the Barley brothers, Toffee and the Wheeler brothers) were caught in the middle, and me too if I was there. I tended to go along with Martin, which Nevan didn't like of course, and Colin might take either side. Colin, being younger than us, just wanted to take part and didn't mind much what was played just so long as he was involved.

Whatever make-believe games were played, though, lack of numbers presented difficulties, in some ways more serious ones than for the sports we played together, because James Rigby Smith, who could nearly always be persuaded to join in with football or cricket, would refuse to play make-believe games. They had no appeal for him at all or maybe it was just that being two years older than the rest of us he'd grown out of them. So they'd be at least one down on numbers when they wanted to play pretend games. Yet make-believe by its very nature can supply things missing in reality and, according to Colin, Nevan and his brother Martin had some terrific make-believe games at times, sometimes entirely on their own, and got on famously. Hearing this did make me jealous, I must admit, because I considered the make-believe, fantasy games Martin and I played in the woods at school were special to us and I wondered about his imaginary games with Nevan – someone he didn't really hit it off with mentally or intellectually – how they could have been a success. I really wanted to hear stories of how Martin and Nevan had *not* got on, how they had disagreed or quarrelled and, happily, Colin had plenty of those.

Some of these stories of discord were more to do with different tastes or opinions which created undercurrents of disharmony rather than head on clashes. For instance, Nevan was a great fan of comics and collected all kinds avidly. War comics and horror comics, in particular. He rarely read books. Martin Rigby Smith and his brothers enjoyed some comics, such as the Beano and the Dandy and they regularly read the Eagle, like me, which included Dan Dare (space fiction), Jeff Arnold (Western), Harris Tweed (character comedy), PC 49 (police stories), but they read books too, mainly adventure stories, again like me, and rather looked down on Nevan for feeding his mind on comics alone and trying to argue, as he did, that you could learn just as much from comics as you could from books.

Martin found Nevan's horror comics grotesque and would laugh at them dismissively and rarely look at them but he would read Nevan's Western comics and sometimes his war comics, and whenever he did Nevan would make something of it and claim Martin was just being hypocritical in his attitude to them. Martin would retort by claiming he only read Nevan's war comics because they were so bad they were funny and he would mock them by mimicking their representations of gunfire and bombs and quoting bits of dialogue from them. The Second World War comics, in particular, came in for satirical treatment, with their zooming cartoon planes and crashes and explosions – enormous stars bursting on the page accompanied by words like 'WHOOSH!' and 'ZAP!' and 'BAM!' and 'POW!' and 'SMASH!' – and German pilots in planes or soldiers manning artillery posts, who were always terrified, as they looked up in the sky and shouted, 'Achtung, Spitfire!' or expleted, 'Gott in Himmel!'

No, Martin really didn't care much for Nevan's obsession with modern war and warfare. Historical warfare was another matter. I remember Martin doing a study of pitched battles between the English and the French in the Hundred Years War, during our scholarship year, which impressed our History teacher. He drew diagrams of the battles and made much of the part that the longbow had played in the success of the English forces against the French. Martin wasn't really interested in guns, except guns in the Wild West, in saloon bars or the main street of the town: six-shooters which you whipped out of a holster in one-to-one duels. It was the competitive confrontation, the sudden death play-off between two individuals which appealed to him, like the opposition of two boxers or batsman and bowler in cricket. The large scale devastation and destruction wreaked by planes and artillery and grenades and bombs didn't appeal to him at all, nor me in fact, so that was something else Rigby Smith and I had in common and where we differed from Nevan.

Colin also told me of differences of opinion and fierce rivalry between Nevan and his brother Martin over tennis. I noted the rivalry myself and saw that it constituted much more of a direct clash than their differences of choice over make-believe games and comics. Nevan had a grass tennis court in his garden and when it wasn't too wet in the summer the Rigby Smiths would play tennis on it with him, instead of using the public hard courts in the park. Sometimes Nevan had tennis parties. He liked friends coming round to play tennis at his house, it made him feel important. He liked to win too, of course, and he often did, which raised his self-esteem further. When there were four or more tennis playing friends at his house they would play doubles. I only played a few times on his court and didn't enjoy it very much because I wasn't very good and usually got thrashed, whether it was doubles or singles. After many defeats, I preferred to watch, though I did like playing Martin (we did play tennis together on occasions), because although he used to beat me he managed to do so without humiliating me. He let me win a game or two, unlike Nevan who once beat me 6-0, 6-0, and hardly let me win a point. Nevan was quite ruthless and his whole manner towards me suggested that he was wasting his time playing with me.

The rivalry between Nevan and Martin over tennis was particularly intense because they were so closely matched. When they played doubles there was seldom a problem because Nevan usually ensured he played with Martin and they would invariably beat any other pair. Singles was a different matter. They were head to head in tense competition. I must say, I was surprised how good Nevan was. I know he had regular coaching but Martin had some coaching too, in tennis classes at Marby College in the summer holidays, so Nevan's coaching alone does not explain why he could match Rigby Smith or even do better than him.

When I first watched them play I thought Martin would wipe the floor with him. I expected him to do so because he was undoubtedly a superior sportsman and he was larger and more physically developed. But I was surprised and disappointed by what I saw. Martin blew Nevan away with powerful serving and ground strokes, his back hand was particularly good, but then he became wild and reckless. He would start doing double faults and over hitting the ball. Nevan was not a powerful player but he was accurate and canny. He made fewer mistakes than Martin, played safe, and enticed Martin into errors.

Martin complained that there wasn't enough room at the back of the court for him to play his ground strokes properly, which was true, but it was the same for both players. The thing to do, I could see, was to develop a shorter back swing or get up to the net and volley as often as possible to avoid, or minimise, playing the ball at the back of the court. Nevan was good at volleying and could adapt his game to his own court much better than Martin, and this angered Martin and severely strained his patience and his temper. He hurled his racket about at times – 'racket abuse' as it's called now – and completely lost his composure, the thing I most admired him for at school. Of course, it wasn't Nevan's fault, I can see that now, but I was inclined to think so at the time. I almost agreed with Martin that Nevan had an unfair advantage playing on his own court and I felt, in any case, that he possessed some extra power when he was at home. It was all part of my general unease at Nevan's.

Pop Music

Martin's and Nevan's love of pop music was a close mutual interest which, on the whole, made for a harmonious bond between them, unlike their fondness for tennis, and it was a bond which I envied. They fell out over one pop singer, though, as I will be explaining later.

Pop music for all of us in the mid and late 1950s was almost entirely rock 'n' roll and skiffle. It all started with Bill Haley and the Comets, with the number one hit Rock Around the Clock, a record you simply had to have, not only to listen to but to dance to. Nevan had this record, of course, and he used to claim he was one of the first people in Marby to get it. He may have been, possibly, but I suspected he just made that up in order to be one up on the rest of us for we were all quite young when Rock Around the Clock first hit our shores.

I wasn't really 'into' rock 'n' roll, in fact, at the time Rock Around the Clock first came out (1954-55) but I was soon sucked into the whole phenomenon by Elvis Presley, who exploded onto the youth scene in America, then in Britain, in the second half of the 1950s. The first record of Elvis Presley's I can remember is Teddy Bear, though I must have heard earlier records like Heartbreak Hotel. There was some film footage of him singing Teddy Bear on the TV news. For the first time I saw the famous Elvis Presley hip swaying. Our parents found it grotesque and ridiculous and the whole Elvis Presley mania bizarre and unwholesome.

Our parents' generation came to expect crazy things to come out of America and tried to take comfort in the hope and belief that they were ephemeral, they would fade away soon enough, that sanity would prevail and time-honoured customs would eventually reassert themselves. In a way they were quite right, for the word 'craze' came to mean inordinate enthusiasm for a product, practice or pursuit which didn't last. In that sense of the word many things that came out of America in the 1950s were simply crazes but Elvis Presley was not a craze in that sense for his impact rippled ever outwards and onwards in the world of pop music.

Nevan became a great fan of Elvis Presley and so did Martin, though less so. Nevan bought every record of his he could; Rigby Smith bought some of his hits and truly loved rocking and rolling to the more energetic ones. Hits such as Jailhouse Rock and King Creole were his favourites when it came to dancing. There soon followed other pop singers, such as The Everly Brothers and Lonnie Donegan. Nevan and Martin loved The Everly Brothers and Lonnie Donegan equally. Actually, all three Rigby Smith brothers loved them, Lonnie Donegan, in particular, and knew all the words of their songs by heart and would sing them together at any time.

Cumberland Gap, Putting on the Style and Don't You Rock Me Daddy-O were probably their favourite Lonnie Donegan numbers to sing aloud and, a little later, The Grand Coulee Dam. Mrs Rigby Smith rather liked Lonnie Donegan, the only pop singer she had any time for, because she found his lyrics amusing and, in the case of The Grand Coulee Dam, very expressive. She found the words of most pop songs utterly feeble and meaningless and she had a great store of traditional lyrics in her head to compare them with, to strengthen her case against them. I remember her once quoting 'Drink to me only with thy eyes' and 'My love is like a red, red rose', and saying, "Now those words mean something and they express real emotion!" But she didn't despise Lonnie Donegan's words and once surprised us by suddenly quoting lines from The Grand Coulee Dam when Toffee asked her what she thought of it, knowing she liked Lonnie Donegan.

"The Grand Coulee Dam?" she replied. "That's not like most pop songs. It's really descriptive!" and she began reciting, not singing, its refrain with great feeling:

In the misty, crystal glitter of the wild and windward spray,
Men fought the pounding waters and met a watery grave:
Why, she tore their boats to splinters but she gave men dreams to dream
Of the day the Coulee Dam would cross that wild and wasted stream.

And she repeated, "Oh, she tore their boats to splinters but she gave men dreams to dream", and then said, with her eyes lit up, "now that's poetry!"

Martin and Colin Rigby Smith singing together made a pretty good sound and they could get quite caught up in an ad lib performance when Lonnie Donegan was mentioned. Nevan would then feel left out and try to get back into the spotlight by asking if we'd heard Lonnie Donegan's latest. He was nearly always the first to hear the latest, of course, and acquire it. Or he'd try other tactics. I remember once when Martin and Colin were in full flow with Don't You Rock me Daddy-O, he sang along with them and then started

193

manhandling me in time with the music, tugging at my jumper, pulling it in different directions:

Don't you *rock* me, Daddy-O, don't you *rock* me, Daddy-O,
Don't you *rock* me, Daddy-O, don't you *rock* me Daddy-O!

On each *rock*, he then pushed me or shoved me. When the verse came which the Rigby Smiths particularly liked, he became even more animated, pushing or pulling me on each 'sing':

My old auntie promised me,
Sing away lady, sing away,
When she died she'd will to me,
Sing away lady, sing away.
She lived so long, head got bald,
Sing away lady, sing away,
She got out the notion of dying at all,
Sing away lady, *sing* away!

Then the refrain came in again: 'Don't you *rock* me, Daddy-O'. At this point Martin and Colin joined in and started pushing me around too in time with their singing. I was being pushed and tossed around between all three of them. It didn't hurt me (much), not physically, and it didn't bother me particularly that the three of them were ganging up on me (you get used to that when you're with other boys and you're small); in the case of the Rigby Smiths, at least, it wasn't malign in any way, but it upset me that the whole thing had been instigated by Nevan. It was another instance of the influence he wielded over Martin who seemed quite oblivious of it at times.

Things were worse with pop star duo the Everly Brothers because Nevan used to make out that he and Martin had some special connection with them. It was as if nobody else knew and appreciated the Everly Brothers in the way they did. I liked their songs too but Nevan used to suggest my liking of them wasn't on the same par as theirs. Just as Martin and Colin would sing Lonnie Donegan numbers together, with James too sometimes, Nevan and Martin would sing Everly Brothers' songs together, not particularly well though, I didn't think, not nearly as well as the Martin and Colin singing Lonnie Donegan. And I always felt Nevan sung the Everly Brothers' songs in such a way as to irritate me as much as possible.

I remember their singing Bye, Bye, Love together and when they came to the line 'Hello, loneliness, I think I'm gonna cry', Nevan would give me a

194

look that seemed to hint the line suited me. Bird Dog, another Everly Brothers' hit song, I felt he definitely did aim at me. The song has the repeated phrases, which are half spoken, half sung, in a lower register, 'He's a dog' and then 'He's a *bird* dog!' Nevan would come closer to me and saysing the phrase at me. It was all just fun, of course, as far as Martin was concerned, he just laughed carelessly, but I wasn't sure about Nevan. He seemed to relish the words unduly, indeed he clearly relished all the words of the song, which included lines such as:

Hey, Bird Dog, get away from my quail,
Hey, Bird Dog, you're on the wrong trail!

He gave me a look, as he sang, which wasn't very friendly, a sort of warning, I thought. But, to be honest, I didn't really know what was going on in his mind.

Nevan and Martin's complete agreement in pop music taste was somewhat undermined near the end of the 1950s when Cliff Richard burst upon the British pop scene. Nevan regarded Cliff Richard as a watered-down British version of Elvis Presley but Martin became a great fan of his believing he had something unique about him. Martin preferred Cliff Richard's body movements to Elvis's, though they were modelled on Elvis's, and Cliff's smoother singing style and clearer diction (*he* thought it was clearer, anyway). Just as Nevan would go and buy every record by Elvis Presley, Martin would try to acquire every record by Cliff Richard.

Nevan, true to form, turned their different preferences into a competitive thing. He would follow the Top Ten closely and continually remind Martin when Elvis Presley was no.1 in the charts. Since he often *was*, in the USA if not always in the UK, that made for a lot of reminders. Nevan would then innocently inquire which number in the pop charts Cliff Richard had reached. In our Penly Grange days, Cliff Richard had only one no.1 hit so this was a game Nevan nearly always won. I do not doubt that Nevan liked Elvis Presley but how much, I used to wonder? Playing the competitive game between Elvis Presley and Cliff Richard was a form of one-upmanship for Nevan. He backed Elvis Presley because he liked to back a winner, that's what I thought.

There was of course plenty of rivalry between *all* of us over our favourite pop stars and songs, and I remember day boys Edland and Scales having a fierce dispute over which was the better version of Singing the Blues – Guy Mitchell's or Tommy Steele's. (I kept quiet because I didn't know there was any version other than Tommy Steele's). But it's fair to say that, in general, pop music, rock music, united us much more than it divided us, and bonded our generation or decade together as the Beatles did on their own for the

1960s. We felt part of this new thing, rock 'n' roll, which was a young people's phenomenon, it was for *us*.

Rock 'n' roll set our generation apart from the adult world. The disapproval by most adults of pop music, and rock 'n' roll in particular, was proof in our minds that they were out of touch, and the world out there, a dynamic new world, was ours for the taking. When we grew up. But how many of us actually wanted to grow up just yet or get out into the grown-up world? To go beyond the safe portals of our schoolboy life? It was all in the mind – in the senses and the feelings and the imagination. We didn't want reality just yet, we were still playing games. New games, true, teenage games, but still games.

One unforgettable experience of the unity that shared enjoyment of music can create occurred at school one afternoon. Social or personal psychology alone could not explain its deeply emotional nature – it was a spiritual, almost mystical experience – though on one level it was simply a peer group response to new recording technology, to a landmark in the history of modern society's access to mass entertainment. How old was I? I must have been about twelve.

There was a space above one of the classroom blocks in the quad, a sort of loft where we were allowed to play games and listen to records. Martin and I went up there one afternoon before the post tea-time lessons and found just about everyone there of any account, including Jock Clayton and Forrest, Westford, Rickmack and Loretti, Honeyman and Spencer, and Jakeman, of course, with his cronies, and day boys Edland and the Barley brothers, and Spilwell, usually ploughing his own furrow, and others of lesser account, such as Norton and Nevan: all gathered together round a small box on the floor with its lid open. It was about six or seven inches high and perhaps ten inches across, about the size of a two-tiered biscuit tin. The box seemed to be owned by, or in the charge of, Loretti, who was putting something into it and then moving his hand over it. Suddenly out came the sound of music, pop music, rock 'n' roll! And it was no ordinary rock 'n' roll music. This was very special music.

We were absolutely stunned. Stunned by the box, stunned by the music. The box seemed like a magic box. We realised it was a gramophone but it was like no gramophone we'd ever seen before. Apart from being so small for a gramophone, there were no handles on it to wind up the turntable, nor any leads to an electrical socket to provide electrical power as in radiograms, with which we were familiar, though not all of us owned one. Loretti's box was, in fact, a battery-driven gramophone for 45 rpm records. Rigby Smith and I, and I daresay most of the others, had never seen a 45 rpm record before. It was strange that Nevan hadn't obtained one of these gramophones before Loretti, but I felt sure he soon would.

196

Although somewhat larger than our CD today, the 45 rpm record was considerably smaller and neater and far less brittle than the 78 rpm shellac record we were used to, which you had to hold very carefully in two hands from the moment you picked it up because it could so easily crack or get scratched. The 45 rpm record, a vinyl record, was much more 'user friendly' – easy to hold in just one hand and far less fragile – and a miracle of the miniature to us, and we soon discovered that in its EP form (Extended Play) a record might last for a lot longer than the usual three or four minutes of the 78 rpm.

With the 45 rpm single and EP came the new technology of the lightweight pick-up arm and its smaller attached stylus needle which did not require constant changing. The new stylus needle lasted a long time, maybe months, before it wore down (though it could get damaged). The brass or copper needles we used at first for our 78rpm records could only be used once. After one playing of the record you had to remove the needle and replace it with a new one, so you bought them in batches like packets of drawing pins. Silver and gold needles, which were obtainable a little later, lasted longer but still only a few more times that the brass ones.

So, this new 45 rpm invention of the record industry, together with the battery-driven gramophone (or 'record-player' as it came to be called) and the stylus needle, was a wonderful technological advance. Yet it was the *music* which issued from Loretti's magic box which was the most wonderful and thrilling thing of all, and which truly united us in an unique way for a few glorious minutes. The record being played was by Buddy Holly and the Crickets. Buddy Holly, a relative newcomer on the pop scene, was loved and respected by all of us who had become acquainted with his music. None of us had a word to say against him and even cynics like Rickmack and the phlegmatic Westford would respond with reverence when his name was mentioned and say in hushed tones, 'Oh, Buddy Holly!' as lovers of pure classical music are famously supposed to utter 'Ah, Bach!'

Buddy Holly's tragically early death in 1959 might have later decked his name with a retrospective sheen of sentimental, romantic awe, but, as we listened to that 45 rpm record of Buddy Holly in the loft above the classrooms in the quad at Penly Grange that afternoon, we had no inkling of his death within a year or so. Quite the contrary, he seemed forever young, never to die. We were swept away by his vitality and raw energy, by the melody of the song, by his boyish, raucous and untutored, yet expressive and distinct, musical voice, and by the accompanying sharp, jangling, clashing sounds of the guitars and vocal backing. The song, which teetered on the edge of anarchy but remained under control (just), was Oh Boy which I'd heard before on Radio Luxemburg, but it hadn't impressed itself upon me so strongly then with its relentless power and reckless abandon, as it did now. The words were fairly typical for a pop love song of the time, nothing special, except for one or two lines which, carried on the wave of their heady, headlong music, fired my imagination:

All of my love, all of my kissing,
You don't know what you've been missing,
Oh boy, when you're with me, oh boy,
The world can see that you were meant for me.

All of my life I've been awaiting,
Tonight they'll be no hesitating,
Oh boy etc. ...
Stars appear and the shadows are falling
And you can hear my heart's a-calling,
A little bit of loving makes everything right
And I'm gonna see my baby tonight ...

The love element, the romantic-erotic language, was of no appeal to me at 12 years old, but that line '*Stars appear and the shadows are falling*' did stir something quite deep within me. It spoke to me of another world, another archway to travel through, into a mysterious land without limits; a realm of beckoning lights and possible adventures beyond. All very vague, and yet, like some of Martin Rigby Smith's fictions, such as the secret tunnels in the woods, very beguiling and captivating. Something yet to be discovered.

Nevan at School

Nevan's impact and influence at school was considerably less than it was at the Rigby Smiths' or at his home. Rigby Smith and I didn't see him in lessons because he was in a lower class than us, nor at Scouts when he gave up Scouts, so he couldn't interfere there. Nevertheless, he was in the same Group as us (E Group) and did Games with us in the afternoon so we usually saw him every day at school, and as time went on he inveigled himself more and more into our unorganised leisure activities, our non-timetabled free time.

I remember him joining in our games in the playground or on the grassy area beside the ha ha – in games such as tag or French cricket – and trying to exert his own influence on them. He made no attempt to take over, he was much more subtle than that, he simply used his own method of selecting who was 'on' or 'in' at the beginning of the game, whenever he got the chance, and in so doing he always seemed to get the result he wanted. The standard rhyming chant for picking the person to be 'on' or 'in' for a game was the rhyme 'Eeny, meeny, miny, mo'. We were totally unconscious of its racism and recited the words regularly to start a game without a second thought:

Eeny, meeny, miny, mo,
Catch a nigger by his toe.
If he squeals, let him go,
Eeny, meeny, miny, mo.
O ... U ... T ... spells 'out',
So *out* you must go.'

You gathered round in a circle and one person recited the rhyme and went round the circle pointing his finger at each boy in turn on each syllable of the rhyme, and when the word 'go' was reached the person being pointed at was singled out to be 'on' or 'out', depending on what you were playing. Nevan always liked to recite the rhyming chant at the beginning of a game and pick the person to be 'on' or 'out' but he had his own little rhyme which he preferred to use. I don't know where he'd got it from, perhaps from the local primary school he'd attended before Penly Grange. It was quite different from 'Eeny, meeny, miny mo'. He made everyone standing round in the circle hold out their fists, and then he went round the circle tapping each fist with his hand, reciting,

'*One* potato, *two* potato, *three* potato, *four*,
Five potato, *six* potato, *seven* potato, *more*'.

He did it with great assurance and authority and no one ever questioned it. Well I did once, and he gave me a withering look which said, 'there's always one, isn't there?' which shut me up. My objection was that since each boy had two fists he was effectively being counted twice and when the rhyme was done at speed, as Nevan tended to do it, or when he sometimes started again for no apparent reason, it was difficult to follow his counting. I noticed he managed to make me 'on' in tig on many occasions, above the law of averages I thought, and I much preferred someone else to do the choosing rhyme and use 'Eeny, meeny, miny, mo' which I could follow. Sometimes Rigby Smith would get in first with 'Eeny, meeny, miny, mo' but Nevan was often quicker off the mark and had us all holding out our fists for his rhyme before anyone else began with the familiar one. It didn't bother Rigby Smith much, it was only a method of getting a game started after all, but I disliked the way Nevan suggested his rhyme was somehow superior to the usual one, as well as the trickery he seemed to use to my disadvantage.

His interventions in some of our other games troubled me much more, however, than his mere influence on the start of our games. These interventions or interferences didn't occur very often, fortunately, but I remember two occasions involving Rigby Smith and me which upset me a lot. I have referred to one of them already – to the time when he forced his way into our Robin Hood game and insisted on being Little John, which I wasn't allowed to be because I was supposed to be too small, yet he wasn't much bigger than me. Since our games in the woods were often related to, or occurred side by side with, our Scouting activities, and our enthusiasm for Scouts was a strong bond between Rigby Smith and me, I didn't want Nevan, who had given up Scouts, thinking he could be involved in them on an equal footing with me. I wanted him to realise that our games in the woods at school were *our* games, they were not the same as the games we played at his home or the Rigby Smiths'. So I wasn't at all happy about him barging into our Robin Hood game.

But the second occasion of his gate crashing a pastime of ours, which I remember particularly well, was even more maddening, though it wasn't in the woods, it was in the paddock. The paddock was beyond the quad and near the lily pond. It was an area of rough, sparse grass and bumpy but fairly soft earth, with wood chippings and sawdust scattered around. It was not much good for ball games but very suitable for chasing around, falling down and rolling around games, including piggy-back fighting.

Rigby Smith and I made a good horse and rider pair in piggy-back fights. He was quite strong and fairly tall, swift moving and agile, and was perfectly happy carrying me on his back because I was light and didn't hang round his neck like some riders and we had a good understanding. We did pretty well together and usually got the better of piggy back pairs like Hodgeson and Radford, and Westford and Timpson. Hodgeson and Westford were good carriers but they were slow at manoeuvring. It wasn't difficult to dodge round them and grab Radford or Timpson from behind and yank them off Hodgeson's or Westford's back with Rigby Smith's help. He would hold me up on his back with one arm and hand and use the other hand to help dislodge the opposing rider. Of course when held up by only one arm and hand, and when clinging to your rider with only one arm because the other was used for grappling with your opponents, it was harder to stay on your 'horse', your carrier, and I did occasionally fall off and lose a fight. If you were removed from your horse or fell off you lost that round of the contest but you could always remount and fight again.

One day I noticed Nevan watching us. He'd been riding on Porter's back and hadn't done too well and Porter had given up for a while and then gone off to play billiards. Rigby Smith and I had had an encounter with Rickmack and Spencer, and Rickmack, who was on Spencer's back and a very tough customer, had managed to yank me off. I wasn't hurt or the slightest bit deflated and I was about to remount Rigby Smith's back when Nevan suddenly came forward and said, "You've had your turn, Mouse, now it's my go." Whereupon he jumped onto Rigby Smith's back and goaded him into action. "Come on, Martin," he said, "let's go!"

Rigby Smith didn't hesitate. He leapt straight into action with Nevan on his back and charged at Spencer and Rickmack. I was absolutely livid. I shouted at Nevan, "Who said anything about *turns?* I'm Martin's rider!" but he took no notice of me and neither did Rigby Smith. Apart from stealing my role in the piggy back fight I was furious with Nevan for calling me 'Mouse' and then calling Rigby Smith 'Martin'. On another occasion in school, amongst other boys, he might have called Rigby Smith 'Berry', like everyone else, not caring that he didn't like it, but now Nevan was just sucking up to him – he knew Rigby Smith liked being called Martin – and he was doing me down me in calling me Mouse not Tim. He should have called me *Tim* if he was going to call Rigby Smith *Martin.*

I was to become even more annoyed when I saw how well Rigby Smith fared with Nevan on his back. The two of them soon despatched Spencer and Rickmack and then got the better of Westford and Timpson who had been going through a successful patch. With Nevan on his back, Rigby Smith charged around with renewed energy. I have to concede that Nevan was very good at staying on Rigby Smith's back, though heavier than me, and sometimes, for brief crucial moments, Rigby Smith was able to use both his hands and help tear the riders off their carriers' backs. Rigby Smith never seemed to tire and the pair of them cleared the field. They were invincible. They were naturally very pleased with themselves, cock-a-hoop, in fact.

I felt totally excluded, and unfairly excluded, because I had always been Rigby Smith's rider before. We had done pretty well together, and even though I had been dislodged briefly in an unfortunate moment I had helped Rigby Smith soften up the opposition, I was sure, which could well have contributed to his success with Nevan. What was particularly galling was that these piggy back fights were one of the few games or sports in which my small size could be used to advantage. (I've mentioned chain tag being another but there wasn't much kudos being good at that, and it was a purely individual thing). My small size and light frame made me an ideal rider for Rigby Smith but now the heavier Nevan had shown he could do just as well as me, even better. Had it been anyone else other than Nevan I might have been able to take it, but such was my increasing rivalry with Nevan I was beside myself with envy and, yes, hatred!

I didn't like to complain to Rigby Smith about Nevan edging in between us. I didn't want to seem the complaining type and I didn't want to appear jealous of Nevan which of course I was. But this time I couldn't stop myself revealing something of my feelings when we were alone together later. I tried to keep the whining, hurt tone out of my voice but it was difficult.

"Why do you always let Nevan push in when we're doing fine together? You're letting him wrap you round his little finger."

"No, I'm not," he responded, "what are you talking about?"

"The Robin Hood game. You let him play Little John and he never even asked. And you said I was too small and he's not much bigger than me." I thought I would mention this first, since, although annoying, it had troubled me less than the piggy back fighting."

Rigby Smith's reply was diplomatic. "Well, we needed someone to be Little John and you were doing fine as Will Scarlet, I thought."

"I daresay, but you always let him get his way."

"No, I don't, not always. It's a matter of give and take. Sometimes he does what I want to do."

"When?" I retorted. "When has he ever done what you want him to?"

"Lots of times. In games at home. And he'll follow my orders too, sometimes."

"Oh, yes?" I said sceptically.

"Yes. Look at the Puppet Club and the Red Hand Gang. He accepted my leadership, didn't he? Everyone did."

"He wasn't very keen, was he?" (I was thinking particularly of the Puppet Club and he knew it).

"He did his best."

There was a sarcastic note in Rigby Smith's voice, almost of contempt, and it raised my spirits a little. It encouraged me to broach the incident that was really needling me:

"You let him barge in and become your rider in the piggy back fighting. We were partners and you just switched to him and ignored me. Left me in the lurch."

"It was all on the spur of the moment, I didn't think about it. Just got on with it. And it gave you a break, didn't it?"

"But you never let him off your back after that, did you? It wasn't just a break."

"Well, we were good, weren't we? Beat everybody hollow. Nevan was terrific at staying on my back!"

I couldn't stop myself asking the next question though I dreaded the answer. "So *he*'s going to be your rider from now on, is he?"

I could see from the look in his eyes that Rigby Smith was caught out. I guessed he very much wanted to have Nevan as his rider because he thought his chances of winning with Nevan would be greater than winning with me but he didn't want to hurt my feelings so he said tactfully,

"I don't see why you can't both be my riders. You're both good and you're both my friends." This concession (that's all it was) was better than nothing but I was still crestfallen and he realised it. He had an inkling of what was behind my objections to his teaming up with Nevan and clearly felt forced to say more:

"I know what you're thinking. About Nevan. Or seem to be. Of course we're friends. I see him nearly every day at home. We do lots together. We have a smashing time sometimes. But it's all up and down with him; I never know where I am with him. He even got Nick Wheeler against me last week. Anyway, so what? You're my best friend. You always have been. You know that."

I suppose I did, and I suppose I was reassured to hear him confirm that I was his best friend. Yes, it was good to hear him say it. And yet at the same time I rather regretted that he'd felt the need to say it. It had always been an unspoken fact before, something assumed by us and everyone else at school. To pronounce it, raised the possibility for the first time of it not being so. His affirmation therefore wasn't entirely reassuring. In any case, I was eventually to learn more about Rigby Smith's friendship with Nevan which would seriously call into question his declaration that I was his best friend.

On (and Off) the Buses

'Lords of the world'

As day boys living in Marby about five or six miles from Penly Grange School, we had to find transport to get us there and back. Well, our parents did. At one time a minibus was hired for us which carried about twelve passengers and another time a rota of lifts in parents' cars was arranged but neither lasted very long. Cost may have been a factor, but in any case, the main problem was organising transport back to Marby, especially in the summer when boys involved in cricket matches or extra practice in the nets often came home later than the others. The train service was no good either way because the nearest railway station to Penly Grange was Tibdale which was two or three miles beyond the school. Our best means of transport, therefore, or at least the one which gave our parents the minimum hassle, proved to be the public bus service from Marby to Tibdale.

The return service – from Tibdale back to Marby – went past the school every half hour. If you were kept at school for whatever reason, or missed a bus through dilatoriness, you simply got the next one half an hour later; other day boys didn't have to wait for you. Once our parents realised the straightforwardness of getting us to school and back to Marby by public bus – at least back to the centre of Marby – it became their preferred method of transport for us, though it wasn't ideal in every respect. I must have spent about four years of my five years and a term at Penly Grange travelling on public transport buses and, on the whole, I loved it, though there were some unpleasant aspects of it, especially in winter.

The Journey

Getting to the bus in the morning could be quite a scramble. I lived on the west side of Marby and had to get to the bus station in Marby town centre about a mile and a half away to catch the Tibdale bus. The Rigby Smiths lived on the north side of Marby about a mile from the Marby-Tibdale road. Sometimes they got a lift to a bus stop on the Marby-Tibdale road from a parent, at other times they had to walk. I usually had to walk. No other boys at Penly Grange lived my side of Marby and although my dad might give me a lift if he was at home and it was convenient, my mother couldn't because she didn't drive (in fact she was a bit of a stay-at-home generally). So I had to look sharpish if I was to get to the bus station before 8.15 in the morning. Any later than 8.15 am and I probably wouldn't make it to school in time.

The Rigby Smiths and others used to join me on the bus about three or four bus stops along the Marby-Tibdale road. At first it was just a matter of Martin Rigby Smith and his older brother James, the older of the Barley brothers (Steven), and Scales and Edland, sometimes the Fenby-Taylors, and one or two others I barely remember. Other day boys must have gone on different buses or perhaps got lifts from their parents. Later, two younger brothers – first Brian Barley and then Colin Rigby Smith – came on board too; then, a year later, Bernie Nevan who was to have such an unsettling effect on my friendship with Martin Rigby Smith.

The bus journey to Penly Grange from Marby took about twenty-five minutes. There was about two miles of Marby and its outskirts and then three or four miles of countryside. The bus stopped at the end of the rough, unmade-up driveway into the school, by the lodge house where the Headmaster lived, and after 50 yards or so joined the main drive into the school. You turned right when you reached the main drive and then had another 60 or 70 yards or so to walk into the school, a bit further if you went to the classroom quad rather than the main building.

On the journey to Penly Grange in the morning, the bus stopped on the same side of the road as the school, so when you alighted you could walk straight into school without crossing the road. That was all well and good but it meant, unfortunately, that going home in the evening, in the other direction, you had to cross the road to get to the bus stop and, moreover, walk round to the far side of the bus in order to get onto it. These factors all added time to the process of catching the bus. There was no question of reaching the end of the driveway as the bus arrived and jumping onto it in the few moments grace you had before the bus moved off again with its new passengers. You had to be in place at the bus stop on the far side of the road if you wanted to be sure of catching the bus.

Furthermore, the school driveway to the bus stop ran between trees and at right angles to the road so you couldn't see the bus coming at a distance, only when it passed the end of the driveway. You could hear it, of course, you came to recognise the sound of the bus, but, by the time you heard it, it was too late. A number of times I remember rushing to catch the bus after school, sometimes with the Rigby Smiths, sometimes with others, occasionally on my own, only to see it shooting past the end of the driveway, my heart sinking, knowing it was now at least another half hour before the next bus. A boring enough prospect in summer but very dreary in winter when it was dark and cold.

Since we had lessons after tea on week days, the earliest bus we could get was the 6 o' clock bus in the evening, so it would always be dark going home in winter. The bus journey to Marby might have been only twenty-five minutes but when we got into Marby we still had to walk home. Often I wasn't back home until 7 o' clock or later. Sometimes, getting home could be very tedious, especially if we had to wait longer than usual for a bus, but there was a good side to the prolonged time it could take to get home.

It was our own time, and because we did sometimes have to stay later at school and occasionally missed buses or they were delayed or not running regularly, our parents accepted that we might get home late. This gave us a certain amount of freedom to dilly-dally on the way if we were so inclined. There were no mobile phones in those days, of course, and although there were public phone boxes in Marby town we hardly ever used them: they were regarded by our parents, as well as us, as often inconvenient or difficult to make use of (either through being occupied by someone else or not working) and an unnecessary expense except in emergencies. For that hour or two, or longer sometimes, between the end of the school day and arriving home, our parents did not know where we were nor what we were up to and had to accept it: they could only assume we were, at some point, travelling on a Tibdale to Marby bus.

Once off the bus and at the bus station in the centre of Marby, Rigby Smith and I should have gone our separate ways because we lived at the opposite ends of Marby, but as I mentioned in the previous chapter we sometimes walked halfway back towards the other's home still enjoying each other's company. More often, though, we spent some time together in the centre of Marby, window-shopping and buying sweets.

Even after most shops were shut, the tobacconists and newsagents would still be open with a good range of sweets for sale, as they are today. Rigby Smith and I would buy bubble gum and gob stoppers and sherbet dips, and sweet cigarettes because of the football and cricket cards in them. We swapped cards and each of us built up quite a good collection. Although I was not particularly interested in the individual players depicted on the cards, unless I knew them by repute, it was fun collecting them because you never knew which cards would appear in your packet. Sometimes you got the same card you'd had before, maybe several times, which was disappointing, but there was always the excitement of seeing a new card, of a new footballer or cricketer, or one you'd seen in some other boy's possession at school but which you didn't have and which went towards the completion of your set. (I'm not sure that I actually ever completed a set).

When Colin Rigby Smith, and then Nevan, started at Penly Grange School they tended to tag along with us, which cramped our style a bit, though I became resigned to having Colin with us, especially once I came to like him and accepted his right to be with us. I never really accepted Nevan. Although I said earlier that Rigby Smith didn't linger so long in town once he had his younger brother Colin to look after, that isn't entirely true. They spent a little time with me buying sweets in a shop by the bus station and then, on their way home, they often stopped off to buy more sweets. Liquorice was a favourite of theirs but only shops on their way home stocked the kind of liquorice sweets they particularly liked, so they said.

The Rigby Smiths weren't particularly rich; I don't think Mr Rigby Smith had a lot left over once he'd paid the school fees for his three sons, and Mrs Rigby Smith wasn't a working mother. Their pocket money was fairly modest, in fact less than mine, but they always had some spare cash for sweets because Mrs Rigby Smith gave Martin and Colin some money for the bus home from the centre of Marby and she didn't object if they spent their bus fare in the shops and walked home. They walked home a lot, as you can imagine! She preferred them to spend the money they saved on stationery, such as writing paper and notepads, but it usually went on sweets, as far as I could tell.

I suggested to my mum that she might do the same for me – give me money for the bus fare and let me spend it on something else if I walked home – but it didn't work for me because my mum knew the buses along our road weren't regular and that I usually walked to the bus station and back, anyway, as a matter of course. She did, however, offer to pay for a taxi for me if I ever needed one to get back home from school when the buses weren't convenient or weren't running. I never needed a taxi except once, when I was ill and had to come straight home early from school. She never paid for a taxi to take me anywhere in Marby but this didn't bother me because I never expected it.

Bus Travel and Bus Seats

Travelling on the buses was usually great fun because we normally had a seat, we were rarely forced to stand amidst a crush of people – my most recent experience of travelling by bus – and, in fact, we often had a pick of seats. As time went on, our favourite seats on the bus changed and we could usually sit in them, though occasionally someone was there before us and we had to accept our second or third choice of seats.

At first on the buses we were like little kids at the fun fair. The buses were double decker buses, nine times out of ten – whenever a single deck bus turned up it seemed rather a feeble effort, as if they'd run out of double decker buses and were calling on their reserves – and we would jump on board, clatter hurriedly up the metal staircase and head straight for the front seat on the top deck. We felt lords of the world up there above all the traffic, on the level with the tops of lamp-posts and upper storeys of buildings and, in the country, with hedges, telegraph wires and some trees. It was scary too, but exhilarating, like a frightening ride on a roller coaster or the Big Dipper. Actually, it was better than a fun fair, because it was completely free – it came with the price of the bus ticket – and it was part of real, everyday life, it wasn't just a game, a leisure activity. What's more, it took place without our parents or teachers being around.

It was scary on the top deck because the bus would sway and swing around when turning left or right, or going round a roundabout, and some bus drivers seemed to drive so recklessly you really felt at times the bus was going to tilt over. We would cling onto the handrail across the front window, or above the back of our seats, to stop ourselves hurtling into the front or side windows, knowing it would do us little good if the bus did topple over. Once out of Marby and on the road which turned left to Tibdale off the Donminster road, there was an additional element of scariness: a railway bridge to go under. No matter how many times the bus drove safely under the bridge, you always ducked when the bus approached the bridge. If you were sitting on the front seat, you couldn't help it; it seemed inevitable the top of the bus would hit the underside of the bridge. Yet it never did and you always felt you'd had a lucky escape.

It was tremendous being on the front seat on the top deck, it gave you a literal as well as a metaphorical 'high', but we soon found out its disadvantages. On the front seat of the top deck, you were furthest away from the exit from the bus, and you would be last off at your stop unless you left your seat very early before your stop came. If you came down the stairs too early, the bus conductor might send you back because there was space for only a limited number of people on the embarkation/disembarkation platform at the back of the bus. Furthermore, when on the front seat, you had to turn round to see what was happening on the rest of the bus and you always presented your backs to the other passengers when looking out of the front window. That meant other schoolchildren could flick pellets at you, or jeer at you, and you couldn't see where pellets or jeers were coming from. There was rarely any fighting on the bus that I can recall, just occasional scuffles and cap grabbings, and flicking of pellets, but there was always potential hostility from boys from other schools, such as Tibdale Grammar, and it didn't feel comfortable knowing they were sitting behind you, and you hadn't got eyes in the back of your head.

Our next favoured spot, therefore, when we became more bus-wise, was the very back seat of the top deck. The seat right by the top of the staircase was the most coveted spot of all. Unfortunately, it was generally recognised as the best seat to have – at least by all schoolchildren – and you couldn't always be sure of nabbing it. For nearly a year after we had decided the back seat upstairs was far better than the front seat or anywhere else on the top deck, this prime seat was occupied each morning by an older boy on his way to Tibdale Grammar School (we tended to see him less often in the evening, though). He looked pretty tough and not the sort of boy to mess with, so we didn't challenge his right to sit there and we sat in the seats in front of him for some months.

Actually, although there was usually no love lost between pupils from Penly Grange and Tibdale Grammar School, we quite liked this particular boy and were impressed by him because he was never unfriendly to us, like some of his schoolmates, and he wore his cap on the back of his head in a ludicrous yet artful way. Schoolboys had to wear caps in those days, it was part of the school uniform: and for many years to come. Some, of course, objected and wore their caps as little as possible, 'lost' them or merely whipped them out of a pocket and jammed them quickly on their heads when someone in authority was watching. Many allowed their caps to become tatty and wore them loosely, untidily and askew, and the goodie-goodies wore them correctly, firmly on their heads with their peaks at the centre, neatly in line with their collars and ties and coat lapels. But this boy from Tibdale Grammar did none of these things.

He had wavy, very carefully combed hair, stacked up high and flowing freely over the top of his head. There was really no place for a cap and wearing one should have interfered with his immaculate hair style, yet somehow he perched his school cap on the very back of his head and managed to keep it there. It was a miraculous feat, unquestionably, but the cap's low and precarious position on the very back of his head of beautifully wavy hair also looked very silly and was meant to. Even at our young, uncynical age (generally), we could read this piece of sartorial whimsy as the boy intended, as the most witty of protests. He was saying, 'all right, I'll follow the letter of the rule, I'll wear a cap but I won't let it interfere with my hair style, I'll wear it my way, and if it looks silly, too bad, that will only show what a silly rule cap wearing is'. His combined fashion statement and satirical comment also conveyed his pride in managing to keep the cap on the back of his head against the odds. We all felt the temptation to knock the cap off his head, of course, but the reason why we never did was not just that he was older and bigger than us; the fact was, we really admired him for his cap balancing act, his subtle defiance not just of school authority but all the laws of gravity and probability!

Eventually, this debonair cap balancer from Tibdale Grammar School must have moved house or school, because we no longer saw him on the bus and were able to take over his slot at the back of the top deck. Not all of us because there was only room for two or three of us on the very back seat and for only one in the place right by the top of the staircase. Rigby Smith tended to sit in that key position when it became available and Colin or I sat next to him, though sometimes Nevan had nipped in first before we knew it. If there was no room on the back seat I would sit in the seat in front of Rigby Smith and turn to talk to him. I didn't mind because I wasn't travel-sick like some of the others.

There were at least three things about the back seat on the top deck which made it so desirable. There was no one behind you so you didn't need to watch your back and you could see everyone on the top deck with the greatest of ease because they were all in front of you or beside you. The view from the back of the top deck was also better than anywhere else upstairs because there was a mirror near the top of the staircase which you could peep into with just a slight turn of the head. The mirror was primarily for the benefit of the bus conductor so that he could see who was about to get on or off the bus when he was upstairs or see who was coming downstairs from above when he was on the bottom deck, but the passenger seated on the back seat of the top deck could also look in the mirror and see who was coming and going in the same way as the bus conductor. This omni-vision, enjoyed without moving from one's seat or turning round, was a pleasant and comfortable experience and gave you a feeling of power, or at least of Olympian detachment, as other people bustled about trying to find a seat or get themselves downstairs in time to disembark at their stop; and, of course, since everyone who sat upstairs had to pass you, coming and going, you saw them all, you could have a good look at them without moving an inch. Furthermore, in your position right at the back of the top deck you could get downstairs, if you wanted to, and off the bus before anyone else on the top deck.

Getting off the bus quickly and easily eventually became one of the most important things for us in our bus travel: it was something to do with feeling in control and having a sense of freedom of movement. That's why, when we were older still, when we were eleven or over, we found an even better spot on the bus. There was an element in our choice, I think, of 'we've done the top deck, the top deck is for kids, we're more mature now', but the main thing was that we'd learnt one major disadvantage of being anywhere on the top deck. Wherever you were, even on the very back seat, you still had to go downstairs to get off the bus and you might not have a clear run down the stairs, someone might start coming up just as you were about to descend, and, even if you were sure of having a clear staircase, you would still have to allow some seconds for making your descent. When you got to the bottom of the staircase, someone downstairs might have got to the disembarkation area at the back of the bus before you, and you would have to wait behind them before getting off the bus.

You were king of the roost upstairs, you were in the equivalent of the directors' box at the football match or Royal Box at the theatre but when you came downstairs you lost your privileged position, you surrendered your vantage point. To whom exactly? To whoever was sitting at the back downstairs, that's whom. They could see you coming downstairs just as you could watch the top deck passengers coming upstairs, and they could be sure of getting to the back of the bus before you, unless you came downstairs very early and were prepared to stand and wait for a couple of minutes (which wasn't very 'cool'); they could also see the approaching bus stop first, at least see it more clearly, and judge its distance better, and were able to stay in their seats until the very last moment before they wanted to get off the bus.

So that's why we started sitting at the back *downstairs*. There were other advantages in sitting in this section of the bus. At the back of the top deck you could see everyone on the *top* deck without effort, coming and going, but by the same token, at the back of the bottom deck, you could see everyone *downstairs* and everyone coming and going there, and you could also see anyone ascending or descending the stairs. So you could cast your eye, even if only briefly, on everyone on the bus; you could see everyone on the bus at some point, apart from those who had got on the bus before you arrived and got off after you. There were very few of those in our case because we travelled all the way to Marby bus station where most people ended their journey or changed buses. We would indeed have been useful eyes for a detective agency if we had cared to use them in a prying way.

Other advantages of the back seat downstairs included the view out of the back of the bus which you couldn't see from the upper deck without turning round and a different sort of travelling sensation from the one you had on the upper level. The swaying around on the upper level and one's elevated position was certainly exciting, but downstairs you could see the ground moving away behind you and gain a better sense of the speed of the bus in relation to stationary objects in the street. There was also some feeling of elevation at the back downstairs since the back seats were raised slightly above the other seats downstairs. Another thing that made you feel the back seats downstairs were different, indeed superior to all the other seats on the bus, was the fact that they faced inwards across the bus and not forwards down the bus, you weren't hemmed in by a seat in front of you, and the

211

window panes opposite you and behind you at the side of the bus were larger than any you would look out of when in other seats on the bus, which added to the feeling of spaciousness around you. Of course, on the buses which were open at the back on the kerb side, most of them in our day, it could be draughty at the back of the bus downstairs but I don't remember that ever bothering us; perhaps we were hardier then.

The Bus Services: Ledderfield and Donminster

I have spoken of the Tibdale-Marby bus as if it were a single bus service. In fact, there were two different bus services and each bus service had its own make of bus and modus operandi. There was the Ledderfield bus which plied a north/south route between Ledderfield and Bellington (in the south), and the Donminster/North Eastern Counties bus which ran from east to west, from Donminster to Marby. I don't remember the precise departure times of either bus from Marby to Tibdale in the mornings, but the Ledderfield bus coming from Tibdale, on its way back to Marby, was scheduled to stop at the Penly Grange bus stop on the hour every hour and the Donminster bus was timetabled to come by on the half hour every hour. So, although there was a bus home for us every half hour, it wasn't the same bus service each half hour.

As far as I remember, the record of punctuality for both bus services was about the same – fair to middling – but there were quite a few differences between the Ledderfield and Donminster buses in other respects and although they were mostly quite small differences they added up to give us a definite preference for the Donminster buses over the Ledderfield buses. Finally, an unpleasant altercation with a malign Ledderfield bus conductor simplified and set the seal on our opinions and judgement of the two bus services. It was basically Donminster buses good, Ledderfield buses bad.

The first thing against the Ledderfield buses wasn't their fault. It was the accident of their schedule. The bus we normally got after school on an ordinary weekday was the 6pm bus; on a half day it was the 4pm bus. Since the Ledderfield bus always came on the hour, it was the bus we usually got. However, sometimes we got lucky (I can't remember reasons why other than last lesson cancelled or Games shortened) and we caught the 5.30pm bus or the 3.30pm respectively. At these times we caught the Donminster bus and so we came to associate the Donminster bus with favoured times, the Ledderfield buses with more boring and routine times. That was hardly fair on the Ledderfield buses as a measure for comparison but there were other factors which were more intrinsic to the buses or bus companies themselves.

First of all, the Ledderfield buses were less attractive in appearance than the Donminster buses. The Ledderfield buses were an off-white colour and the dirt showed up on them more, they looked grubby and drab, whereas the Donminster buses were a much more appealing green and yellow. We also preferred the layout of the seats on the upper deck of the Donminster buses. On the Ledderfield buses there was an aisle between the seats upstairs as well as downstairs. This made it easier for the conductor to collect his fares: with just two to a seat on either side of the aisle he didn't have to reach very far. On the other hand, on the Donminster buses, the aisle on the top deck was down one side of the bus, the right side, and there was just one continuous undivided seat on each row to the left of the aisle for four or five persons. This was not so convenient for the bus conductor who had to reach across three or four persons to get his fare from the passenger by the left window, but we liked this arrangement of seats. It kept us closer together and it was cosier and more fun jostling around together on one seat.

Another difference between the Donminster and Ledderfield buses lay in the type of tickets which each used. The Donminster bus tickets were made of fairly firm paper, similar to the paper of cinema tickets; they were separate tickets and of different colours and were kept on a clipboard which the bus conductor carried. When he handed you a ticket you felt it was your ticket. One little craze we had was counting the separate digits of our bus ticket number. If they added up to 21 it was regarded as a great stroke of fortune, like a lottery win. Occasionally, a few seconds after a boy had received his ticket, you might hear an exclamation of triumph and delight when he discovered his ticket number added up to 21. The lucky boy would then keep his ticket as a collector's item and see how many more tickets he could acquire with a number adding up to 21.

The Ledderfield bus ticket, however, wasn't worth keeping even if it had a number adding up to 21. It was just a torn off piece of paper dispensed from a metal roller machine with a handle. The bus conductor turned the handle and out came a very flimsy piece of paper, thinner than toilet paper, with small blotchy numbers on it in blue ink. Every ticket was identical and was utterly characterless, there was no ticket design, which the Donminster tickets had, even though a basic one. If you tried to keep your Ledderfield bus ticket it would become quickly scuffed up, curled up and scruffy and would defy preservation as a distinct artefact unless you stuck it in a book or onto a piece of card. Some day boys kept their Ledderfield bus tickets (or tried to) if their numbers added up to the magic 21 but I never bothered and nor did the Rigby Smiths or Nevan.

During the time of our travelling by bus to Penly Grange, the new make of bus with automatic opening and closing doors came into service – on the Ledderfield buses. We didn't like the automatic doors because whether you were wanting to get on or off the bus, you had to wait for the doors to open which they did with a pist-shoosh of air. (We never liked that pist-shoosh of air, it was too mechanistic and impersonal, a force you couldn't argue with or appeal to). Of course the automatic doors made the buses safer than the open-at-the-back ones we were used to, but the price of safety, as is often the case, was freedom and we resented our loss of freedom.

With automatic doors, you could not leap on or off the bus at the last minute as you could with the open-ended bus. Leaping on and off the bus at the last moment was something we rarely did (we weren't stupid, not usually) and of course bus conductors always tried to discourage it, but sometimes you were compelled to do so to avoid missing your bus or be taken further than you wanted to go. In the case of the former, jumping on, it was good to know you could always rely on the steel pole on the platform near the stairs to steady you and hold you up when you leapt on at the back. And the knowledge that you could get on or off, at the last minute, and weren't imprisoned on the bus until the automatic doors were opened, made us feel more free, gave us more scope in the timing of our movements. The Donminster buses did not change over to buses with automatic doors, not in our time, so that was yet another reason for our preferring the Donminster buses to the Ledderfield buses which soon all had automatic doors.

The Bus Conductor

As far as I remember, we got on reasonably well with bus conductors, on the whole. They could be brusque, bossy and short-tempered sometimes, ordering us to sit down when we stood up and not leave our seats to get off the bus before they decided we needed to. They could also be impatient when we took ages to dig coins out of our pockets to pay for our fare (I don't ever remember having a bus pass or season ticket), but we got used to most reprimands and even came to like one or two bus conductors on both bus services. Unfortunately, the one bus conductor we clashed with in a memorable way was a Ledderfield bus conductor, which only confirmed our view of the Ledderfield bus company.

In mentioning this unforgettable clash with a bus conductor, I say 'we' but, in fact, the Rigby Smiths and I (and Nevan, I assume) were really only spectators to the drama that unfolded between two day boys and a Ledderfield bus conductor one winter's evening. The day boys in question were the two Fenby-Taylor brothers. I suppose we must have been about eleven or so and they must have been about twelve and thirteen.

The Fenby-Taylor boys were eccentrics like their father. Mr Fenby-Taylor had an unkempt beard, a wild, swirly head of hair going grey at the sides, wore a crumpled, green corduroy jacket, and was the Liberal candidate for Marby North. (In those days Liberal candidates were usually regarded as no-hopers, cranks, or oddballs). He was noted for driving very fast and recklessly in an old banger, a black Morris Minor. He was reputed to have once hit the roundabout a mile or from Penly Grange at such speed that he went round it on two wheels, keeping the car under control only by a miracle. Rigby Smith told me that he'd once had a lift home with the Fenby-Taylors in a much more powerful car than the old banger, a sleek Riley in fact, and they'd touched ninety miles an hour. They'd got back to Marby in about five minutes! I'd never been in a car which had done more than seventy miles an hour and that was exceptionally fast to us then. Ninety miles an hour on a B road, which is all the Marby-Tibdale road was then, seemed insane (and not exactly sensible on an A road either).

The Fenby-Taylors lived on the east side of Marby in a large, ramshackle house and seemed to live matching ramshackle lives. The Fenby-Taylor boys never attended school regularly and often turned up late for things and, as far as I could tell, were never punished. They were scattered-brained, lackadaisical and happy-go-lucky, but it didn't seem to matter because they were accepted unofficially as 'characters' and given some latitude as a result (I suppose it *was* unofficial, unless was there some special arrangement between the school and their Liberal candidate father to be more tolerant with them for some extenuating circumstances). They were both tall and thin, with long, dishevelled hair, long fingers and long, flat feet and they wore droopy clothes. They used to tell tall stories to the younger boys and were sometimes believed.

There was a third Fenby-Taylor brother, an older boy who had left before the incident I am about to relate occurred. He told whopping fibs and set standards in tall storytelling which his younger brothers obviously attempted to emulate. I remember this older brother told me once when I was still quite new that the reason why his feet were long and flat was that a double decker bus had driven over them. At the time I believed him and used to look at his feet in awe and wonder, like a religious devotee looking at a saint's relics. Those feet had been flattened by a double decker bus! What amazing feet! But hadn't it hurt when it happened? He never said.

The Fenby-Taylors were so easy-going and laid-back, I was surprised to find them one winter's evening on the homeward journey to Marby in some bitter

215

conflict with the Ledderfield bus conductor. Their usual manner and demeanour tended to be relaxed and jokey, so their serious mood and unmistakable antagonism towards this bus conductor was all the more marked. The bus conductor in his turn looked sullen and reproachful towards them. No, more than that – he was aggressive towards them. He was not a bus conductor I recognised, nor did the Rigby Smiths, yet from the way he treated them he seemed to know the Fenby-Taylors. The Fenby-Taylors attended school so irregularly that it was perfectly possible for them to have met a conductor that we had never seen before. But what was his problem? Why did he 'have it in for' the Fenby-Taylors? We didn't know. It only seemed to us, when we realised that there was friction in the air and pricked up our eyes and ears, that the bus conductor was threatening the Fenby-Taylors in a rather sinister way.

We had reached the edge of Marby and the Fenby-Taylors stood up, ready to move to the back of the bus to get off at their stop. (We must have been sitting downstairs). The bus conductor told them to sit down, in no uncertain terms, and said that they were not going to get off the bus until he said so. He seemed to know perfectly well where they wanted to get off and I assumed he would ring the bell for their stop and then let them get up and get off when the bus reached it; that he was only trying to show that he was in charge and that they shouldn't be so hasty. However, he didn't ring the bell and the bus was about to go straight past their stop. The older Fenby-Taylor got to his feet and tried to reach the bell button a few feet further down the bus.

"Leave it!" snapped the bus conductor. "You ring that bell and I'll wring your neck!"

The bus continued on past their stop. The Fenby-Taylors were soon half a mile away from where they wanted to get off and were livid.

"We're reporting you!" said the older Fenby-Taylor.

"Yes," said the younger Fenby-Taylor, "what's your number?"

"My number," said the bus conductor fiercely, "is here!" and he thrust the lapel of his bus conductor's jacket into the younger Fenby-Taylor's face. Pinned onto the lapel was a round disc and on that disc was a number, the bus conductor's number. If this was a challenge to the Fenby-Taylors then they were equal to it. In a matter of seconds, they had collaborated in finding paper and pencil – quite an achievement for boys normally so scatterbrained and inefficient – and the younger brother had noted it down. They didn't have long to do so, for the bus conductor, with a look of cynical scorn, soon moved away from them towards the back of the bus which had stopped at the next bus stop without the prompting of the conductor's bell because there were people at the bus stop waiting to get on. The Fenby-Taylors leapt out of their seats and tried to get down the aisle to the back of the bus but the bus

216

conductor blocked their way. He allowed the new passengers to get safely onto the bus and then he pressed the bell *three* times!

It was a very dramatic moment and a sickening one for the Fenby-Taylors. For the benefit of those who do not know the code of bell ringing on buses I shall explain. One bell ring tells the bus driver to stop, two bell rings tells the driver it's safe to move off again towards the next stop, and three rings tells the driver to move off but not to stop again at the next bus stop even if there are people there waiting to get on. The three bell rings are intended to inform the bus driver that the bus is full, that there is no room for any more passengers, so he must continue until he hears just one ring again from the bus conductor for the purpose of letting people *off* the bus only.

This time the bus was not full, certainly not to capacity, and the bus conductor should have given just two rings and allowed the bus to stop at the next bus stop if there was anyone waiting there. Usually when we heard the three bell rings we felt how lucky we were to be on the bus already, together with a token feeling of sympathy for those waiting at the next bus stop who would see their bus sailing heartlessly past them. We knew what it felt like, it had happened to us sometimes. The feeling lucky emotion, of course, usually predominated over feelings of sympathy for those waiting for a bus but this time we knew what was behind the three bell rings. The bus conductor was spitefully denying the Fenby-Taylors any opportunity of getting off the bus, and we did not feel lucky. We shared some of the Fenby-Taylors' outrage and indignation, though we were less upset than them because our destination was the bus station anyway. (Occasionally I got off earlier to go to the bike shop or the library but the bus station was my usual point of disembarkation).

Yes, that's where we were heading, without any more stops: the bus station in the centre of Marby. Only then were the Fenby-Taylor brothers able to get off the bus. They had come one and a half miles out of their way. Even when they got off at their right stop they had about a mile to walk home so they now had to walk two and a half miles home unless they waited for another bus to take them back the way they had come. That meant both time and money. If they phoned home from a phone box, would they be able to get a lift home? Would one of their parents be in? We didn't know nor did they. Their parents kept very irregular hours.

The Fenby-Taylor brothers made remarks to the bus conductor like, "we'll get you for this, you blankety blank, you're going to regret this!" and the younger Fenby-Taylor brandished the piece of paper in his hand on which he'd scribbled the bus conductor's number. The bus conductor was smirking. He had a supercilious, 'that'll teach you' look on his face. He calmly examined his ticket-dispensing roller machine and then started jangling the money in his bus conductor's bag at them, in a defiant, dismissive way. He seemed to be saying, 'Complain as much as you like. I'm getting on with my job, you can go hang!' He evidently didn't know their father was the Liberal candidate for Marby North!

In the 1950s, adults did not pay much attention to complaints from children, quite the opposite to today. Perhaps the bus conductor was banking on that but if so he made a mistake. A few days later the younger Fenby-Taylor approached us with a triumphant look on his face; we hadn't seen either of them for a couple of days.

"Our dad did complain", he said, "about that 'so and so' conductor, and they've sacked him! 'Ring that bell and I'll wring your neck!' he said. Well, they're wringing his neck now!" It sounded good, very good, but we were cautious in receiving the news because the Fenby-Taylors could tell fibs or maybe it wasn't fibs as such but just wishful thinking on their part.

"How do you know they've sacked him?" asked Rigby Smith.

"They said they would look into it and deal with the matter. That's what our dad said."

"But how do you know they've actually *done* anything ?" I asked. I wasn't so sure they had or would.

"My dad says they have," replied the younger Fenby-Taylor. There were no doubts in his mind.

Later, the older Fenby-Taylor confirmed what his brother had said and he added with smiling confidence, "I don't think we'll be seeing that conductor again."

We all looked out for the conductor on every Ledderfield bus thereafter, at every time of day, in both directions. None of us ever saw him and it became plain that the Fenby-Taylors were right. He'd either been sacked or, at the very least, moved to a different bus route. We were delighted. Delighted that a complaint from a schoolboy, one of us, had been upheld; delighted that a nasty, vindictive, bullying adult had been rebuked and, it was now safe to assume, disciplined, perhaps severely. Whenever I had recalled the whole episode in future years and that bus conductor, I had a picture in my mind's eye of a dark, swarthy man with black eyes and an evil scowl on his face. All that was missing from the picture was a scar on bus conductor's left cheek. Otherwise he was the perfect villain. But was he? Was he really just the baddie in a straightforward good versus evil encounter?

Before writing all this down, I had never thought to explore the question *why* the bus conductor was so set against the Fenby-Taylors. At the time, the answer, in so far as the question was asked at all, was simply that he was a nasty piece of work, was in a bad mood and was picking on the Fenby-Taylors. But on reflection, now, I have to ask whether there wasn't more to it. He seemed to have met the Fenby-Taylors before. Had they given him some gratuitous cheek, some 'lip' on another occasion, maybe on more than one occasion? Was his preventing them getting off the bus his way of getting back at them? Was it his only way, apart from reporting them to their school which he may not have wanted to do? Too much hassle, he might have thought, especially if they withheld their names, as the independent-minded or pigheaded Fenby-Taylors (take your pick of adjectives) would probably have done, though they were only too ready to take his number.

When you take a broader view, and let those above-mentioned questions into your frame of thought, a different picture begins to suggest itself. Bus conductors, especially on double decker buses, were always under a lot of pressure: seeing passengers got safely on and off the bus, ensuring orderly behaviour and collecting fares on both decks of the bus, weaving through the dense jungle of bodies when it was standing room only; sometimes, additionally, having to store push chairs and luggage under the stairs at the back of the bus and perhaps having to decide when the bus was full, when no more passengers or luggage could be accepted, which might make you very unpopular with members of the public, a further source of stress.

With such demands on the bus conductor, even if on the night of his clash with the Fenby-Taylors the bus was not packed to the gills, is it likely that any bus conductor would add to the difficulties of his job by stopping two schoolboys getting *off* his bus? Unless something had driven him to it, perhaps? Could that something have been the stresses and strains of the job, causing him to suffer some sort of breakdown and begin behaving in an unreasonable way? Or were those two schoolboys, the Fenby-Taylor brothers, not just random, innocent schoolboys who happened to be on the bus when he snapped, but mischievous schoolboys who had wound him up *before* and had contributed to his 'flipping his lid'? Not that provocative behaviour on their part would justify his holding them on the bus against their will and lengthening their journey home considerably as result, but it would shed a different light on his behaviour.

I have used the past tense when referring to a bus conductor's life because the bus conductor is now a more or less extinct species; kept alive for a long time by the London Routemaster buses but now even they have reached the end of the road. Nowadays the poor bus driver has to do the bus conductor's job as well as drive the bus. Sitting in his cab at the front of the bus, the point of entry to, and exit from the bus (though some buses now also have central exit doors), just as the rear end of the old buses used to be, with control over the automatic opening and closing doors, the bus driver can refuse passengers entry into the bus if they won't pay the fare or appear drunk and disorderly, but once they are on the bus he (or she) has no control over them, for he has to concentrate on driving the bus. The passengers ring the bell, they order the bus to stop, and they are left to their own devices on the bus.

There are rules of conduct on board, of course, but the bus driver can't enforce them whilst the bus is in motion. I've seen crushes of school children today, swarming around the front of stationary buses, pushing, shoving, swearing, shouting and screaming as they wait to get on, and, once on board, no less unruly. I've seen that helpless, powerless look on the face of the bus driver, knowing he is going to have to transport the whole bunch of them through the streets without any means of restraining their behaviour or any sanctions over them. I'm sure the ordinary bus driver today would love to be able to stand over an unruly child on his bus and curb the child's behaviour with a weighty reprimand or warning. But stuck in his driver's seat and facing forwards, as he must, with all his schoolchildren passengers behind him, he can do and say nothing. If things get completely out of control, all he can do is stop the bus and phone for assistance. Our nefarious bus conductor on that Ledderfield bus all those years ago misused his powers and authority (such as they were) but at least he had some power and some influence over what happened on his bus. Today's double role, driver-come-conductor, must envy the drivers and conductors of old, even if the wages are a little bit better now. (Unless, perhaps, he/she only wants to drive the bus and prefers minimal contact with the passengers).

We continued on the buses until we were thirteen years of age when we left Penly Grange School and moved on to Marby College which was only two or three miles away from our homes. There were no bus services to Marby College in the south and we cycled there. So ended our era of bus travel as schoolchildren. It afforded us much pleasure and excitement but some less pleasant moments too, such as when, in the cold and the dark of winter, we sometimes waited ages for a bus, and then, when on the bus at last, the journey in the dark – with nothing to look at except the other occupants of the bus and no sure way of marking one's progress until Marby was reached – seemed to take ages. Why was it that at those times too the unsavoury smell of stale tobacco, lingering in the bus, seemed then more noticeable than ever?

Yet even the dark nights of winter created something good for us on the buses when we were open to their unique atmosphere and allowed them to cast their nocturnal spell over us. You only needed to relax and use a little imagination as the bus drove through the night. You were on a space craft hurtling through the darkness and vastness of space. That worked well if you closed your eyes and gave yourself to the motion of the bus, to its throbbing and vibrations, to the sound of the engine and to its oily-petroly smell. Or you could simply look out of the window and notice all the seats in the bus and all the occupants in the seats on the bus – in fact everything on the *inside* of the bus which you could see – *outside* the bus, rushing through the countryside. You knew there were trees out there, telegraph poles, farmhouses, barns, fences, railway lines and bridges and other obstructions, yet, miraculously, you and all your fellow passengers sped through them all, quite unhindered and unharmed, as if your bodies had no mass or weight or substance. You were dreaming, you were in a fantasy movie, in a parallel universe, another life, it seemed; except you weren't, you were just sitting on a bus and you'd done this journey many times before.

But why should I say 'just' sitting on a bus? Aren't buses and the movement of buses miraculous enough in themselves? We thought so when we first travelled on them. And why do we dismiss the added wonderful sensation of flying through the world outside the bus on a dark night, by rationalising it, by saying that it's 'only' the *reflection* of the light inside the bus? Isn't light and the reflection of light a wonder too?

I cannot say when precisely I began to lose my childlike wonder and awe and my acceptance of things at face value; when I stopped taking natural phenomena and events literally and uncritically and began to analyse them and attempt to explain them rationally and scientifically. It certainly began to happen whilst I was at Penly Grange and overlapped with, indeed must have been part of, my gradual separation of fact from fiction. I do know that at the age of twelve, and even a little older, I was still enjoying some pretend games in the school woods with Rigby Smith, which included imaginary secrets, invented by us, then half believed by us because we wanted to believe them. We did not yet find all such games foolish and childish, we could still go along with some of them, at least.

All would have been well, I'm sure, we could have grown out of this semi-believing phase together, had Rigby Smith not had other things going on in his life. But, as I was to discover, he was growing up faster than me, and not just physically. He was entering another realm – an 'emotional' one for want of a better word – before me. This was going to shake me because we had been so close for so long and I was going to feel left out (again). There was another reason too why it was going to hurt and I never saw it coming.

The Dark Side of Rigby Smith

'Nae man can tether Time nor Tide'

Whon I talk of the 'dark side' of Rigby Smith I am not referring to a morally shady side but rather to a hidden, unknown side of his character and life: like 'the dark side of the moon', so called because it's the side of the moon which can't be seen from the Earth (owing to the peculiarities of its orbit and rotation). Rigby Smith had his weaknesses and defects, which I have described, but I do not believe he had a bad, sinister side which he deliberately kept concealed from me. However, there were things about him which I couldn't understand, connect with, or reach, and which he wouldn't or couldn't share with me.

Religion and Confirmation

One thing that baffled me was the fact that he was very religious. He liked talking about religion whenever he got the chance and was very forthright about his beliefs. I was surprised he was so keen on religion because I thought it would be superfluous to him. There was so much else going on in his life that I didn't know why he needed to be bothered with it. I suppose I thought religion was for old people or for young people who were a bit feeble and lacking in self-confidence or talent; that it was a sort of substitute for living life to the full here and now. I wasn't irreligious myself but I didn't see the need to think a lot about religion. Going to school chapel for five or ten minutes at a time in the morning and discussing religious topics in Divinity lessons seemed OK to me but nothing to get excited about. Religion was a topic, a subject, like any other, that's all, though of less relevance or interest than many other topics. In any case, success or acceptance at school were the only things that really counted, apart from friendships, and I didn't see where religion came into that unless you believed you needed God on your side to do well or be accepted, and perhaps Rigby Smith believed that.

He was, though, I know, genuinely religious. He was not just a nominal believer: it was an integral part of his life, certainly of his weekend life at home. In fact, it was a basic, built-in part of all the Rigby Smiths' lives at the weekend and at Christian festivals and holy days. Although the Rigby Smiths were always very welcoming whenever I went round to their house, my lack of experience of church and enthusiasm for worship did make me feel more of a visitor on Sundays rather than virtually another member of the family which I felt any other day of the week I was there.

I remember in the early days of my friendship with Rigby Smith suggesting once that we got together to play football on a Sunday morning. He stared at me as if I were an idiot and said he always went to church on Sunday morning with all the family. It was the only thing to do on a Sunday morning, apparently. He invited me to come along to church with him and the family, and I did go once or twice with them, and Mrs Rigby Smith was pleased to have me along but she wondered about my parents. She was concerned about my coming to church with Martin and the rest of their family rather than going to church with my own family. I reassured her on that point. My dad never went to church and my mother only went to church at Christmas and Harvest and, perhaps, Easter, and then she would go to St Winifred's in Marby town centre which was high church: she liked all the ritual, incense and candles and things. My brother and sister, both much older than me, had more or less left home by then and so weren't relevant to the question. They weren't churchgoers anyway when they were younger.

St Margaret's, where the Rigby Smith family went – a church with a tower, built in the late Victorian era – had candles on the altar and a robed priest and choir but didn't have incense and they didn't parade around with candles. They didn't have representation of Stations of the Cross round the church or a statue of the virgin Mary or anything like that, nor the choir fenced off from the rest of the congregation, as at St Winifred's. There was also less stained glass at St Margaret's, more clear glass and broader windows, and so, all together, it didn't have such a holy atmosphere as St Winifred's and I was less overawed by it as a building.

However, the stained glass window over the altar at St Margaret's did impress me considerably. I found it moving but also rather disturbing. It showed a Crucifixion scene and depicted Jesus hanging on a large cross between two thieves on lower crosses, with bystanders or spectators beneath the crosses looking up at them. Your eye, of course, was trained on Jesus, suffering on his cross in the centre of the picture. The bystanders included Roman soldiers and well-to-do people. All the clothing of the people in the scene was richly coloured, purples and reds, I remember, and there was quite a lot of blue sky above the crosses. This stained glass tableau was a strange mixture of the beautiful and the grim. It didn't convey any religious meaning to me (at the time, anyway) but it gave me a strong sense of some bizarre, dramatic, mysterious event and I have never forgotten it.

St Margaret's was on my side of town and only a ten minute walk from my home so it was easy for me to get to on a Sunday morning. My mum was happy for me to go to St Margaret's – on my own. It wasn't her choice of church but since I had been christened as a baby, it was good for me to go a church, she felt, and she recognised it was closer and more convenient for me than St Winifred's. Actually, I didn't go to St Margaret's very often because I just didn't feel very comfortable there. The Rigby Smiths were always very nice to me, perhaps a little too nice and a little too kind, especially Mrs Rigby Smith and James Rigby Smith, which only enforced my feeling that I was not really part of their church life, I was an outsider.

Whereas they always knew at every point in the service when to stand up and sit down and which page in the service book to turn to, I always had to watch and follow the rest of the congregation closely. With characteristic care and consideration, Mrs Rigby Smith would always make sure I was on the right page and at the right place in the Prayer Book but I would rather have been able to find the right page and place for myself. Mr Rigby Smith was a churchwarden at St Margaret's so we sat in the churchwarden's pew which was in the front section of the pews. I suppose sitting in the churchwarden's pew did make me feel quite important, especially since I was with the Rigby Smiths, but I would have preferred sitting at the back of the church (just as I came to prefer sitting at the back of the bus) where I could see everyone else and they couldn't see me: not without turning round and you don't do that in church, do you?

I liked singing hymns at St Margaret's, just as I liked singing hymns in the school chapel, hymns like 'Immortal, invisible, God only wise' and 'Guide me, O thou great Redeemer' (Cwm Rhondda) but there were quite a lot of hymns I didn't know which the Rigby Smiths all knew, of course, and they sung much more loudly and confidently than me. James Rigby Smith sang particularly loudly, sometimes in a strange, falsetto voice, which I found rather unnerving. When the Rigby Smiths stopped pressing me to join them at church, probably sensing my unease, and just invited me to play football with them in the afternoon in Belcombe Park, I was really quite relieved. (Mrs Rigby Smith didn't play football, I should point out, but the rest of the family did: all three sons and Mr Rigby Smith, whenever he was free on Sunday afternoons).

What struck me about the Rigby Smiths was not so much that they went to church but that they actually enjoyed it. I found church essentially dull and lifeless, a mechanical routine in old fashioned, creaky language, despite the sense of occasion which it provided, a bit like being in the theatre but at a boring play, and the brief pleasure afforded by the singing of one or two hymns. Had I not known the Rigby Smiths, I would have maintained that people went to church merely to be socially respectable. I'm sure many people did back in the 1950s, but I knew there was more to it than that for them. Did I try to discover what *was* in it for them? I don't think I tried very hard, but I know that Rigby Smith's – Martin Rigby Smith's – attitude to his faith aroused mixed feelings within me.

On the one hand, I could not fail to be impressed by his faith. It was strong and sincere, and since I admired him, anyway, for other reasons, I could not ignore it, I had to take it seriously. On the other hand, his absolute certainty in his religious beliefs was a bit off-putting. He allowed no scope for doubt. He would discuss such things as the nature of God, the will of God, heaven, hell, the afterlife, the end of the world etc., but he didn't see the point in discussing the existence of God. It was a 'given', an indisputable fact for him. I remember on one occasion, in the dining room one lunch time, Rickmack expressed an atheistic view, not necessarily his own, and Rigby Smith laughed. "No God?" he said, "you've got to be joking!" He gestured all around and above him. "Where does all this come from? Did it create itself? Did we create ourselves?" On another occasion he blew away all scepticism with a little rhyme: 'If the sun and moon should doubt/ they'd immediately go out!' Something that he'd got from his mother, I daresay. He picked up a lot from her; not that he didn't make her quotations his own, I'm sure they often were, or came to be. This one, I learnt later, was from William Blake.

When Confirmation time came, during our last year at Penly Grange, I expected my lack of religious belief, compared with his, would stand out more and become more of an issue between us, but it turned out not to make much difference and I discovered eventually we had something in common in our response to Confirmation.

Confirmation at Penly Grange was (and still is, as far as I know) a religious ceremony or rite open to all pupils who had been baptised. We were told that the ceremony we were to take part in was a renewal of our baptismal vows, that it was about making our own decisions and faith commitment as mature moral beings, but it seemed to me to be more about joining an ancient ecclesiastical club called The Church of England, about doing the accepted, respectable thing. It was an important rite of passage in our parents' and teachers' eyes but to some of us (quite a few of us, I think) it was more of a hoop we were expected to jump through rather than another welcome archway leading to a larger life of unexplored, grown-up possibilities, as it surely should have been.

Most of us at Penly Grange School had been baptised, or 'christened' as we more commonly called it, so we were eligible for Confirmation, and most of us went through the process of Confirmation there before we left, when we were 12 or 13. It was the done thing. We all got something out of it, I think, including me, though I'm not sure what. Although, as I've indicated, I wasn't really religious, I wasn't an unbeliever or atheist. I didn't mind going along with it all, not really. I didn't object to it, it just didn't mean very much to me. If I thought about Confirmation at all deeply, I found it rather bewildering and so I had no wish to talk about it outside Divinity lessons and Confirmation classes. Unlike Rigby Smith. He was only too happy to rattle on about sin and the devil, and sacraments, and the Old and New Testament, with Westford, Rickmack or Spilwell. I felt completely out of my depth when Rigby Smith was wittering on with one of them about some theological point or other and their talk didn't capture my interest in the slightest.

I must admit, I did quite enjoy the day of the Confirmation itself. It was built up into a very special event at school and as the main participants in it we were made to feel important and were the centre of everyone's attention. And we got Confirmation presents. It is true to say that most of the presents were books which I was never going to read (except for a modern translation of the Bible which I still dip into from time to time) but it was nice to be given them and have the inscriptions inside them marking the Confirmation Day, and it was good to have the Bishop of Donminster's signature in a 'Companion to Confirmation' book, given to us by the school chaplain, Henry Hewey. The Bishop of Donminster signed the book and a Confirmation card and certificate – 'Ronald Donminster' – in the Headmaster's study.

It was a little weird being in Teddy Eldin's smoky study, scene of canings and reprimands in the past, looking out, as then, on his secluded garden, but knowing that this time I was in a favoured, privileged situation and could be certain Teddy Eldin would not be going over to the bookcase to extract a cane from the frosted glass-fronted cupboard beneath it for the purpose of meting out his routine punishment on my backside. Not in front of the bishop and all the others, surely? No, I cannot say I was *certain* it would not happen, only that it seemed unlikely. Teddy Eldin's study never quite lost its heavy atmosphere of guilt and fear whenever I was in there, even during our last year when Teddy Eldin treated us, by and large, much more kindly.

What was Confirmation all about? Apart from making those Confirmation vows to 'renounce the devil and all his works' etc.? It was essentially about the coming of the Holy Ghost or Holy Spirit and the taking of Communion, the sacrament of bread and wine, the 'elements', for the first time. The sacrament of bread and wine was somewhat strange to me, but at least bread and wine were tangible and taking Communion, though very formally done, involved a simple, everyday thing – eating. The Holy Ghost, being an invisible, spiritual force, was a much more mysterious and unintelligible thing and rather frightening. But I needn't have been frightened or apprehensive in any way. In the event, the Confirmation experience, at least for me, was rather tame.

The Bishop laid his hands on our heads and we were supposed to receive the Holy Ghost, the Holy Spirit, rushing through us (though we were told we might not be conscious of it); later, we ate a wafer and had a sip of wine from a chalice which represented the body and blood of Christ. I'm sure that some of the Penly Grange Confirmation candidates really did receive the Holy Spirit (or what they believed to be the Holy Spirit) and that the bread and wine really was for them the equivalent of the body and blood of Christ. But I cannot honestly say that I was conscious of either the Holy Spirit or the presence of Christ. Maybe I wasn't ready, maybe I was too young for this particular rite of passage, as with other things. Maybe I just lacked the necessary faith. I certainly lacked faith.

I expected that Rigby Smith, on the contrary, would be on a religious 'high' after his Confirmation, but going home in the car afterwards (it was a Sunday and Rigby Smith's parents had brought us in their car – my mother and me) he seemed strangely subdued, more so than usual, and he could be quite sombre and thoughtful at times, especially in his last year. Later, he confided to me that he had not really felt the Holy Spirit pouring into him, and he didn't know what to make of the wafer and the wine he'd received. He seemed disappointed and, perverse as it may sound, I was pleased to think he had not had a special experience which had been denied me. Or didn't appear to have done.

And so, all in all, that part of his dark side which was bound up with his religious nature came to separate us less, I thought, as we matured, though he remained a strong believer and I a very weak one. Conversely, another part of his dark side which was at first seemed trifling and innocuous came to acquire much greater significance in time and finally became quite critical. I am referring to his interest in the opposite sex, in girls.

Girls

Had Rigby Smith's interest in girls been merely a matter of curiosity about sex and sexual things it wouldn't have concerned me or affected me much, I don't think. We were all curious about sex (though few of us were as curious as Spilwell) and as I grew older I noticed more lewd allusions to women or girls in boys' conversations. Sometimes I heard boasts about alleged exploits with girls but it was all mere talk and juvenile bravado, as far as I was concerned, and mostly crude and animalistic. When I speak of Rigby Smith's interest in the opposite sex, I mean his interest in, or his preoccupation with, girlfriends; I mean something much more romantic and sentimental. I say girlfriend*s*, in the plural, because although I knew of only one girlfriend in his Penly Grange days, Jennifer Danvers, there was another girl he met before Jennifer who seems to have had some hold on him for quite awhile.

I first learnt of this previous girl when we were in the middle of a conversation about holidays we were going on in the near future. He suddenly broke off, went into a sort of reverie and then asked me, quite seriously, whether I had a girlfriend. He was only eleven or ten at the time and I found it a very odd question coming from him to me. It was odd coming from him because I didn't think he had the slightest interest in girls, in fact I thought he despised them, and odd he should think that I, at my age, even younger than him, and in a very limited social circle (which he must have been aware of), might possibly have a girlfriend. By way of answering his question, because it was put so earnestly, I mentioned my friend Caroline, the daughter of a friend of my mother's, with whom I sometimes played cards and board games because she lived very close and there weren't any boys for me to play with nearby, but I had to admit she wasn't a girlfriend in the way he meant.

He fell silent for a moment and then returned to the subject of holidays. He started to tell me about his summer holiday in Devon that year. He'd mentioned it before but given me no details of it. He began opening up about it now. He was full of it, what a smashing time he'd had, but in his account of this holiday he was holding back on something and I had to deduce what it was, though the more he talked the easier it was to make the deduction, and I think he wanted me to infer what it was anyway. He couldn't tell me outright, he'd feel foolish, confessing he'd fallen for a girl, but that's what I gleaned had happened. And the girl's name was Sandra.

In late August, Rigby Smith had gone with his family for a fortnight's stay in a hotel in Devon which catered especially for families (not so many of them about in the 1950s). Spring Field Hotel it was called. There was a games room in the hotel, Rigby Smith told me with great glee, where you could play table tennis and darts, and fiddle around on a tatty piano, playing little jingly tunes with one stabbing finger, 'chopsticks' and things like that, which you picked up from the other kids; sometimes you hammered out very simple duets with them. There were quite a lot of youngsters at the hotel, both girls and boys, and they nearly all congregated in the games room, using the games facilities provided or just generally messing about together, the slapdash use of the piano being just one example of this. A gang of young ones, an informal club, soon formed and played out in the garden as well as the games room, playing tennis and croquet together, and chasing and piggyback games. Sandra was not a guest in the hotel, she was the daughter of the proprietor, but she joined in many of the games with the children staying there and became part of the gang.

The Rigby Smith family would go to the beach, less than a mile away, when it was fine, and walk on the cliffs, but Rigby Smith told me he preferred being at the hotel because it was such fun being with gang, who never met or played on the beach for some reason, only at the hotel. It was such fun being with the gang – I read between the lines – because Sandra was one of the gang. Her name kept cropping up when Rigby Smith talked about the gang and what they did, and whenever he mentioned her name he tried to sound offhand but, on the contrary, a new note entered his voice, a note of excitement, exhilaration even.

Sandra was nearly a year younger than Rigby Smith, I gathered, so she could have been no older than ten or nine when he first met her. A very tender age, you might think, to be the object of romantic passion but I have since learnt that Dante fell in love with Beatrice, the love of his life and inspiration of his poetry, was she was only just nine, and he was not quite ten, which gives food for thought here. Sandra was slim and fair-haired, pretty, headstrong and proud. I gained this impression of her partly from what Rigby Smith said and remarks his brothers made about her, and partly from a ciné film I once saw of their holiday, which Mr Rigby Smith had shot and in which she featured briefly, rushing up and down the hotel steps, along with other members of the gang, with a sharp and scornful look on her face. Was that disdainful look of hers for the camera or for someone else, I wondered? I also learnt from Rigby Smith that Sandra was fond of horses and he would often watch her riding her pony – Starlight or Stardust – in the field behind the hotel. She lavished a lot of attention on Starlight, it seemed, and I got the impression he was jealous of that pony.

The Rigby Smiths returned to Spring Field Hotel for the next three years. I daresay Sandra could have become Rigby Smith's summer holiday girlfriend but I don't think she ever was. She doesn't appear to have cared much for him. Rigby Smith once showed me a postcard he'd had from her. He seemed to treasure it but it was only an ordinary postcard, a small postcard, with a rather dull picture of the hotel on it, and it had only a few brief lines of pencilled scrawl on it, that's all. I don't think he ever had a proper letter from her. If he did, he never showed it to me, which I think he would have done, since he'd shown me the postcard; he would have shown me the envelope of the letter at the very least if he'd had a letter from her, I'm pretty sure.

One story, in particular, which he told me about the hotel gang, and one pop record which he owned and seemed to have a special affection for, were sufficient to confirm all the clues I had that his feelings for Sandra were not returned: that it was unrequited love.

It seems that the hotel gang had a running around game, a form of tag, in which all the boys chased all the girls. It was called Kiss Cats and was played on the hotel lawn by the tennis court in the evening twilight. If a boy caught a girl and said 'kiss cats!' he was allowed to kiss her, within a ten second time frame, then he had to let her go. According to Rigby Smith, the girls were quite good at eluding the boys and even if a boy caught a girl he might not exercise his right, being, sometimes, too shy or embarrassed. So not much kissing actually occurred, heightening the excitement when it did. The fun was partly that in the dark you might not know who had been caught or by whom, therefore not know which boy might be kissing which girl or, perhaps, not kissing at all.

Rigby Smith went after Sandra, he admitted to me, though he tried to make it sound a random decision on his part. I don't suppose she had a chance of eluding him, even in the dark, with his speed and determination. However, when he caught her and said 'kiss cats!' Sandra did not let him kiss her, she did not give him his ten seconds, she just wriggled away from him and ran off defiantly into the gathering darkness. Rigby Smith didn't pursue her, though he could have done, for she'd broken the main rule of the game, and nothing subsequently happened. It wasn't much of a story but it obviously meant something to him and he felt compelled to tell it. I sensed he had felt spurned by Sandra's reaction and had taken it very much to heart, and in telling the story he hoped to ease the hurt somehow.

The significant pop song was called It's Only Make-believe. It was a no.1 hit and first recorded in the late1950s by a pop star who rejoiced in the name of Conway Twitty. Later it was recorded by several other artists. I knew Rigby Smith had a special regard for this song because whereas with most other pop songs he would gyrate around and sing along noisily with the words (karaoke style), for this one he remained very still, closed his eyes and barely moved his lips. He went into a sort of trance as the monotonous, mesmerising tune, carrying the repeated, echoing phrases of the song, built remorselessly to a climax of unfulfilled longing – in the drawn out refrain of each verse, 'It's only make-believe!' The word 'only', in particular, in that last line, was stretched out to express all the yearning in the song. It is sufficient to quote the first verse, after the introductory lines, to give the gist of the lyrics for the next two verses were similar:

My one and only prayer is that some day you'll care,
My hopes, my dreams come true, my one and only you,
No one will ever know how much I love you so,
My only prayer will be some day you'll care for me,
But it's only make-believe!

I would have been just guessing this song had any connection with Sandra, for he made only cryptic comments about it meaning something special to him, had I not noticed one word he'd written in small block capitals letters at the bottom of the record's dust cover – ARDNAS. He used anagrams in secret messages to me (not top secret messages because they were too easy to decipher) and I knew without a doubt he meant SANDRA. Much later, I discovered ARDNAS had been firmly crossed out. I never knew whether that meant he wished to conceal his association of the song with Sandra or whether his feelings for her had come to an end, or both.

Sandra was only a remote, faint figure for me, whom I never met and knew only at second hand through anecdotes and that short piece of ciné film. I knew she'd had made quite an impression on Rigby Smith but how could I ever have suspected that she foreshadowed a more permanent change in him, that she sounded a warning note, provided a hint that he was moving into new emotional territory, on his own, opening a gap between us again?

I had, indeed, no inkling of it then but neither did I detect any signs of any significant change when he became acquainted with Jennifer Danvers whom I did meet and came to know moderately well. Jennifer Danvers entered the scene when we were twelve years old or so, about two years after Rigby Smith first met Sandra. The social scene in Marby, that is. It was more Rigby Smith's scene than mine, he being the more outgoing, sociable type, and going to more parties than me, but I went to some of those parties too and I encountered Jennifer Danvers and her friends from time to time. I don't think they took much notice of me, I was too small and shy, but I noticed them, particularly Jennifer Danvers who was not small and shy.

Jennifer Danvers was a farmer's daughter who lived a couple of miles outside Marby (to the north) and she'd got to know the Rigby Smith boys through her cousin and best friend Fiona Roberts whose father was a doctor. Jennifer had short, dark hair and was quite tall for her age. She had lively eyes and was very playful and full of energy. You might say she was 'bouncy'. She was not quite so volatile as her red-haired friend Pauline Patterson who had a tennis court and gave tennis parties (and was also crazy about horses) but more so than her bosom pal Fiona who was a quieter character with light brown hair and a serene air and the most attractive of the girls I knew then. Not that I was much affected by the looks of any of the girls. I wasn't interested in girls then in the way Martin Rigby Smith was.

Jennifer took a shine to Martin as soon as she met him and made no secret of it. Unlike most of the girls, she did not simply huddle in corners and whisper and chatter at parties, she was 'proactive'. When the MC at a party ordered everyone to get into pairs for a game, she didn't wait to be asked, she took the initiative. I remember her grabbing Martin's hand, at their first meeting, and dragging him into the circle where 'pass the parcel' was about to be played. Thereafter, she would always try to stand near him too for games such as 'postman's knock' and musical chairs.

Martin didn't seem to mind. He quite liked it, I think, though when it came to finding a partner for dancing rock 'n' roll, he seemed to have his eye on another girl with long fair hair, called Valery, who caught the attention of one or two other boys too. I remember there was an occasion at a party when Cliff Richard's record Move It was being played. Martin became very animated and started rocking 'n' rolling with Jennifer who was equally excited, but all the while he was glancing across at Valery who was not dancing and was taking no notice of him; whether deliberately or because she really wasn't interested, it was difficult to tell. Some girls were very good, I thought, at feigning indifference to the boys, though sometimes, maybe often, the indifference was perfectly genuine.

Whether Martin really preferred Valerie to Jennifer I couldn't say. As time went on, however, Martin came to be more and more associated in people's minds with Jennifer and they eventually became an established, recognised pair – Martin and Jennifer or Jennifer and Martin, depending on whether you spoke to a boy or a girl in the social set. I didn't take it very seriously because Martin himself didn't seem to take it very seriously. After a while, he didn't deny Jennifer was his girlfriend and he certainly liked her quite a lot, but he used to imply he was only stringing her along for the time being, that she wasn't 'the one'. Did he still hanker after Sandra? I just didn't know.

Why should his relationship with Jennifer have made much difference, anyway? She was at boarding school and only around in the holidays and half terms, and even then only at parties, as far as I knew, and parties weren't that frequent. At school, in the term time, our friendship was still firm, despite Nevan's attempted incursions upon it, and totally solid, I felt, and in one way in particular. Even though we were now not quite so close in our academic schoolwork, concentrating more on our special subjects for our scholarship exam (History and Latin for him, Maths and Science for me) and we were becoming gradually further apart in sport as Rigby Smith began to play in the school First teams and I never got near them, except as touch judge and cricket scorer, we still had one thing that bound us uniquely together – the woods.

The Woods Again

What with schoolwork and Rigby Smith's sport (training, as well as matches, and constant practice in the nets in the cricket season), we didn't get much time to go to the woods but we went there quite often in Scouts on Fridays, which enabled us to keep an eye on our dens and secret places, and on half days when there weren't any matches we went there as often as we could. As we grew older, our games in the woods changed – by mutual agreement – our tastes and outlook developing at about the same pace, and we could easily adapt to each other's ideas. We pursued his ideas more than mine, I daresay, but he occasionally took up my suggestions and we continued to collaborate well.

We began to abandon our pretend games in which we took on the personae of such figures as Robin Hood and his Outlaws, D'Artagnan and the Three Musketeers, The Range Rider and Dick West, Dick Turpin and his Gang or The Black Brigand and his Band – heroes of legends, novels, comics or TV. In any case, fictional adventure play based on heroes such as these required several people to be any good and you couldn't always be certain how many boys you could get to join in your play nor how far they would go along with your own imagined scenarios. We wanted more and more to be ourselves in our self-devised fictions, to invent our own mysteries involving hidden dens, secret meeting places, codes and passwords; partly in competition with the XR gang who had their own little secret schemes, and partly to make use of the woods' natural, intrinsic qualities, rather than use the woods loosely as stage scenery for imaginary locations which could be anywhere.

We believed, or believed sufficiently anyway, that there were real mysteries latent in the woods. However, as we became more and more familiar with the woods, the element of the unknown and the mystique of the unexplored began to diminish somewhat. And that's why the map, Rigby Smith's map, of conjectured hidden tunnels in the woods became so important to us. The map embodied a possible secret, an almost plausible, real secret which we could wholeheartedly believe in (or persuade ourselves to believe in) and take perfectly seriously, when other pretend adventures were beginning to lack conviction and therefore genuine excitement. Above all, the map was something we could investigate together, on our own. We needed nobody else.

We took Rigby Smith's map into the woods a couple of times and tested it, after a fashion, like amateur surveyors. We paced out distances of the projected tunnels and took bearings and examined square yards of ground where two or more tunnels could theoretically meet. Sure enough, we found mounds of earth or sunken ground in one area which might have been the result of systematic excavations. Some points where tunnels might have hypothetically met were too overgrown to be explored properly without tools and we planned to get hold of some. Nothing in our initial investigations, however, contradicted the postulated secret network of tunnels. It was, we convinced ourselves, just there to be discovered.

Rigby Smith suggested some historical research next to find out more about the Sellersby Estate in the last century. We both got very excited by the prospect of opening up a historical dimension to our search. It raised the vague possibility of ghosts in our mind too, of spirits from past days lingering on somewhere underground (we still thought in fantasy terms like that) but I was looking forward, even more than that, to unearthing artefacts, uncovering physical evidence and becoming an archaeologist!

"Yes!" I said, "find out if there are any records of tunnels being made like the ones at Kellwick!" The Kellwick Estate, near Marby, which was closed to the public but had been used at one time as a military training base, was known to have a network of subterranean passages built a long time ago by the Duke of Exford who once owned the Sellersby Estate. And part of the Sellersby Estate now formed the site of Penly Grange School. That was a fact! I felt intellectually inspired now as well as exhilarated by a real mystery to pursue in the woods. Rigby Smith said he would look for information in Marby public library which he could walk or cycle to from home, and maybe the Tibdale library too if he had time and could get transport there. I offered to look in the school library. We were both fired with enthusiasm for our secret investigation. We were real detectives now!

Other things then intervened, inevitably, to delay our inquiries or distract us from them. Work for our scholarship exam never got any lighter, quite the contrary, and sport took up increasing amounts of time, especially for Rigby Smith: in the spring term he was playing both rugby and hockey, and doing athletics and cricket in the summer term. I did a lot of swimming especially in the summer term but I seemed to have more time available than him and I pressed on with my own historical research, or tried to. I scoured all the historical and reference books in the library which covered the last two centuries but found nothing relevant. I didn't want to ask Mr Carrow or Mr Barnet about the topic, both of whom might have been helpful, because I didn't want to reveal what Rigby Smith and I were investigating. It was our private project. When Rigby Smith told me he hadn't had time to go to Marby library I didn't blame him, I simply went myself.

I found out some interesting stuff about the Sellersby Estate, and Nablock, part of the Sellersby Estate, where we went for weekend camps, but nothing about any tunnels in the woods. However, I learnt that a previous owner of the estate had been given to the construction of odd buildings or follies in Nablock woods – we'd come across the remains of one or two when camping – and the full extent of his building exploits on the Sellersby Estate was not known apparently. Although very vague, this fact was enough to encourage me and gave me something to take to Rigby Smith, to show him I'd been hard at work on our investigation and to give our secret research some impetus.

Our research certainly needed impetus because Rigby Smith's enthusiasm was waning a little and he began to pass over what I thought were good opportunities to visit the woods and continue his search for the tunnels. At first I thought he was simply too busy with other things when he couldn't find time to go to the woods but I sensed something was definitely wrong when he received my news about possible buried follies in the woods with almost total indifference. A folly was not the same, of course, as a tunnel, but it was something historically possible, not a fantasy: a credible line of enquiry to pursue, with a possible link worth exploring. In any case, wasn't he supposed to be interested in history, wasn't it his favourite subject? I had expected him to seize eagerly on my information, and, ignoring its tenuous connection with any tunnels say, "Let's go and see if we can find any buried stones from old buildings, let's see if there's a link with our tunnels!" but he hardly reacted at all when I told him, his mind seemed a million miles away.

He was obviously distracted by other things but it couldn't just be schoolwork and sport and Scouts (he was working on proficiency badges now) for he'd had all those preoccupations before when we were exploring the woods together on a regular basis. I noticed, though, that he was now spending more time than usual talking with Nevan at school, during break especially, and on the bus going home. It was just-between-the-two-of-them, 'in' talk, the sort they sometimes engaged in at home but it had always been generated before by Nevan and I got the impression Rigby Smith only went along with it to please him. It was Nevan's little game and Rigby Smith was uneasy about it when I was around, knowing it cut me out. But now he was indulging in private duologue with Nevan quite happily, ignoring my presence, as if I wasn't there or didn't need to be included in their private conversations.

These private conversations were primarily about girls. They talked about the latest pop songs, as ever, and crooned Everly Brothers' songs together, sometimes Buddy Holly, but they now related particular songs and their lyrics to girls they both knew. The same two girls' names kept cropping up in a playful way. It was always Nevan, I noticed, who seemed to initiate this little naming game. He would say with pointed emphasis things like, 'Jennifer told me she thinks All Shook Up is Elvis's best song: she said it makes her think of someone. I wonder who?' … 'Do you know what Jennifer thinks of Cliff's latest? She told me, you know' ... 'Jennifer didn't say much at Pauline's last party, did she? Why was that? I can guess' ... 'What was that 'love heart' Jennifer gave to you? [heart-shaped sweet with a love message on it]. Was it *Don't Wait* or *Chase Me* ? Or was it, perhaps, *Try Me?*'

Rigby Smith would evade his questions about Jennifer and ignore his teasing comments and retaliate by mentioning Fiona's name every time he mentioned Jennifer's name. That's how I learnt that Nevan fancied Fiona although he always dismissed the suggestion, not by outright denial but more subtly by damning her with faint praise. 'She's all right, I suppose, not at all bad,' he would say. 'Yes, I must say, she's quite nice looking. Not as good looking as Jennifer, of course', and so turn the focus of conversation back to Jennifer. That's how, in fact, I first discovered that Rigby Smith and Jennifer Danvers had become attached in other people's eyes, and he soon ceased to deny it, as I've said. Even so, as I've also said, I didn't think Jennifer was more than a holiday pastime for him, and Nevan's insistence on bringing up her name in school-time whenever he got the chance I found forced and contrived and extremely irritating. And I wasn't the only one. Rickmack and Loretti didn't like it either.

As far as his liking for Fiona went, I didn't think Nevan had a chance. Unlike Rigby Smith, who was quite tall, dark and handsome and who could comb his hair up into a big wave which made him look like a pop star, Bernie Nevan was rather pale, small and weak-looking, with unremarkable, light brown hair and hairstyle. He was quite neat and tidy in his appearance, I admit, and he managed to display a cool manner and convey an air of enigma and intrigue which might have had an appeal to girls who like a man of mystery and who easily fall for that sort of thing, but there were other more masculine, hunky and good-looking boys who fancied Fiona whom she was bound to prefer, I thought. In any case, it was uncertain how much Nevan really liked Fiona; I sometimes thought it was just another make-believe game he was playing with Rigby Smith, an exclusive game for two players, but this time a more grown-up kind of make-believe, he kidded himself, because it was to do with the opposite sex and involved real life girls.

Despite all their talk, therefore, about Jennifer and Fiona, I didn't believe either Jennifer or Fiona were especially important to Rigby Smith and Nevan, it was just a form of display, showing off how mature and socially advanced they were to be on terms of easy acquaintance with girls, when many boys at Penly Grange had little or no contact with girls. For their part – Jennifer's and Fiona's – although I had noted how drawn Jennifer was to Rigby Smith at parties I'd been to, I didn't think it amounted to anything very deep, nor could I imagine, as I've said, that Fiona could possibly fancy Nevan. Yet I was quite wrong about all this, and I was to discover the truth (a hard truth for me) in a most unexpected way.

It was the summer term, our last summer term. It was sometime after I'd suffered the surprise and disappointment of Rigby Smith's complete lack of interest in my discovery of the possible existence of follies in Penly Grange woods about a hundred years ago. We were both doing quite a lot of homework in the evenings in preparation for our scholarship exam and Rigby Smith was having cricket practice in the nets every afternoon, both batting and bowling. It must have been no later than the middle of May, for as far as I remember we had not yet had any cricket fixtures and Rocky Craggs' faith in Rigby Smith's cricketing ability, particularly as a batsman, had yet to be borne out. I knew very well that Rigby Smith was as concerned about his performance in cricket matches as he was about his performance in the scholarship exam, in June, and so I accepted his preoccupation with cricket when he wasn't studying for the scholarship exam. After all, I was as keen for him to do well as he was himself. Almost.

One day, however, it rained heavily all morning and the cricket pitches and the nets got very wet, and so even though it stopped raining after lunch there was no question of anyone playing any cricket. Surprisingly, because on similar occasions we'd been made to do extra PE in the gym or go on a school run, we were given free time following the afternoon lessons (afternoon lessons in the summer term were always from about 1.30-3.30, not after tea as they were during the other two terms), and even the First Eleven cricketers were given time off and not made to do any fielding practice as they were usually required to do in such circumstances.

We were allowed to go swimming, an option which many boys grabbed eagerly, but, more importantly for me, even though I loved swimming, we were allowed to go into the woods because the sun was now coming out. It seemed a great opportunity for Rigby Smith and me to get back into the woods and explore the evidence for the hidden tunnels. I put it to him but he seemed slow to respond, as if the idea hadn't occurred to him and he needed to assimilate my proposition for a few seconds. He couldn't offer cricket practice as a reason for not going in the woods this time because there *was* no cricket practice and he'd effectively been handed about an hour and a half of unforeseen free time on a plate. He looked closely at his watch, then at me, and seeing how eager I was and realising he had no excuse for not taking up my suggestion, he nodded.

"OK," he said, but without sounding very eager. "It'll be a bit wet, though, after all that rain. Maybe we could go in for half an hour or so, but I don't want to be late home, I want to get the 4.30 bus."

237

"Homework?" I asked (I knew he was doing extra work for History and the General Paper). It seemed the obvious reason for getting home early, though if he'd had his cricket practice he couldn't have expected to get a bus any earlier than 5.30 or 6.00pm.

"Yes," he replied, "... and other things".

His 'and other things' was a giveaway that he was not being entirely frank with me. Rigby Smith never told an outright lie. If he wanted to avoid the truth, he qualified his statements and added vague riders like 'on the whole' or 'that sort of thing', 'you might say that' or 'I suppose so'. The addition of 'other things' to his otherwise plain 'yes' came into this category of half truth or evasion on his part, I could tell. But before I had time to question what his 'other things' were he became suddenly decisive.

"Come on then," he said, "let's go, let's get in there!" He said this more in the tone of someone who wants to get something over and done with rather than out of any genuine enthusiasm, I thought, so my pleasure in getting him to come exploring the woods with me again (other than on Fridays in the company of other Scouts) was somewhat tempered. He didn't have his boiler suit with him – I did – but fortunately he didn't let that deter him. He said he hadn't got time to change anyway and he wasn't bothered about the rule about wearing boiler suits: he was a monitor, wasn't he, and had expected to be playing cricket, hadn't he? I was a monitor too but I thought it might be better to wear my boiler suit and Rigby Smith had to wait a couple of minutes while I got changed into it. He kept looking at his watch impatiently while I did so which I didn't like.

"Where do you want to look first?" he asked, as we entered the woods, in a manner which suggested this visit was purely for my benefit. Why can't he relax and enjoy it too? I wondered. What's on his mind? I proposed the area near the two sycamore trees used as a base in French and English games. These sycamore trees were on the north side of the woods and I had once come across a square grey stone, half sunk in the ground about fifty yards away from them. I had not thought much of it at the time but, since learning about the possibility of there being follies in the woods in the last century, I thought it was worth exploring the spot to see if there were any other stones like that which might be the remains of an old building, and, if there had been a building there once, to investigate whether or not they might be related to any tunnel construction.

I explained this to Rigby Smith and he seemed prepared to search the undergrowth in the designated area for a short while at least. I located the stone I'd found before, and after five or ten minutes of scrabbling around in soggy undergrowth we found what could have been another stone of the same kind, but it was buried too deep in the ground for us to be certain.

"We'll need a spade to look at that one properly," said Rigby Smith, "In any case, we haven't got time to explore anymore now. And anyway," he added, "I'm not sure how this spot connects to our network of tunnels." He wasn't really applying his brain to his plan of the tunnels but *I'd* given the matter some thought. I thought this spot might lie along Rigby Smith's blue coloured tunnel line which ran diagonally from the north west fence near the sycamore trees to the south east of the woods where there was a grassy area along the edge of the woods, sometimes used for pitching tents when training for Scout camps. If there was any evidence of a tunnel in that south east area we hadn't seen it but if Rigby Smith's hypothetical network was right there should be a tunnel running somewhere in that vicinity.

"It would be on the blue tunnel line, wouldn't it?" I remarked.

"Not the yellow one?" Rigby Smith looked puzzled. Doesn't the yellow tunnel run here? Isn't it coloured yellow on the map?"

"Well you ought to know, it's your map, isn't it? Have a look at it!" I urged him. Rigby Smith always carried the map with him (it was about 8 inches by 6 inches), folded up in his red and green wallet, his most cherished possession, and he often had it ready in his hand when we were exploring, but for some reason he hadn't thought of getting it out this time.

"Well of course!" he said. "Let's have a look at it!" and he put his hand in his pocket to bring it out. Some papers spilled out of his pocket and fell to the ground. "Whoops!" he exclaimed, "that's not the map." He looked embarrassed and bent down to retrieve the three items on the ground. But I stooped more quickly than him and picked them up before he could. It was true – none of the items was the map. They were two photographs (black and white) and a letter. I just had time to notice Martin Rigby Smith's name and address on the envelope in neat, round, feminine handwriting, before he grabbed it out of my hand.

"Just a letter," he said, "I got recently," it looked very recent to me, "from …" – he paused for a moment, wondering whether or not to be secretive about it, but obviously decided against it – "Jennifer Danvers. I've got to answer it." He was trying, unconvincingly I thought, to make it sound like a moral obligation. He saw me looking now at the two photographs and explained: "Some pictures I took with Jennifer's camera. At that party in our garden. And in Belcombe Park. She's just had them developed."

Studying the garden party photo, I saw Brian Barley and Toffee playing some game in the background which I knew to have been darts. Jennifer was the main subject of the picture and was standing in front of a volleyball net. I noted her short dark hair, clear-cut features, and the impish look on her face. She was wearing a longish dress and a thin cardigan, and was holding her arms behind her back in a slightly self-conscious pose. It was quite a good likeness of her, I thought. She certainly looked her bright and lively self.

The other photo, however, made a greater impact on me because of its far greater implications. It showed Jennifer, on the left of the picture, sitting on a bike, with ruffled hair, grinning confidently at the camera. She was on what looked like a country road, though in fact it was in Belcombe Park, as Rigby Smith said, and there was no other traffic to be seen. That in itself did not mean a great deal except that it indicated Rigby Smith was going on bike rides with Jennifer Danvers and not just seeing her at parties. What was in the rest of the picture, however, was much more significant to me; or, rather, *who* was in the rest of the picture.

Standing close to Jennifer on her bike, was a barefooted Fiona, graceful and exceptionally pretty Fiona, in knee length skirt, holding her shoes with no bike of her own in sight (somewhat puzzling). She too was smiling but not at the camera. She was gazing across at a third person who was sitting on a smart bike in the foreground of the picture on the right. That person was Nevan. He was in jacket and tie, though on a bike ride, and was wearing his cool, sly, inscrutable, slightly disdainful look. I was stunned for a moment and then felt a rising rage within me. If the picture had been a 'live' one I would have punched his face.

I knew there was more to my anger than simply my resentment at Nevan worming his way, literally, into the picture again. What was clear to me from the photo was that Fiona, despite my scepticism, liked Nevan, maybe a lot, and Martin Rigby Smith and Jennifer, and Bernie Nevan and Fiona, had become a foursome. A foursome in which there was no need for anyone else, certainly not me.

Nevan had got the better of me yet again – that's how I saw it. I had accepted that in the holidays and at weekends in Marby, Nevan could compete with me over friendship with Rigby Smith and he often had the edge over me, certainly in his own home. But at school, in the term time, I held the trumps. There was no question that I was Rigby Smith's best friend and he'd said so himself, hadn't he? No doubt he would still maintain he was but how could he maintain it now, when Nevan was making such evident inroads into his school-time thoughts and preoccupations too? Not just Nevan, no, it was Jennifer too, she was taking over his mind, they were in it together, squeezing me out. Sadly for me this wasn't just paranoia or an inferiority complex – though the conspiracy theory was a fantasy I came to realise – because my worst intimations were confirmed by what followed next.

Rigby Smith took the photos out of my hand and replaced them with the map which he had now found. "Look," he said, "take the map and see how it fits in with these stones in this area. See whether it's the blue or yellow tunnel that runs here. I've got to go now." He added, "You can come back home with Colin if you like, he's swimming I think."

It was amazing that he should hand his map over to me so casually, his precious map that he was normally so possessive about. I began to suspect that he now had something in his pocket that was much more precious to him. Was it the photos or the letter or both photos and letter? He had grabbed the letter back more swiftly than the photos but what was he doing carrying any of these things around with him? They had been sent to his home in Marby, why did he need to bring them to school? To show Nevan? Possibly, but he could have shown them to him at home, couldn't he? It seemed just as likely to me that he had brought them to school because he wanted them with him, he couldn't bear to be separated from them. Could those 'other things' he had to do tonight possibly be part of all this? Was he impatient to answer that letter from Jennifer Danvers. Was that it?

As he left me, almost running, I felt my heart sink further into the ground. If he'd lost interest in his network of tunnels in the woods, his pet project for the woods from his own imagination, it was only one small step towards his losing interest in the woods altogether. Not the woods for Scouting but the woods for mysteries and secrets and make-believe games, the special playground which we two had shared, and just us two, even if others had tagged on at times to make up the numbers in one or two adventure games.

As I watched Rigby Smith moving away from me and out of the woods, through the tall green trees, all come, or just coming, into leaf, I felt left behind in more ways than one. Remembering that moment now, I see it as if he were passing through the pillars of another sort of archway, into a realm of experience where I could not follow him then. What was that realm or of what did it consist? Sexual bewitchment and intrigue? Another secret game? 'Relationships'? Romantic love? However you described it, it was an area of experience I was not to enter for many years to come, nor did I want to. And I never understood how it might possibly supersede deep friendship – the type of friendship Martin Rigby Smith and I had enjoyed for five years – or simply sweep it aside.

After a cursory glance at the map, not caring about it, not taking it in, I went back into school to get my books for the evening's homework. Parker was on his own in the library/classroom, seated at a table near the window, head down, working away at something. He ignored me at first, then looked up and spoke,

"You've been in the woods with Berry, haven't you?"

"Yes," I said. It was pointless to deny it.

241

He threw me his know-all look. "You've been investigating something, haven't you? Doing some sort of research?" I didn't respond to this and he continued, "What have you found out? Or is it all a big secret?"

"Not much," I said. For a moment I felt inclined to tell him more. It would have been good to speak confidentially to someone, to unburden myself to someone. But I couldn't. Not to Parker. I had nothing against him and we had something in common, both of us being swots, but Rigby Smith wasn't a fan of his and we just weren't close enough. Parker continued looking at me quizzically, waiting for me to say more. I did.

"It is a secret, yes. Supposed to be. But I don't think we'll be doing much more about it. Not now."

"Why not?" asked Parker, seeming quite interested.

"Berry is too busy."

"Oh yes, he's got his cricket as well as the scholarship exam, I know."

"He has, that's true, but it's not just that."

"What is it then?"

I swallowed hard and tried to mask the rising hurt and bitter disappointment in my voice.

"It's *other things*," I said. "*Other things.*"

My instinct, my gut feeling, was regrettably proved right. As it turned out, we never investigated the secret network of tunnels again. For several weeks Rigby Smith never even asked for his map back. I don't think he ever consciously decided to give the whole thing up, though, because at lunch once he suddenly asked me if I had the map safe and when I assured him I had, he said, 'Good, look after it, won't you, till we get another chance to go in there.' But we never did have another chance. Too much happened that final summer term, and any spare time which Rigby Smith had, he did apparently spend it on 'other things'.

Colin confirmed he was writing regularly to Jennifer Danvers, as I suspected. According to Colin, he was writing long letters to her and spending ages on them some evenings. Colin also confirmed what I had deduced about Nevan and Fiona. Colin thought it was very amusing, in fact it was the funniest thing he'd ever heard, he said. Fiona fancied Nevan (Bernie to her) and had written to him. Colin couldn't understand what Fiona saw in him unless she'd been taken in by his air of mystery which was the only thing I could think of too. Colin didn't know if Nevan had written back to Fiona but he'd sent her a photo of himself in his tennis kit, and he and Martin were constantly swapping gossip about what Jennifer and Fiona were talking about at their school, St Catherine's, and planning to do in the summer holidays.

I was losing out in every way. Although I kept in touch with the First Eleven cricket team through being the scorer, Nevan was now closer to Rigby Smith when it came to both cricket practices and matches because he was actually in the team with Rigby Smith, not just a spectator, and sometimes they batted together as well as fielding together in matches. And they seemed to be getting on better and better together at school as well as at home. Throughout that summer term, therefore, despite the fact that Rigby Smith and I still had most lessons together and did Scouts together most Fridays, I felt more and more that Nevan was replacing me as Rigby Smith's best friend. The fact that Nevan was being increasingly nice to me didn't help at all. It only made matters worse. It suggested to me that he regarded the rivalry between us as no longer necessary since he'd won the contest over who was Martin Rigby Smith's closest friend.

There was one occasion, however, I'll never forget, which showed there was still something special and unique between us despite the fact that in practical, everyday terms, we were no longer best friends or, at least, no longer sharing things in quite the same way we used to do. It happened towards the end of the summer term and it amounted to no more than the briefest of conversations. The occasion was a cricket match. Unlike the ones I have already described in detail in an earlier chapter, it was not regarded as a memorable match by most people, and yet to Rigby Smith it certainly was, and I realised it too. The match was against Marby College away and resulted in a draw. Rigby Smith scored another half century but it wasn't a very self-assured innings; he'd batted much more fluently in other matches. And yet, in its own way, in an unspectacular way, it was a triumph. That was because of the context of the match.

Only a fortnight earlier, Rigby Smith had sustained a nasty injury. In a home fixture against St David's, a ball he was intending to sweep on the leg side jumped up off the pitch and hit him full in the face. He was knocked unconscious for a few seconds and then had to be carried off the field. He got an enormous black eye and played no further part in the game nor could he play again for over a week. The game against Marby College for which he was just about fit enough was a big challenge to him because he'd lost a bit of his usual confidence in playing fast bowling and he was going to be up against the fastest bowler he'd yet had to face, a lad called Naseby, whose pace and swing and accuracy were astonishing for a fourteen year old.

Marby College batted first and scored a huge total of over 160. It didn't look like we had a chance and, as feared, when *we* batted, Naseby started to skittle our batsmen out. There was no question of our winning the game only a question of whether we could hang on for the draw. Rigby Smith played a nervy innings, riding his luck, snicking Naseby through the slips and miscuing some hits which just cleared the fielders' heads, surviving a couple of dropped catches and somehow keeping his stumps safe. He hung on whilst other batsmen came and went, gaining runs here and there and dealing with the few bad balls, and we held out for the draw with only one wicket left to fall and fewer than 100 runs on the board.

Rocky Craggs and some of the boys in our team were joking afterwards about Lady Luck being on Rigby Smith's side and he smiled too knowing he had indeed been lucky. But there was more to it than that. The crucial thing, not generally recognised, was that the injury to his eye, though it had done no permanent damage, had shaken him up considerably, and from a remark he made to me before the game I got the impression he would have gladly missed the match against Marby College and the fearsome Naseby, but he felt as captain he couldn't get out of it. In securing that drawn result against Marby College he had, as the commentators say, 'dug deep' and played a true captain's innings. I would have thought Rocky Craggs and even Teddy Eldin (although he wasn't at the game as far as I remember) would have thought more highly of this gritty innings, but apparently not, as I discovered a few days later when I got the chance to talk to Rigby Smith on his own. I felt compelled to compliment him on his innings against Marby College although my scorebook had recorded mostly singles and very few boundaries, nothing outstanding.

"Your innings against Marby College," I said, "and Naseby in particular ... I reckon it was your best. All things considered."

"Really? Despite all those snicks and streaky runs?" he seemed surprised but not greatly.

"You held on, though, didn't you?"

"Yes." He smiled appreciatively at me. "You're right. And you know what? No one else has said that. That it was my best innings. It had to be you, didn't it? You're the only one who really knows me, aren't you?"

He paused and I thought he was going to say more. About our friendship. I thought he seemed a little sad and he was about to express regret that things between us weren't quite as they had been. But it might have been just my imagination, something I wanted him to say. Actually, it wasn't a time for him to express regret or feel sad about anything. Apart from his injury from which he was continuing to recover, things couldn't have been going better for him. He'd learnt he'd won a scholarship to Marby College (like me) and, following his winning of his colours at rugby and hockey, his winning of all the track events in athletics, and a brilliant cricket season in which he had acquired a batting average of over 80, he was due to receive the Best Sportsman of the Year Award. He'd also gained a Scout cord in Scouts, an award which went well beyond the First Class badge (only two other boys in the school had achieved it), and had won the school chess tournament. He wouldn't have forgotten either that earlier in the year he'd had the leading role in the school play. On top of all this, his 'other things' seemed to be going well too and he must have been looking forward to the summer holidays when he and Nevan could get together with Jennifer and Fiona again and do more than merely correspond.

Far too many positive things, therefore, were happening to him and preoccupying him for him to have any time or inclination to think about what he was losing, or had already lost, by growing older and giving up his childhood attachments and pursuits. So I shouldn't have been surprised that he did not, in fact, say anything more about our special friendship. I could take some comfort, though, from the little he *had* said: about being me the only one who really knew him; even though it wasn't entirely true because there were some things I did not know or understand about him, as I've made clear.

I mulled over what he might have meant. Was he simply saying that we had been friends for a long time and so had got to know each other better than anyone else; was he just making a general point about the longevity of our friendship and our familiarity with each other's ways? Or was he being more specific? Was he thinking of particular things or experiences? We had our common love of the woods which was, or had been, a unique part of our friendship but that was now fading and I wondered what else he might be thinking of, apart from the woods, something special to our relationship, my knowing him in a special way?

I reflected that there were times when he had laid bare his soul or I had had glimpses of his deeper self. They were usually moments associated with sport or physical prowess. There was the time he told me he was going to be a professional sportsman and there was the time I witnessed the agony he felt when he did so badly in the Group cross country race. There were the fights I saw, his humiliation at the hands of Burton and then Jakeman, and later the restoration of some pride when he got the better of Jakeman in the unforeseen re-match with him. There was the fiasco of the rowing on Lake Windermere, which I'd witnessed, indeed been involved in, when he made a complete fool of himself, and I'd been permitted an inkling of him making a fool of himself in another way – over love, over a girl who, I believed, had rejected him or cold-shouldered him. He had not confided in me openly about that but he'd told me enough for me to draw my own conclusions about his heartache, which is what he wanted me to do, I'm sure.

In all of these incidents I had seen him in some sort of crisis of self-confidence and self esteem. And then I realised the full significance of the cricket match against Marby College. His bouncing back after his injury was not just important for his cricket but for everything else. Whenever he'd taken a knock to his confidence he had sought to make a comeback and he usually had. That was what really mattered to him. And the fact that I recognised this, or appeared to, and no one else did, had confirmed for him that I knew him, knew about him, in a way no one else did. No, not even Nevan, for all his closeness to Rigby Smith, through circumstances, through living so near to him and seeing so much of him, and now, through a trick of fate, it seemed, of related girlfriends.

I drew some consolation from this realisation and tried hard to resign myself to the way things were now. But, I wondered, would I be able to withstand the emotional pressure of the end of term service, which would be sure to bring all my thoughts about Rigby Smith and the whole of my life at Penly Grange to a head, and confront me with the stark truth, the sharpened awareness that my life was soon to change even more radically ... and irrevocably?

The End of Term Service

'God be with you till we meet again'

Until my last two terms or so at Penly Grange, I always sat lightly to the gravity of the end of term service. It was meant to be both a touching and inspiring occasion, especially at the end of the summer term. This was the term most boys left Penly Grange, at the age of thirteen, and even for those boys not leaving the school, the end of the summer term still preceded the longest break between terms in the whole school year. The end of term service, therefore, in the summer term, when we were gathered together for the last time that school year, marked a separation between close friends and schoolmates of at least two months and possibly a permanent separation for those who would not be coming back to Penly Grange the following term. A sad occasion then, surely? No, not for me nor the day boys I knew. Not normally.

The implicit mood and tenor of the end of term service, what we were supposed to feel, was that that life outside school was going to be tough and challenging, harsh and inhospitable, and that leaving school was like leaving home. This presumption was particularly amusing to us day boys, for we never regarded school as home in any way; we had our own homes and went back to them every day. Moreover, we felt most of the fears, dangers and challenges in life occurred *at* school rather than anywhere else: whether it was the threat of bullying from the likes of Burton and Jakeman, or the compulsion to do well in schoolwork or sport, or the fear of punishment for losing or forgetting your books or your games kit, or the general oppressiveness of the school routine with its rigorous timetable and no mercy shown if you were late for anything. We felt much safer and more relaxed away from school and all its pressures. The coming of the holidays spelt unalloyed joy. Well, almost.

There was some sadness, a minimal amount, at the thought of not seeing boarding school friends again for a while, but I could still see day boy friends, if I wanted to, during the holidays since we all lived in or around Marby and many of my friends were day boys. It is true that I saw less of Rigby Smith in the holidays but I could still see him a fair amount, if I made the effort, and the end of term service never signified a separation from him in my mind. Of course, after Nevan had established himself as a close friend of Rigby Smith's, I regretted the fact that he saw a lot more of Rigby Smith than I did in the holidays but I wouldn't be thinking of that during the end of term service. Just the joyful prospect of the holidays which meant release from all the strictures of school. The only downside to the holidays was that occasionally I was bored, but that wasn't often. I had my model railway set to keep me occupied, my aero-modelling and stamp collection, when I couldn't get round to the Rigby Smiths' or they were away, and there was always Caroline to play with, a board game probably, if I needed a companion.

For boarders, the holidays meant something fundamentally different. Whereas we day boys came home every night to our families, so that we had two lives during term time, school life and home life, boarders had just one inescapable life – school life. For three months at a time, they woke up together in dormitories, washed, ate, had lessons and breaks, ate again, got changed for Games or for Scouts or 'fieldwork', got washed and dressed afterwards, had tea and more lessons, played their own games in their 'free time', ate supper, did prep (homework), engaged in further hobbies and pastimes, then went back to their dormitories to wash or bath and sleep once more till the cycle began again.

Of course, there were away matches for those in school teams and there were occasional school outings and weekend camps in the summer for those in the Scouts, so life for some boarders was not completely restricted to the confines of Penly Grange, but whatever the boarders did it was in the company of other pupils and mostly supervised by teachers or matrons (in the evening); they were under almost constant scrutiny which was not always benign. There was seldom any let-up for them from the relentless, unforgiving march of the school routine; frequently cheek by jowl with others, in the public eye, compelled to be in a particular place at a particular time whether they liked it or not, and with the right implements, equipment or kit, whether they had it or not, day and night: for day boys, it was just the tyranny of the daytime routine.

True, each term had a half term weekend break of two nights and there were usually two 'exeat' weekends a term when a boarder was allowed home for the Saturday night, returning early evening on the Sunday, but some boarders could not go home for various reasons, such as living too far away to make it worthwhile or parents abroad, and even for those who could go home, just four nights altogether per term away from school was small respite amidst a stretch of ninety nights in the autumn and summer terms, mercifully somewhat fewer in the cold Spring/Lent term. For boarders who were unpopular and picked on by staff or boys, or were simply solitary types, loners like Beddoes or Critchley, living so long in the unforgiving company of other boys was, at best, irksome, at worst, a living hell. Term time for such boys was a prison sentence and the holidays were remission, time out on parole. For them, the end of term service signalled total freedom and an even greater joy than we day boys felt, save for the thought they would have to return to school, to their overcrowded prison cells, after all too short a time out.

Conversely, those boarders who had good friends and who, by and large, enjoyed the communal school life, might find leaving school for a couple of months quite a wrench. Then there were the boarders who were not especially happy at school but who were more unhappy at home, due to family circumstances or just having nothing to do at home. They too would find the end of term and the end of term service an occasion more of sadness than happiness.

Since I was normally in the '*happy*-at-the-end-of-term' camp, I could easily indulge in some sentimental nostalgia at the end of the summer term for the passing of another school year, whilst at the same time, because I wasn't deeply affected, study the faces of boys in the school chapel during the service to note signs of sadness there, perhaps actual tears. I wasn't the only one who did this, by any means. For some of us it became a spectator sport, a game to pass the time in an otherwise largely boring ritual. The sport or game was to 'spot the emotional weakling who can't hold back his tears': for of course if you felt any sorrow at the end of term you were not supposed to show it, our schoolboy ethic was to be stoical when upset for any reason and certainly it was not *cool* to cry about leaving school even if it were for the last time.

The End of Term School Hymn

Keeping a straight face and a stiff upper lip, if you were truly sad at the end of term service, would probably not have been too difficult, even at your final end of term service, had the service consisted merely of a few prayers, exhortations from the visiting preacher to go out bravely into life ahead, a reading or two, and formal farewells, accompanied by the moralistic ramblings of Headmaster Teddy Eldin. What put a rueful boy's stoicism really on the rack, however, and strained it to breaking point, was the traditional hymn we always sang at the end of term – 'God be with you till we meet again'.

God be with you till we meet again;
By his counsels guide, uphold you,
With his sheep securely fold you:
God be with you till we meet again.

God be with you till we meet again;
'Neath his wings protecting hide you,
Daily manna still provide you:
God be with you till we meet again.

God be with you till we meet again;
When life's perils thick confound you,
Put his arm unfailing round you:
God be with you till we meet again.

God be with you till we meet again;
Keep love's banner floating o'er you,
Smite death's threatening wave before you:
God be with you till we meet again.

Neither the somewhat lightweight, jingly tune of the hymn (Randolph), though the third line has an affecting rise and fall, nor the old-fashioned Victorian words, of somewhat simplistic, sentimental piety, were particularly potent on their own, but together, and in the context of a farewell service in the chapel where all the school were gathered, they made a compelling combination and were an almost irresistible tear jerker for the emotionally sensitive. I had sung this hymn over a dozen times during my time at Penly Grange, quite enjoying its imagery of battle, challenge and danger, but reciting the words without paying much attention to their import, apart from their general good wishes to everyone for the months ahead lived away from Penly Grange.

However, during my last year at Penly Grange some of the lines of the hymn began to mean more to me, and as that final summer term raced towards its conclusion after the scholarship exams I began to realise that at the impending end of term service, my last end of term service, I would not be able to remain as detached as hitherto. I began to realise that if the scales of happiness and sadness at the end of term had, for me, always been firmly tilted towards the former, to happiness, this time they were likely to be tilting the other way, to sadness.

I say 'tilting' only because up to the very last week of term I was experiencing very mixed feelings. On the one hand, I had good reason to be very content and quite pleased with myself. I had won a scholarship to Marby College, doing particularly well in Maths, Science, English and French. The English and French were a bit of a surprise, but very gratifying, particularly the French, since I'd been so bad at it at the beginning and I always thought my progress in the subject had been rather slow. I was now a school monitor (prefect) and a patrol leader in Scouts. I had achieved a lot in Scouts, in fact, having gained five proficiency badges, as well as the First Class badge, including the quite tough Backwoodsman badge (which involved gutting a fish and skinning a rabbit and building and sleeping in a bivouac in the woods). I had got my Master Certificate for swimming and done well in the swimming sports and I been commended for my chess playing and my scoring for the First Eleven cricket team. I was looking forward to being publicly honoured with the other leavers at the end of term for my successes and my various contributions to my Group and to the School.

Furthermore, in some ways I was quite looking forward to leaving Penly Grange and moving on to Marby College. Marby College would be a newer, bigger world. It was a world much spoken of, and alluded to, into which many of those older boys we looked up to had passed (whom we had seen with our eyes or knew by repute) and who had achieved great things, the young Mr Barnet, our favourite teacher, being one of the most notable and admirable. It was natural we should want to follow in their footsteps. I was certainly looking forward to the intellectual challenge of Marby College, particularly to the more rigorous science teaching I expected there, feeling most teachers at Marby College had little more to offer me academically. On top of all these reasons to savour the end of term, there was the prospect of the summer holidays to come: a Scout camp which I always enjoyed (usually), and then a further seven or eight weeks of freedom. My cup was running over … but it was also emptying.

For there was, of course, another side to the end of this term. And as the last day of term came ever closer, and with it the end of term service, I became more and more aware of what was coming to an end in my life, of what I would be losing, relinquishing for ever.

On the penultimate day of term we had the usual hymn practice and sang through 'God be with you till we meet again' in a perfunctory way, though we were told, as ever, to pay more attention to our diction (to put the 'd' on 'God' etc.). I couldn't help thinking seriously about the words, especially the first and third verses, and applying them to my situation and to all of us who would be leaving Penly Grange at the end of term.

'With his sheep securely fold you' runs the third line of the first verse. This line seemed very relevant now for we had all been in a sort of sheepfold, snugly together. This hadn't really come home to me before. On the contrary, during the last year, and especially this last summer term, I had been feeling increasingly independent and rather proud of it. I was a bit of a swot, perhaps, but everyone had accepted that for sometime now and my scholarship conferred honour on it and put me in a select group of boys, for only five boys out of forty had won scholarships (Parker, Rickmack, Thorpe, Rigby Smith and me). Although I played chess both for my Group and the School, and always wanted to do well for them, chess is a solo game and you win and lose on your own; and it was essentially the same for swimming, for you competed on your own against individuals from other Groups or schools unless it was a relay race and even then you swam your stage of the race on your own.

Likewise, my cricket scoring was a solo activity. It linked me to the First Eleven and I certainly felt their ups and downs but I wasn't in the team, I was apart from them, doing a unique job on my own. I felt more self-reliant too in Scouts now, being in charge of my own patrol and, particularly, since completing my First Class Journey test with just one other boy (Westford) and being just one of a handful who had gained the First Class badge. Moreover, although I had friends at Penly Grange and liked most of the pupils in my form and my Group, the only friendship I really valued was my friendship with Rigby Smith which I never believed was dependent on Penly Grange School for it had always extended beyond it. No wonder then that I felt a self-sufficient and independent schoolboy.

But it was now dawning on me that my independence was an illusion. I was not, in fact, a detached, separate individual, not when I thought about it. The end of term hymn expressed the wish or prayer that the dispersed community should be kept together in spirit 'till we meet again', but hitherto I had thought of the scattering of the community of Penly Grange as only affecting the boarders in any serious way and it had hardly concerned me at all. In singing the hymn I had paid only lip service to the sentiment, but now I saw it applied to all of us, all leavers, day boys as well as boarders. We would all be scattered at the end of term and there was no coming back to Penly Grange, this time, no return to the sheepfold, as before, next term.

'Till we meet again' was all the more poignant a phrase because we would not, in fact, be meeting again at all, not as members of Penly Grange. If we did see each other again, and many of us would *see* each other again, at Marby College, it would be under new and very different circumstances. A chill was creeping into me, infiltrating the warmth of my cosy prestige at Penly Grange. Though not as academically brilliant as Parker nor reaching the dizzying heights of Rigby Smith's all round success, I had come close to the top of the tree at Penly Grange in some ways. I had been accepted and recognised for who I was, and even, in my last year, esteemed. After Penly Grange, I now realised, I would have to start again from the bottom. Yes, I had won a scholarship but how much would that mean once at Marby College? Would I be accepted there? I couldn't help comparing myself, on this point, unfavourably, with some of the other leavers, like Westford, Rickmack and Rigby Smith.

Westford would be OK. He was solidly built and good at rugby, so important at Marby College. He was shrewd and self-confident in an unassertive way, as a monitor he had always been obeyed without question and as Captain of School he'd been liked and respected by all. Rickmack was a thinker, not just academically bright, and he was also good at Games, especially rugby, better than Westford in fact. He had a toughness and independent-mindedness I always admired, as did others; his short stature seemed to do him no harm at all. And Rigby Smith, equally good at work and sport, so that he would doubtless please both teachers and boys, was of above average height, physically quick and agile and able to take care of himself, if necessary, as his final encounter with the domineering Jakeman had demonstrated.

But what of me? A swot and below average height: physically weaker than many boys of my school year and a bit younger. Though keen on sport, not good at sport, except swimming, and how far would that get me? Swimming was not a major sport at Marby College, as far as I knew. I couldn't think of any friends who had gone on ahead of me to Marby College who might be allies or supporters when I arrived there, and I envied Rigby Smith for having an older brother (James) who was already at Marby College, paving the way for his younger brother and providing a ready social connection for him, since Martin would almost certainly be going into the same House as him (they were called 'Houses' at Marby College not 'Groups' as at Penly Grange). As for those friends coming with me to Marby College, would I end up in the same class or House as any of them? Was there any chance at all – what I really wanted – that I might be put in the same House or class as Rigby Smith? I just didn't know.

My day boy links would continue with those Penly Grange day boys going on to Marby College, and most of them were, but they'd be no more travelling on the buses together. There was no public transport to Marby College and it wasn't far enough away (just 2-3 miles) to merit the laying on of a special bus for us. In fact, most day boys cycled to Marby College and I was to become part of quite a close knit cycling fraternity but I didn't realise that whilst still at Penly Grange. What I did know was that there was talk of Rigby Smith becoming a boarder at Marby College. If that happened it would sever the first and most lasting bond between us. It was the discovery of that bond which had helped us to 'click' at our first meeting, my very first day at Penly Grange when I was so scared about being a new boy and longing to be accepted, when much to my surprise and delight, the self-assured and well-established Rigby Smith had welcomed me into the fold, the day boy fold, with those wonderfully heartening words: "You're one of us!"

I would always be grateful to Rigby Smith. He, above all others, had helped me to settle in at Penly Grange and had remained my closest friend (though regrettably I did not think I was *his* best friend any more) but would he, or could he, do the same for me at Marby College, in a bigger and, I feared, harsher world where there was 'fagging' and where school prefects could cane you if you stepped out of line (or maybe just didn't like you)? Certainly not if he were in a different House and form from me, both perfectly possible. And would there be anyone else to take his role as guardian? No, never, I could never expect to get that lucky again, could I? I would be on my own.

And what of the intervening time? The immediate future after Penly Grange but before starting at Marby College? In other words, the summer holidays, the rest of July, the whole of August and first half of September. There was Scout camp first, somewhere in the Yorkshire Dales, where I would be a patrol leader and would see the likes of Thorpe, Parker, Honeyman, Spencer, Westford and Rigby Smith. That would be good, that would maintain my link with Penly Grange for ten days. But after that I would be in a less secure social world. Not a hostile or threatening world, as I feared Marby College might turn out to be, as well as a challenging one, but a social world which would be indifferent to me.

I would still be welcome at the Rigby Smiths', I knew, but I would have to play second fiddle to Nevan all the time now as far as Martin Rigby Smith was concerned, and in his new, mixed social circle, featuring Jennifer and Fiona and Pauline and others, I would at best be on the margins, the periphery of his attention. I might get invited to an occasional tennis party, I might go swimming with all the others at Marby College baths, actually enjoying the swimming more than the socialising (the other way round I suspected for Rigby Smith and Nevan), I might even drop in on The Cosmos Café on the south side of Marby and join Rigby Smith and Nevan and their mixed gang, and drink frothy 'espresso' coffee and play a record or two on the jukebox. I might go. I would not be rejected, I would be accepted, after a fashion, if only as a friend of Martin Rigby Smith's.

But then again I might *not* go because I would only be tolerated, I wouldn't really be part of the gang. I hadn't got a girlfriend nor had I any wish to acquire one. I had more in common with Colin Rigby Smith who, I knew, wasn't interested in girls either but was interested in similar things to me, like sport and stamp collecting, and aeroplanes and trains and adventure stories (e.g. Gimlet and Biggles by Capt W.E. Johns and John Buchan novels), the hit parade, especially Lonnie Donegan and Johnny Duncan, and exchanging jokes. He had a joke book in which he was collecting jokes; Martin had done that once but had now stopped doing it. Whenever I saw Colin at a social event I found myself gravitating towards him though he was two years younger than me. Being on the fringes of Martin's social circle, like me, I felt we had a lot in common. I liked his company anyway, as I've said before: he was good fun.

What I really wanted was for things to be as they used to be with Martin Rigby Smith before he cared tuppence about girls, before he'd met Jennifer; no, before he'd met the elusive Sandra, for she had first aroused his interest in the opposite sex, far too early. It would have been better still had I been able to put back the clock to the time before Nevan had appeared on the scene and had started to divert Martin's attention away from me. But that time was gone and would never return and I had to accept it, like Martin's attraction to girls: doubly galling that Nevan should be part of that too.

Nevan, as it happened, had been irritating me near the end of this final term in a new way, with his perpetual reiteration of Buddy Holly's last song It Doesn't Matter Anymore. He'd been doing it in a facetious, mocking manner, I thought. Sometimes he'd just hum the tune, sometimes sing the words. Whenever he sang the words, he included the line, 'Well, you've left me here so I could sit and cry' and the refrain, 'But I guess it doesn't matter anymore'. Who was he mocking? I was never sure whether Nevan was aiming the song at me, for I had foolishly told him something of my misgivings about leaving, or at himself, for although the same age as me he was staying on at Penly Grange for another term or two. I don't know who had made this decision, the school or his parents, or maybe it was by mutual agreement, but he'd entered the school later than me and they must have thought he had some catching up to do academically. Anyway, the immediate significance of this was that the end of term service this summer term would not be *his* last end of term service. He could therefore remain more easily detached from the emotion of final farewells (whether he would have actually felt any emotion, anyway, I couldn't say). He could watch the rest of us and see how we reacted, and I was sure he would be watching us, me especially, very closely.

This made it even more imperative for me not to show any emotion. I did not want Nevan deriving any entertainment from the slightest sign of tears on my part. If only we didn't have to sing the usual hymn at the end of the service! The line I was most worried about, I realised, was the third line of the third verse – 'When life's perils thick confound you/ *Put his arm unfailing round you*'. When singing it with everyone else in the school chapel, it always gave me a warm feeling of comfort and reassurance. Hitherto it had just been a passing, sentimental thing. I didn't feel I actually needed an arm round me to comfort or console me any more than I needed a back massage when I hadn't strained my back, though, like a back massage, even when unhurt, the sensation is always a very pleasant one. This time, however, now that I was contemplating saying goodbye to the whole of my life at Penly Grange and reflecting on how a major era in my life was almost at an end – how I would be going out into an uncertain future and having to face up to

255

the fact, once and for all, that my friendship with Rigby Smith, already not what it was, would doubtless continue to weaken outside Penly Grange School – I really felt the need for a loving arm around me. So, no doubt did other leavers, though I couldn't say how many felt insecure like me and how many were largely carefree, raring to go like Rigby Smith, Westford, Porter and Honeyman.

I don't know how much religion there was in the hymn for me: how much I believed God would put his arm around me and all of us, whether he was there at all even, but it was a most appealing thought. I only knew for certain that when sung communally in Penly Grange chapel those words did give me a strong sense of belonging and that when singing them this time I would be acutely aware that it would be for the last time, that the belonging, and the collective comfort which that belonging gave, would be coming to an end when the singing was over.

Knowing this, would I be able to hold back the tears when singing the hymn on my last day at Penly Grange? When I reached that third line of the third verse, especially? Disguising my feelings wasn't going to be easy since I was singing in the choir and choir members were all too visible, being seated at the front of the chapel and facing sideways across it, not in forward-facing rows like the rest of the congregation.

I devised my strategy of concealment, my cunning subterfuge. I was going to have a very nasty cold. Nasty colds are unusual in the summer but they do happen, and mine, as it turned out, was a particularly nasty one. Or maybe it was a bad attack of hay fever (though I don't usually suffer from hay fever). Whatever it was, it was so nasty I had to blow my nose frequently during the end of term service, then go and sit at the back of the choir, in a less conspicuous position, out of consideration for others. It so happened that, for some reason, I found myself having to blow my nose longest and hardest during the singing of the hymn, but since the hymn came at the end of the service and the congregation had by now got used to my blowing my nose, they did not notice anything different in my behaviour and reactions during the hymn. That was what I counted on, anyway.

I hoped nobody noticed – or if they did thought nothing of it – that during the third verse of the hymn my handkerchief was spread more extensively over my face than ever:

God be with you till we meet again;
When life's perils thick confound you,
Put his arm unfailing round you:
God be with you till we meet again.

We did not meet again in the chapel of Penly Grange – ever – and met only once more in the dining room, in the library/classroom (those of us in the scholarship form) and on the playing fields, watching a friendly cricket match between an augmented staff team and the First Eleven; I was not scoring on this occasion.

In the late afternoon of that final day at Penly Grange, and after my final swim, I walked ... out from the quad through the archway, my satchel stuffed with my PT kit and swimming gear, past the chapel and across the playground where we'd so often played 'tig' in the early years, past the lawn on the right with the stone bird bath, then down a section of the rhododendron-lined drive and left through the trees to the bus stop on the Marby-Tibdale road ... for the last time. I remember being on my own, though I don't know why. That archway through which I had walked *into* the quad, to begin my five years and a term at Penly Grange, I had now walked *out of*, away from, to begin, in earnest, the next major phase of my life – my teenage years. Though they were to be significant and interesting enough, they were not to prove so rich and memorable, so character-forming and soul-shaping as my Penly Grange years. But then, nor would many other phases and years in all my life to come.

Postscript and Different Perspectives

'There's a divinity that shapes our ends'

Marby College and Beyond

To write about my life at Marby College and thereafter, and the subsequent futures of my Penly Grange friends and acquaintances – notwithstanding that I know or remember very little about many of them – would require another book and would probably be another kind of memoir. However, I can offer the reader a few notes on some of the boys who have featured in my Penly Grange memoir, beginning with Martin Rigby Smith.

Rigby Smith did well at Marby College but not superlatively well. He got his school First Fifteen rugby colours, played hockey for the First Eleven and was in the school athletics team: he was a good middle-distance runner. He was unvanquished at boxing. The fact, though, that after winning his weight at boxing (light middleweight), when aged 14 or 15, he gave up boxing altogether, did, of course, help him to preserve his clean sheet of no defeats. He failed to make his mark in school cricket which surprised everyone, eventually turning to athletics and to tennis, a minor sport at Marby College. He did not do particularly well at tennis, though he was in the school team and showed occasional flashes of brilliance.

At some point he gave up his ambition to be a professional sportsman and he told me he was thinking of becoming a monk! Interesting that, because he was still 'going steady with' Jennifer, I believe, when he told me that. He was very keen on her, I know, though he used to pretend he wasn't. I know he was keen on her because when she suddenly stopped writing to him after two years of being his girlfriend he was very upset. He said very little about it (in any case we didn't talk much together at Marby, just long conversations on rare occasions) but the way he told me about it reminded me of the way he talked to me about Sandra – very guarded and cryptic and trying to batten down his emotions, yet eager to confide in someone, to unburden himself in some way. Incidentally, Nevan and Fiona split about the same time, perhaps earlier, so the foursome which had been so strong for a time was completely shattered. I got no satisfaction from that, I should add, not by the time it happened.

As at Penly Grange, Rigby Smith's two best subjects were History and

English and he couldn't decide between them when applying for university. History had always been his favourite and he won the History prizes both years in the Sixth Form but then he applied to read English at Cambridge. When he didn't get into Cambridge for English he switched back to History and won a place at Oxford, though he ended up studying French and Spanish. At Oxford, he saw Parker at Christian Union meetings. Parker, as I had expected, did brilliantly in academic work and music at Marby College and won a scholarship to Oxford to study a science subject – Biochemistry, I think.

As I had feared, Rigby Smith and I were not in the same House at Marby College and he *did* become a boarder so the Group and day boy links we'd had at Penly Grange were not maintained and we were inevitably more distant from one another at Marby College and forged links with other friends. I don't think, though, that either of us found a friendship to match that friendship we'd shared at Penly Grange. Rigby Smith's close comradeship with Nevan continued, at home in Marby, at least, but at Marby College their friendship had little chance to develop, especially when Rigby Smith became a boarder whilst Nevan remained a day boy like me. Although in the same House, they never saw each other in lessons, Nevan being in a lower year, and they only did sport together when playing House matches.

I saw quite a lot of Rigby Smith in class during the first two years because we were in the accelerated 4A Form, and did several 'O' level subjects together, like English, Latin and French (in different sets for Maths and Physics, though). At 'A' level, however, he went for Arts subjects and I chose Maths and Science subjects (Biology and Physics), so our paths seldom crossed in the Sixth Form. I would like to have done English Literature 'A' level with Rigby Smith, Rickmack and Loretti, having enjoyed English with Mr Carrow at Penly Grange and then with Mr Jeffers at 'O' level, especially Orwell's Animal Farm, though I'd found Twelfth Night a bit tedious to study, and I enjoyed reading classics of English Literature, especially novels and lyric poetry, and always have done, but in our day there was no mixing of Arts subjects and Sciences, it was one or the other, and my forte was definitely Maths and Science. After Marby College I went to Imperial College, London, and read Applied Maths, so we went our separate ways at university too.

Over the years we have been in intermittent contact. I have been in touch with Colin too, who, incidentally, did medicine at Edinburgh and became a GP in Bradford. Occasionally we have met at the Rigby Smiths' home where his parents have remained and where I have always felt welcome. When my mother died, however, I had no reason to return to Marby on a regular basis and have done so only rarely, just to one or two Reunions at Marby College. My meeting with Martin and his older brother James, about ten years after we'd left Marby College, to visit the terminally ill Robert Barnet, our most inspiring teacher, I have recorded in an earlier chapter of this memoir.

Martin Rigby Smith did not become a monk, nor a clergyman like his brother James, but he did become a missionary of sorts and taught abroad in a school in Jordan for a time. Later, he taught in France and married a French girl and had children. Much later still, he turned to publishing of some kind; I not sure what exactly but something to do with French educational books. As far as I know, he is planning on staying in France. I believe his children have left home now and are married, like mine, or have partners. (I don't know whether he has any grandchildren yet). About eight years ago, at a Marby College Reunion, Martin told me he was going to write a book about his school days which would interest me. I think he actually said the book would be *based* on his schooldays which implied it might be fictional but he told me very little about his intentions and I've heard nothing more about it since.

Nevan did not go to university but entered the furniture retail business and then went into advertising, at least for a time. Rigby Smith went to his wedding in Donminster in the late 1960s/early 1970s, but didn't keep in touch with him much after that. However, he did occasionally hear from him and also picked up snippets of news about him from Pauline Patterson who kept in touch with many people in her tennis and rock 'n' roll party circle, and she told him Bernie had gone to the Far East and was establishing business contacts out there. That was ages ago, though.

Westford did even better at Marby College than he had done at Penly Grange. He did well at rugby as before and became Head of School as at Penly Grange but his schoolwork exceeded his academic achievement at Penly Grange (he had not been put in for the scholarship exam) and he won a place at Cambridge to study natural sciences. After university he became a captain of industry, a director of a firm manufacturing technical instruments. Rigby Smith and I went to his wedding but hardly kept up with him after that. He was due to come to a Reunion once at Marby College. Rigby Smith and I had asked to be seated next to him at dinner but he never showed up and we never found out why.

Rickmack has disappeared without trace which I very much regret. I continued to be quite friendly with him at Marby College but saw less of him in the Sixth form, as with Rigby Smith, because he did Arts 'A' levels (English and, I think, French & German). He did well in rugby as before and was extremely good at English, as before, but it seemed to me he became increasingly surly and cynical as he got older and full of doubts about life, his life in particular. When I asked him once what career he had in mind he gave me a pained look and said, "The trouble is, Mouse, I know what I *don't* want to do, but I don't know what I *do* want to do." He made no attempt to get into Oxford or Cambridge and, as far as I know, though I may be wrong about this, he didn't go to any university, which was odd because he certainly had outstanding intellectual ability.

I twice tried to discover Rickmack's address from the Marbian Old Boy secretary but he didn't have it, and no one I questioned at the last Marby College Reunion I went to knew what had happened to him or anything about him. Neither did Rigby Smith. If Rickmack ever reads this memoir, maybe he'll get in touch with me. He is the one Penly Grange Old Boy whom I have lost touch with that I would particularly like to meet again. I admired him and respected the quality of his mind and his staunchly independent character.

Tom Thorpe, whom I saw a fair amount of in the Sixth Form because he did Maths 'A' level with me, read Law at Cambridge and eventually joined a firm of solicitors. Recently I met up with him and we had a good chat about Penly Grange. It was quite an important meeting for me and my memoir, as you will learn.

Burton Update

And what of Burton? Max Burton? Burton the school bully: the Old Boy whom I had met in hospital and who had triggered the writing of my memoir? What had happened to him since that meeting? The answer to that question is very little: as far as I know.

I had vowed to return to the hospital and have a talk with him, and then, maybe, if things went well, open up a discussion about 'the old days' at Penly Grange. If he wanted to face up to the truth about his behaviour at Penly Grange, I was prepared to help him. If he didn't want to talk about it that was fine too: I didn't really see myself as a confessor figure or therapist, trying to winkle out confessions from him for his self-improvement and mental or spiritual health, though I had felt a bit like that briefly when in hospital with him. But if he did want to talk about his school days and he persisted in hanging on to his deluded view of his bullying ways at Penly Grange what would I do? Surely I would not shy away from telling him the truth; I couldn't let a distorted view of the past go unchallenged, could I?

As it happened, I did not have to make any response to him at all because when I went back to the hospital he wasn't there. The nurse had said he would be in hospital for many more weeks, so I thought I had maybe two or three months in which to visit him. I put it off for awhile because I had plenty on my plate preparing for my early retirement, and perhaps, also, because I was becoming less enthusiastic about talking with him again and more interested in recollecting all the other characters at Penly Grange as I got deeper into my memoir.

I'd had my operation in October, and by December, though busy at work, I had somehow managed to write the first chapter and plan most of the others. I was looking forward to March when I would be retired and able to spend much more time on the memoir. I knew I would have to take a break from writing over Christmas: that juggernaut which knocks everything out of its way. I knew that at Christmas I would have to spend more time with my family and friends and on general socialising, and it was then I decided the time was ripe to visit Burton. Christmas was, anyway, an appropriate time for renewing old acquaintances.

But he wasn't there. I was told he'd gone home for awhile and was due to be moved to another hospital in the New Year. The hospital wouldn't give me his address nor could they tell me which hospital he was being moved to; they said they didn't know. When I explained I had been in the same ward with him and he was an old school acquaintance, they were unmoved. They had their rules, they said. Protection of personal data and all that. They said I should try Friends Renuited or write to the school in question. That made me laugh. I couldn't see Burton having kept up any contacts with the school or being interested in Friends Reunited. He didn't have any friends at Penly Grange, unless you included Jakeman but he was more of a henchman than a friend, I would have thought.

I did make a perfunctory effort to trace Max Burton. I went on a few websites and put his name into one or two searches but, as I expected, just got masses of useless and irrelevant information. After all, Burton is not such an uncommon name. I then put Burton on the back burner for awhile. Time passed, and when my early retirement began in March I settled down to an extended period of writing my memoir. Burton faded in prominence in my recollections of Penly Grange and therefore, inevitably, in my present day thoughts. When I thought about him now, I realised that although he had always loomed large in my memories of Penly Grange – my bad memories of the school – he had only really existed at the uppermost layer of my mind. He had been terrifying at the time and cast a blight over my school life but he'd only been a year or two at Penly Grange and his lasting impact on my life as bitter adversary and enemy had, in fact, been slight compared to someone else's. To Nevan's.

Of course I had always remembered perfectly well that Nevan and I had been rivals over our friendship with Rigby Smith, but until I started to write about Nevan in my memoir I had not realised the extent of my antipathy towards him and my jealousy of him. I had not remembered how deep my rivalry with him ran, how much his gradual ousting of me had rankled. But, as I wrote about Nevan and re-read what I had written, I could see the bias in my writing and I began to perceive him differently, as someone with similar needs to mine. I could even respect the way he'd chosen to assert himself in a schoolboy world which is unforgiving of the physically, emotionally or mentally weak.

I would not, however, alter what I had written about him, I decided – though I might add some qualifying or extenuating remarks about his behaviour in places – because that's what I felt about him at the time.

Then I had my meeting with Thorpe.

But, before that, I revisited Penly Grange.

Return to Penly Grange

'But no one descended to the Traveller'

It is an extraordinary fact that I had never returned to Penly Grange School since walking away from the archway, chapel and playground, and down the driveway to the bus stop on the main Tibdale to Marby road, well over forty years ago. Extraordinary, because over the years I had returned regularly to Marby to see my parents whilst they were still alive and I been to occasional Reunions at Marby College. The journey from Marby to Penly Grange was an easy one and less than half an hour by car. I always travelled to Marby by car, so why had I never bothered to make that simple journey down the road from Marby to Penly Grange?

Furthermore, I had on more than one occasion driven past the school to visit a friend who happened to live near Tibdale, but I had never turned off the road and driven up to the school to have a look around. And I can't really explain why. My reluctance to see all the inevitable changes to the place and my resistance to the indulgence of nostalgic impulses, some sort of emotional block, are only partial explanations, as is the contrary feeling of apathy or indifference about the past, which I've sometimes felt, especially when far more pressing circumstances in the present have preoccupied me. Shortage of time might have been a factor, I was always short of time until I retired, but how long does it take to drive half a mile off your route and have a quick look at your old school from the outside. I had never even done that.

When I began writing my memoir, a return to Penly Grange was put off a bit longer by my decision not to go back there until I'd finished it. I wanted to preserve in my head my picture of it as it was in the 1950s, uninfluenced by subsequent changes to the site and buildings. That was my intention, anyway. But things turned out differently.

I needed to do some research into the historical background of the school – which I had only known somewhat hazily – to add to my first chapter about the school. I thought I could do this at a distance but it didn't prove all that easy. I didn't particularly want to contact the school directly so I visited their website, but it turned out to contain very little information about the school's history. It just went on about the school's superb modern facilities and the well-qualified, 'caring' teaching staff, and on other pages mentioned recent school successes and forthcoming school events – the future not the past.

So I decided to visit Donminster library which I'd learnt from my internet searches now housed all the official school archive material in the county. I had time to visit Donminster, several hours away from my home, now that I was retired, and I found sufficient there for my purposes. However, I was keen to know more, for most of the stuff in Donminster library was about Marby College rather than Penly Grange. It was, in fact, my eagerness for more historical information about Penly Grange which led to my returning to Penly Grange before I'd finished the memoir, despite my decision not to do so.

It was Tom Thorpe, though, who triggered the train of events which actually led to my return. He contacted me in June, quite out of the blue, by email. He'd learnt my email address from a mutual friend and was interested to know how I was getting on. It was a long, long time since I'd seen him and it was funny he'd chosen to contact me now when I was writing my memoir. Could this be just a coincidence? It was certainly very timely, anyway. Thorpe was quite happy to have just a quick chat on the phone and then exchange email messages but I was eager to speak to him face to face, have an expansive conversation and hear some of *his* memories of Penly Grange, and he agreed to meet me and share what he could remember.

He was working in York and I was due to come north in July to visit my daughter, so we arranged to meet in the evening in a pub outside York which we both knew. (I would be on my own because my wife was still working:

264

not due to retire for a couple of years). Checking my route to York from the south, I realised I could easily take the road to Tibdale on the way up north and there might be time to divert a mile or two from the main road and visit Tibdale Library. It was still only a small library, as far as I knew but, I thought, being the local town to Penly Grange School, it might possibly have something about Penly Grange which wasn't in the Donminster library.

I made the journey as planned and when I was within a few miles of Tibdale, I glanced at my watch and saw that it was about 5pm. It was a pleasant afternoon in early July. York wasn't far away, and I had plenty of time to make my appointment with Thorpe, but I wasn't sure for how long Tibdale library would be open. It was a Wednesday and that might be a day when Tibdale Library closed early, it suddenly occurred to me. I instinctively put my foot down on the accelerator and found myself speeding past Penly Grange School at about 70 miles an hour. I reached the outskirts of Tibdale a few minutes later but did not drive into Tibdale. Contrary to my initial plan, I turned the car around and drove back to Penly Grange School.

I had suddenly been struck with the absurdity of what I was doing. I had raced past Penly Grange School to visit a library which *might* contain a few facts about the school which I didn't know and which *might* be of value to the historical background of my memoir, but which *might not* even be open! I had time to spare if I didn't visit Tibdale library and I was very close to Penly Grange School itself. Surely the time had come to visit it again. It would be ridiculous to pass up such an easy opportunity to see the real physical thing itself. However much changed by time, it couldn't have changed that much, surely? And, anyway, I wanted to see it now.

And so it was that on a cloudy bright July day, warm but not hot, with a light breeze blowing – in the late afternoon – I returned to Penly Grange after more than four decades. I deliberately drove past the east entrance, down to the west entrance, so that my approach to the school would bring me into the school from the direction I had always taken in the past.

The driveway was very much as I remembered it, with the beech hedge on the left, and trees and rhododendron bushes on the right, but the road surface was much improved, and when I reached the junction where, in the past, a right turn took you back via a rough track to the main road and the Headmaster's lodge, it had become a well surfaced crossroads where a smooth new road to the left led to an area of the site which had been extensively developed, and I glimpsed a smart new brick building less than a hundred yards away in a slightly raised position.

I drove past the neatly mown grassy patch, bounded by a high stone wall,

265

which formerly had a circular stone bird bath in its centre, now completely bare but otherwise looking very similar to how I remembered it, and onto the terrace in front of the main school building, the old Victorian manor house. I didn't know whether it was all right to park there. There were no other cars there, but there was plenty of space and there was no sign indicating any alternative parking area so I parked the car just a few yards from the main building and got out to survey the scene.

As I had approached the terrace in my car, I had glanced at the grounds to the right of the main building and beyond, which spread out to the games fields where we had played our rugby and cricket and other sports, but I thought I would defer a closer look at them until later. First of all, I would look at the front of the main building, then I would go left and make my way to the quad through the archway, if it was still there.

I expected to have to declare myself to someone in an office and check that it was all right for me to walk round the school; even if it were, and they really believed I was an Old Boy, in these security-conscious days I would probably have to wear a label saying 'VISITOR'. As it happened, the front door of the main school building was firmly locked and there was no one around. The place was completely deserted and very quiet indeed. Penly Grange had obviously begun its long summer break, but even so I was surprised there was no sign of any groundsman or caretaker keeping an eye on the place. When I did start wandering around I was quite prepared for someone to pop up from somewhere and ask the seldom-welcoming question to the stranger, 'Can I help you?' But no one ever did. I felt like an intruder, getting away scot-free with my intrusion, yet not really guilty of an offence because this place had once been a part of my life; I was no ordinary intruder.

I spent some time looking at the main school building, the former Penly Grange Hall, to see how far it resembled my description of it in my memoir. In many respects it was not much different. It still had the ivy and was still quite imposing but I had not been entirely accurate in calling it a stone building. The mullioned windows were stone, leaded in the top quarter, as I had said, but the main fabric was brick and a very orangey brick too which I was surprised I hadn't remembered.

Since the place was locked it was evident I wouldn't be able to see inside the building, and since there was clearly no one to report to for permission to look round the site, I thought I would take myself round the outside of the school premises on an unguided tour of my own (I had plenty of memories to guide me). I started with a visit to the quad area. I decided that if anyone challenged me I would tell them the plain truth: I was an Old Boy visiting my old haunts, though I wouldn't tell them why. As I've said, no one ever did, which pleased me. It was nice to think that Penly Grange had not yet succumbed to the 'machine guns and barbed wire' mentality of many institutions, both public and private, with CCTV cameras everywhere and warnings to visitors about their every move being monitored, signs stating 'no unauthorised personnel', 'trespassers will be prosecuted', 'dogs patrolling at night' etc.

Whilst quite enjoying my solitude as I wandered around, which left me free to my own thoughts, I felt at the same time I would like to have shared some of my thoughts with a suitable person, a sympathetic person, preferably a contemporary of mine, someone with common memories. Who at Penly Grange today would be interested in my memories or find them in the slightest bit significant, save perhaps for the odd boffin or pedant interested in school history? I was aware of the enormous gap between me and the present day inhabitants, the pupils and staff of Penly Grange School today.

The site was now slumbering, at rest, but it was a refurbished site from my days, I knew, and I could guess that in term time it would be full of life and buzzing with the latest educational trends and activities. It was an educational world far apart from mine: a world with a very different ethos from the one I knew. In this happy new world, the teachers would be benign and 'caring' (they had to be), and if not satisfied with their pupils' behaviour or concentration would never dare even to tap them on the shoulder for fear of being sacked or sent to prison. In our day, we the pupils were subject to fear of the teachers if we overstepped the mark, and how easy it was to do so. Now the boot was on the other foot, and the teachers were the ones living in fear, fear of overstepping the rigid bounds of behaviour governing any form of physical contact whether malign or benign.

Had the less caring and unrestricted physical discipline and conduct of our generation of teachers led directly to this state of affairs? Was it simply a case of the 'whirligig of time bringing in its revenges?' And was it a wholly good thing? This sense of the vast gulf between today's teachers and pupils and ours – and today's generation and ours generally – was sharpened for me as I walked round the site of Penly Grange School by the sudden appearance of the only people I saw during the whole of the time I was there, half an hour or so. Two children. On the move.

Making my way to the quad by a deliberately circuitous route, in order to take in more of the site, I walked down part of the new section of the drive and then moved right, towards the central portion of the school again. As I followed the road round to the right, two children came past me on small bicycles, one after the other, a distance of ten yards or so between them. They could not have been much older than I was when I first started at Penly Grange, i.e. eight years old. They were not travelling very fast and they wore cycle helmets. They totally ignored me. They came past me again later, on a different part of the site, and again took no notice of me. I assumed they were children of the staff and I think they were boys but I couldn't be sure because of their helmets and the fact that they were wearing jeans.

At the time they passed me by on their bicycles, I was thinking it might be quite interesting to talk to a current resident of Penly Grange and hear what they had to say about the place, perhaps mention the past, maybe not; after all, although I never force myself on anyone I'm not an unsociable person and I quite like to hear what people have to say about places I visit. A current view of Penly Grange today was not exactly what I was after but would not be without interest. However, communicating with these children would, I realised, be an impossibility. Not only because I was a middle-aged man – an old man to them – and a complete stranger, and not only because there were two generations between us, but because I felt sure their childhoods, although unfolding in the same place as mine, were totally different from the childhood I'd had. I spoke English like them, I came from a similar social background (probably), had been to the same school (I assumed they both attended Penly Grange School) but, for all that, I was from a foreign culture. And those helmets they were wearing typified for me a major element in the differences between their culture and world and mine.

We never wore helmets when we were cycling, we never even considered it. We cycled through the busy town traffic of Marby, over pot-holed dirt tracks around Marby, and crashed down the steep slopes of the woods near Marby College. Coming down hills we might reach thirty miles an hour (some claimed to have done forty). Perhaps we were foolhardy in our neglect of safety considerations and certainly we were lucky we never suffered any serious injuries, but there was something almost comical about the way these children (at their parents' instigation, no doubt) had gone to the other extreme. These two children were moving at speeds of only a few miles an hour, about jogging speed, on smooth, quiet, private roads, without a single vehicle in sight, yet they had their helmets firmly in place. I wondered about these safety-conscious children. Would they ever be allowed to do anything dangerous? Would they be allowed to climb Helvellyn and clamber over rocks and across scree when they were eleven, as we did, and if so would they be required to wear their helmets? And would they be allowed to go anywhere without their mobile phones? Was safety everything now?

I made my way to the quad, approaching first the converted barn on the left which had been the chapel where we sang 'God be with you till we meet again' at the end of term. It didn't look like a chapel anymore, more like some sort of storage building. I went through the archway, still there as before, though the tunnel was a little longer than I remembered it. And then I was in the quad. It was a bit of a come-down, I must admit. Not just because it was a bit smaller, for I expected that, but because there were no classrooms there, indeed there was nothing of a school-like nature there at all. The gym and classrooms had all been converted into small mews accommodation, presumably for the school staff, possibly the domestic school staff rather than the teachers, though I had no means of knowing that without asking someone. If an adult had been strolling around I might have asked him or her about the buildings now, but I had no intention of knocking on anyone's door to ask questions about the buildings now or Penly Grange School today.

Since seeing the children, I was feeling even more like the unnamed Traveller in Walter De la Mare's mystery narrative poem The Listeners, which we read and studied with Mr Carrow. The Traveller in De la Mare's poem returns to some derelict house in a forest, and the inhabitants of the house, whom De la Mare describes as 'phantom listeners', do not respond when he knocks on the door and enquires whether anyone is there. In some way, however, in their uncanny silence and 'stillness', they do convey telepathically that they have heard him; they just won't, or can't, communicate with him directly. It's as if he is a being from a totally different age or an alien from another world.

Had I knocked on the door of anyone living at Penly Grange today, I sensed I would have received an equivalent response to the one the Traveller received from 'the listeners', if I'd told them I was returning from the 1950s. Their response would have been politely expressed, I'm sure, by word or look or silence, but their message would have been essentially: 'Go away, you are not of our time and you have returned too late. We cannot relate to your time and we have no wish to talk about it. Those moth-eaten stories of the past. Those Dark Ages. We have nothing in common now, the world has moved on. Goodbye.' As Walter de la Mare commented on his poem, so I learnt, it was the Traveller, in fact, who was the ghost not the present inhabitants of the apparently empty house.

Outside the quad, to the right, there were some gardens. The orchard had gone, but beyond the gardens, I knew, the woods were still there, or what was left of them. I didn't go and investigate. Instead, I came back into the quad, went out through the archway and returned to the main school building. Then

I went to have a good look at the other side of the site, the spacious side, which stretched out towards the green playing fields some one hundred yards away or more from the main school buildings. Actually, it was all green grass on the left of the drive and looked even smoother, more expansive than before, because the ditch, the ha-ha, had been filled in. (So there was no more fun to be had leaping over it now. Too dangerous?).

The magnificent cedar tree, twenty yards or so from the cricket pavilion, still retained its gracious air but was not quite so broad and majestic as I remembered it. What surprised me about it, however, was the way it was tilted over to one side, to the right. I hadn't remembered that. Perhaps it was something that had happened in the last forty years? Perhaps it mirrored the bias of my memories? That was only a casual thought as I gazed at the cedar tree. It was only later, after seeing Thorpe, that I reflected more deeply on the substance and nature of my memories.

The pavilion was completely new, a small, brown-framed, cabin-like construction, with no character whatsoever, quite different from the much larger green and white pavilion I remembered. The biggest shock of all for me, however, was the absence of the enormous beech tree which had stood beyond the cedar tree and had towered over the back of the pavilion. With the removal of the beech tree, which made the cedar tree look more isolated, the area of the playing fields near the pavilion had undoubtedly lost some grandeur.

I couldn't help now looking beyond the cedar tree and the pavilion to the woods behind them, but, reluctant to contemplate them too closely, I next turned my gaze to the area behind the main school building, to see what, if anything, had happened to the Headmaster's study which had looked onto the secluded ornamental garden, glimpses of which I'd enjoyed, after a fashion, when being caned.

In some respects the study and the garden were no different. The French windows, with their square, white window frames, looked almost exactly as I remembered them and the garden still had the same shape and general layout. What was different, though, was the fact that the garden was no longer enclosed. There was a low evergreen hedge on the far side but the hedge on the near side had been removed so that the garden, which was singularly lacking in flowers considering it was July, was completely exposed to public gaze. The privacy, secrecy and mystique of the garden were gone, along with all the canings in the study, I safely assumed. In so far as the mystique and the seclusion of the garden were bound up with Teddy Eldin's canings, this had to be a good thing, but it was a pity that the source of my archetypal secret garden images had been eliminated too.

But there was something far more important to me than the Headmaster's garden. The woods, of course. Once again my eye travelled towards them, beyond the 'modern' dining room which ran parallel to the near end of the Headmaster's garden and which looked exactly the same as it had done over four decades ago, though surely the roof had been replaced since then? I could see the tops of the taller trees in the woods, like ash, beech and sweet chestnut, but there didn't seem to be many of them and I knew I could not bring myself to go and have a closer look. I knew the woods would be not at all as I remembered them. They would have been stripped down too and exposed to more public view. Their size and wildness, larger than life in my memory, would be reduced to almost nothing now, I felt certain. Much of the woods would doubtless have been cleared for easy management and for the installation of controlled and organised outdoor pursuits.

There would probably be a smart woodland 'centre' and a climbing wall and a mini assault course. There'd be a cyclo-cross trail and sports such as archery (if not thought too dangerous for children), perhaps clay pigeon shooting. There would be no area, no inch of the woods, unused for a specific purpose, unaccounted for, unregulated. There would be nothing wild left over for the creation of dens: no dense, unexplored undergrowth, bushes and trees for the imagination to play with, to invent fictions about, I knew. But I was not going to have a look and see. I was not going to have my fears and suspicions confirmed. I would keep those pictures in my mind of the woods as I remembered them, and keep alive in my memory, untarnished by present day realities, the great times I had had in the woods with Martin Rigby Smith: our making of dens and our games of French and English in Scouts, our skirmishes with the XR gang and make-believe games with anyone; above all, our search for those hidden tunnels never completed, in fact barely begun, so who's to say they never existed?

As I stood looking towards those woods which I was not going to revisit, I felt even more of a stranger, out of place, isolated by my personal memories, an interloper into a totally changed regime, despite the abiding, unchanged external features of its setting. I felt a strong desire to talk with someone of my own time and place, someone who knew Penly Grange as I knew it. I reminded myself that there was such a person and that I would be seeing him soon, namely, Thorpe, who was little more than half an hour away, traffic permitting.

The thought of seeing Thorpe, a man of my time, raised my spirits as I got back in my car and drove away from today's Penly Grange School: an up-to-date prep school of the twenty-first century, shorn of much of the past I knew, in ethos and educational practice, though still an appealing place *to the eye* in a broadly similar way. My meeting with Thorpe, though, was not going to prove quite so supportive and endorsing of my memories as I'd hoped. Not altogether.

Meeting with Thorpe

Although I hadn't seen Thorpe for about thirty-five years, I had no difficulty recognising him when I walked into the pub where we'd agreed to meet. He was a bit taller than I remembered him and his hair had gone grey and was fringed with white, which should have come as no surprise but for a moment it did, before the reasoning part of my brain kicked in and reminded me how much older we both were since we last met (though I didn't believe I was nearly as grey as him). His face was just the same – if it was lined I scarcely noticed it – and he wore the same thoughtful expression with the same little glint in his eye.

Since we'd already communicated by email and on the phone at some length we didn't need to catch up on where our lives were now; we knew all the basics about our families and careers and where we were living. He knew, for instance, that I had two grown-up daughters, one married (no children yet), and that my wife had not retired like me but was continuing working – for the Inland Revenue. We were able to get onto the topic of Penly Grange almost immediately. I had told him about the memoir I was writing and he was happy to supply me with some of his own memories of Penly Grange but he warned me he couldn't remember very much. Talking to him, it did seem he didn't remember as much as me. Every so often he would exclaim during one of my reminiscences (only told to draw him out), 'Wow! What a memory you've got!' but he did remember a few little details about the school and its characters which I'd forgotten or never known before.

His memories of Teddy Eldin were similar to mine, especially in regard to his sex education. Thorpe grinned when we got onto this topic. 'Yes,' he said. 'We were told he was going to teach us about *the birds and the bees* and then he really did teach us about the birds and the bees – and not much else!' That was spot on. Thorpe also remembered thirteen year old Spilwell's enthusiasm for the subject of sex and added to what I remembered of his outlandish character and behaviour which was quite a lot already.

Strangely, he did not remember much about Teddy Eldin's canings, nor Mr Swales' dubious corporal punishment practices such as Tickle Tibby. He did remember he was called Slasher Swales, and Thorpe called him the

272

Tubby Tyrant, and a little Mussolini. He well remembered the Tubby Tyrant's habit of having half holidays cancelled but he reminded me of something I hadn't mentioned in my section on him in my memoir: what a good organiser Swales was of school events, things like the Whitsun Fete, the Summer Dance, Parents' Day and, above all, Bonfire Night.

Oh yes, I remembered Bonfire Night all right, a superbly organised event where we were given dark brown treacle toffee, invited to eat toffee apples dangling on strings and then, in our boiler suits and wellingtons, we gathered in the dark on the edge of the playing fields, like army units grouping in silence for a night attack, waiting for a signal to charge an enemy position.

In our Bonfire Night exercise, the enemy position was the roaring bonfire at the edge of the playing fields near the woods, and I think the enemy was supposed to be Guy Fawkes in flames on the bonfire but I was never sure about that. When the signal came for the charge across the fields towards the bonfire – a solitary firework, a streaking rocket – it was the moment to run very fast and make a lot of noise, firmly believing our shouts were penetrating the night sky above, stars and all, and somehow disturbing the universe. The shouting, though, was not just an empty rant. It was an expression of genuine excitement because the full firework display was soon to follow, after we had taken up prearranged positions near the bonfire and the cordoned off area where the fireworks were to be ignited. We were kept at a safe distance from the fire and fireworks; or what seemed safe to us, though no doubt by today's safety standards we would have been required to stand much further off. We had 'jumping jacks' too in those days which are banned now (the only rule with 'jumping jacks', like bangers, was that you couldn't throw them at anybody, which was known to happen at private firework parties at people's homes as well as in the streets).

Having begun with a rocket swooshing up above the tallest trees in the wood, the Penly Grange firework display ended in a similar way with a single, solitary rocket. During the display we had snow fountains and Catherine wheels and Roman candles and other fireworks which fizzed or spluttered but not a very wide range of fireworks by today's standards. In comparison with today's public firework displays our fireworks would be regarded as very feeble but we found our firework show truly dramatic and magical, and we were more than just spectators at an event as people are today at firework displays.

Indeed, as well as that collective charge across the dark playing fields, we had further involvement in the whole show. Although Swales and Mace lit the fireworks, we provided the fireworks – four or five from each boy were permitted and put into the general coffers – and we were allowed to light sparklers and, after the last rocket had streaked into the sky, swirl them around in the night air. Sometimes we had mock sword fights with them. It was amazing that the normally repressive Swales tolerated this and that having laid down the procedure for the night's activities he did not boss us around but let the nocturnal event take its course.

I had remembered only the petty tyrannies and sadistic punishments of Swales, but to be fair to him, on Bonfire Night, although the event was strictly marshalled – certainly when the fireworks were being lit – he did create an adventure for us, he allowed us to enjoy the sensation of being out of doors in the dark on a momentous historic occasion, unrestricted except for our military-style instructions which were all part of the game anyway. Not that we thought much about the actual historical events of Bonfire Night, but we did get the feeling of its being a great tradition. And Swales set it all up for us. He took away our half holidays sometimes, but in staging Bonfire Night, in particular, as well as other large scale leisure events, he went some way towards making up for his killjoy character. I can see that now.

Thorpe remembered Carrow: his being a stickler for tidiness, and coming to the Lake District once with the Scouts, and also his *Hamlet* production, but he didn't remember much about his poetry lessons. Timmerton and Nailsworth he recollected only hazily and the name Lampton meant nothing to him at all until I supplied him with some reminders, including his bloodshot eyes, and then he exclaimed, "Oh, that lunatic who used to swing a rope around in the gym! He didn't last long, did he?"

He remembered the chaplain Henry Hewey's flippant Divinity lessons quite well and his jocular, 'Hells, bells and buckets of blood!' but in contrast to his easy-goingness Thorpe also remembered having fears about the End of the World, engendered by something Hewey said in one of his lessons. Mind you, he remarked, it might have been in Nailsworth's Divinity lessons, he wasn't sure. The young Robert Barnet he remembered as a 'breath of fresh air' in a stuffy school atmosphere, which confirmed perfectly what I'd written about him, but I was amazed to discover that he had not heard about his early death. How could he have missed the news? I wanted to consider this with him and reflect more on it but there was not a great deal of time left for us to talk and I still wanted to hear what he could remember about some of the boys, apart from Spilwell.

For a minute or two, though, I let him expatiate on Charles Bracken, French teacher and scoutmaster, whom he remembered 'fondly'; not for his French teaching but for the Scout camps and walking expeditions he organised. Thorpe described the Striding Edge walk up Helvellyn in the

Lake District – which I well remembered myself and have alluded to already – as a formative experience for him which led to his later interest in walking, cycling and kayaking and, indeed, going back to the Lake District many, many times. He was very grateful to Bracken for pointing the way to these great outdoor pursuits through Scouting.

I cut him short on Bracken, because he wasn't really telling me anything new, and asked him which of our fellow pupils he could remember. He said he remembered brain-box Parker – The Mekon – being an even bigger swot than him and me, and he remembered the phlegmatic, self-contained and composed Westford, Captain of School, who seemed to keep control of the younger boys effortlessly when he was a monitor. He remembered school bully Burton and being delighted when he was expelled, but not Jakeman, until I described him and then he said, 'Oh, yes, the pushy boy who was always boasting and showing off and combing his hair!'. A little surprisingly, he'd remembered nothing of Jakeman's talent for inventing nicknames. He recalled Crawford from Marby College days, but not as Jakeman's henchman at Penly Grange, and Rook, the other gang 'ringleader', he couldn't remember at all.

The two boys I was most interested to hear Thorpe's memories of were Martin Rigby Smith and Nevan because they featured so prominently in my memoir and I was curious to know if he had any recollections of them that were different from mine. I was particularly interested to hear what he had to say about Nevan because by the time I met Thorpe I was beginning to feel that maybe I'd been a bit hard on Nevan and I wondered whether he had a different angle on him or whether, after all, my assessment of him was about right. Above all, I wanted to know what he had to say about Nevan's friendship with Rigby Smith. What could Thorpe remember of it? How close did he think it was? But I was intending to work round to that. First of all, I mentioned Rigby Smith and Nevan separately. His response to both their names gave me a bit of a shock, particularly his response to Nevan's name when I brought it up.

"Rigby Smith? Berry he was called, wasn't he? He was good at chess, I remember," said Thorpe. "Used to win most of his matches, didn't he?"

"Is that the main thing you remember about him?" I replied, somewhat surprised this should head his list of things he remembered about Rigby Smith.

"Well, yes, we were in the school chess team together. You were in it too, weren't you?"

"Yes. Can you remember anything else about Berry?"

Thorpe paused for thought and then said, "He did Scouts, didn't he? He used to go on the Youth Hostelling trips with Bracken I was just referring to. And he was quite bright at some subjects, though I can't remember which ones."

"And sport? Can you remember nothing about his sporting ability?"

"No, not much. He was quite good, was he?"

"Quite good? He just happened to get the Best Sportsman of the Year Award in his last year, that's all."

"Ah, well that wouldn't have made much of an impression on me. I wasn't very keen on sport, team sport."

"Didn't you watch the cricket in the summer term?"

"Well, I knew it was going on in the background. When we were having our strawberries and ice cream round the boundary. I remember it always seemed to be hot, dry and sunny in June and July when we had our strawberries on certain match days and watched the cricket – supposedly. It was 'flaming June' every June, I thought, especially at Whitsun." He grinned. "But do you know what? I recently saw an old Penlian school magazine for one of the years we were there and that particular year the Garden Fete at Whitsun was a complete wash out. Torrential rain! Which I'd completely forgotten! Maybe we only had a couple of good summers and they're the ones I've remembered, so all the summers were like that in my memory."

"And you don't remember Rigby Smith's batting at all? All the runs he made?" His observations on his memories of the weather were interesting but I wanted to get him back to the subject of Rigby Smith.

"To be honest, I can't remember a single cricket match at Penly Grange – I just wasn't interested in school matches."

I wasn't getting much out of Thorpe on Rigby Smith and I thought the time had now come to move on to Nevan. What Thorpe had to say about Nevan was what I really wanted to know. I was still writing my chapter on Nevan and what he had to say about him might prove useful. Whether I could use it or not was another matter. I leaned forward and made my question sound as pointed as possible,

"And Nevan?" I asked. What do you remember of him?

His face went blank and he seemed to struggle to register the question. "Nevan?" he said, more to himself than me.

"Nevan?" He scanned his memory files and came up with nothing on the name Nevan. "Not Norton?" he proffered.

"No," I replied firmly. "Nevan. Bernie Nevan. Small boy with cunning eyes. Always pretending he had a secret he was keeping to himself. Very conspiratorial. Liked gossip and intrigue and stirring things up. And he used to talk about girls a lot." (I knew this was subjective and somewhat exaggerated but I needed to use large brush strokes and bold outlines in depicting Nevan if Thorpe was having difficulty in recalling him). Then I added: "He was a close friend of Rigby Smith's." There. I'd said it now. Surely that would trigger some memories. But Thorpe wasn't very helpful, not on Nevan.

"*You* were Rigby Smith's friend, Berry's friend. What did they call you? Berry and his Mouse, wasn't it? You were always together. I don't remember anyone else." He paused for thought again. And he thought long and hard. Then he said, "No, I don't remember anyone called Nevan." He was quite sure about it. Since writing about Nevan in my memoir, he had been looming very large in my Penly Grange memories and I was astounded that Thorpe had no recollection of him whatever. This was over and above my disappointment that he could offer me nothing at all on Nevan to confirm what I'd already written about him or provide another slant on him.

Shortly after this negative exchange on Nevan, Thorpe and I parted company, promising to keep in touch. (Incidentally, he knew nothing of Rickmack either). He said he'd write or email me if he thought of anything else but we both knew he probably hadn't got anything else, or nothing else I could use in my memoir. I made my way further north, stayed with my daughter for a couple of days and then returned home, back down south, to continue getting used to my retirement (not difficult) and to complete my memoir.

Thorpe's failure to remember Nevan became easier to understand when I thought about it and, more importantly, it contributed to the final phase of the complete turnaround in my feelings about him. When I thought about it, it was really not so surprising that Thorpe didn't remember Nevan. They were not in the same class and they were not in the same Group. Thorpe was a boarder not a day boy so he wouldn't have seen him on the buses and he wouldn't have played in any of the school teams with Nevan because Thorpe wasn't in any school teams. Nevan dropped out of Scouts when he was about eleven so Thorpe wouldn't have remembered him from Scouts. They might have fought side by side with Rigby Smith in some of the battles in the woods with the XR gang but Nevan was not noted for his fighting prowess and would probably not have done anything special to make him stand out in the memory.

I don't think Thorpe had ever been to the Rigby Smiths' house and he would have seen nothing of Nevan and Rigby Smith's friendship at home. As for Nevan exercising more and more influence over Rigby Smith that last year and especially the last term of all, I was prepared to admit I might have exaggerated it in my mind when I recollected it. The truth was that Nevan's real influence over Rigby Smith applied mainly to when they were at home, though that didn't mean I was altogether wrong about him trying to edge me out at school in such things as the Robin Hood game and the piggy back fighting which had really upset me – when he'd taken over from me as Rigby Smith's rider without so much as a 'by your leave' and denied me a great opportunity to prove my worth in a physical contest.

I had relived all that and worked through it all, and now, as my memoir drew to a close, at least the first draft, I reflected more deeply on Thorpe's not remembering Nevan, also his not remembering some things about Rigby Smith and others. For my part, I had remembered virtually nothing about the Luke brothers whom he'd mentioned to me at one point in our conversation and would evidently quite like to have talked about, but I had nothing I could say about them.

It's generally recognised that we all remember the same events differently, we all have our personal slant on them, but what was coming home to me with greater force than this truism was the fact that we also remember quite different things, even when we live at the same time and share a common life; in this case the life of Penly Grange School in the 1950s. We remember them largely according to how important they were to us at the time, for our memories are bound by the strength of our original experiences, and how narrow and personal those experiences and memories often are! This does not explain everything we retain from thirty, forty of fifty years ago – sometimes the most trivial things stick in our minds for no apparent reason – but I believe it explains many of my memories. Why I remember Nevan so well, for instance.

Nevan was a small boy, almost as small as me, and unremarkable in many ways. He notched up few notable achievements at Penly Grange, except in sport, and even in sport he didn't match up to the likes of Jakeman, Rigby Smith, Rickmack or Porter. Yet Nevan was a huge figure in *my* memory, and not only because we were at loggerheads over Rigby Smith, though that was an integral part of it. He was huge because of the enormous influence he exerted on people and events in my small circle. At the time I had always seen his influence as something negative and malign but looking back on what he'd done, on what he'd been, especially in the light of Thorpe's not even remembering him, my perceptions of him were undergoing a sea change into something truly rich and strange.

To my astonishment, I found myself feeling sorry for Thorpe for not having known Nevan as I had known him and missing out on those dramatic moments and dangerous escapades he'd engineered with the Gribley gang and others and, intentionally or not, with Mr Hay. Perhaps he'd been behind the unexplained hostility of the rough-tough boy who had laid about Brian

Barley – I'd only just thought of that – which had goaded Martin Rigby Smith into action, putting his fighting qualities on display and eventually involving several of us in a lively incident on an otherwise unremarkable day. Even some of our petty squabbles at the Rigby Smiths', which had annoyed me so much at the time, seem to take on an almost rosy glow when I imagined a Nevan-less time in Marby. A more contented time of easy-going friendship with Martin Rigby Smith, it certainly would have been, but, maybe, it would also have been a less colourful, less memorable time, I have to admit.

Divine Conspiracy

'Immortal, invisible, God only wise'

I began to reflect more broadly on the writing of the whole of my memoir, on its initiation and development and on how it had affected me. There had been something going on behind it from the beginning, some unseen influence at work, it seemed to me. My memoir had been triggered by my surprise meeting with the arch bully Burton in hospital. Could that meeting have been just an accident? Would I have written the memoir anyway had I not met him? I found myself having to answer 'no' to both questions. I had quite enough to do in my retirement, including gardening and exploring my love of opera and folk song – a book on one of those subjects I might seriously have considered – without writing any kind of autobiography.

Yes, I might have jotted down some of my more amusing memories of school life, for fun, to circulate to some people, perhaps, but I would never have attempted a full length book about my school days, I'm sure, had I not been challenged, by Burton's distorted memories, to set the record straight. Yet my memoir had entailed much more than merely setting the record straight: much more than my account of Burton and his sidekicks, and the harsher, Dotheboys Hall side of school life at Penly Grange which he'd condemned from his hospital bed; more, even, than a fully rounded portrait of Penly Grange School in the 1950s, good as well as bad, for it had expanded beyond school to life in Marby at the Rigby Smiths'. And once I began to write about the Rigby Smiths in Marby, it was inevitable that Nevan would become a major character in my story, yet I had never thought of writing much about him at the outset. I never expected him to take centre stage, with Martin Rigby Smith, in the way that he had, nor could I ever have imagined my view of him would become transformed in the process of remembering.

Evidently, much good had arisen out of the writing of my memoir. Firstly, I no longer harboured vindictive feelings against Burton. Since he'd been the catalyst to get me started on the memoir, he'd more than made amends as far as I was concerned. In any case, the memoir had revealed he was not my deeper, longer-lasting opponent: that 'honour' had gone to Nevan. And now I had come to terms with Nevan in my mind. I felt reconciled to him and was glad, privileged even, in a way, to have known him.

Furthermore, the writing of the memoir had brought home to me what I owed to others – to my friends, especially Martin and all the Rigby Smiths, and to several teachers. It had also brought me much pleasure to recall and relive some of my past experiences. There was some pain too, some regret and disappointment reawoken, but the uplift and satisfaction gained in setting it all down had been far greater.

So you will understand, I hope, when I say it seemed clear to me that the force behind my memoir was a wholly benign one and that I needed to reconsider my religious beliefs which were basically agnostic, though never firmly so. I have always been more of a *non*-believer, I would say, than an *un*believer. I have not been hostile to religion, at least not to genuine Christianity, but apart from school chapel, which was compulsory, and my visits to St Margaret's in Marby with the Rigby Smiths, which I eventually discontinued, I have never been a church-goer or someone who prays (except in a crisis) and have rarely, if ever, sensed, in a definite, meaningful way, any divine presence or direction in my life. Not until now.

Some spiritual seeds were sown in my prep school days, no doubt, through my contact with the devout Rigby Smiths, which had also led later on to my hospital visit with James and Martin to the terminally ill Robert Barnet, a true Christian who was ready to die. That visit, and what James had said, had made a deep impression on me, more so in retrospect. Probably something had rubbed off on me in my preparation for Confirmation and the event itself in Penly Grange chapel, along with the end of term services there, though I was hardly aware of it at the time; and, I daresay, I drew something of spiritual value from the Rev. Nailsworth's earnest instruction in Biblical law in the library/classroom during my last year at Penly Grange. It's perfectly possible, too, that even Henry Hewey's lightweight, cavalier lessons conveyed something of lasting significance to me, in their fleeting moments of serious religious teaching and occasional profound, if throwaway, comments on faith.

Were those potential spiritual seeds – if really planted in me – germinating now, triggered somehow by recollection? Or is that far-fetched? I only know that in revisiting and re-creating my Penly Grange days, some fifty years on, I had become aware of a spiritual reality, a divine dimension, underlying my life and influencing it in a discernible way. I was conscious, indeed, of a higher Power having played a part not only in the initiation of my memoir, and in driving it forward, but also in the shaping of it. I have mentioned how the book had grown far beyond my original intentions but there was also the mysterious phenomenon of things coming into my mind unbidden and then falling into place in my record of the past in quite unexpected ways: I experienced a sort of ghostly guidance in my writing. Consequently, I had much to ponder on, intriguing religious questions to answer, but as far as the memoir itself was concerned there were no doubts about it, I decided. It was inspired and sanctioned in some way, it was *right*.

But my total confidence in my memoir and my version of the past did not remain unchallenged or untested for long. Before I'd finished it, I got a bit of a jolt. A greater jolt, in fact, than I'd had in my meeting with Thorpe. The jolting came in the form of a phone call from someone I didn't know.

Or thought I didn't know. The person at the other end of the phone spoke in a suave, self-assured voice and called himself Bernard something. I thought he must be an insurance salesman or perhaps a sales rep for a pension investment fund. It took me awhile to latch onto who he was; he had to repeat his name several times and in slightly different forms before his identity finally sunk into my brain:

"... Bernard Nevan. Nevan, you know. Bernie Nevan. From school? You must remember me – Penly Grange and Marby College? We were there at the same time."

"Of course!" I said, when I had readjusted my preconceptions of the person speaking to me and the penny dropped at last, "I remember you, I've just been ..." and I was going to blurt out, 'I've just been writing about you' or say 'talk of the devil' when I checked myself, realising it would be better to keep quiet about my memoir, certainly for the time being. So I altered my remark to the much vaguer, "I've just been thinking about my schooldays, funnily enough." I sounded fairly calm, I hope, but actually I was shaken by the fact Nevan of all people should contact me now (was this providence too rather than coincidence?)

"Have you indeed? said Nevan. "What sort of things do you remember?" He gave a sort of laugh. "A big question, I know."

Well, I thought, I'm not going to condense the whole of my memoir for you in a few sentences, so I simply said, "Teddy Eldin, of course, and some of the other teachers. That sort of thing." I was trying to avoid any immediate reference to him or Martin Rigby Smith; I'd rather he introduced the topic himself if it was going to come up. And it certainly would sooner or later. But he talked about me first.

"You were known as Mouse, weren't you?"

"Yes, at *school*." I wanted to emphasise that; I had another life outside school he ought to have remembered. "It was Jakeman's nickname for me. Because my name is Moss."

"Oh, was that it? I don't remember why, except you were small and a bit shy. Like me."

I thought: small, yes, but shy? You Nevan? That was certainly a new angle on things. I thought about my being called Mouse and it suddenly struck me that Nevan never had a nickname. He was always simply Nevan; except at the Rigby Smiths' where he eventually became simply Bernie. How did he escape having a nickname, I wondered, when Martin and I both had one? That was very clever or lucky of him.

Nevan turned to the present. "What are you up to now? Still working?"

"As a matter of fact, I've recently retired. From the Civil Service. I've taken early retirement. Got quite a good approved pension package." (Actually, it wasn't brilliant but it was OK).

"Oh, very nice. All right for some. Mind you, I don't want to retire for awhile. I like my work."

"What do you do?"

"I work for a sportswear company. Sales and marketing."

"Sounds good." (It did indeed, compared to the Civil Service; I wasn't just saying that).

"It is. I get to travel a lot. I've just got back from Kenya." Nevan changed his tone of voice. "I'll tell you why I'm phoning. I've just got your contact details from Martin. Martin Rigby Smith. You remember him, of course? And his brothers."

"Oh, yes, quite well."

"Well, there's going to be a Penly Grange Reunion in November. Did you know that?"

"No." (I never seemed to hear about Penly Grange Reunions, only Marby College ones).

"Well, there is, and I daresay you'll be able to come now that you're retired?"

"Probably, yes."

"Good. I thought it would be a good idea if some of us got together before the Reunion and had a drink before the main event. Caught up a bit, you know. Those of us who were at Penly Grange in the 1950s. The Reunion is for all Old Boys in the 50s, 60s and 70s, so we 50s boys need to stick together, don't you think? I got in touch with the Barley brothers not so long ago: Brian can come, I'm not sure about Steven. Martin can't come, though. He's in France, you know?"

"Yes, I did know."

"Well, he suggested I got in touch with you which I have now." (Does that mean he would not have bothered with me if Martin had not suggested it, I wondered?). "I thought we'd meet in the Red Dragon in Tibdale, just off the Marby-Tibdale road. Early evening. The Reunion's on November 18th. Does that sound reasonable to you?"

" Sounds fine to me: a good place to meet."

So far the conversation was going along amicably enough. I was particularly pleased that I was having this conversation after I'd radically revised my view of Nevan. Had I talked to him a few months ago when the embers of my resentment against him were still glowing, I daresay my exchange with him now would have been a lot more forced and uncomfortable. Unfortunately, though, when I asked him who else he knew was coming to the Reunion, the conversation took a decided turn for the worst. Not immediately but fairly soon after.

"Martin's brothers might be able to come: Colin and James. They might be able to tie it in with a visit to their parents in Marby. Mine died but theirs are still around and living in the same place."

"Yes, I know." (I didn't say my parents had died too).

"You remember Colin and James, of course, especially Colin?"

"Yes, indeed."

And then Nevan uttered words, ingenuous words for him but which jarred on me in their inaccuracy, like out of tune singing, and proved the prelude to an even more discordant remark.

"You were best friends with Colin at Penly Grange, weren't you?"

"No, not really. We were friends, yes, but I only knew Colin through Martin. I was Martin's friend first and foremost. Colin was two years younger than me." How could Nevan have forgotten that! I was staggered. But worse was to come.

"Were you?" said Nevan, airily, dismissively, I thought, though you can't always tell on the phone. "Well, Martin and I were best mates, of course. The very best. All our time at Penly Grange. We were thick as thieves. The two of us."

I was rocked back on my heels by this confident pronouncement of Nevan's. For a few moments, I felt some of the good will I had built up towards Nevan beginning to seep away. That phrase, 'the two of us', in particular, grated on me. Old anger and resentment – no, not really resentment so much as indignation – was rising within me, against the voice of common sense, the voice of the mature adult, trying to point out to me that such a reaction to mere memories of friendships long past was childish and absurd. But, I protested, against the voice of reason and adulthood within, Nevan is wrong. Even if he and Martin became best friends that last year at Penly Grange, they weren't before that, and certainly not at Penly Grange. Why, Thorpe couldn't remember him at all! Nevan was just deceiving himself. He was looking back through an extremely limited lens, a very narrow archway, which gave him a blinkered view of the past.

He would not have witnessed my friendship with Martin the first two years of my life at Penly Grange – he wasn't there – but he would have been well aware we were already firm friends when he first got to know Martin himself. He would have been very conscious, then, that Martin and I travelled to school on the bus every day and were together most of the time at school and that when in Marby, at the Rigby Smiths' and his home, we were rivals in our friendship with Martin. But in associating me more with Colin than Martin, perhaps because I tended to stick with Colin in the mixed Marby holiday gang, all that had gone from his memory or been filtered out somehow.

When my conversation with Nevan ended and I put the phone down, I continued my musings. Of course my view of the past was restricted too. I never knew the full story of Martin's relationship with Nevan that last year at Penly Grange. I never knew precisely what part Jennifer Danvers and her cousin Fiona had played in strengthening their bond. I assumed the two girls had played some part in it but I never knew what difference they really made. All I knew was that in being excluded from their foursome I had felt further removed from Martin than ever. Yet when we had talked briefly about his shaky performance in the cricket match against Marby College, such a crucial one for him, he had spoken to me as if I were, unquestionably, his closest friend; that cricket match, late on in the final summer term, had taken place after the foursome had formed.

The question was did it all matter? It was all a very long time ago, all water long under the bridge. Did it matter who was best friends with whom in the past? More precisely, who was best friends with Martin, in what way and when? And the answer was emphatically 'yes', it did matter. To me. It mattered to me because although I always had friends at other times of my life I never had a friend quite like Martin Rigby Smith. And I did not want that friendship devalued, brushed away under the smooth carpet of the commonly agreed past, reduced to the level of a typical childhood friendship 'we've all had', with a dismissive smirk from the worldly-wise! It was special our friendship, unique, for a number of years: our time spent together, what we knew about each other, certainly what I knew about him (though it wasn't everything). But I did not need to argue about it, I suddenly realised with some relief, because it's plain to see in my memoir. Let the memoir be read, all of it. It's all there, including Thorpe's testimony. It's not the past seen only through one archway.

I *would* go to the Penly Grange Reunion in November, I decided, looking forward to meeting some of my Penly Grange contemporaries and friends, such as Colin and James Rigby Smith, if there, and the Barley brothers, even Bernie Nevan himself, though that would be strange; but I would keep my counsel, listening to the memories of others before proffering any of my own. I might possibly use others' recollections in my memoir, if I could blend them in, but I didn't really need any more material and I aimed to finish the work before Christmas. Whether I would tell anyone at the Reunion that I had almost completed a written memoir of my Penly Grange days was something I would have to think about, together with the question of how and when I would publish it.

Naturally, the Rigby Smiths' response to my memoir, when published (or perhaps in draft form if I allowed them a preview) would interest me most, especially Martin's response. He would recognise much of it, and approve it, surely, in essence, if not in all its details. Would it, perhaps, prompt him to produce his own book now? That book which he had said he was going to write about his boyhood, over eight years ago. Had he already written it and was it a novel or a memoir? I would love to know. And maybe I shall.

If, and when, Bernie Nevan sees the memoir, I hope he won't be put out by my revelations of our rivalry – which he seems to have completely forgotten – nor my feelings about him all those years ago. I hope he will take it all in good part, especially since I come out in his favour at the end. But, as I've commented before, you never know with Nevan: I couldn't predict his reaction.

I cannot, of course, be sure of anyone's reaction to my memoir, nor what repercussions (if any) might flow from it, but still believing, as I do, that Providence set it in motion and also had a hand in the writing of it, I have a hunch, a hope, that same benevolent Power, that higher Hand, will steer it through publication and see that its consequences for others too are all for the best.